PRAISE FOR *WEREGIRL*

"... a perfect fit for balanced and justice-seeking Libras"
—*Teen Vogue*, 'Must-Read YA Book of the Month'

"Supernatural fans of all ages will thoroughly enjoy the exciting, dramatic saga of a young woman's dual quest to master her own wild gift and uncover the sinister secret lurking within her dilapidated hometown."
—*Midwest Book Review*

" ... a solid story with engaging characters"
—*Publishers Weekly*

"Multiple, complex wolf characters."
—*Kirkus*

"A medical thriller, a teen supernatural story, [and] a cautionary tale about powerful drug companies and corporate greed ... a decent initial effort by a team of authors."
—*School Library Journal*

"With a keen eye for how real teens act and talk alongside a heartgripping story of danger and magical transformation, Bell has created a wildly appealing tale about the dark side of the human relationship to the natural world."
—Eliot Schrefer, two-time National Book Award Finalist

"Move over Michael J. Fox, there's a new teen wolf in town and this time it's a GIRL. *Weregirl* will not disappoint. Yes, you can pretend it belongs to your tween if you're really that self-conscious. But I say own it. This is way better than *Twilight*."
—Laura Pyle, *Environmental Health News*

"A combination of Van Draanen's *The Running Dream* and Henry's *The Girl Who Was Supposed to Die*, *Weregirl* is a satisfying blend of fantasy and mystery."
—Ashlyn Duke, *Killer Nashville*

"Throw out all your preconceived ideas because the story morphs into a mystery thriller that is appropriate for teens but so well written that adults will be hooked. I would love to read more! (hint, hint, Ms. Bell!)"

—Tanya, *LitBuzz*

"Ultimately, Nessa feels like a real girl, with all of the flaws, desires, and confusing feelings that real girls her age have — and rather than treat this as something monstrous, as many werewolf stories have done in the past with both male and female heroes, *Weregirl* allows her space to navigate her transformation for herself and come out the other side a stronger person."

—Victoria McNally, *Revelist*

"I really liked the relationship between Nessa and her best friend Bree. Bree helps Nessa figure some things out about her werewolf transformation and their bond becomes stronger as the story progresses. The female characters also don't degrade each other, which is refreshing, even though Nessa faces a competitive environment at school."

—Farid-ul-Haq, *The Geekiary*

"Filled with humor, romance, adventure, and a real-world relevant storyline that tackles the effects of corporate chemical pollution and DNA manipulation, *Weregirl* is a breathtakingly fun, not-to-be-missed addition to one of today's most exciting literary genres—crafted by a truly feminist team of authors."

—*Broadway World*

"This was such an amazing read! I really loved it. Honestly, I inhaled it, I couldn't read it fast enough... The problems in *Weregirl* are scary real and make a great balance for the paranormal elements."

—Courtney Dion, *The Violent Vixen*

"For those tired of the typical supernatural YA novel, this book is your answer. I was left constantly turning the page, anticipating the reveal of what's really happening in this town where Nessa lives. *Weregirl* is like a superhero origin story and a mystery wrapped in a supernatural guise."
　　　　　　　　　　　—Jennifer Lutton, Bookseller at VJ books

"The team of women who wrote this together really captured shapeshifting and the consequences of being a werewolf while maintaining school, social, and home lives in a way that I had a very difficult time disagreeing with."
　　　　　　　　　　　—Sara Modal, *Bean's Bookshelf and Coffee Break Blog*

"The wolf pack Nessa enters into is beautiful and they were easy to connect with."
　　　　　　　　　　　—Sarah Fairbairn, *The Adventures of Sacakat Book Blog*

"Loved it! I fist pumped the air and started cheering when I finished."
　　　　　　　　　　　—Snow, Goodreads

"The plot was refreshing and stepped away from the tropes that often come with werewolf books. It wasn't predictable and I was sitting on the edge of my seat getting ready to see what was on the next page . . . It's one paranormal book you don't want to miss."
　　　　　　　　　　　—Marne Smith, *A Book Tropolis*

"I've read my fair share of werewolf fiction and this was not a repeat of previous tropes. The interaction with real wolves was a good choice that I hadn't seen before."
　　　　　　　　　　　—Taylor, Goodreads

"*Weregirl* is an exciting and thought-provoking novel that will make your heart pounds as you read more of it. A simple, thrilling story."
　　　　　　　　　　　—Alyssa Janine Busia, *Book Huntress' World Blog*

CHIMERA

A WEREGIRL NOVEL

C. D. Bell

CHOOSECO™

WAITSFIELD, VERMONT

Book design: Stacey Boyd, Big Eyedea Visual Design
Cover design: Dot Greene, Greene Dot Design

For information regarding permission, write to:
Chooseco
P.O. Box 46
Waitsfield, Vermont 05673
www.weregirl.com

ISBN 10: 1-937133-58-3
ISBN 13: 978-1937133-58-0

Published simultaneously in the United States and Canada
Printed in the United States

10 9 8 7 6 5 4 3 2 1

Publisher's Cataloging-In-Publication Data
Names: Bell, C. D. (Cathleen Davitt).
Title: Chimera: a Weregirl novel / C. D. Bell.
Description: Waitsfield, Vermont: Chooseco, [2017] | Series: [Weregirl series]; [2] | Interest age level: 12 and up. | Summary: Nessa returns home from a run with her pack to find an FBI raid and the shocking news that her mother, Vivian, is being arrested for violations so serious she may be facing life in prison. What did Nessa's mother, a small-town vet tech, do to threaten Homeland Security? Vivian's secret past leads Nessa to discover there is more to her story than she ever imagined.
Identifiers: ISBN 978-1-937133-58-0 | ISBN 978-1-937133-59-7 (ebook) | ISBN 1-937133-59-1 (ebook)
Subjects: LCSH: Teenage girls—Juvenile fiction. | Werewolves—Juvenile fiction. | Cross-country running—Juvenile fiction. | CYAC: Teenage girls—Fiction. | Werewolves—Fiction. | Running—Fiction. | LCGFT: Thrillers (Fiction)
Classification: LCC PZ7.B38891526 We 2017 (print) | LCC PZ7.B38891526 (ebook) | DDC [Fic]—dc23

To our packmates Gracie, Pippa,

Sydney, and Monday.

The elixir of life is a chimera.

— Mary Shelley, *Frankenstein; or,*
The Modern Prometheus, 1818

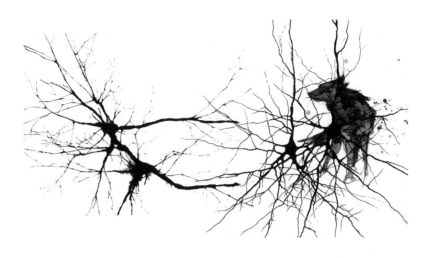

CHAPTER ONE

atch me if you can, Luc seemed to say, flashing his signature move—a quick fake to the left—to start a game of tag.

Yeah, right, Nessa thought, sticking to the trail and the hunt. She didn't have time for games today. It was her job to fix dinner for her younger siblings, Nate and Delphine, and she had to get home soon. Her mom, a vet tech, was working late, helping Dr. Morgan with the monthly spay/neuter clinic.

But when Luc circled back and then brushed past Nessa as he took off out in front of her again, she couldn't resist. Sometimes you just have to run.

And for Nessa Kurland, "sometimes" was more like "most times." A cross-country runner, she loved the feeling of her body lifting up off the earth, the lightening in her feet, hips, and shoulders. She felt the lightening now, her toes barely touching the damp ground and melting patches of snow, the branches bending and snapping as she ran through them.

Luc had a few lengths on her but Nessa knew she could catch him. He wanted her to. If he'd been running to outpace her, he would never have looked back, teasing, his tongue hanging out of the side of his mouth.

Was he laughing at her?

Nessa laughed herself, then swallowed, redoubling her pace, digging in with her shoulders. Two or three leaping movements later, she had come even with his midsection and was launching herself sideways, throwing Luc off course.

He rolled onto his side, and then sprang back to standing, turning to face her. Expecting Nessa to play.

But Nessa had frozen in place, lifting her nose to a gentle breeze that had just started to stir the branches around her. It was carrying an odor Nessa was always on alert for, even as she dreaded it.

A Paravida wolf.

Wait, no, not wolf.

Wolves. There were two at least.

And not far away.

Nessa glanced at Luc to be sure he was registering the scent too. He was, and when Nessa took off at a trot toward the east, he fell in beside her. They chose their route carefully, keeping their distance from the dangerous Paravida wolves, but also cutting off the wolves' path toward town. The last thing Luc and Nessa wanted was yet another human-wolf encounter.

The Paravida wolves were not natural wolves. They'd been

raised by human researchers in secret labs on the Paravida corporate campus north of town. Because they'd been bred to be hyper-aggressive—and because they'd been isolated from one another in individual cages instead of being allowed to form packs—they had never developed the survival skills of wolves in the wild.

The Paravida wolves had escaped into the wild last fall, and many of them had fought and killed one another. Others had starved. The ones that hadn't were living on garbage. They were thus attracted to humans, whom they associated with food.

All winter, Nessa and Luc had tried to keep the Paravida wolves out of town—staging battles when they needed to, but mostly using scent markings, night singing, and other classic natural wolf maneuvers to let the Paravida wolves know: This Place Is Not for You.

But inevitably, some Paravida wolves had occasionally broken through. They had eaten livestock, stalked farms. They'd been spotted on the edge of the golf course outside of town. A group of three wolves had showed up on the playground at Tether's elementary school, causing the administrators to institute indoor recess for the rest of the winter season.

By mid-February, snowmobilers were calling in wolf sightings a few times a week. It was becoming standard for anyone heading for a hike or a ride to arm themselves, which had already led to injury. Guys drinking beer and driving snowmobiles in the woods around Tether weren't exactly James Bond–caliber. When you added the fear of a wolf attack alongside a loaded gun and a vehicle speeding over an unpredictable course you were asking for trouble.

Luc was hoping a balance would eventually return, that

the Paravida wolves would become absorbed by the local wolf population, or at least learn how to survive in the wild so that they would leave the humans alone.

Nessa wasn't so sure.

"Assimilation," Luc would say. He would never quite rise to the bait in an argument. He'd shrug as if to say, "Facts are facts."

"See?" he'd said when they first figured out that the Paravida wolves were mating with natural wolves. Even in the pack Nessa and Luc sometimes ran with, a young female had given birth to wolves fathered by a Paravida wolf.

"'Atta boy," Luc had said.

Which was funny, until it wasn't. Just a few weeks earlier, a truck driver delivering to a Walmart forty miles east had backed his truck up to the loading bay, gone inside, and come out ten minutes later to find a pair of wolves ripping through a pallet of cereal boxes. Which hadn't scared him nearly as much as when the second wolf had jumped on him—apparently that one must have been guarding the "kill." The driver had managed to scramble back inside, holding the door closed with his body while calling for help. The attack made the evening news in Detroit.

Luc stopped now, his nose deep in a patch of snow. Nessa came over to check out what he'd smelled. She raised her head, asking him a question and his stare answered her.

Blood.

Not a lot, Nessa telegraphed. *Just a few drops.*

She sniffed again, really digging her nose into the snow this time. She detected another odor besides the blood. Something Nessa recognized. She couldn't identify it though. There were things she knew only as a human that sometimes didn't carry over into her wolf brain, and for now she couldn't remember.

Luc moved on, following the scent trail of this other wolf, and Nessa followed it too. The wolf had been moving fast but erratically, and then had slowed. Like a doe or a buck who had been shot, running itself to death.

Luc must have been following the same train of thought because he lifted his snout and blew air out of his nose. To a human, the gesture might have appeared derisive, like he was scoffing at an idea, but Nessa knew it was just his way of saying, *Not possible. There's not enough blood to explain the stumbles and quick turns this wolf is making. Whatever is slowing him down isn't a gunshot wound.*

Scenarios ran through Nessa's mind. Okay, if there wasn't enough blood for the animal to have been shot, then what? Was he sick? Was that what she had smelled?

She stopped trying to understand because just then she caught the odor again. Without thinking, she was running, Luc right behind, all sense of play gone, the game forgotten, just the impulse of running together remaining.

They arrived at a clearing, noting the way the tracks the wolf had left here were dragging deeper and deeper into the snow.

And then, there. They'd found it. A fresh depression in some soft mud, an overwhelming trace of smells that announced the wolf's collapse.

But that wasn't what had gotten Luc's attention. It was the human odors that were causing the hair on their backs to stand on end. The smell of boot leather and shampoo, tissues, couch upholstery fibers laced with fire-retardant chemicals, and cat hair—as familiar to Nessa as the smells of her own home.

There had been a lot of activity in the area where the wolf had collapsed. Recent activity. The smells were not more than five or ten minutes old.

So where was the wolf now?

Here, Luc seemed to say, taking off toward the road. This was not good. The road meant town. More people.

What was going on?

She followed Luc, realizing that the wolf had been dragged. How was that possible?

And then the puzzle pieces snapped together.

Nessa realized what the smell she'd been getting before had been. She recognized it from cleaning cages at the vet's—it was the smell of an animal coming out of surgery.

Anesthetic.

This wolf had been shot with a tranquilizer gun, not a rifle.

By the time they reached the road, found the tire tracks, and concluded that the wolf was gone, Nessa was sure that the animal had been captured, not killed.

But why? Who had done this?

Whoever it was, Nessa hoped they were armed, because when one of those hyper-aggressive wolves came to and realized it was trapped, the kidnapper was going to be in for the fight of their life.

Ten minutes later, Nessa and Luc were approaching Luc's cabin. Or at least, the cabin he'd claimed as his own when he had found it in the woods behind his house and fixed it up. His dad traveled a lot for work and his mom spent a lot of time back in the Upper Peninsula, where they'd moved from the year before.

As they reached the clearing that surrounded the cabin, Nessa watched Luc's wolf body as it seemed to accelerate without actually moving forward, blurring, each step a shifting of shape and color and light. What shook out as he slowed was an arm and then a sneaker and then his track jacket: the human form of Luc.

Nessa always forgot how much she loved the way Luc looked in human form. As a wolf, Luc was gray, dignified, older-seeming. As a human, he was ganglier, tall with dark shaggy hair and a runner's thin hips and legs, broad shoulders. And he had a way of taking up space without apology that made Nessa feel instantly comfortable.

She felt the familiar tingling sensation that signaled her own transformation. Although it looked like a speeding up from the outside, on the inside it felt like a slowing down, and Nessa struggled to keep her balance as if she were lurching out of deep surf at the beach.

Then there they were, Luc and Nessa, both human again, breathing heavily from the workout they'd just had, looking at each other as they always did after transforming together, that *Can you believe we do this?* expression on their faces. Luc had taught Nessa about transformation—how to suppress it, how to make it happen when you needed it to. She still had to transform at the new and full moons, no matter what, but over the winter, she'd gotten to a point where she could move in and out of wolf form at will. Thinking about her family was her trick for returning to human shape. To become a wolf, she had only to think about the way she felt when running, or the way she felt in the woods.

Generally after a run they were both starving, and this time was no exception. Pushing open the cabin door, Luc filled a kettle with filtered water and Nessa lit the camp stove. He pushed the sleeves of his jacket up to his elbows, showing off muscular forearms. They'd been dating since January, but still sometimes the most basic things about Luc made Nessa catch her breath. He'd been so quiet in the beginning of the school year she hadn't thought much of him, but the more she got to know him, the more she wondered how she hadn't seen his coolness—and how simply beautiful he was—from the outset.

Focus, Kurland, Nessa said to herself. It wasn't her style— or Luc's—to go too mushy. She dug through the plastic Rubbermaid box that held packets of hot chocolate and ramen, peanut butter, and crackers. This time she scored: granola bars.

Luc had found the cabin back in the fall and worked hard to make it nice: replacing the window glass, sanding and varnishing the exposed wood walls, bringing in cushions and sleeping bags, cleaning and repairing the woodstove and chimney. Even in the very cold, they'd been able to use it, lighting fires in the woodstove and cozying up inside sleeping bags. Over the winter, they'd spent a lot of weekend afternoons out here, doing homework while watching the snow fall outside.

Nessa poured hot water into the waiting mugs, the cocoa powder rising to the surface until Luc dipped the spoon and started to stir.

"So... someone is hunting Paravida wolves?" Nessa ventured.

"Yeah," said Luc. "But that wolf wasn't dead. I don't get it. It had been shot, but there wasn't a lot of blood and still it went down."

"That's because they were using a tranquilizer gun," Nessa

said. "I smelled the anesthetic when we were out there, but couldn't think what it was until just now."

"A tranq gun?"

"It's sodium thiopental. Dr. Morgan uses it all the time as a sedative, and in high doses it'll knock you out—even kill you." Nessa's mother, Vivian, had gotten Nessa a part-time job cleaning cages at the vet's office so she was familiar with the basics. "Biologists use it to bring down animals so they can tag and radio chip them for studies."

Luc tasted the cocoa; passing one to Nessa, he took another sip of his own. "Biologists," he said. "That sounds like the scientists from Paravida. You don't think they're recapturing the wolves, do you?"

"I wish," Nessa said. She took a sip of the hot chocolate. It never failed to strike her how good food tasted after she transformed. "This is so good," she marveled.

"I know, right?" Luc said, taking another deep sip of his. For a second they locked eyes and Nessa felt the charge that was always there between them.

Luc placed his mug on a tree stump table and sprawled out on cushions pushed up against the wall, patting the spot next to him. Nessa knew she should be going home, but couldn't resist collapsing into it. He loved resting and it was contagious. Nessa felt her most relaxed around him. They hadn't taken time to light a fire, but the cocoa was warming and it felt so good to sit down. Luc smelled of woodsmoke and pine trees and the tea-tree soap his mom bought.

He wrapped an arm around her shoulders and leaned down to kiss her. She kissed him back, feeling a tingle come up through her arms and legs, traveling deep inside her. She snuggled in, feeling the warmth of his body even as they both broke away to laugh at the sound their windbreaker running jackets made rubbing up against each other.

"Do you ever wonder what it would be like?" she asked. "If I stayed with you?"

"Stayed in the cabin?" Luc said. "Like overnight? You know it's never going to happen." Ever since late last fall, when Nessa had come clean to her mom about her and Bree's "investigation" of Paravida—Nessa was the one who had discovered the horrible research the company had been doing on wolves—Vivian had been extra careful, developing a sixth sense about when Nessa was saying she was at Bree's when she wasn't really there. Not exactly convenient timing for Nessa to have her first real boyfriend. She would have appreciated a little more freedom.

"Well, not just overnight at your cabin," Nessa said. "There's that. But what if we stayed as wolves overnight?"

Luc disentangled himself. Sat up. Scooted forward, his back suddenly straight and stiff. "No," he said. "This is not for you."

"Why not?" Nessa said. "It's okay for you but not me?"

Luc stiffened and Nessa knew she'd broken his code of never referring to the fact that one day, in the not-too-distant future, Luc would merge into the wolf population forever. He'd first transformed when he was little, and always assumed he would complete that transformation when he got closer to adulthood. This was his family's way—in every generation there was an uncle or an aunt who got the call.

Some people got jobs after college. Luc would go into the woods, Nessa thought to herself, but she didn't dare joke about it out loud. Luc had made it clear that the total transformation was deeply important to him and also deeply private. He didn't want to talk about it, and he certainly didn't want Nessa to come with him.

The truth was, Nessa *had* thought about what it would be like for her to go too. She loved running as a wolf. She loved being inside the mind of an animal, letting her animal self out to play. "It would be cool," she said now, guardedly. "You always say you'll know what it's like to really *be* a wolf. To eat meat you helped hunt. To—I don't know—I could have puppies someday. Really be part of a pack."

"That's not why I'm doing it," Luc said. He still had his back to her. "I'm doing it to make a real impact on the lives out there. To help restore the balance."

"So why not me too? Let's face it, Earth doesn't need any more people, but wolves are endangered."

Luc laughed. "Are you hearing yourself? You just said 'endangered.'"

"Well, they're endangered only at the species level," Nessa sputtered. "Individual wolves aren't affected." Luc said nothing. "Okay then, why is it okay for you and not me?"

"Because I've always known this was who I would be. I was meant for this." Luc had told Nessa early on that he'd been a wolf nearly as long as he could remember. Some wolves were chosen, the way Nessa was—bitten by wolves who needed help. Others were born into it. "You do realize that if you became a wolf for life, it would be, like, I don't know—dying?" he said. "You'd leave everyone behind. Your family. All your friends. What would they think? That you'd run away from home or something?"

"You think *your* family is going to be okay with it?" Nessa countered.

"They *know*," Luc said. "It happens. It's an honor."

He finally turned and looked at her. Luc looked like old Luc, the guy she'd first met last fall, the distance runner on her team whose times were untouchable, the new kid at school who didn't seem to have or want to have friends.

"Luc, I'm sorry," she said immediately, scooting forward to put a hand on his back. "Is this . . . hard for you?"

Luc looked at her then, too, and when his gray-green eyes locked on hers, Nessa felt her skin turning electric.

"I don't know—" he said. His words seemed to get stuck in his throat. "I don't know how I am going to be able to leave you."

If he hadn't been looking at her in just such a way, Nessa might have said, "So don't." But she could feel how serious he was about this. She didn't want to mess with that.

"Luc," she said, pulling herself forward to kiss him in a way that reminded her of so many other times, but also felt 100 percent exciting and new. She knew he didn't want to talk about this anymore. She knew it would be merciful to change the subject. "My mom is going to *kill* me if I'm not home to help out with Nate."

Luc drew away. "Yeah, okay," he said. He breathed a sigh of relief. He was back to himself when he said, "So what about this tranq gun situation?"

"I don't know," Nessa said. Sliding her feet into her sneakers, she laced them up with quick, practiced motions. It was nice to be able to run without the ice-traction cleats she'd been strapping on to her shoes all winter. "I guess I could ask around at Dr. Morgan's. See where you even go to get that stuff. Find out who might have access to it?"

"That sounds good," Luc said.

"But Luc," Nessa added. She was holding the door open and sucking all the warmth from the cabin but she had something else to say. "The Paravida wolves. There are so many of them. What happens if we can't keep them away from the town?"

"We can," he said. "They just need time. Trust me, okay?"

Nessa rolled her eyes. "Trust," she said. "Right." As someone who had grown up in a town poisoned by a greedy chemical company, trust wasn't exactly her strong suit. She pulled the door closed behind her before sprinting away, down the trail toward home.

Or maybe not so much sprinting as jogging. Track season would start up soon—she was going to have to start training. All winter, she'd been running in wolf form, but slacking off when she ran as a human.

A half-mile into her trek, she heard Luc behind her, running as a wolf. Seeing him, she couldn't help it, she transformed back into her wolf-self as well. They sprinted back to her neighborhood, capturing some of the speed and joy, even as the temperature dropped and the weather seemed to remind them: Winter was not over quite yet.

It was then that she noticed the faintly pulsing light coming from the direction of her neighborhood.

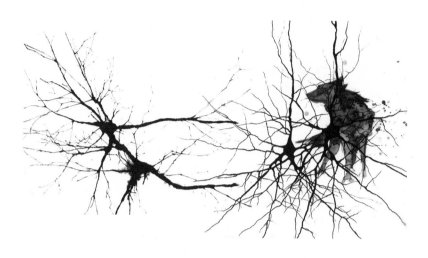

CHAPTER TWO

Nessa transformed out of wolf form a quarter mile or so behind her house, watching Luc continue on down the track they'd worn between their houses. She made her way gingerly through the half-frozen mud and matted leaves, hoping to avoid soaking her sneakers. She also wanted to avoid the motion-activated lights in her backyard. She was late, and on the off chance that her mom had actually beaten her home, it was a bad idea for Nessa to announce the fact that she was coming in through the backyard. Vivian didn't know Nessa was running as a wolf, but she knew Nessa was spending more and more time in the woods—supposedly training—and she didn't like it.

Nessa gave a little gasp when the path turned around a hill and she could see that the lights in her yard were already on. In fact, they were blazing. And then she realized that the lights she was seeing were not coming from the few outdoor spotlights hung behind the roofline.

These were floodlights, the kind you'd see set up next to the scene of a car accident on the highway. Nessa felt her stomach clench. Why were these lights set up in her neighborhood? And so close to her house?

She quickened her pace, slipping out of the woods a safe distance from her house, so it would look like she'd been running on the road. She hoped she'd see a crew of town construction workers digging up a water pipe or doing emergency work on the gas line. Anything that didn't affect her family.

As her house came into view, Nessa saw bright blue state police cruisers were rocked up over the curb onto the front lawn, their flashing red lights casting a surreal glow over the front of her house. An armored Humvee marked 'Homeland Security' was parked in the driveway like a tank.

Nessa strode quickly across her front lawn, weaving among the parked vehicles. Men and women in windbreakers were shuffling in and out of the shadows the lights cast. When one of them turned, Nessa saw unmistakable block lettering on his navy blue windbreaker: FBI.

She felt her heart beating twice as fast as usual, heard the sound of blood rushing in her ears. Nate and Delphine were inside. She had to make sure they were okay. The sight of her mother's beat-up Ford in the driveway gave her a tiny morsel of hope. At least Vivian would be there.

She headed for her front door, not stopping when she heard

voices calling out "Miss?" and "Hold on!" She was also able to hear snippets of whispered conversation that most people—people who are not also wolves—would not have been able to.

"Can she go in there?"

" . . . attempted damage control . . . "

" . . . timing is crap . . . "

Delphine was the first person Nessa saw on entering the house. Nessa's younger sister was standing just inside the front door, her hands limp at her sides, weeping like Nessa hadn't seen her weep since they were both little, saying, "Nessa, my God, Nessa." Nate was tucked in the corner of the old plaid sofa, hugging his knees to his chest, shaking and rocking, whimpering with his eyes squeezed shut.

She heard her mother's voice, from the kitchen. "Put that down. What the hell do you want with my Grandma Kay's recipes? My God, you think I was hiding something in the flour bin?"

Following the sound of Vivian's voice, Nessa made her way past men and women in suits, guns in holsters on their belts, opening drawers and running something that looked like a Geiger counter over the carpeting.

"Mom?" she called out as she rounded the corner and entered the kitchen. "What's going on?"

Vivian was sitting at one of the padded chairs at the round, Formica-topped kitchen table, straining forward. Her hair that she wore loose and full had fallen into her face, but when she saw Nessa she looked up, her hair falling away to show the piercing blue eyes Nessa had inherited. She was still dressed in her vet tech scrubs with the kitten pattern on them. "I don't know what you're looking for, but that's cat food!" she was shouting at a woman opening the giant Tupperware of Purina Vivian kept under the kitchen sink to feed the cats she occasionally treated in the garage. An agent was running the Geiger counter-looking device around the edges of the open oven. A second agent, wearing gloves, was going through the trash.

Nessa's mind felt fogged. Clearly, she was missing something, but information was not processing the way it should. Nessa could not tell what she was supposed to pay attention to. That her mom was dressed in her work scrubs as Nessa would expect her to be? That her shoulders were oddly hunched? That she was sitting when she normally would have been standing? That the house was filled with FBI agents carrying boxes?

Then Nessa saw that Vivian's hunched position could be explained by the fact that her mother's hands were cuffed behind her back.

For a moment Nessa thought it was a joke. A giant prank to make her feel guilty for being late to cook Nate and Delphine dinner.

At least, she thought that until the pair of officers flanking Vivian lifted her by the elbows to a standing position, and Nessa managed to repeat her question. "What's going on?"

"I'm—" Vivian started. She cleared her throat, lifted her head. "I guess I'm being arrested." She almost laughed as she said it and Nessa knew right away the seriousness was making her mom a little insane. She felt the same way.

"Look," Vivian said, as if the reality were sinking in for her just as it was slowly dawning on Nessa. "I—" She stopped to think. "I can't think. Call Aunt Jane. She'll come for you." Vivian paused and pursed her lips. "Her number is in the roll top desk.

Until then, please take care of Delphine and Nate."

"But—"

"I'm assuming this is some kind of—" Vivian glared at a man in a suit with red receding hair and angry skin, infected from eczema or acne—"grave mistake."

The man ignored Vivian's look, gesturing to the officers flanking Vivian. They started to lead Vivian out of the room.

"Wait!" Nessa shouted, but the men didn't stop moving.

Nessa's only choice was to follow. At the door to the house, Vivian struggled to turn back one last time. "You should make sure to call Dr. Morgan," she said to Nessa, craning her neck back in an attempt to turn. "See if you can pick up extra shifts. With me gone, tell him you can take over those extra jobs I'd been working on."

"Wait, what?" Nessa asked. What extra work? Nessa wasn't licensed to do the tech work Vivian did. Not to mention that after all her years at the clinic, Vivian was way more than a tech. She practically ran that place, and could diagnose and perform any procedure as well as Dr. Morgan.

Nessa followed Vivian as far as the front door, feeling a brief flash of guilt for leaving Nate on the couch, but knowing she just had to stay with her mother as long as she could.

In the driveway and yard, the lights were shining directly into the open garage. Nessa still couldn't understand. It was like a strange dream. Why were men in SWAT uniforms carrying boxes of the Kurlands' Christmas ornaments out of the garage and loading them into their van, their radios broadcasting static and unintelligible questions?

Delphine joined Nessa in the doorway and they watched together as one of the officers closed the sedan door on their mother and moved around to the passenger side in the front to let himself in. His partner got in behind the wheel and the car began to roll away, the detective with the red hair standing at the end of the driveway and watching it go.

Delphine pushed past Nessa and ran out to the spot where the car had been, slipping slightly in the scrim of mud that lay on top of the partly frozen ground.

Was Delphine going to follow the car? Shooting a look back at Nate, who remained curled up into himself on the couch, Nessa caught up with her sister at the mailbox. Nessa put an arm around Delphine's narrow shoulders. Delphine was pretty and popular—at school, Nessa would pass her table in the cafeteria and see Delphine laughing in the center of a group of her friends, boys stopping by the table to steal their French fries. But she wasn't laughing now. Her face had turned fierce. "I want all of these people out of our house," she near-growled.

"Why are they even here?" Nessa asked. "What did they say when they came?"

Delphine shuddered. "It all happened so fast," she said. "One minute, I was hearing sirens, you know? I thought it was a fire."

Nessa nodded, looking at the cars now parked up on their lawn and at their neighbors'.

"I thought it was a fire *at someone else's house*," Delphine clarified. Her eyes filled with tears. "Then I went to the window and it was just this . . . convoy. Car after car, and trucks, and by the time I realized they were actually coming to our house and I was calling to Mom—I guess she was in the kitchen?— these SWAT guys were storming down the door and if it wasn't unlocked they probably would have broken it down. They all had guns, Nessa. They had so many guns. They were pointing them at us. At me and Nate. I was so scared that Nate wasn't going to understand. That he'd do something stupid without knowing and they'd shoot him."

Delphine wiped at her running nose with the back of her hand. "And then they were rushing over to Mom and saying, 'Is your name Vivian Kurland?' and the second she said, 'Yes,' they were telling her she had the right to remain silent and pulling her arms behind her back and she was telling them there must have been a mistake and yelling at me not to look and to call you. So I ran in the living room to get my phone and that's when you came home."

"Oh my gosh," Nessa said.

"I know," said Delphine. "And Nessa, they've been taking so much of our stuff with them. Weird stuff. A box of broken lamps. My old cheerleading uniform. Old clothes going to Goodwill that I helped Mom pack up."

"More like *forced* her to pack," Nessa said, just to coax a smile out of Delphine, who was worrying her right now.

Delphine didn't drop her focus. "That man," she said. "The one in the suit?"

Nessa nodded.

"He wouldn't tell Mom what she was being arrested for. She kept asking him. At first, she was giving him hell." Delphine smiled weakly at the memory. "You know Mom."

Nessa nodded. Vivian was amazing with animals, but when it came to people—people who weren't her children—you didn't want to get on her bad side. She was a fighter. Teachers who ignored the fact that Delphine was a math whiz just because she wasn't a boy, coaches who didn't invite Nessa to be on the elite squad because they didn't think she could afford the cost of the uniforms or fees—they experienced the full force of Vivian's ire. She had gone toe-to-toe with state agencies for years, getting Nate the services he needed for his autism.

Thinking of Nate, Nessa remembered that he needed her now. "We should probably go back inside," she said.

"I just—" Delphine said. "Why would they take Mom?" She was crying again.

"I don't know," Nessa said. She tried to make her voice calm and comforting. She told herself: *Don't cry. Don't feel.* She had to stay strong. She was the one who had to take care of Delphine and Nate.

As Nessa was leading Delphine inside, Sheriff Williams, Vivian's distant cousin, pulled up and came to a hard stop in front of their house, seeming to jump out of the car before the engine had turned off.

Nessa had rarely seen him look angry before but he looked angry now, the fur-trimmed hood of his parka bouncing, the open jacket flapping at his sides as if his very life force caused the winds to blow. "Girls," he said, touching Nessa lightly on her shoulder. "Go inside. I'm going to find out what's going on and I'll be in, in a minute."

If explanations were to be given, Nessa wanted to hear them too, but then she thought about Nate and passed through the door even as she heard the sheriff bellowing, "What the heck is going on here?" to someone she couldn't see. She could see him interrogating a group of SWAT guys stowing equipment in their armored truck.

Nessa squeezed her eyes closed, trying to keep the rising panic at bay, trying not to think. She opened her eyes and saw that Delphine, sitting on the couch next to Nate, had laid a hand on his arm. He swatted it away, and Delphine scooted back. It was freezing in the house from the door being propped open so long.

"Hold on," Nessa said, heading over to him. She pulled a blanket off the back of the couch and snapped it open, stretching it between her two hands, then wrapped it around Nate's shoulders, pulling the ends together and taking him by the shoulders. This was something she'd seen Vivian do before. She knew not to try to stop his rocking, only to let him know by the pressure on his arms that she was there.

Just as he was settling, leaning against her, Sheriff Williams entered the house, carefully wiping his boots on the mat, crossing his arms in front of his chest, like people do at a funeral when they don't want to be there. He shut the front door after one last agent had brushed past him.

Through the window, Nessa watched the stream of vehicles leaving. After the noise of the crackling walkie-talkies and idling engines, the night felt empty. The silence seemed to underscore the awful fact that their mother—who belonged here, in this house—was gone.

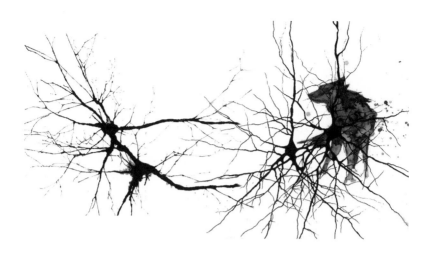

CHAPTER THREE

ell, kids," Sheriff Williams said. "I just got a chance to talk to Agent Lonegrin. I don't have very good news for you three." He sighed and took a seat facing them, on the opposite end of the old sectional sofa, the only furniture in the living room aside from the TV and the table that held the souped-up computer Delphine had rebuilt almost entirely out of old parts.

"Your mom's been arrested, and though I don't know the whole story about what she's going to be charged with, I won't lie to you. If Homeland Security and the FBI are involved, it's pretty serious. We'll know more tomorrow when she goes before a judge to hear the charges. But the most important thing is that right now, you three are going to need a place to go."

"Go?" Nessa said. "What do you mean?" They were home. They didn't want to go anywhere.

"Are we going to get arrested too?" Delphine asked.

Sheriff Williams actually laughed. "Not to my knowledge," he said. "You just can't be alone without some kind of guardian present. The state's already got a social worker on the way."

"Why?" Nessa said. "I'm seventeen!"

"You're still a minor. If there is someone you can think of you'd like to be with, we should give them a call now and get the paperwork in place while the social worker is here on site. It's the best thing to keep you out of foster care, to get you switched right now to a family member you all are going to feel most comfortable with."

At the words "foster care," Nate lifted his head. The Kurlands knew kids in foster care.

"We're going to foster care?" Nate asked.

"No," said Nessa, opening her phone. "We're calling Aunt Jane."

As the line rang, Nessa prayed that Jane would pick up. Jane didn't have a family or even a boyfriend and she loved movies and concerts and restaurants and plays and all that city stuff there was to do in Milwaukee. She was often out.

But she answered, her pleasant, surprised "Nessa!" seeming to come from another time. "Uh . . . I . . . Aunt Jane?" Nessa felt dangerously close to tears and realized she just could not do this. She couldn't describe what had just happened. Sheriff Williams took the phone out of her hand.

"Jane," he said. He identified himself—of course, they knew

each other as Jane was his second cousin too. Then he said, "I'm calling about Vivian. Now, she's all right, but I'm with her kids because there's been a bit of a situation."

Nessa could hear Jane's tone of alarm through the phone as Sheriff Williams kept talking, answering questions, explaining, mostly talking about all the things he *didn't* know.

As she listened, Nessa remembered how Sheriff Williams had been the one to take her and Vivian out to the Paravida plant last fall, after Nessa and Luc had broken into it. Nessa had told Vivian about the labs she'd seen there—labs where children supposedly taking part in a long-term health study were being used for medical experiments, labs where wolves were being used to grow human organs. Sheriff Williams had listened to Nessa's story without trying to convince her she must have hallucinated it all, and even after they got to Paravida and found the labs completely emptied of any incriminating evidence, he'd been kind. Or maybe, he'd known on some level there was more going on than there seemed. Sheriff Williams had been the one to spot a single bloody matted piece of wolf fur that the cleaners had managed to miss.

Paravida, Nessa thought. They had resources beyond compare. If they'd been able to remove all traces of a lab overnight, could they have orchestrated her mom's arrest as well?

Nessa wandered out of the room as the sheriff and Jane's conversation turned to logistics. She made her way down the hall, ending up in Nate's room. She looked out the window, toward the woods, which she could just make out in the darkness. She thought about Luc, wishing he was with her. Was it possible she'd been running out there with him only an hour before? That her life had been turned upside down so quickly and suddenly?

Craving normality, she thought to text her best friend Bree. But Sheriff Williams had her phone. Besides, the words she'd need to explain what just happened were too stark, too wrong.

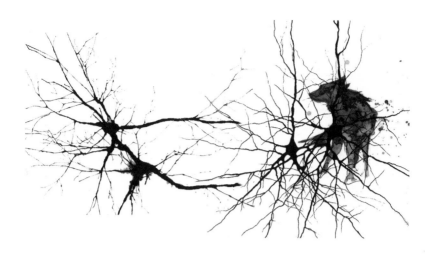

CHAPTER FOUR

The situation felt no less surreal when Nessa woke up on the couch five hours later. Jane was there, shaking her shoulder.

Nessa pushed herself into a sitting position, giving Jane a bleary hug.

It took Nessa's exhausted brain a few moments to get around to remembering why Jane was even there. What had happened.

And then she did remember and she could feel the air pushed out of her chest all over again. Her mom had been taken away. For no real reason that Nessa could think of or name.

"Honey? Nessa?" Aunt Jane said. She was smaller than Vivian. Her hair was straight and red, where Vivian's was blonde and wavy. Their personalities were different too. They were basically polar opposites, but still, there was something about having Aunt Jane open her arms at the exact moment that the events of the evening before came back in her mind that invited Nessa to break down.

But Nessa didn't break down. She knew she had to be strong. She reminded herself: She was a wolf. She had to stay alert.

Aunt Jane gave her a suspicious "I know you're upset and I won't believe otherwise until you've had a chance for a good cry" look, then turned to the social worker who had arrived during her drive and said, "As far as I'm concerned, these kids are never going to foster care, so let me know what I need to do and say, and I'll do and say it."

After a few more hours of not enough sleep, Nessa woke to see Aunt Jane up and cooking breakfast. Nessa couldn't help it. She laughed.

Aunt Jane was *not* a cook. But there she was, standing at the stove, dressed in a kimono, sliding sunny-side-up eggs (that were basically raw) onto a plate, her thin hair tucked behind her ears, her glasses sliding down her nose every time she slid the spatula into the pan.

Jane was chatting and talking a mile a minute about her drive the night before—how she'd managed to stay awake thanks to a sharing-size package of M&M's and a cup of coffee as tall as her forearm. Her bag was still in the living room, an oversized tote stuffed full with a jumble of things she must have pulled together at the last minute. Nessa saw bungee cords, a yoga mat, an umbrella. When Vivian traveled, she brought only what she could carry. Jane was likely to bring everything she owned, up to and including the kitchen sink.

"Look!" Jane said, holding out the plate for Nessa's inspection. "Eggs!"

"Thanks, Aunt Jane," Nessa said, with as much enthusiasm as she could muster. Even as she looked at the gelatinous substance Jane scooped onto her plate—Jane broke the yolk as she served it—Nessa was grateful to her aunt for coming. She was also grateful that Aunt Jane kept the conversation light. Nessa wasn't ready to talk about her mom.

As Delphine and Nate emerged, Jane moved from the story of the enormous coffee cup to the traveling guitar-toting folk singer she'd met while buying the coffee and his advice on mixing caffeine and NoDoz. (Short answer: It's a bad idea.)

"Now, guys," she said, after Nate had zipped up his winter jacket and hiked his backpack onto his shoulders—his bus came to the house first and would arrive any minute. "I'm going to see your mom today—Sheriff Williams told me she will be seen by a judge and maybe even released this afternoon—so I might be gone when you get back.

"I'm sure she's crazy worried about you three," she continued, "so I'm going to be sure to tell her that everything here is going fine. Not that I'll need to. I'm sure they'll release her right away. But just in case she isn't able to get home by the end of the day, let me know if you have any messages for her. I'll be happy to deliver them."

Nate just stared. He didn't like it when you dumped a lot of information all at once.

"No messages?" Jane asked him, cheerily.

"Tell her we don't believe she did anything wrong," Delphine said, tossing her hair back and looking defiant. "No one will."

"Tell her I'm going to talk to Dr. Morgan today about the extra shifts," Nessa said, remembering her mother's curious instruction from the night before.

"And you Nate?" Jane said, looking at him hopefully, her eyes opened wide. "Do you have any message you want me to pass on?"

"Uh . . ." Nate said. Ducking his head, he mumbled, "My bus is here," and pushed his way out of the door.

Just then, Nessa heard what sounded like music to her ears. The unmistakable roar of the Monster, a.k.a. her best friend Bree's car. It had earned its nickname because of its monolithic size and the fact that its engine sounded like a monster's growl. It was safe though—that had been Bree's dad's number one concern when he bought it for her.

"Is she giving us a ride?" Delphine said hopefully. "I'll brush my teeth!"

"I didn't call her," Nessa said as she left the kitchen. Inwardly, she thought, *because I couldn't bear to tell her what happened.* She dreaded doing it now, as if saying it out loud would make it more real.

Before Nessa even reached it, Bree poked her head in the door, her tight curls bouncing. She had her eyebrows raised, shaking her head in horror and wonder, her dimples showing as much when she frowned as when she smiled, which under normal circumstances was all the time.

"Nessa, your mom!" she said.

"You know?"

"My dad heard about the police car convention at your house over his radio. One of your neighbors called my mom, too, so . . . " She looked around as if not expecting to see the room looking so much like itself. "I figured this might not be the day you'd want to deal with riding the bus to school. Nessa, *the FBI was here?*"

"Yep," Nessa said.

"And . . . your mom? They . . . took her?"

Nessa nodded again. She could feel a lump start in her throat.

"Did they take the box?" Bree said, in a low voice.

For a second, Nessa didn't know what Bree meant. "What box?" she said.

Then, she remembered.

The Paravida box.

Late last fall, after they broke into the health clinic in town, Nessa and Bree had made off with a folder of potentially incriminating files describing Paravida's involvement in a health study of Tether's kids. They'd hidden the file after reading it, knowing it was probably chock full of evidence they'd be able to use against the corporate giant someday. All winter, Bree had been arguing that they should use the contents to return to the investigation. Nessa had been too busy patrolling the woods for Paravida wolves, and given Vivian's increased level of vigilance, a good time had never presented itself.

"Oh, God," Nessa said now. "That's why they were taking all that stuff out of our attic and garage. Why didn't we move it when we had the chance?"

"Because we were busy," Bree said. "But as soon as I heard about what was happening, I thought about it. It was obvious to me that's what they'd come for. Nessa, I'm guessing they just arrested your mom for show. They'll release her on a technicality but somehow portions of the 'evidence' they took will be missing."

"Oh, wow," said Nessa. "That hadn't even occurred to me." But she had to admit, Bree's theory made perfect sense.

Last fall, after they'd broken into the Paravida facility itself, Nessa had expected the company would go after her, but when November turned into December, and December turned into January, she'd let herself believe she was small potatoes. "But why take my mom? Why not me?" she asked. It still did not make tons of sense.

"Who knows?" Bree said. "Remember, there are judges and a chief of police on Paravida's board. They can take whoever they want to."

Just then, Jane stepped into the front hallway from the kitchen. "Bree!" she said. "I've missed you!" and as if it were the most natural thing in the world for Jane to be cooking eggs at Nessa's house on a Monday morning, Jane started asking Bree for updates on her love life—the last time they'd seen each other was the previous summer, when Bree had still been breaking up with Sad Matt.

Bree mouthed the words "Talk more later" to Nessa as she returned Jane's hug. After catching up, Bree, Delphine, and Nessa headed out to Bree's car, even as Jane raised the egg-slimed spatula in the air and called, "Tell your mom I say hi!"

"You bet," said Bree.

Nessa shuddered. It felt so wrong to have Jane here, funny stories or no. She just wanted her mom.

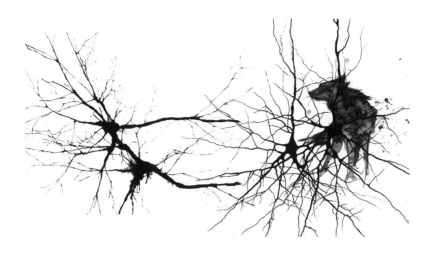

CHAPTER FIVE

ree's dad was not the only one who had picked up on the news of Vivian's arrest via the police radio scanner. Tether was the kind of town where news spreads fast, especially if the news involves an arrest, half the Michigan state police, Homeland Security, and the FBI.

As Bree's car pulled into the parking lot of Tether High, kids stayed collected in groups to be there the minute Nessa and Delphine arrived. Even when they were still in the car, Nessa could see kids bending down to catch a glimpse of her through the windows.

She had experienced unwanted celebrity before, but this kind of attention was new for Delphine. As they climbed out of

Bree's car, Nessa saw her sister gamely trying to keep her chin up and act like she wasn't noticing the silence and the stares—looking exactly like Vivian as she did so—but she could also see the flush rising up Delphine's neck and into her cheeks.

Nessa looked to Bree. Maybe they should get back in the car and run everyone over? Bree shook her head slightly. There was nothing they could do.

But then as Nessa turned in Delphine's direction again, she saw that Delphine was not alone. Luc had emerged from somewhere—had he been waiting for them?

He placed himself in front of Delphine, blocking her view of the staring crowd. His dark hair was falling over one of his eyes and he had his hands shoved into the front pockets of his jeans, his shoulders lifted as if he were mulling over a decision.

Over the top of the car, he caught Nessa's eye and winked. He then pulled a hand from a pocket and made a big gesture of throwing his arm over Delphine's shoulder, and walked her toward the school entrance like he was the older brother she'd never had.

A path cleared for Luc and Delphine, and walking a few steps behind, Nessa could hear Luc asking Delphine for fashion advice and Delphine laughing. Nessa decided Luc was a genius.

"Thanks," Nessa said to him later after he'd walked Delphine to her locker, hung out with her while she put her stuff away, and then took her to her first class. He'd caught up to Nessa where she was waiting for the Physics room to open.

He pushed his hand up through his hair and looked out at the streams of students passing by, then back at Nessa. For once, Luc looked a little worried. "*You* okay?" he said.

Nessa thought about being brave and lying, but her

self-control deserted her. "Not really," she confessed.

"Yeah," he said. "I wouldn't think so."

"Why didn't they come get *me*," she said. "Bree thinks they were sent by Paravida."

"Yeah," said Luc. "It makes no sense. What could they possibly think your mom *did*?"

"Nothing," Nessa said as the bell rang. "Which is why they'll probably send her right back home this afternoon."

"Yeah," said Luc. "By the end of the day, maybe it'll feel like none of this ever happened."

"That would be nice," Nessa said. But she doubted she'd ever forget how awful she felt just then.

In some respects, being in class helped. The known routine of answering questions, writing things down, changing rooms, listening to kids answer questions—it calmed her. But at the same time, she couldn't focus.

Everyone wanted to know what her mother had done. Teachers who weren't calling on her were whispering behind her back. Kids who weren't making eye contact were saying, "If the FBI is at your house, you've done something. I don't care what you say," and "I'll never let that woman treat Torrance again," as she passed. Her supersonic wolf senses only made it worse.

And then this happened: Walking to her third-period class, she found herself staring at a poster someone must have hung up in the hallway the night before—it showed a wolf inside a red circle with a slash diagonally through it. On the top it said, "When an endangered species gets dangerous: Lift the wolf-hunting ban in Tether." There was an email address at the bottom: WolfNoMore@gmail.com

Ten feet down the hall, she saw another poster, just like the first, except this one was in the midst of being masking-taped to the wall. By Tim Miller, who she knew from cross-country.

"Hey, Tim, what is this?" Nessa said. "You know you and the rest of the idiots who want to go after these wolves are just going to get yourselves killed, right?"

Oh, no, she thought. She hadn't meant to come off so angry, but she could hear that she was almost growling and Tim was a good guy. He'd helped Nessa and Bree with their Paravida investigation back in the fall—explaining how hospital morgues operated—and he had always had a bit of a crush on Nessa.

Now his eyes were widening in shock and surprise. "Sorry," Nessa muttered. "Maybe on a day when my mother hasn't just been arrested, I might be more diplomatic," she continued.

"Yeah, Nessa, I'm so sorry—" Tim said. And then, as if he couldn't help himself, "Do you know what they think she did?"

"I don't know, okay?" she said. Or maybe shouted. "They don't tell you apparently. And besides, she didn't do anything. It was a mistake. She's coming home today."

Tim just stared. Nessa turned and walked away.

She had fourth period free and, looking for sanctuary, she stumbled into Coach Hoffman's classroom, which was always empty at this time of day. Kids from cross-country used the room to catch up on homework or hang out and talk about running strategy.

Coach was just getting off the phone as she walked in. "I've told you, I don't know anything about it!" he was saying, his voice rising with frustration.

Nessa wondered vaguely who he was talking to. He'd been fighting the uniform suppliers since February when the new running tanks they'd sent had been emblazoned with the words "Lether High."

"Nessa, I'm glad to see you. Sit," he said, pointing to a desk in the front row. He looked at her for a minute, like he was trying to think of something adult and comforting to say and then he just blurted, "What the heck am I even supposed to say to you? I'm so sorry."

Nessa tried to think of something to say in reply but came up empty also and just shrugged.

"You know what?" Coach said. "I'll just say that I know your mom and I like your mom and whatever they think she did, I don't believe it." He held up two hands, palms facing Nessa in the "stop" gesture. "Enough said."

Nessa smiled. Maybe for the first time all day. "Coach," she said. And then she couldn't say anything else. This was the man who had caught her when she'd run so hard she hadn't been able to stand up after finishing a race. She didn't want to cry here, so she sat on her hands and stared at the clock on the wall above her head.

"But I gotta tell you," he went on. "That was Paravida on the phone, calling about the award status."

"Oh, yeah, right," Nessa said. The Paravida Award. After winning at States last fall, Nessa had been awarded the coveted prize. At the time, she'd already had her suspicions that the company was up to no good, but she hadn't been aware of the full extent of it. She'd appreciated the free sneakers, the swag, and the scholarship to running camp, even if it meant she had to enter all her running times on the app they maintained on the website. Sneakers and camp were critical if she was going to win a college scholarship.

Nessa nodded, going cold inside. "It's because of my mom, you mean?" she said. "They're going to take away the Paravida Award? Is that even possible?"

"Nah," Coach said. "They're just freaking. They don't give away sneakers and camp and uniforms from the goodness of their hearts. They do it to—" (he made giant air quotes) "—enhance the brand. Anything that isn't squeaky clean is probably giving some executive vice president a coronary somewhere. It'll all blow over. Sheriff Williams called me—he knows I'm your coach—and he told me this whole thing was probably some horrible mix-up and your mom's likely to be home in time for dinner."

Nessa nodded, trying to look comforted for Coach's sake. Trying to remind herself that Paravida was a big company, and the award people were probably not aware of the other, more sinister sectors of the company. Coach Hoffman seemed calm—she should follow his lead.

But would he be so calm if he knew the things about Paravida that she did?

"So Paravida's gonna squawk for a day or so about some technicality. They say you aren't filling in your training times using the web tool they provided."

Nessa shook her head.

Coach sighed. "This is not a big deal," he insisted. "I know I don't have to ask you if you're running, because I know how disciplined you are . . . Just write it down when you have a sec, okay?"

"Thanks," Nessa said. She wasn't running. She'd been too

busy patrolling the woods to make time. But Coach didn't need to know that. "I will."

"And if you need anything, just let me know. Margery's always happy to have team members sleep in our guest room. Your brother and sister too. Just in case your mom has to stay another night or two."

"Thanks," Nessa repeated. "But my Aunt Jane is here. My mom wanted her to come, probably because Nate—" Nessa followed Vivian's practice of never using the labels that had been assigned to Nate, his "diagnoses." To her, they didn't have anything to do with who Nate really was. "With Nate especially, it needs to be family."

"Good," Coach said, leaning forward, slapping his desk like the issue need not be spoken of again. "I'm sure once this has been cleared up, we'll all have a good laugh."

"Yeah," said Nessa. "Ha."

At her locker, just before lunch, she saw she had a text from Jane.

Heading to Grand Rapids. Hearing's sometime after 2 p.m. Fingers crossed!

Nessa did cross her fingers, and then pushed her phone deep into her pocket. All she had to do was get through lunch, two more classes, going to the library to study, and then she could go home. Her mom would be there. This nightmare would be over.

But at lunchtime, Bree was waiting for Nessa at the entrance to the cafeteria, pink slips of paper in hand.

"What are those for?" Nessa said.

"Duh," said Bree. "They're our out-to-lunch passes."

"I can see that," Nessa said. "But um . . . you want to go out? Today?" The last thing she wanted was Bree's favorite Slushie for lunch.

"No," Bree said. "I want to go to your house. We've got to look for that box in your garage."

Yes, Nessa thought. *Of course.* Pulling one of the slips out of Bree's hand, she turned on her heel, booking for the nearest exit.

"Don't you want to get your coat?" Bree asked.

"Let's just go."

While Bree was navigating the Monster out of the parking lot, Nessa worried she was going to transform into a wolf right then and there—occasionally it would happen at points of heightened emotionality or fear. She took a deep breath. She had to calm herself down. To think.

"But we're not going to find it," Nessa said. "You realize that, right? They're the *FBI*. If all they came to get was a box in the garage, they'll have found it."

"Unless all those agents and squad car guys were just pretending to be FBI?" Bree said. "And they're really just people who work for Paravida?"

Nessa took a minute to think that over. "No," she said. "I don't think being part of the FBI's that easy to fake." She glanced at Bree. "Especially when it comes to my mom being in an actual real jail and showing up today in an actual real court. Jane's gone to see her, so she's got to really be there."

"I can tell you one thing," Bree went on. "Whether it was the real FBI or not, whoever was at your house yesterday was *sent* by Paravida. And the only reason Paravida would have sent someone to your house was because of that box."

Lunch period was only thirty-eight minutes long. The girls knew they didn't have much time at Nessa's. The second the Monster rolled into Nessa's driveway, Bree slammed the gearshift into park and they had the doors open almost instantaneously. Tearing up the front walk, Nessa scrabbled at the lock with her house key, her hands shaking. Once they got the door open, they rushed through the kitchen and into the garage, turning on the lights.

And then they saw what the garage had become.

"I don't know how we're going to find *anything* in here," Nessa said, feeling defeated all over again.

The agents had really done a number on their not-always that-well-organized garage storage area the night before. It was a mess. The single fluorescent fixture cast deep shadows behind the boxes and shelves and old tires and, in one corner, the exam table and crates Vivian had set up for the animals she sometimes treated there.

Bree sighed. "This is going to be harder to find than I thought."

"And we've got to get back to school in a half-hour," Nessa reminded her. "On top of all that, we're probably looking for something that isn't here anymore."

"Well, let's start by assuming it is," Bree said. Nessa led her toward the back corner, behind the lawn mower, where she had put the box back in November.

The back corner was now dominated by a small mountain of camping equipment and old paint cans where the agents must have emptied the entire contents of a utility shelf onto the floor. Nessa started digging through the tents and sleeping bags and camp stoves and tarps, Bree moving in behind her to stack the paint cans back on the shelves they'd been stored on.

At the bottom of the pile, Nessa thought she saw something. She didn't want to get her hopes up, but she remembered hiding the files in a plastic bin, and there now, behind a tower of empty appliance boxes, stacked on the TV cart that they used before they got the flat screen when Nessa was still in middle school, she saw something blue.

"Look," Nessa said, pointing. "That might be it."

She dragged it out into the center of the garage and she and Bree lifted off the cover together. There, inside, were the file folders they'd taken, a mix of personnel documents, retirement plan updates, pictures that might have been tacked to a cube wall at some point, and the other files they hadn't gone through yet.

"It's all here," Bree said, in the hushed tone of someone contemplating a mystery beyond her comprehension.

After looking through the entire box again, trying to remember if there was something that had been here before but they weren't seeing now—there wasn't—Nessa sat back, resting on a white plastic lawn chair.

"I don't get it," she said. "Why would Paravida want my mom's Goodwill donations and Delphine's cheerleading uniform but not this?"

"And why would they take your mom, not you?"

"Yeah," Nessa said.

"Unless ..." Bree said. She screwed up her eyes as if she was squinting into the distance.

"Unless what?" Nessa prompted.

"Unless your mom actually did something wrong?"

Nessa looked around at the contents of the garage, the bikes and abandoned toys and discarded rowing machine someone had given them but Vivian had never had time for. She saw the jumble of tools that never seemed to help them repair the leaks in the plumbing or frayed electrical wires or holes in the cheap wallboard of their house. It was a testament to Vivian's life: helping animals, giving her kids everything she had, trying to scrape by without ever having enough money.

"My mom?" Nessa said. "A criminal?" She shook her head. "Think again."

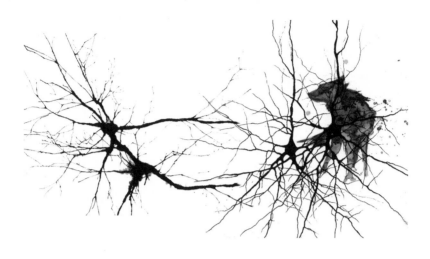

CHAPTER SIX

unt Jane's text had said the hearing could happen as early as 2 p.m. and Nessa started checking her phone at 2:28, which was when school let out. There was nothing.

Nessa went to the library to study. She picked a quiet cubicle in the far corner, cracked open her AP Bio textbook, and pretended to read, but within moments, she was checking her phone again. Still nothing.

She remembered to call Dr. Morgan's office, feeling weird the whole time. His receptionist, Ashley, picked up the phone. "Oh, hi, sweetheart, how are you holding up? Have you heard from your mom? We're all so worried about her."

She's acting like Mom's in the hospital, Nessa thought, *instead of in jail.* "She's only going to be gone one day," Nessa explained. "She'll be back by dinner."

"Oh, then, that's not so bad now, is it?"

"I—uh," Nessa said. "My mom said I should call and see if Dr. Morgan needed any extra help. I could come in after school or something. Track practice hasn't started yet."

"Great idea. Let me check with the boss," Ashley said. On hold, Nessa listened to the recorded messages about the importance of primary care visits for your pet, and supporting the mobile spay/neuter clinic her mom had started a few years back. It was interrupted by Dr. Morgan's voice on the other end of the line.

"That you, Nessa?" he said.

She was used to Dr. Morgan looking up from a suture he was sewing or listening to an animal's heartbeat to say, "Hey, runner, how's the treads?" Now, his voice over the phone, the familiarity of it, the association it held of her mom being just in the other room, was comforting.

But he didn't sound like himself. His voice was softer, and he was forming his words slowly, like he didn't quite know what to say. "Nessa, I'm so sorry," he said, and for a second she thought she might want to remind him this wasn't his fault. But why would he think that, anyway?

"I don't know if you knew, but the FBI searched the clinic at the same time they were at your house last night. I had no idea they were coming. I got a call from Sheriff Williams and I got myself over here, but they wouldn't talk to me. Do you know what's going on? What they're looking for, I mean?"

Nessa explained that Jane was finding out and after she'd finished answering Dr. Morgan's questions, she added, "The reason I'm calling is that, you know, one of the last things my mom said to me was to call you. She said maybe I could help you with the extra shifts?"

Dr. Morgan cleared his throat, getting back to business. "Ah, yes, well I certainly could use some help. What with the raid on the clinic, there's a lot to do. How's tomorrow after school?"

"Okay," Nessa said, and then she blurted out. "Do you know what my mom would have meant by extra shifts she's been doing lately? Are there any new tasks I could help with, things she might have been working on?"

There was silence on the other end of the phone. It went on so long that for a second, Nessa wondered whether they'd lost the connection. But no, Dr. Morgan was still there.

"Why would you ask that?" Dr. Morgan said.

"It was just something Mom said. When I saw her last night. As she was leaving. She said to ask you."

"Oh, she did?" Nessa could nearly hear the gears turning as Dr. Morgan thought this through. "I have to say, I don't really know what your mom was referring to," he answered eventually.

"Okay," Nessa said. But really, she wasn't okay. The whole conversation had made her feel only weirder about the whole thing.

After ending the call, she immediately checked her texts, even though she would have heard if one had come through. Why hadn't Jane checked in?

There was still nothing ten minutes later. Nothing at 2:46. Nothing at 2:54. Nothing at 3:07.

At 3:13, a text came in, but it was only from Luc.

You there?

Nessa texted back.

Yup. What's up?

We running?

In sneakers? Nessa wrote back. Or barefoot?

"Barefoot" was a code word Nessa and Luc sometimes used to refer to transforming.

Barefoot.

Nate was at after-school enrichment. Delphine was at Lego Robotics. So technically, Nessa could have joined him. And she was tempted. When she and Luc were in wolf form, she felt whole in a way she rarely did otherwise. But then she'd have to separate from her phone.

I can't. Waiting to hear about my mom.

K.

Nessa felt too anxious to sit still, however. Remembering Coach's instruction about logging her running time, she changed into her running clothes and ran a shortened loop through town—avoiding the woods, carrying her phone in her hand the whole time. She ran an 8-minute pace, which was slow for her. At least she'd used up some time. Her watch now showed 4:09. She took the late bus home. Delphine got dropped off by friends a few minutes later. "Did you hear from Aunt Jane?" Delphine asked.

Nessa shook her head.

That was at 4:47. At 4:51, she checked again. Nothing. No text at 4:57. Or at 5:03.

And then there was something: Nessa heard a car. Aunt Jane's Volkswagen. She and Delphine ran to the living room window, peering into the driveway as the car turned in. Was her mom in it? Nessa was hoping to be able to see through the car's windshield, but there was a glare. It seemed to take a year for Jane to open the driver's side door. Was that because she and Vivian had been finishing a conversation they wanted to keep private? Would the passenger door open next? Would her mother climb out?

When Aunt Jane turned away from the car, her head bent, her narrow shoulders stooped, and entered the house alone, Nessa still did not stop hoping that her mom was still going to open that passenger-side door.

Even after Jane shook her head, put down her purse on the coffee table, collapsed onto the end of the sectional, and said, with tears in her eyes, "I know I should have texted but I wanted to be here to tell you in person," Nessa refused to believe it.

She caught Delphine's look of distress and tried to stay calm for her sake.

"They're keeping her," Jane finally said out loud.

"But you said—" Delphine started, closing her eyes as if trying to avoid the scary part of a movie. "Sheriff Williams said that because of us—because of Nate, they'd never."

Jane shook her head slowly. She leaned forward, resting her elbows on her knees. "I met your mom's lawyer," she said. "His name's Zachary Chandler. He just got assigned to the case this morning—you have the right to a free attorney but he looks . . . So. Young." She took a deep breath. "He had only just found out what she was charged with."

"What is it?"

Aunt Jane swallowed. She looked pale. "Delphine," she said. "You'd better sit down." Aunt Jane made room on the couch and took Delphine's hand in one of hers and Nessa's in the other.

"First, your mom looks fine. I wish she was home. I wish none of this was happening, but I just want to tell you that she is okay. She's herself."

"Okay," said Nessa, already wondering how bad Jane's news had to be to merit this kind of a lead-in.

"The other thing to know is that she has that lawyer. Sometimes you have to wait a week for one to be assigned to you, but your mom got one today, so even if he looks young, that's a good thing." Jane paused to swallow deliberately.

Lawyers . . . the government . . . Nessa nodded, though she could tell she wasn't taking any of this in. "Aunt Jane," she said. "What do they think she did?"

"I'm going to tell you," Jane said. But then she still didn't. "She's—look, last night, we all knew this had to be some kind of mistake, but in the back of my mind, I was also thinking, 'Maybe Vivian's gotten in some kind of trouble. Maybe with her taxes or something, maybe from running her own vet clinic out of the garage.'" Jane closed her eyes as if contemplating something that made her insides crawl.

"Dr. Morgan said the clinic was searched last night also," Nessa volunteered.

Jane nodded. "I'd heard that. That gave me the idea that this could be some sort of code violation over at the clinic. Maybe there's a law they were breaking without realizing it."

"Is that what happened?" Delphine asked. She pulled her

hands away from Jane's so she could pull her hair back. With a practiced, unconscious gesture she divided it at the back and began to plait one side after another into braids. "She's in trouble at the clinic?"

Jane shook her head. "No," she said. "It turns out the charges have nothing to do with the clinic. They have nothing to do with anything. They're not anything your mom has done or even has come close to doing. Which means she's completely innocent. Unless she has become someone who is not the sister I know, there is no way she would have come close to doing the things she's accused of."

Aunt Jane squeezed their hands again. "Girls, your mom's been charged with grand larceny. The lawyer says they're thinking of charging her with crimes that are even more serious. They got this one thing past the grand jury and now they're going through the evidence they collected yesterday, looking for more."

"Grand larceny?" Delphine whispered. Wrapping one of her newly formed braids around a finger, she squinted forward, like she was trying to focus on something that was too far away to see. "What does that mean?"

"Well," Jane said. She was stalling, Nessa could see that. What could Vivian have been accused of that would be so bad? "They basically believe she stole."

"She *stole*?" Nessa said. "Like what, shoplifting?"

"More serious," said Jane.

"They think she broke into someone's house?" Delphine tried.

An image shot into Nessa's mind—her mom, dressed all in black, her blonde hair tucked into a Navy watch cap, climbing out of a window of one of the other houses in their neighborhood, a fistful of necklaces in one hand and a computer monitor tucked under the other arm. Nessa couldn't help it. She laughed out loud. "They think Mom's a burglar?"

Delphine smiled too, nervously.

"They don't think she broke into anyone's house," Jane said, smiling along with them as if grateful for the opportunity. Then her smile disappeared. "They aren't saying what she stole or from whom—in federal court, they don't have to. But her lawyer told me that generally, theft cases seen in federal court involve the theft of public property. This could be documents or information—anything that's public property."

"But Mom never goes anywhere except work and here," Delphine said. "When exactly do they think she would be stealing public property?"

"I know, I told you, I think this is just . . . wrong," Jane said. "It's either a mistake or I don't know. With computers, maybe they think she's hacking into government websites. Maybe someone else did that and stole your mom's identity so it looks like it was her. It's going to get straightened out. I told the lawyer as much. I told him that there was just no way any of this could be true."

Nessa felt like she'd missed a step at the bottom of a staircase and didn't know where the ground was. "Did he believe you?" she said. "The lawyer? Does he believe Mom?"

"It's his job to believe your mother," Jane said. And then she clapped her hands together, looked at her watch. "Look, we can sit here all night but I know your mom wouldn't want that. Nate's going to be home any minute. We have to keep to the routine for his sake. Homework, right? Dinner? I've got some

KFC in the car."

Dinner? Nessa thought. *Impossible.*

"Girls," Aunt Jane said, like a nurse talking to a patient she's afraid will slip into shock. "The bond hearing is in two days. It's likely your mom will come home then, and at least we'll know more. We can talk to her face-to-face. We've got to hope for the best."

"How are we supposed to do that?" Nessa asked. "I feel like I'm going to throw up."

"Me too," said Delphine.

"You fake it," Aunt Jane said, for once sounding like Vivian herself. "You fake it 'til you make it. It's not going to do your mom one lick of good to have us crying and moaning. It's two more days. Don't think of it as anything more than that."

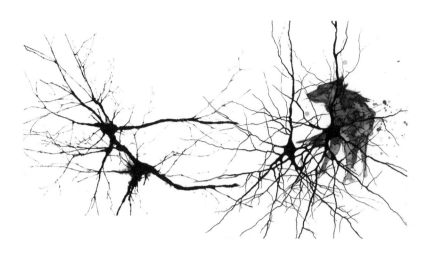

CHAPTER SEVEN

essa and Delphine did as Jane said. They ate the KFC. They talked about "Mom coming home soon" with Nate, and then turned on one of the videos he liked to watch before bed. Nessa forced herself to go through the motions of her regular nighttime routine. She put on headphones and finished her AP Bio homework at the kitchen table. Jane took the couch, powering up her laptop and trying to catch up on work. Delphine headed toward the room she and Nessa shared.

At first Nessa couldn't focus; the words on the page and in the diagrams she was looking at made no sense at all. But then she did manage to digest the difference between plant cells and animal cells. She needed to commit the diagrams to memory to prepare for a quiz, but it wasn't that hard to learn—plant and animal cells were almost identical.

Chewing on the top of her pen, Nessa let her mind wander for a minute, contemplating. There was a half-dead spider plant on the windowsill that no one ever watered. Strange to think that at its core, the spider plant was made up of building blocks that were nearly identical to the building blocks that made up Nessa's own body, that made up the potatoes and chicken she'd had for dinner.

At the thought of potatoes and chicken, Nessa realized she was hungry. Actually hungry this time. While Jane was helping Nate get ready for bed, picking out his clothes and packing up for the next day—these helped reduce morning anxiety— Nessa went back to the bucket of KFC.

All alone in the kitchen, eating contemplatively, Nessa replayed in her mind the moment of walking in on a cuffed Vivian. The situation had been surreal to say the least, but she couldn't shrug off the strange things her mom had said to her. *Pick up extra shifts at Dr. Morgan's?* Okay. *Find Aunt Jane's number in the roll top desk* when of course Nessa knew Jane's number. Jane was the Kurlands' #1 Emergency Contact and had been for years.

Besides which, Nessa knew Vivian didn't keep anything in the roll top desk. It was a piece of furniture Nessa's grandpa had restored during the woodworking-as-hobby phase of retirement. Vivian kept it because it reminded her of him, but the drawers were too small and would stick in hot weather. It was mostly just a place to stash mail. Nessa had checked again just to be sure and found nothing. Even the FBI had figured out it was filled with useless detritus and left behind the unwanted mail-order catalogs, pencils with hardened erasers, and screws that had come out of some long-forgotten appliance.

Just as Nessa was polishing off the last drumstick, Delphine walked into the kitchen.

Nessa looked up at her. Her eyes were still red from crying.

"Last piece, I'm sorry," Nessa said sheepishly, checking the bucket to confirm that, yup, she'd had the last piece. Well, the last three pieces. "You know I get hungry."

Delphine's expression did not change.

"There's still some fries?" Nessa tried. "They aren't bad if you nuke them, but only do ten at a time because if you don't eat them right away, they turn into rubber. Look." Hoping for a smile, Nessa lobbed a fry from the bucket onto the floor and it jumped back up before settling on the linoleum.

"This isn't about food," Delphine said. "It's about—I mean, Nessa, I feel like they didn't just take away Mom, they took away everything. At school, everyone is talking about it. And looking at me funny. And I don't know what to say to them."

Nessa felt anger rising up inside of her. Her first instinct was to say, "Who? Who is looking at you funny?" But then she looked at Delphine and realized that maybe there was one way she could help her sister.

"Delphine," she said, almost in a whisper. "I'm sorry. I wish I could protect you."

Delphine sniffed. She looked at Nessa and narrowed her eyes in a way that Nessa recognized—Delphine had something to say. "What is it?"

"Well, I don't want to betray Mom or anything," Delphine started. "But once, last month, when I was home sick, something came in the mail. I was watching TV on the couch. I don't think

Mom thought I was paying attention, but it was this envelope, it had a blue stripe on the back, and just the way she looked when she opened it . . . I knew it was upsetting. I didn't think too much about it, but then, when I came back from the bathroom, she jumped up."

"Jumped up from where?"

Delphine leveled Nessa with a meaningful gaze. "She jumped up from putting something into the roll top desk."

"Grandpa's desk?" Nessa said stupidly. It wasn't like they had more than one item of roll top furniture in their lives.

"When the FBI was here, I watched them search the desk. I was thinking they'd find whatever it was Mom stuck in there. I could see that Mom was watching too. Her face got all scared when the agents were over there."

"And did they find it?" Nessa said. She felt breathless, as if the moment were replaying for real.

"They never did," Delphine said. "All they took from the desk was the rubber-band ball."

Nessa couldn't believe Delphine was explaining this fact with a straight face. It was a family joke that the rubber-band ball always had to be hidden because Delphine got freaked out by the way dirt could collect in it. "Aren't you kind of glad about that?"

"Nessa," Delphine said, ignoring her question. "They never found that envelope."

Nessa pushed the bucket of congealed fries and chicken crumbs away.

She could see from the glimmer passing over Delphine's eyes that they'd had the same thought at the same time. They were heading toward the roll top desk before the glimmer was gone.

They shuffled through the desk and found a few photos, odds and ends. They opened and closed the sticky drawers, pulled them out, felt into the creepy dark spaces behind them. They prodded with a pencil in the area under the roll top, where you could theoretically slide a paper or two. Nothing.

Then, while sliding a drawer back into place, Nessa felt the piece of wood joining the flat part to the angled part at the back wiggle. She pressed the board, moving her fingers closer to the edge. "Wait, hold on," she said. She felt the board depress. It was on a spring and when she had pressed it as far as it could go—about an inch—she felt it click into place, leaving access to a compartment running just beneath the desk's surface, behind the center drawer. She pushed her hand into the opening and touched paper.

"You got something?" Delphine asked breathlessly. Nessa nodded, pulling out an envelope and holding it for a moment before she and Delphine went wordlessly back to the kitchen table. Sure enough, there was a blue stripe across the envelope's back.

Would whatever was inside this envelope seal Vivian's fate? And why was Vivian keeping *anything* secret? It was so unlike her, who had no problem being direct. Nessa felt too nervous to open it on her own, and passed it to her sister.

The envelope was already slit open at the top, and Delphine removed a thin stack of paper and slid it across the table, pushing the KFC bucket to the side. Nessa helped herself to two more fries. Delphine grabbed the bucket to move it away. "Pay attention!"

Nessa snagged a third fry and stuffed it in her mouth, then

leaned over the top page.

It looked like the same kind of bank statement Nessa had been receiving once a month since she'd started working at Dr. Morgan's and opened an account. Except where Nessa's balance never got much higher than $100—any savings were depleted when it was time to buy school supplies or new running shoes for cross-country—the total deposits on this account formed a number so large that at first Nessa thought it might be the account number. Or a phone number? It was nine digits long.

Then she noticed that one of the digits was a dollar sign.

Nessa looked at the statement again. The total on deposit was clear: $842,763.15.

"Is this . . . Mom's?" Nessa asked.

Delphine stuck her pointer finger on the page with enough force to slide the paper an inch across the table. "Look," she said. "There's her name."

And sure enough, there it was. Next to Delphine's slightly chubby finger, with its bitten-down nail and Claddagh ring, heart pointed up, was the name "Vivian J. Kurland, FBO Vanessa Kurland and Delphine Kurland."

"Mom," Nessa said, swallowing, "has this much money?"

Delphine answered by flipping the first page over. The back was covered with all kinds of fine print. "This looks real, right?" she said.

Nessa started looking through the statement's pages, trying to find something that might show that this was just a sweepstakes offer or a credit card scam. But it looked legitimate. Scanning the account activity, she saw that no one had made any withdrawals but there were regular deposits into the account from Daniel Host, President, Chimera Corp.

Moving to sit next to Nessa, Delphine said, "This can't be real, right?" She reached for a fry now herself. "Because if Mom really had this money, then why didn't I get to go to coding camp last summer? Why isn't Nate getting the second speech appointment his school wanted him to have?"

"And why did Mom sit me down and tell me I was going to need to score a scholarship for college, even if I stayed in-state?"

Delphine was still holding the fry she'd picked up and, absentmindedly, she put it in her mouth. And then moved to spit it out as if it were so hot it was burning her. "Nessa, this is inedible!" She carried the bucket of cold fries to the trashcan and dumped it in. "No one should eat these."

"Hey!" Nessa said, torn between feeling grateful for her sister's purposefulness and wishing she could have just one more fry. Even if they were making her feel a little disgusting.

Delphine returned to the table, picking up the statement again. "What's Chimera Corp.?" she mused, holding the statement close to her face as if there might be a watermark on the page. "What does 'FBO' stand for? And who," she asked, looking up at her sister, "is Daniel Host?"

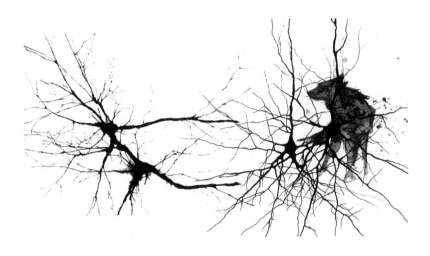

CHAPTER EIGHT

Nessa and Delphine had a hard time getting to sleep that night in their shared bedroom, coming up with all sorts of theories to explain the bank statement. That it was a fake, somehow planted in the desk by Paravida, to be found by the FBI.

That Vivian had done something wrong and was being paid by whoever she was working for.

That she had won the lottery and was waiting for the Disney World tickets to arrive before breaking the news.

$842,763.15! What was Vivian doing with that kind of money? She had clearly hidden it. And she had clearly pointed Nessa and Delphine toward it as well.

Finally, first Delphine and then Nessa dropped off to sleep. When Nessa woke, Delphine was still out. It took a second for her to remember the sad facts of the past thirty-six hours: her mother's arrest, the charges, the mysterious bank statement. Nessa could see a crack of light beneath the dark window shades—in spite of the continuing snow and the cold temperatures, sunrise was earlier now. It was almost April and the birds, returned from their winter migration, were making a racket.

Nessa lay still for some time, watching Delphine's string of pink globe lights over the window begin to glow as the sunlight outside intensified.

Finally, she summoned the energy to check the time on her phone and she saw that she had a text from Luc.

Got something to show you. Can you make it out for a run? I'll wait for you on North and 2nd in the truck in case you can.

Nessa groaned and rolled out of bed. If Luc was calling a morning meet-up, it must be important. He didn't like to wake up early any more than she did. Less, actually.

Noiselessly, she opened the bottom drawer of her dresser without waking Delphine, pulled out her running things, and closed the door softly behind her.

North and 2nd was a few blocks away, and Nessa saw that Luc was already waiting at the corner with his truck running when she got there.

"Hey," he said when she slid into the passenger door. He kissed her on the cheek, leaning in sleepily. "I hate this," he murmured. "Running is for losers." Nessa laughed. Mornings were not Luc's specialty. In fact, his mom had given him a mug that read:

I hate morning people.

And morning.

And people.

As he pulled himself back to an upright position, he took a sip of coffee out of that very mug.

"You sleep okay?" he said.

Nessa knew Luc was asking if she was okay generally, but she didn't want to think about the answer to that question. She didn't want to explain what it felt like to have Vivian not come home—she'd texted him the facts of the matter the night before—Bree too.

"I can't talk about it," she said, and Luc, knowing her, let it go. As always, she appreciated his not going overboard with emotions. Being awake at six in the morning was bad enough without someone gushing about how sorry they were your mom was in jail for some crazy trumped-up crime and you were one step away from foster care.

Luc was wearing track pants with the ankle zippers open, a red down vest, rag wool gloves. He hadn't shaved. She gestured with the back of her hand up and down to show him she was talking about his outfit. "You're looking very backwoods this morning," she said.

He half-smiled and really looked at her for the first time.

"It's frigging freezing," he said. "Supposedly we're in spring. What gives?"

"Tell me about it," she said. In the dark of her bedroom, she hadn't been able to find her Turtle Fur and was hunching her shoulders in an effort to close off the draft around her collar.

Luc held up an arm, inviting Nessa to slide over next to

him. She did, and when they hit a hill and she could hear the gears of the ancient pickup starting to strain, she said, "Now?" and on Luc's nod, popped the stick shift into fourth gear. They drove this way a lot and Nessa felt right now that being with Luc, being in sync with him—this was better than sympathy.

"So my text," he said, after a minute had passed. "I want to show you something."

"Okay."

"Something in the woods."

"Okay."

"Let's just say, if you weren't already considering joining me in the woods for spring break, you should," he said. "This is what we're going to be doing."

Ten minutes later, Luc and Nessa were climbing out of Luc's truck, which was parked off the side of the road at a trailhead popular with hunters during deer season. Luc parked as far into the woods as he could, making sure the truck was out of sight. With all the wolf sightings, people in town had been warned not to go hiking or exploring in the woods and Luc and Nessa knew better than to make a public event out of the fact that they were still heading in.

Footwear, stretching—it was Luc and Nessa's routine to run a few miles into the woods before transforming. This was one of the precautions Luc had taught Nessa to take. She'd also learned how to leave behind smells in certain locations and mask them in others—Luc was thoughtful about who was upwind of you and how close they were, as well as never forgetting the fact that you had no idea who was below you, wind-wise. He'd explained that they needed to be careful, even if most wolves would let them pass. Wolves didn't think of Luc and Nessa as half-human as much as they thought of them as guests.

As they ran, Nessa realized Luc still hadn't told her where exactly he was taking her. However, as with many of the questions she sought answers to while in her human form, she lost track of them in her wolf mind. As a wolf, she didn't need to know *where* Luc was going because Luc was *here*. *Here* was with her. *Here* was the woods. *Here* was together.

And then she did know where, because they stopped at the edge of the natural wolves' territory. They sat down next to each other and called out to let the natural wolves know they were close by. This was their pack, as much as it was possible for a human to have one.

They sang something short and simple and once they'd heard an answering call, they continued toward their pack's inner sanctum. It was a den where Sister had dug a hole underneath a rock structure at the edge of a clearing where she had given birth to her pups. A place to keep them safe as she fed them throughout the late winter months.

When Luc and Nessa reached the clearing, Nessa saw that there was something gray and feathery moving over the ground. Almost like smoke, it separated into small pieces and then came back together again. And then she recognized the mass for what it was. Pups! One was in serious pursuit of a blowing leaf. Another was rolling in dirt. A third was chewing on its paw.

Nessa turned her head to look at Luc as if to say, "They're out from the den?"

Luc nodded, and with a bound leapt ahead of her, jumping

into the puppies' midst. Within seconds, the puppies were jumping up themselves, trying to climb onto his back, biting at his legs. He lay down and rolled over and they climbed up on him, or at least attempted to. The smallest couldn't quite manage the challenge and ended up rolling back to the ground, where he stretched lazily as if the slide had been intentional. Seconds later, the puppy had forgotten all about it, biting his back left haunch. Then he was up again, hurling himself at Luc as if the idea were just now presenting itself.

Nessa saw Sister watching protectively as her pups explored and played. Their coming out of the den for the first time must have been a significant occasion because all the wolves in the pack had gathered—or maybe that was because the puppies were so vulnerable that this was an all-hands-on-deck situation?

The six puppies were nearly impossible to keep track of. They still looked identical, too—downy gray fur with spikes of longer black hair poking through where new coats were growing in. They had tiny snub noses and wide-spaced, staring eyes. Two trotted past Nessa like they were soldiers on patrol. Sister literally sat on top of another, who was biting her ankle. When Big One rolled over like Luc had, the puppy trapped beneath Sister's belly squirmed out to join two others in play biting and climbing him as if he were a mountain.

Tentatively, one girl puppy approached Nessa. For a second, Nessa wasn't sure what to do. But then the puppy bowed to her, opening her mouth into what started out looking like a lion's roar and ended up as more of a yawn. The puppy made a squeaking sound. She must have caught sight of the back end of her tail as she did so, because suddenly she was spinning in a circle.

Nessa flopped down on the ground, letting the puppy sniff her all over; then she jumped up, a bit amazed at how surprised the puppy looked. The puppy went into a crouch, but she was still so wobbly that her legs splayed to the side. Nessa laughed a wolf laugh, which looked a bit like panting. She caught Luc watching her. He raised his head as if to say, "See what I'm saying?"

She didn't have time to answer because another of the pups had found her.

"Ow!" she yelped as his teeth bit into her back left ankle. She spun on him and without knowing how she knew to do this, put his face in her mouth, not biting down. This gesture would have sent an adult wolf into fight mode, but crazily enough, it seemed to make the pup happy.

Nessa didn't know how long they stayed, playing with the puppies. She noticed that the pack was fully sharing the responsibility for keeping them from wandering away, and even feeding them with bits of food that they were regurgitating and spitting into the puppies' mouths.

Which was possibly the most disgusting thing Nessa had ever witnessed.

After the puppies dropped off to sleep, either finding their way back into the den or being pushed or carried there after they'd collapsed, Nessa and Luc did some check-in play with Big One and Mama, who remained the alpha pair even when it was Sister's pups the pack was caring for.

On the way out, Luc and Nessa crossed the scent of the pups' dad, Jack, the Paravida usurper.

Ugh, Nessa thought. He creeped her out.

He just didn't act like a natural wolf should. He wasn't hunting to feed the pups. He wasn't helping to care for them or raise them. Thinking about him now, Nessa shot Luc a look that she meant to communicate: *What kind of a deadbeat lets seven other wolves raise his pups?*

Luc shot a look that she knew meant: *At least he's hanging around. Considering he's a Paravida wolf, that's more than you might expect.*

They continued the debate in human form in the truck ride back to Nessa's, with Luc arguing, predictably, for the rehabilitation of the Paravida wolves, and Nessa holding out that they could never be trusted. But then they got sidetracked trying to figure out which puppy was which. In her mind, Nessa named the girl who had climbed on her belly Princess. The boy who had bitten her ankle was Biter. The soldiers marching in step? That was easy—the Brothers, Junior.

By the time Luc dropped her at the end of the driveway, heading back to his house to shower before school, they were laughing. It was the best Nessa had felt in a while.

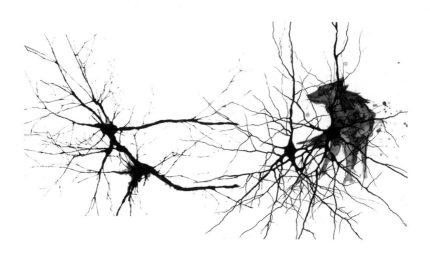

CHAPTER NINE

*I*n a hushed conversation while they were getting dressed, the girls decided not to tell Aunt Jane about the FBO bank account—Delphine had found out it meant "for benefit of," an account to be used only for the persons named on it. "We need to learn more about it first," Nessa said. "And we should ask Mom, before blabbing about it to Jane."

Delphine nodded her agreement. "After all," she added, "Mom's going to be home tomorrow night. She can explain the bank account to Aunt Jane herself."

Two days, Nessa thought, repeating Jane's calming mantra. *We only have to get through two more days.*

In the kitchen, Jane was cooking pancakes, looking

somewhat frayed. She sounded cheerful, but the pancakes were burned. And raw. "How is that even possible?" Jane said, pushing her glasses up her nose.

Nessa gobbled up four of them anyway.

After school, Bree decided to come along to Nessa's extra cage-cleaning shift at Dr. Morgan's.

"You really don't have to," Nessa said. "I'll be okay by myself." It had only been two school days and she was already full-on sick of everyone treating her like she might be contagious with the plague, or falling all over themselves to express sympathy.

"Oh, I'm not going for *you*," Bree said. "I heard they brought in a stray who had kittens."

"How do you even know that?" Nessa asked. "I swear, Bree, your handle on Tether town gossip—if you could harness that power for good, you could probably create world peace or something."

"Kittens . . . World peace . . . How can you *not* see the connection?"

Nessa laughed. "Point taken."

When they got to the clinic, it felt pretty much business as usual. They checked in with Ashley, but before Nessa could even go to the utility closet where the rubber gloves and cleaning supplies were stored, Dr. Morgan emerged from an exam room, leading a two-year-old greyhound rescue out to a waiting client. "Nessa, good, I'm glad you're here," he said. "Before you start, I want to talk to you. Follow me."

Cheerful and healthy, a big cross-country skier, Dr. Morgan had the year-round tan a lot of people in Tether got from working outside. Nessa had always liked him—he'd been in the periphery of her family's life forever, showing up occasionally for Thanksgiving or a Sunday afternoon football game.

Dr. Morgan gestured up the hall. Nessa assumed they were heading to his office, but instead, he led her past that door as well as the ones leading to the exam rooms and into the kennels. Bree, after a quick glance with Nessa, joined them.

"Um . . . kittens?" Bree mouthed, broadly pointing to the door to the small kennels, where small or old animals needing quiet were housed.

Nessa shook her head and made a praying gesture to show she was asking Bree to stick with her. Maybe Dr. Morgan was about to tell her about the "extra work" her mom had been doing?

Bree shrugged, turning back to follow Dr. Morgan, stopping with him while he checked in on a cat coming out of anesthesia. Then he kept going, heading for the clinic's back door. Nessa knew where he was taking them: the mobile spay/neuter clinic, which lived in an RV behind the main building. It felt like a miniature version of the vet's office, but with a generator, a rudimentary surgical setup, and a long row of kennels along one side.

Nessa knew it well. Setting it up had been her mother's idea. Vivian had raised the money for the unit after investigating how it could vastly reduce exploding feral cat populations that were endangering populations of songbirds, and reduce mass euthanasia of unwanted animals. Eventually they'd expanded the operation to include pet cats and dogs, and they spent a day or two a month in neighboring towns. Nessa would have assumed this was Vivian's extra work, except it wasn't exactly new. The mobile clinic had been in operation for more than two years.

Dr. Morgan opened the door to the RV and Nessa and Bree followed him inside. Nessa was expecting the bright, cheerful space she was used to, but when she entered, the lights were off and inside was a mess. It looked like her garage, with the cabinet doors open, their contents spread out randomly throughout the space, boxes of medical supplies, glass vials of medicines, and packs of shrink-wrapped surgical instruments scattered everywhere.

"As you know," Dr. Morgan explained, snapping the lights on, "the FBI did a pretty thorough search of the clinic. I have no idea what they were looking for or whether they found it, but they focused a lot of the search here and certainly made a mess of things. Meanwhile, we're scheduled for fifteen appointments on Saturday over at the Marblehead Apartments. I don't know how I'm going to get the surgeries done without your mom there, but priority number one is getting this place cleaned up. Can you organize?"

"Sure," Nessa said, picking up a bag of saline, checking for punctures before laying it down on the counter.

"I'll help," Bree volunteered.

Thanking them, Dr. Morgan left, and Bree and Nessa got to work, sorting through supplies, repacking cabinets, and tossing any package with a broken seal into a box to be taken to the trash.

"Maybe this will help us understand what the FBI, or Paravida, or whoever, was looking to find," Bree said after a while. "That could be a clue to what they think your mom did."

"Good thought," Nessa said.

Nessa dug in with renewed purpose. But most of what they found was completely innocuous: the forms owners would fill out at drop-off, gloves, drapes, masks, the instruments, the anesthesia. At some point, the idea that they were supposed to "read" the mess the FBI had left behind as if it were tea leaves seemed absurd.

"Somehow I don't think my mom's gone to jail for putting too many dogs in the 'cone of shame,'" Nessa said, as she sorted the cones by size so they would fit back into the box they came in.

Bree laughed. She held up a roll of "I ♥ my pet!" stickers. "Maybe the FBI was mad because she over-distributed stickers."

"Yeah," said Nessa, laughing now too. "Maybe she gave one to someone who wasn't a kid? They're only supposed to be for children, you know."

Bree shook her head. "I know, right?" she said. It felt good to laugh. Then Nessa moved to the next cabinet and her laugh died.

"Look," she said. Bree got up so she could peer over Nessa's shoulder, into the cabinet where anesthesia was stored. Nessa passed her back a laminated card, first removing it from the Velcro tabs that were used to stick it to the cabinet door. There were cards like this on every cabinet that served as an inventory list of everything that was kept inside.

"Look at the list," Nessa said. "There's supposed to be some Telazol in here and some sodium thiopental but I'm not seeing either."

"What are they?" Bree asked.

"Sedatives," said Nessa. "They use them for knocking the dogs out. It's weird they stock the Telazol here, because I didn't think Dr. Morgan used it for spay/neuter. He used them for euthanasia."

Bree shuddered.

"Yeah, I know—so sad," Nessa said, thinking of all the times she'd seen pets who looked ready and the owners who looked . . . not so ready. "But there's something else." Nessa told Bree about the sodium thiopental she'd smelled in the woods with Luc, where they'd found the wolves who had been picked up by humans. "Someone was using it to tranquilize the Paravida wolves," she said. "I wonder if that's connected to what's going on here?"

"Or what if it's all those people in town who are lobbying to lift the hunting ban on wolves? Maybe they're the ones shooting them."

"But why the tranquilizer gun? Why not just kill them?"

"Because it's against the law?" Bree said. "Maybe they're killing them somewhere hidden away, where there won't be evidence? Like dig a big hole somewhere, collect all the wolves, drive them to the hole and then shoot them?"

"Bree!" Nessa said. Looking at Bree's dimples and curls, you would never be able to tell that she had the mind of a hardboiled detective. "I swear, if I ever need to kill anyone I'm going to hire you to plan it out for me."

Bree blushed and smiled, like Nessa had just told her she was great at flower arranging or another hobby that didn't involve killing people. "But if that was happening, maybe whoever was trapping the wolves in the woods was stealing the drugs they needed from here? You can't just order them online, right?"

They decided they'd bring up the subject of the drugs with Dr. Morgan. "Maybe he'll tell us something about them that will help us figure out what's going on," Nessa said.

"Good idea," Bree agreed. "But let me do the talking, okay?" Bree was a little better than Nessa at teasing the truth out of people without revealing her intentions.

Once the RV clinic was cleaned up, Nessa and Bree stopped in Dr. Morgan's office, handing him the list Bree had made in her neat, bubble letter handwriting of everything that would need to be restocked before the mobile clinic was ready to go. Surprisingly, the girls found they didn't need to raise the subject of the missing drugs—Dr. Morgan immediately raised his eyebrows at the list.

"This is weird," he said, scanning it over. "We don't even keep Telazol in the RV. Must be a mistake."

"Is the sodium thiopental not supposed to be there either?" Nessa asked. Bree stepped on her foot, a reminder to try to be a bit more subtle.

"It's just that these are drugs we don't use that much. They have their purpose, but we don't keep a stockpile this large. It would be more appropriate for a high-kill shelter, somewhere that was euthanizing on a daily basis."

Bree gave Nessa a significant look.

"Whose job was it to order them?" Nessa asked, suddenly wondering if the wolves being tranqed in the woods might be connected to someone working at Dr. Morgan's clinic. Or even Dr. Morgan? If she'd learned nothing else from the Paravida adventure in the fall, it was that you couldn't trust anyone— even people you'd known all your life.

"Your mom managed the ordering and resupply, actually," Dr. Morgan said.

There goes that idea, Nessa thought.

"Maybe she had some kind of bulk pricing opportunity?" Bree suggested. "Can you get sodium thio-whatever at Costco?"

Dr. Morgan smiled. "Hardly," he said. "These drugs are highly regulated."

As he walked with them to leave the clinic, Dr. Morgan held the door for Nessa and looked her right in the eye when he asked, "Have you heard from your mom? Is she all right?"

"We're hoping she'll come home tomorrow," Nessa said.

"Please tell her I'm thinking about her. Let me know if there is anything I can do to help."

"Thanks," Nessa said. "I just don't understand what's happening."

Dr. Morgan shook his head. "Me neither," he said. "But I'll tell you something, and I'll tell it to anybody. Vivian Kurland is one of the most upstanding, honest people I've ever known. Whatever they think she may have done, they're wrong."

Once they were in the car, Bree turned to Nessa.

"He's hiding something," she stated flatly.

"Dr. Morgan?" Nessa said, turning to give Bree a full look and laughing at the idea. "Cross-country skiing, always-chipper Dr. Morgan?"

"He's not always chipper," Bree said. "Remember that time you used the hand soap instead of the cage soap and there was all that lather spilling everywhere?" This was one of Bree's favorite stories. There had been clouds and clouds of soap lather filling the kennel room. Dr. Morgan had slipped and fallen and yelled "fiddlesticks!" so loudly the girls hadn't been able to keep from laughing.

"Okay, he was annoyed. But you heard him in there. He's worried about my mom. He's hoping for the best for her."

"Yeah, I'm sure he is," Bree said. "But there was something he wasn't saying too. I'm sure of it. And that's the thing we need to understand."

Nessa knew enough about Bree's instincts to be worried. But she already was worried. She said nothing.

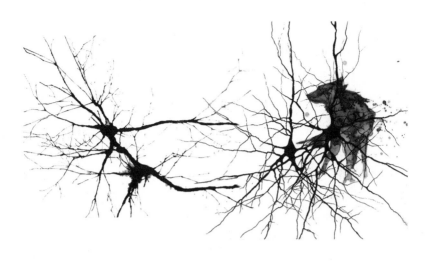

CHAPTER TEN

t least this will all be over soon," Aunt Jane said, her knuckles white where she gripped the wheel at 10 o'clock and 2 o'clock, like she was still taking driver's ed. "Whatever they think your mom did or didn't do, after today, we'll get her home where she can talk to us and we'll figure this all out."

Nessa found herself looking sideways at Jane, even as the highway disappeared behind them in the side-view mirror. Her phone buzzed—a text from Luc:

Good luck today.

She texted back a thumbs-up emoji. Then a worried face. They were heading to Grand Rapids, where the closest federal court building was located.

"Are you sure you want to come in?" Aunt Jane said. She looked worried, biting her lip and glancing at Nessa. "It might be upsetting for you."

Nessa laughed. "Not as upsetting as sitting in English class while all of this was going on."

Aunt Jane passed Nessa her phone. The browser was open to a fact sheet about what to expect in federal court. "Read this," Jane said. "You should know what you're going to see."

Nessa did read. She learned that the hearing today was not about whether Vivian had committed whatever "larceny" she was being accused of, but about whether she got to wait at home for the trial to start or stay in jail. If she wasn't dangerous or a flight risk, the government would most likely let her go home, setting a dollar figure she'd have to pay if she tried to make a run for it and got caught. Jane had a folder of documents: the title to the house, the mortgage, a valuation of Vivian's car, and statements from Jane about money she was prepared to sacrifice.

If Vivian had been hiding the money in that bank account, she must have had a good reason. Still, it was hard to listen to Aunt Jane talk about turning over her life savings, knowing there was this fortune sitting in an account somewhere that Vivian could access if she needed to.

"It's not going to feel like a courtroom on television," Jane said. "It's kind of more like going to the DMV. Expect to be bored. Nothing at all exciting is going to seem to happen."

But as soon as they'd passed through the court building's metal detectors, Nessa noticed about a half-dozen people gathered by some benches and a potted palm tree. *Are they from the news?* she wondered. Some of them were carrying cameras. Just as Nessa was halfway through a follow-up thought, that there must be some high-profile case on trial to explain the media presence, one of the reporters detached herself from the group and headed in Nessa's direction.

"Nessa Kurland?" she said, meeting Nessa's eyes, the microphone thrust in her direction. Nessa jerked her head back. Was this someone she was supposed to know? An old friend of Vivian's? Some distant relative she'd met once and didn't remember?

She felt Jane's hand on her arm, clutching. She didn't understand why.

"Nessa, how do you feel about the charges against your mother?"

Who was this woman? Why did she seem to know Nessa when Nessa did not know her?

"Were you aware of your mother's alleged criminal activity when you were competing at States last fall?"

Now there was a bright light shining in Nessa's eyes. It was the reporter's camera—a man had come up behind her—pointing the camera in Nessa's direction. Nessa squinted and put her hand up, like she was blocking the sun.

And then there wasn't just a single camera, a single light blinding Nessa in the gloomy lobby. The whole crowd of journalists had moved over now, shouting essentially the same question in Nessa's direction, shining their lights, clicking their cameras.

All this time, Jane had been pulling on her elbow, trying to lead her away, but there was no "away." The crowd of cameras had them surrounded. Until suddenly a figure broke through the circle, pushing camera people aside. "This way," he said. It was a young man in a gray suit. He took Nessa's elbow on the left. Jane was still holding her tightly on the right, and Nessa felt herself pushed through the crowd.

Nessa looked at the man. She wondered if he was a volunteer at the courthouse. A college student? Were there student volunteers stationed at courthouses to help people like her who had been swarmed by reporters?

The young man let them into a room a few doors down, which he was able to open with a passkey. Inside it looked like a conference room and the quiet felt sweet and immensely welcome.

"I'm Zach Chandler," the man said. "Your mom's lawyer."

"*You're* the lawyer?" Nessa said, unable to keep the tone of surprise out of her voice. "I thought you were in college or something."

"I know," he said. "I look young."

He pulled a pair of glasses out of his jacket pocket and put them on. Nessa wondered whether they were even prescription lenses or if he just wore them to try to appear older. "But I'm good. I know what I'm doing."

"Zach!" Jane gasped. "What *was* that out there?"

"I don't know," Zach answered. "I'm sorry you had to pass through it. If I'd remotely suspected there'd be a media circus today, I would have arranged for you to come in the back."

"I thought maybe they were here for another case," Nessa said.

"They shouldn't be here at all," Zach told them. "The charges against your mom are serious, but not newsworthy." He sent a text on his cell phone quickly. Its thick protective case was the same one Tim Miller had. Nessa grimaced. "It could be that with Nessa having been state champion, the press could be looking for some juicy connection. I just let my boss know what happened. He'll get someone on this . . . find out if somehow the press knows something we don't."

He checked his watch. "Meanwhile, look, I wish I had more time to tell you what to expect in there, but we have to go in." He looked Nessa in the eye. "I'll try my best to get your mom out of there and home to you. Whatever else is going on in her case, there's absolutely no reason why she shouldn't be released today."

Young or not, Nessa decided she believed Zach Chandler. She nodded. "Thanks," she said.

Zach gathered up an accordion folder stuffed with documents and a spiral-bound manual. "Okay," he said. "Let's roll."

The courtroom was smaller than Nessa expected. The ceiling was low. The carpet was old. The paneling was plain, rather than carved and ornate like in the movies.

There were only about a dozen or so seats for spectators in three rows behind the tables, and they were crowded with the reporters Nessa had seen in the lobby. Cameras or recording devices were not allowed.

Nessa and Jane found seats in the front, Nessa sliding in next to a man in a baseball hat scribbling notes on a small notebook. In spite of the scribbling, she decided he wasn't a reporter. He didn't look up at her when she sat down or try to talk to her. He was wearing a baggy gray sweater, old jeans he could have worn while painting a house, and canvas sneakers with duct tape reinforcing the back of one heel. He had a shaggy moustache and gray hair. Nessa noticed he crossed his legs, something men in Tether generally did not do. For a second she wondered if he was a college professor. She noticed the line of dirt on the cuff of his sweater. Maybe he was just a down-on-his-luck guy, coming in out of the cold to warm up and to get a little entertainment here in court?

Zach Chandler passed through the low swinging door. Taking over the table on the left, he began unpacking files from his accordion folder. On the right, Nessa saw what looked like a team of lawyers doing the same. She noticed one who seemed to be in charge. He had a thick neck, like the softball coach at school, and he was leaning back in the chair, an ankle crossed over the opposite knee. He was scrolling through something on his phone while the other lawyers at his table organized the file folders, occasionally showing him pages or asking him questions.

Occasionally Nessa would pick up a word or two from what they were whispering to each other—"disclosure," "forbearance," "prior claim"—but nothing made any sense. It felt like the Spanish she heard on Univision, over at Bree's when her grandma was visiting from Detroit.

A door on the right side of the room opened. "All rise!" Nessa heard, and a man with black hair and a black robe strode into the room. He greeted the attorneys at the tables and then, after everyone was sitting, he said in a low voice, "Bring her in now" to the bailiff. A different door opened, on the opposite side of the bench. A moment later, a U.S. marshal led Vivian into the room.

Vivian's eyes were opened wide, scanning, and Nessa

remembered what it was like when her mom used to come to pick her up at the end of After Care when she was in elementary school. Sometimes Nessa would see Vivian before Vivian had seen her, and she'd get to watch the way her mom's face changed when she spotted Nessa, breaking into a smile that was one part greeting, one part relief.

Nessa saw that same sun-coming-out glow of recognition now. She felt her own returning smile. Nessa lifted her hand to wave, and Vivian raised her eyebrows. It had only been three days since Vivian was taken away, but Nessa realized that she maybe hadn't taken a full breath of air the whole time.

Vivian was taken to the table where Zach Chandler was sitting. Then her mom turned, and Nessa saw that Vivian's hair was tangled and dirty. Did she not have access to shampoo and a hairbrush in jail?

Jail. Seeing her mom in the brown jumpsuit, the idea of jail felt more real.

"As we have a crowd today, let me just start by saying that I want this hearing conducted in a polite, respectful manner," the judge began, speaking toward the spectator area. Then he proceeded to address Vivian directly.

"Ms. Kurland, at this hearing, a determination will be made as to your detention, bond, or potential release. Do you understand what that means? Has your lawyer explained this to you?"

Vivian nodded.

"Now," the magistrate went on, pausing to open a folder and scan through the first few pages. He put on reading glasses to do this, and when he looked up he gazed over them at Vivian. "You are a mother and sole parent to three minor children, I see, and have many ties to the community . . . " He looked down again, continuing to read. "I see you're employed."

Before Vivian could answer, the thick-necked attorney from the other side of the room stood. "Your honor," he said.

The judge turned to face him, rolling his eyes impatiently at the interruption, and spoke testily. "I'll get to you, counselor," he said. "I was about to advise Ms. Kurland that given her file, I had every expectation the government would be offering a bond package involving a mortgage on her house and a lien on future earnings." He said this in a way that gave Nessa the understanding that the magistrate was basically telling the government attorney what to do. The magistrate suppressed a yawn. "Is that in fact what you plan to offer?"

"Your honor, the government is asking for detention." The attorney had a clipped, no-nonsense way of speaking. "Without release on bond."

Nessa saw her mother's back stiffen. Zach Chandler's head swiveled toward the prosecuting attorney as though he'd just heard a loud noise. "No release on bond?" the judge said. "I see no prior criminal record."

"We feel the prisoner is a flight risk," the thick-necked attorney continued.

Zach Chandler was standing before the thick-necked attorney had gotten halfway through this statement. "This is absurd!" His voice cracked with the effort of his objection, and Nessa felt a cold wave of fear seeping into her body, even as she wished her mother's lawyer didn't sound quite so much like a teenage boy just entering puberty.

Zach Chandler continued on. "We're talking a single working mother who is the sole support for a disabled child." He pulled a folder from the top of the pile on his desk and opened it as though he was going to find a paper had magically appeared there explaining away what the thick-necked attorney had just said.

The thick-necked attorney cleared his throat. "We believe her to be in regular contact with representatives of foreign governments and non-state actors hostile to the interests of the United States."

"What?!" Zach Chandler said. "What are you talking about?" He turned to the judge. "We've heard nothing about this."

His voice was high and bright again. He looked like someone whom the thick-necked attorney could pick up and throw across the room, in WWE fashion. If the setting had been the cafeteria, she knew whose lunch money would be lining whose pockets.

Nessa felt slightly cheered when Zach Chandler recovered himself enough to reiterate his point more calmly. "I have received no evidence of these alleged relationships, nor has my client indicated any propensity to flee. I have fifteen character witnesses, including her employer, willing to testify that she is not a flight risk nor does she pose an immediate threat of harm."

"Is there a father on record?" the magistrate asked.

Zach Chandler cleared his throat. "He did not receive custody or visitation in the divorce agreement. He has not pursued a reinstatement of either at any point since the agreement was made. The defendant refused to appeal to him for child support at the outset and none was required by the state." Vivian whispered something to Zach Chandler and he went on. "Additionally, it should be noted that the youngest of

Ms. Kurland's children, Nathaniel Kurland, has no paternity records on file with the state."

Nessa felt her face growing warm. Even though he was reading from his notes as if this were a clinical study of some kind, Nessa recognized the facts of her family. Everything he had said was true. Yes, Nessa barely remembered her father—a few shadowy recollections at best. Vivian didn't talk about him and evaded direct questions, and Nessa had assumed he'd abandoned them, though sometimes she wondered whether he was even alive.

"After the defendant was detained on an indictment from the grand jury for larceny," the thick-necked lawyer said, his spiky hair and the folds of flesh on his neck moving as he nodded for emphasis, "considerable evidence was found at the scene of the arrest. The grand jury, which had already issued the larceny indictment, has now had the opportunity to consider this new evidence and has issued a further indictment of a much more serious nature. I request permission to name those additional charges now to elucidate our request for detention without bond."

The courtroom, where up until then someone had always been talking, rustling papers, whispering behind a raised hand, or tapping on a keyboard, went silent. Nessa saw the bailiff, sitting in a regular desk chair at the door Vivian had emerged from, stop jiggling the chair.

"Go on," the magistrate intoned.

The government attorney did, rumbling along in his thick Michigan accent. "Your honor, we will show that the defendant is a skilled genetic researcher who has both the competence and knowledge to experiment with genetic alterations to animals. Without going into specifics that might jeopardize our case, we will make available to you the sealed transcript of the grand jury proceeding, in which we presented evidence to suggest Vivian Kurland created mutated versions of a local wolf species, essentially weaponizing these . . . uh . . . wolves, and then held meetings with representatives of foreign governments and non-state actors hostile to the United States, with plans to sell these weaponized wolves to the highest bidder, while using them to engage in domestic acts of terrorism on U.S. soil."

In the stunned silence that continued after the attorney's speech, Nessa felt fear take over. She had no control over the shaking. She was sweating. She felt Jane begin to tremble.

"This isn't real," she wanted to stand up and shout to the room. "This is my mom you're talking about."

When Nessa looked down, she saw Aunt Jane's hand squeezing hers. But Nessa could hardly feel the pressure. Of the two hands clasped she couldn't tell which one belonged to her.

Her hand, her body—nothing felt real anymore.

"Your honor, I—" Zach Chandler began, but he looked just as surprised as the rest of them. Finally he was able to sputter out, "This doesn't make any sense. I can't possibly be expected to respond to these charges on the fly. It would have been a matter of courtesy for the government to inform us prior to this hearing." He gestured to the spectator area and added with sarcasm, "Clearly the *press* has been informed."

The judge shook his head. "Given the serious nature of the indictment and the potential for a flight risk, I am ruling for the government, detention without bail."

Vivian nodded, as though expecting this decision, and then

the marshal led her out of the room. She looked back at Nessa as she walked out, one look that there wasn't really time for and Nessa could not read.

Watching her go, Nessa couldn't help but think about the bank account. How *had* Vivian suddenly become rich? She hated to think that maybe Vivian had been paid for something she wasn't supposed to be doing.

The man in the dirty baseball hat was still calmly scribbling away on his pad, even though the world had just been turned upside down. The second hand was clicking on the clock above the door. It was over. Nessa felt like she'd been punched. She felt like she didn't even know what had happened.

"Oh dear," said Aunt Jane. Nessa realized Jane was still squeezing her hand. "Oh dear, oh dear, oh dear."

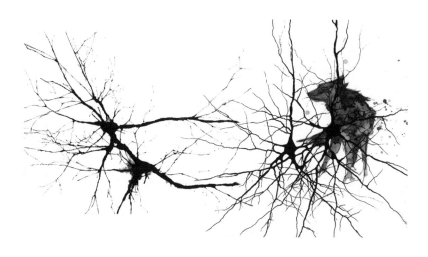

CHAPTER ELEVEN

Nessa was running. This wasn't a dream. It was real. She was running away, running toward, running from, running herself into the ground.

She could feel her paws striking the soft ground of the trail, her powerful hind legs pushing her forward as she leapt into a sprint. With each lunge forward, her fur soaked in more of the night's damp. It was cold out but her heart was beating strong, her breath steaming warm. She stopped to read the smell patterns she was encountering: squirrel, raccoon, chipmunk, cat, deer. She shook her body all over, nose to tail, resetting every muscle, wishing she could do the same with her thoughts.

Her mother was not coming home.

Her family was broken.

Nessa ran alone. When Bree had texted to ask how the hearing had gone, she'd only texted back:

Not good.

She hadn't answered Luc's text with the same question. She didn't tell him she was going into the woods.

The moon was neither new nor full, not the kind of moon that begged for transformation, but she felt like her own feelings were aglow, as if her feelings were burning bright enough to illuminate the world.

She could hear her own breathing.

Nessa did not know how long she'd been running when Mama and Big One suddenly joined her, one on either side. Without having to explain—because wolves didn't—she knew they felt her pain. As if she'd been bleeding or limping, they could see that something was wrong, and it didn't matter that they didn't know what. They couldn't fix it—they weren't trying to—but having them flanking her made her remember that she was not alone, and that calmed her.

Mama and Big One parted ways with Nessa at the trailhead at mile marker 12, and when Nessa returned to the parking lot at the side of the road, Luc was waiting for her. He was sitting on the picnic table in chukka boots, jeans, his parka that was lined with huntsman's orange. His black hair was lit up at the edges in the glow of his truck's headlights.

"How'd you know where to find me?" Nessa asked.

Luc gave her a "C'mon" look. "You're not that hard to track," he said. "You need a ride home?"

Nessa took a deep breath. She knew she should head to Luc's truck—the sooner she got home, the better—but instead she let herself fall onto the picnic table's bench.

Almost as though her body was no longer her own, Nessa watched her hand form a fist and then slowly release it. She formed the fist and released it again. "Something very bad is happening to my mom," she said. "They're saying she's . . . well . . . some kind of a terrorist. Like the Paravida wolves are her fault. Like she made them."

Luc didn't respond, just looked at her in a way that let her know he was listening. Nessa thought about telling him about the money her mom seemed to have come into possession of, but stopped there. She didn't want him to know. *She* didn't want to know.

"I think it's up to me to fight this. To find out what's going on and make it stop."

"How?"

"I don't know yet," she admitted. "But I promise you, Luc, if it's the last thing I ever do, I'm going to get my mom out of that jail."

Luc dropped Nessa off at home, where Jane was packing. She wanted to leave for Milwaukee that very night. She explained that with the publicity breaking, they had to get out of Tether. All of them—she'd take Nate, Nessa, and Delphine with her to Milwaukee.

"So . . . " Nessa said, standing in the kitchen as Jane put all the cereals and snack food Nate liked into boxes. "Doesn't someone need to stay near Mom? Find out what is happening to her?"

Jane pushed her glasses back up on her nose, tucked her red hair behind her ears. "You're thinking that should be you?" she said.

Nessa nodded firmly. In the light of day, she had decided: No matter how bad things looked for Vivian, Nessa believed in her. And only someone with that kind of faith could fight for Vivian for real.

"Nessa," Jane said. She pressed the button on the teakettle. "Look. Sit down." She set two mugs down next to the basket of loose tea bags. "There are some things that you should know. Things about your mom."

"What things?" Nessa said, pulling out a chair from the kitchen table, sitting down.

"Well." Aunt Jane checked the water in the kettle to see if it was nearly hot, pulling the milk from the fridge.

"You should know that some of the things they said about her in court today. They weren't wrong."

"You're saying Mom's a terrorist?!" Nessa blurted, jumping up from her seat. She realized she was practically shouting.

Jane held up a hand. "Go easy," she said. "I'll tell you. Your mom is not a terrorist. But there are things she's never told you." Jane poured the hot water into the mugs. "Here, drink this," she said, handing Nessa one. "Sit."

Nessa's stomach was churning. She took the tea and sat back down. And waited for Aunt Jane to speak.

"When we were growing up, your mom and I weren't close," Jane began. "By the time I got to middle school, she was already off at college."

"Okay," Nessa said. She knew this part so far. The University of Michigan. Where Vivian was an honors student. But something had happened. Something her mother didn't talk about much. All Nessa knew was that Vivian had never finished. She didn't have a degree. Which was why she worked as a vet tech. Which was why Nessa was so determined to get to college herself.

"I know this," Nessa said. "She went to Michigan, but dropped out after two years. Get to the part about how you think she's a terrorist."

"That's not exactly how things went," Aunt Jane said. She sighed. "Your mom told you she dropped out, but really she *graduated* after two years. Nessa, your mother was one of the smartest students to come out of Tether High. Ever. She'd been taking college-level classes and got to college with a lot of her basic requirements completed. She wanted to study Biology— I think she was planning on becoming a doctor, but what I remember is that instead of going to medical school, she went off to graduate school."

"She . . . *what*?!" Nessa said. She suddenly had an image in her head of her mom in a cap and gown. Not a younger version of her mom, but her mom as she was now—dressed in her scrubs, carrying bags of groceries in from the car, lifting a lasagna out of the oven.

"I was so young, I wasn't really aware of how remarkable this was," Jane continued. "She was brilliant in the lab apparently, got hired onto this professor's research project early on in her freshman year, and pretty soon was staying at school during all her school breaks, caught up with lab work. I remember seeing her name on her first published scientific paper. It was far down the list of names—that's a big deal in science writing, what order the authors' names are in—but she was still an undergrad at the time, I think, and everyone else on the list was a post-doc or higher."

"Wow," Nessa said.

"It *was* 'wow,'" said Aunt Jane. "Meanwhile at home, we'd basically stopped seeing her. She would come home for the day on Christmas or something, but she seemed so absorbed in her work. Once she showed up at Thanksgiving with a man in tow. We couldn't even tell if he was her boyfriend. He was on his cell phone in the car the whole time. We thought he might have been a lab assistant.

"When you were born a few years later, no one knew if he was your father or what. She was living in Seattle when we got your birth announcement. I remember I called. I was in school by then. I wanted to be close to her. She's my sister, after all. I suggested I come out and meet you, but your mom said it wasn't a good time. I asked about your father, and your mom said it was someone from work. She said they were together, but she didn't talk much about anything. I think she wanted to be closer to me too, but she had a fellowship in Japan coming up. She was there for two years."

"But—" Nessa said, then realized she didn't know what was weirder. That her mom had a Past. That her mom had been to Japan. (That *she'd* been to Japan?) That she hadn't known any of this.

"During that period, Dad—your grandpa—well, that was when he got sick. He had cancer, and eventually he went into hospice. We called Vivian to tell her, and a few days later she showed up in Tether with you—you were three—and Delphine, who was just a baby. Everyone assumed it was a visit, that she had come to say goodbye. But then she rented an apartment and by the time Dad passed, Dr. Morgan was starting up his vet practice, he hired her, and the rest is history."

"I don't understand," Nessa said. "How could people in town forget about her being in graduate school and becoming a scientist and all that? No one has ever even mentioned it to me. Didn't people know?"

Aunt Jane sighed. She took her last sip of tea, staring at the bottom of the mug as if she couldn't believe the cup was already empty. "Small towns work in funny ways," she said. "Your mother never talked about her past. Never alluded to it. Never flaunted her education or talked about her work. She was living on a vet tech's salary. She was really struggling. That became the reality for the town. It became the reality for her. People live inside the stories they tell themselves. Others see about you the things that you believe."

Nessa spun her empty mug on the table. She'd been drinking out of this mug—the one with the daisy—all her life. It suddenly looked as foreign to her as if she had never seen it before.

The familiar made strange.

Her mom had been a scientist.

Her mom had finished college in two years.

Her mom had done all of the things Nessa dreamed about doing herself, and Vivian never told her about any of it, never explained that it was possible. Never explained how to keep whatever happened to her from happening to Nessa.

Delphine's eyes filled with tears as Jane and Nessa explained what had happened in court that day. As they explained that it was time for Delphine and Nate to leave for Milwaukee. As they explained that Nessa would not be coming with them.

"You're not coming?" Delphine cried.

"I can't switch schools in the middle of my junior year," Nessa said. "Not if I want colleges to take my application seriously." As much as she felt bad for lying, she felt worse in so many other ways that her guilt barely registered. "And track season starts in a month—I have to be here to train. Bree's parents said I could stay with them for a while. Maybe I can go see Mom."

"You think Mom's going to be in jail that long?" Delphine asked. "Couldn't we stay too?"

"I'm sorry, sweetheart," Jane explained. "But I think it's going to be very hard for you and Nate in Tether for a little while. There's going to be some anger. It's best for us to get out of town as soon as possible."

Delphine stood. She looked at the clock over the microwave. "It's 5:15," Delphine said—the clock showed 5:22 but everyone in the Kurland family knew it was seven minutes fast. It occurred to Nessa that this was one of the many little familiarities their family would be missing soon. Who knew how fast or slow Aunt Jane's clocks ran? "I'll be ready by six."

When Nate came home, Aunt Jane kept the explanation simpler. She was learning, Nessa saw. Nate could not understand fuzzy units of time, like "longer than we thought" or "a little while." "Your mom will be gone for two months," Jane said. "You and Delphine will live with me."

"We'll bring all your videos and trains," Nessa added quickly.

Nate scowled. "I don't like this," he said.

"That's good, saying your feelings," Nessa replied, just like her mom would have done.

Nate's scowl softened slightly.

"I would like you to program my DVR," Aunt Jane said. "I have never set it to record any shows."

Nate nodded.

Everyone loaded Aunt Jane's hatchback to the gills and she promised a fast-food dinner on the road.

By 6:15, they were gone.

After she watched Aunt Jane's car back down the driveway and then disappear into the just-getting-dark night, Nessa stood for a minute with her hand on the door. Thinking.

She put on pasta water to boil, packed her clothes, her running stuff, stuff from the bathroom. She stirred the pasta through the murky water, bracing herself against the counter with one hand, and thought back to the crazy things Aunt Jane had told her.

There are things about your mom that I don't think you know.

Now, in the empty house, Nessa finally had time to digest what she had learned.

Not that it made any more sense.

What was Aunt Jane trying to tell her? That Vivian could have done what the government said she had done? But she wouldn't have. Nessa was sure of that. Vivian wouldn't have wanted to.

Would she?

Nessa stood, straining the pasta and dumping a tablespoon of butter and Parmesan cheese into the pot. She speared a few rotini with a fork and shoved them into her mouth, eating straight out of the pan. Why bother with a bowl when no one was home?

Chewing, carrying the pot in one hand and the fork in the other, she walked down the hall to her room, put the pot down on the carpet, and, opening the drawer on her bedside table, pulled out the bank statements. Taking another bite of pasta, she read through the one on top, looking for signs or clues, something to explain what it was. She brought it to the table in the kitchen. As she ate, she stared at the pages. The number. The names. Hers. Delphine's. Chimera Corp. Daniel Host.

Looking at the bank statement, Nessa had to know. Where had all this money come from? Could she use it to save her mom?

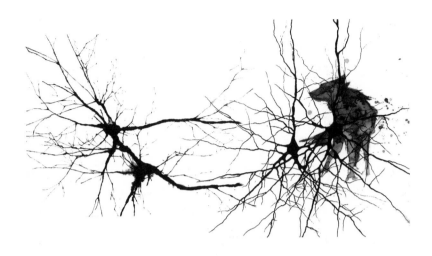

CHAPTER TWELVE

ree pulled up at the curb and Nessa dragged her bag down the front walkway after being careful to close and lock the door to the house behind her.

"Check it out," Bree said when Nessa tossed her bag in the Monster's back seat. "My mom feels so sorry for you she gave us money for ice cream."

The change in atmosphere was almost electric: going from eating plain pasta out of the pan, contemplating the possibility that her mother stole industrial secrets and sold them to foreign governments, to being in Bree's warm car and suddenly feeling like this was a sleepover. Nessa felt her body warming, relaxing. She actually laughed out loud when Bree said, "Sun-DAES!"

and hit the gas, the Monster peeling away from the house.

Nessa punched the power button on the radio. All she wanted was music. She would wake up and fight all this tomorrow. Right now, she just had to forget.

"Did your mom authorize M&M topping?" Nessa asked. "Whipped cream?"

Bree nodded. "Trust me. We're getting the works."

An hour later, the girls were sitting with enormous bowls brimming over with chocolate Breyers, hot fudge, caramel, towers of whipped cream, M&M's, cherries. Bree's mom, Stephanie, usually defined dessert as some light agave over a bowl of granola and yogurt, but even she had served herself a scoop of chocolate in a coffee cup. Bree's dad, who had just gotten back in from what Bree had referred to as a "civic meeting" in town, was still at the counter, making a sundae to rival the girls'. After about five bites, Nessa felt better than she had in days.

"What was your meeting about?" Nessa asked Ted, Bree's dad.

"For the group that's trying to get the ban on wolf-hunting lifted."

A cold bite of sundae stuck in Nessa's throat and for a moment she thought maybe she wasn't going to be able to swallow. Or breathe. She looked at Bree, who had her face screwed up in such a way that Nessa realized Bree had known exactly what meeting her dad had gone to and had been hoping Nessa would not find out.

Bree's dad, Ted—nice, reliable, relaxed Ted—had joined the

anti-wolf movement in Tether?

What was he going to say when he learned about the accusations against Nessa's mom?

What was everyone in Tether going to say?

"How many people turned out?" Stephanie asked, taking a new small bite. "Did they get a good showing?"

"I'll say," said Ted. "They just about filled the gym to capacity. People were standing in the back."

"Sheesh," said Bree, glancing anxiously at Nessa again. Nessa knew she should give her a look to show that she was okay.

But was she okay? She looked down at her sundae, the ice cream melting into the fudge. What had ever made her think it was something she'd enjoy eating?

"Yeah, they had this rep from the National Guard come in," Ted was explaining. "I guess the governor wanted us to know that they're taking this seriously." He laughed, gruffly. "Keep a bunch of hicks out of the woods with their guns, getting into all kinds of trouble."

"They've called in the National Guard?" Bree said. "They think that's necessary?"

"Not yet," Ted said. "But they wanted us to know that it's an option. First they had someone from the state's natural resources agency dishing out a load of hooey about the wolf population helping to establish balance in the natural ecosystem of the woods, and how we had to allow for adjustments in the preda-tor-prey cycle as the wolf populations reestablish themselves. Blah blah, all that environmental bull crap about how nature takes care of its own and how it's really okay that good men are out of logging work as long as the great horned owl's not going to have to move his nest. That lady nearly got booed off the podium." Ted chuckled at the memory. Bree gave Nessa another glance of horror-stricken apology. Nessa just stared as Ted went on explaining to Stephanie.

"But the National Guard fellow, people liked what he had to say. He showed this satellite map of Michigan and zoomed in over Tether and there were all these red dots, right? Like, dozens of them. It uses a new technology Paravida's testing out." He stopped, organizing his next mouthful. Nessa put her spoon down on the table. She'd never noticed the cameras.

"So the red dots," Stephanie said. "They show where a wolf has been spotted?"

"No," Ted said, his mouth full now. "The images are *live*. The map links up the data from the cameras with real-time satellite imagery—apparently they have access to this government satellite that reads heat, so they could see where they are through the trees. And when the National Guard rep told us that, we started to see that the dots were *moving*."

"How many would you say there were?" Nessa choked out. "How many wolves?" She and Luc had thought there were at least twenty Paravida wolves in the vicinity. Including the pack, that would make close to thirty.

"About seventy," Ted said. "But the guy said only a month ago, they were seeing only forty."

Nessa's spoon clattered to the floor. "Sorry," she said.

"Don't be," Ted said. Digging back into his sundae as she got up to rinse her spoon, Ted added, "That number's terrifying. Granted, they're spread out over hundreds of square miles, but it's way more than I think anyone in that room had anticipated. Frankly I'm surprised no one's gotten killed yet. I've stopped asking why they're coming; now I want to know what's keeping them away?"

"Ugh," Stephanie said. She pushed her ice cream away as if she'd just lost her appetite. "It sounds like a horror movie."

"Yeah," said Bree. "Like when you open the door to the attic and it's crawling with spiders or snakes or something." Her enthusiasm for horror movies momentarily outstripping her awareness of the interpersonal dynamics in the conversation, she waved her spoon in the air. "Wall. To. Wall." She took another tiny bite of whipped cream with one M&M perched on top.

Ted was staring at her, his face white. Stephanie was looking at Ted. Nessa looked down into her ice cream bowl. Family moment.

"Um, Bree?" Stephanie said.

Bree looked at her mom. Stephanie reached out with a napkin to wipe a dab of whipped cream off Bree's nose.

"The wolf situation in this town is not funny," Ted said.

"Jeez," Bree said. "You guys really know how to take the fun out of my sundae sugar high."

Ted shook his head.

"This is serious, Bree," Stephanie said. "These wolves. We need to believe that you understand the danger."

Bree lowered her eyes to the table. "I do," she said.

Stephanie didn't answer, just stood up to put her mug in the sink, then headed for the stairs.

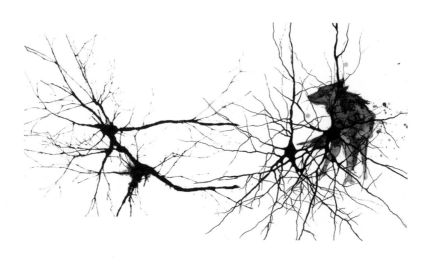

CHAPTER THIRTEEN

orry about my parents," Bree said while Nessa unpacked. Even though it was late, Bree had insisted on giving Nessa a tour of the towel rack she'd assigned to her, the drawers she'd emptied, the air mattress she'd inflated. She'd even given Nessa a little desk on the windowsill, with pens and newly sharpened pencils in a cup. "They're kind of freaking out about the wolves."

"Imagine how they're going to feel when they start thinking my mom's the one who created the problem?" Nessa said. "Are you sure it's okay with them for me to be here?"

"Oh, yes!" Bree said. "They're so glad they can help in some way. And they already do know. Actually—" Bree braced for impact. "I think everyone in town does?

"My parents, though, they don't believe it. Well, I told them not to believe it, and I don't think anyone else in town will, either. People here *know* your mom, Nessa."

Nessa felt a knob form in her throat. "She didn't do those things. I know she didn't."

"Of course not," Bree said. "This whole thing is just so obviously an attempt by Paravida to mask the fact that they were responsible for releasing dozens of hyper-aggressive genetically altered wolves into the environment. I mean, your mom? A geneticist? Come on!"

"Oh, wow," Nessa said. Bree took a look at Nessa's face and saw that this was going to be important. "I guess there's something I better tell you."

"What?" Bree said.

"That geneticist part? She kind of is."

"No way," said Bree. And then it poured out: Vivian's incredible education and budding scientific career. Her mysterious return to Tether. Even the bank account Nessa and Delphine had found, with the insane amount of money Vivian had never breathed a word about.

After Nessa finished explaining, she watched as Bree stared at her, her face a mask of concentration. "Okay," Bree said, counting off on her fingers. "First of all, you're rich. And more to the point, your mom is a scientist. You never suspected it?"

"No!" Nessa said. "I mean, she always knows a lot of stuff, but doesn't every mom? Like, you ask her why the sky is blue and she explains about the spectrum of light and the way light bends as it enters the atmosphere . . . and, yeah." It was weird, to have everything you'd known and thought require reorganization by your brain. In a new tone of enlightenment, she added: "That's not normal, is it?"

"Nessa," Bree said, leveling her with a glance. "When I asked my mom why the sky was blue, she said God had run out of yellow paint after he was done with the sun."

"Okay, yeah," said Nessa, laughing. "I guess that should have been a tip-off."

Bree started refolding Nessa's clothes and organizing them in the drawer she'd cleared out. "Nessa," she said. "They're so glad you're here. I told them it's going to be like having a sister."

"That," Nessa said, smiling wryly, "is the kind of thing only an only child would say."

Bree smiled. "Nessa, don't look so glum. Your mom is a genius! I'm so impressed."

"I don't know if I'm quite there yet," Nessa said. "I feel like I have more questions to answer before I can be excited."

Bree smiled mischievously, her fingers poised over the keys of her laptop. "Maybe Daniel Host—" as she spoke his name, she was typing the letters, "—of Chimera Corp.—" Bree hit the Enter key emphatically, "—can answer some of them?"

"Wait, don't—" Nessa said. She didn't want to start this now. What if Bree's internet searches were being watched? What if the FBI came and took away Bree's computer, the way they'd taken Delphine's?

But it was too late. Bree had already pressed Enter. The girls watched the monitor, waiting for the results to load. Bree, who was closest, was able to scan them first. She squinted, scrolled down, and then back up, her smile gone.

"Oh, my goodness," Bree said, looking at Nessa with a pained expression in her eyes. "I guess he's a professor, but except for this one link to his faculty page at Stanford, there's almost nothing out there about him." Bree turned the screen around and showed a very unusual search page—there was only a single item on it.

"You're right," Nessa said. "That does look weird. Almost suspicious."

She clicked the link, and it went to a Stanford University faculty page. The spot where a picture would have been showed only a broken icon. A three-sentence bio:

Daniel Host, an innovator in biological science, holds the Dwight Thomas Chair for Medical Research. He consults on dissertation study design as well as teaching a seminar in the spring semester. He has been a member of the faculty since 2009.

"You know what that means, right?" Bree went on.

"Uh . . . he's a fake? Like those people who try to friend you on Facebook but have, like, one picture?" said Nessa.

"No," said Bree. "If that were the case, he wouldn't be able to set up a page on the Stanford website. That's a real university. What it means is that he must be a really big deal."

Nessa was confused. "Because he teaches at Stanford?"

"No," said Bree. "Because no one real gets to have this small a presence on the internet. He must have hired a security firm to eliminate every link out there that mentions his name. I saw something about that on *60 Minutes*. People who want that much privacy online have to pay for it."

"Really?" said Nessa. "*60 Minutes*? I think it's much more

likely he's just not real. Or not that important."

"What would you bet," Bree said, her eyes narrowing, "that Daniel Host is connected to Paravida in some way?"

"You think Paravida wants to give my mom almost a million dollars?"

"Maybe they were trying to buy her off and when that didn't work, they found out about her scientist past and framed her for the creation of the wolves. Killing two birds with one stone. Or maybe the whole account is fake, meant to be part of the evidence to frame your mom."

Nessa had to admit, that sounded likely. Except for the part about being bought off. Vivian was the kind of person who would bring a dollar bill to the cashier if she had found it on the floor of the grocery store while shopping.

For the rest of the night, the girls were quiet, working on the last bit of homework before they turned out the lights and went to sleep. Nessa entered her running times in the Paravida Award database, brushed her teeth, and changed into her pajamas. She saw Luc had texted her.

Get some sleep, he wrote. You'll need it.

Given the number of open questions flooding her brain, she assumed she never would, but she texted him back

g'nite :)

In fact, the second her head hit the pillow, she was out.

The next morning, while Bree was in the shower, on a whim, Nessa called Daniel Host's office. She got connected to a recording, a clipped British-sounding voice announcing that this was the voice message box for Daniel Host at Stanford BioSciences.

It was surprising, Nessa thought—given that she was almost certain Daniel Host was a fake person—that the recording sounded so much like one a legitimate person would have. She thought about leaving a message. What would she say? "I know you're working with Paravida. Come clean or I'll bring in the police"?

That wasn't likely to hold water. The police were probably working with Paravida too, just like the FBI. Before the beep sounded, she hung up.

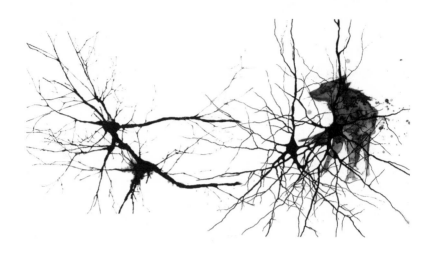

CHAPTER FOURTEEN

rue to their word, Ted and Stephanie never mentioned the accusations that had been leveled at Nessa's mother.

But Bree couldn't put a gag order on the rest of Tether. On Thursday morning at school, the parking lot silence was deafening. Crowds parted in the hallways when she walked by.

By lunchtime, Nessa was ready to explode with anger. "My mom has lived in Tether nearly her whole life," she growled to Luc at lunch. "She's grown up with these kids' parents. She's taken care of their cats and dogs. They know her, and not one person believes that she might *not* be behind the wolf invasion."

"They don't know what to think anymore," Luc said, sounding not like he was trying to console her, but like he was just making an observation about human nature in general. "They're scared. The stuff they're reading—it's convincing."

"I guess," Nessa said. She wished she could be as philosophical as Luc. Mostly she just wanted to transform, overturn a few lunch tables, show her teeth, and growl at everyone whose whispers she could hear until they were cowering in corners. The idea was the first thing that had made her smile all day. See what people would be whispering about *then*.

Nessa was grateful, Saturday morning, not to have to go to school. She and Bree spent the morning in their pajamas playing Candy Crush while following a ridiculous student council group text that mostly involved a series of emojis sent by Bree and her newest crush, Andy Carlisle, who was having a party that night.

Nessa called Nate and Delphine, Skyping with them and Aunt Jane, and then eventually, around eleven, she hauled herself up and out for a training run. As she stretched at the front door, she saw Ted out in the driveway, tinkering with the engine of his car. Stephanie called out to her from the kitchen. "Nessa," she said. "Hold up a sec. Can I ask you a question?"

"Sure," Nessa said, one hand on the doorknob, her legs feeling heavy and tired, not at all ready to go. She took the five steps backward toward the kitchen.

Stephanie was sorting laundry on the kitchen table, folding socks. She gave her a look that was as full of questions as it was sympathy, disarming Nessa momentarily. *Bree is right*, Nessa thought. *People in Tether aren't bad. They're like Stephanie. Confused. Scared.*

"You're not going to run in the woods, are you?" Stephanie asked. She smiled and looked down. "I know that's always been kind of your thing."

"No," Nessa said, though in truth, she'd been thinking about it. But as she looked Stephanie in the eye, she decided she would stay on the roads for sure. "I'm not. And Stephanie—?"

Stephanie looked down briefly to pick up one of Ted's tee shirts. "Yes, sweetheart?"

"Thanks for having me. I know it's probably not easy."

Stephanie dropped the tee shirt, moving quickly around the table to stand next to Nessa. She put a hand on her shoulder— Stephanie was shorter than Nessa so it was a bit of a reach. "Of course! I can't imagine how hard this is for you and, well, whatever is happening, I want you to know there will always be a place for you here."

Nessa nodded, and because she felt unwanted tears springing into her eyes, she said, "I gotta go," and busted back out the door before they could be seen, clocking yet another not-impressive time: 19:35. Her best 5K race last fall, at States, had been 14:53. True, she'd been reveling in the beginnings of paranormal-level abilities, but the recruiters who had practically chased her home from the race were going to expect a lot more than this.

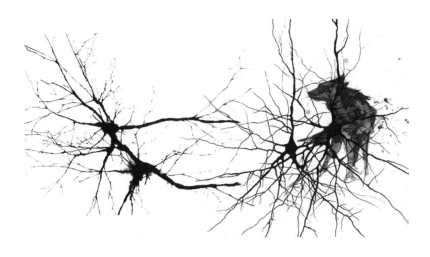

CHAPTER FIFTEEN

unt Jane had been right that the pressure of gossip was overwhelming. When Nessa made the colossal mistake of tagging along with Bree to the bonfire party in Andy Carlisle's backyard, she finally slipped into the shadows at the end of the woods. She still heard what everyone was saying—having wolf hearing comes with unwanted perks. A lot of the insults didn't bother her, but the one that most rankled was "I guess she deserves what she got."

But it wasn't until the next morning that Nessa felt the full impact of the town's ire. Pulling up in front of Dr. Morgan's, rushing slightly to make up for being a minute or two late, she was surprised to see Dr. Morgan himself rushing out, almost as if to meet her.

"Nessa!" he called out.

"Good morning," she said, assuming he'd pass right by her. She had the momentary thought that perhaps he had left something important at home, like his glasses. Except Dr. Morgan didn't wear glasses and he wasn't passing by her. He stopped, blocking her path to the door.

"Have a second?" he said.

Nessa felt a fluttering, nervous feeling rising inside her stomach. She knew—somehow, instinctually—that she was in trouble.

Dr. Morgan's face was bright red. "I—uh—well, there's no way to say this but I've been getting complaints."

"You have?" said Nessa, feeling a rush of relief. She wasn't in trouble! If Dr. Morgan had been getting complaints they couldn't have been about her. She knew she did a good job cleaning cages and even if she didn't, the owners never saw the insides of the crates, anyway.

"What about?" she said, preparing herself for Dr. Morgan to unload his concerns about how the clients reacted to his treatment of their animals. Maybe this was the kind of thing he used to discuss with her mom but now that she was in jail, he was turning to Nessa?

"You've got to understand. People are afraid. That's what happens when they don't understand. I don't believe it but they do." He was rushing his words and Nessa could barely register what they meant.

"Dr. Morgan," Nessa said. "What are you talking about? Afraid of what?"

He rolled his eyes up to the sky, then looked back at Nessa.

His hair was thinning and his skin, normally wrinkled but in a healthy, tanned, outdoorsy way, had an almost ashen look to it. But his amber eyes were the same—direct and bright, handsome. Dr. Morgan had always been kind to Vivian and helped out whenever he could. "They're afraid of your mother," he finally said. "I've been getting phone calls. People canceling appointments. I'm afraid that until all of this settles down, I can't have you work at the practice. If I did, I'm not sure I would *have* a practice any longer."

He laughed at this lame attempt at a joke, but Nessa did not. This wasn't a personal betrayal. That she could have understood. This was a betrayal of her mother.

"Fine," she said, turning on her heel and storming away.

The rest of the day, the only other person Nessa saw was Luc. He picked her up that afternoon and they ran in the woods. She was hoping for some relaxation—she was so filled with bad feelings she thought she was going to explode—but there were so many more Paravida wolves on the prowl, the afternoon became a high-octane game of hide-and-seek. At one point, they found themselves face-to-face with a pair of Paravida wolves and it looked like they were going to have to fight them. One lunged at Nessa and got his teeth into her shoulder. But Jack, the Paravida wolf who was the father of Sister's pups, emerged out of nowhere and stood with Luc. Suddenly, the fight was three on two and the Paravida wolves slunk away.

Luc and Nessa returned to his cabin, both out of breath. "Did you see that?" he shouted across the clearing the moment he'd transformed. He was pointing to the woods they'd come from. "Did you see my boy Jack?"

Nessa rolled her eyes but it was impossible not to feel his enthusiasm.

"He had our backs!" Luc was running in circles around the clearing, taking a skip-like hop every few steps. He looked like the guys on the soccer team when they managed to score. "He's getting it! He's starting to understand what a pack is." In his excitement, Luc let out a whoop, throwing his head back and nearly baying at the sky.

Nessa followed his gaze. Looking up into the patch of blue she could see through the branches of the still-bare trees and joined in, sending her own whoops up into the empty-feeling forest along with his. Luc was right. It was a big deal that Jack had stood with them. It was a big deal that the weather was getting warmer. She felt . . . good for a fleeting moment.

Eventually Luc stopped whooping and turned and reached for her waist, pulling her toward him. She closed her eyes and breathed in his musky smell. She wished they could stay just the way they were forever.

It was hard to believe that everything that had happened to Nessa—to Vivian and to the entire Kurland family—had all taken place over the course of a single week. Vivian had been arrested on a Sunday night and by Wednesday night, Nessa had moved in with Bree. This morning she'd basically been fired from her job, and now she stood whooping it up in the woods with Luc.

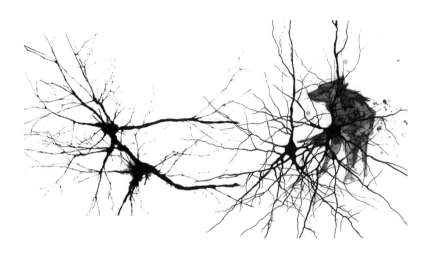

CHAPTER SIXTEEN

ime to go to school and make like I can't hear everyone whispering about my mom!" Nessa said with sarcastic cheer Monday morning, as she and Bree headed out the door toward the Monster, one of Stephanie's tasteless oatmeal-flax-chia breakfast bars wrapped in unbleached wax paper for the ride to school.

But the whispers at school weren't entirely Vivian-centric. There had been more wolf sightings over the weekend and the term "wolf invasion" was tripping off the lips of students and teachers alike. News traveled fast: Kevin James, who owned Kelly's Bar, had seen a wolf going through his dumpsters late Saturday night. Cats were missing, and though no one could say what had happened to them for sure, the suspicion was wolves.

And on Sunday morning at Grace Lutheran, the service had come to a halt as one parishioner after another caught sight through the large windows of a pack of six Paravida wolves trotting lazily through the parking lot, sniffing the swing set. One lifted his leg on the bench where, every fall, a professional photographer took pictures of all Grace parishioners for the annual church directory.

That night at dinner, when Ted announced that he was turning down a driving job because he didn't feel right leaving Stephanie and Bree alone, Bree accused him of being paranoid. Upstairs in Bree's room, Nessa let Bree vent about how her parents needed to start trusting her.

Inwardly, Nessa thought Ted was just being smart. He drove Stephanie to work now, dropping her right at the door to the building where she worked in an insurance adjustor's office in an industrial park outside of town. *Again*, Nessa said to herself privately, *a smart move*.

On Tuesday she ran a 21:05, in part because her shoulder was killing her from the Paravida wolf bite—she'd told Bree the shoulder was fine but in truth, she could barely move her arm without pain. On Thursday the shoulder felt worse and she ran a 22:19. On Friday, Coach Hoffman called Nessa into his office for a check-in meeting about her training. It was against the rules for cross-country coaches to hold practices out of season, but there was nothing wrong with meetings during which they discussed a runner's strategy one-on-one. He looked at her times. "Okay, let's start thinking about interval work," he said. "Maybe you should consider the schedule you were on over the summer."

Nessa nodded, then asked the question she'd been dreading hearing an answer to. "Because my mom's in jail, do you think the recruiters—" she began. "Are they still—?"

"Interested even after what's been happening with your mom?" he said, filling in the question for her. He leaned back in his chair and let out a heavy breath. "Look," he said. "You get your times back down, they're going to be interested. Not to mention the fact that this is going to turn out to be one hell of a college essay."

Nessa called Aunt Jane almost every night, checking in on Nate and Delphine. Delphine sounded like she had been completely absorbed into her new school, where she was being treated like a celebrity guest. She had made a new friend—also a fashionista—who was including her in everything. Nessa wondered why she'd ever worried about her sister. Imbued with all the family talent for making friends and influencing people, Delphine had the ability to make herself at home wherever she went.

Aunt Jane tried to talk to Vivian at least every other day, and she relayed Vivian's messages. Vivian wanted Jane to find an occupational therapist for Nate in Milwaukee. She wanted Delphine to have unlimited access to the internet and she reminded Jane to install parental controls. Jane told Nessa that Vivian was opposed to Nessa's staying in Tether, wanting Jane to bring her to Milwaukee too. "She doesn't want you facing the blowback alone," Jane said.

"I'm not leaving," Nessa said and she could almost see Jane's shrug through the phone line. Jane had enough on her mind without having to enforce Vivian's dictum on this one.

Jane sent a check to the jail to deposit in Vivian's commissary account so Vivian could buy the personal items the jail did not provide—a comb, a toothbrush, cough medicine. "Your mom sounds sicker every time I talk to her," Jane reported. "The cold she's picked up isn't moving."

Nessa's only way of communicating with her mother was by letter. Writing the letters, she thought of a million questions she wanted to ask, but couldn't: *Why didn't you ever tell me you were trained as a scientist? What happened with my dad? Is he still alive? Why did you leave him? Why is the government saying you were accepting money from foreign governments hostile to the United States? What did you leave behind at Dr. Morgan's? Who is Daniel Host?*

But these were questions she had to ask her mother in person. So she wrote letters that were fully fact-based, sticking to the details of her new life at Bree's, her running, what she was learning in school.

She wanted to tell her mother so much more. How, in the courtroom, Nessa had felt powerless. How she'd kept fantasizing that she'd transformed on the spot, bitten the U.S. marshal guarding her mom, and then herded her mom out the door, past the armed security guards at the courthouse entrance. How cruel it was that her mom had been visible, but not reachable. She hadn't been able to talk to her or touch her, and then Vivian had been gone.

She wanted to write Vivian and say, *What if I found out where the magistrate lived and went and begged him to let you go, explaining that our family is normal, that none of this makes any sense?*

Could she tell her that rather than following Vivian's instructions to help with her mysterious new duties at Dr. Morgan's, she'd actually gotten herself fired?

She couldn't tell Vivian these things. It wouldn't do anything to help her. Nothing Nessa could do would help.

Aside from waiting for updates from Aunt Jane and hoping for a window of opportunity to return to the vet's, Nessa had no choice but to resume life in a way that felt as close to normal as possible.

If normal could be described as sitting there staring at a permission slip for the class trip at the end of June—the deposit was due now—and wondering who in the world she could ask to sign it.

If normal could be described as conversations in classrooms stopping when Nessa entered, as if she wouldn't know kids were talking about the wolf-defense militias their dads were forming, as if she hadn't very well just heard Angela Crawley say, "We can't sit around waiting for the National Guard," or Jacob Kelly try to impress his new girlfriend by telling her about the weapons cache his dad was stockpiling.

Tim Miller, who had taken to wearing a button showing a wolf beneath an X made of two semiautomatic rifles, turned away when Nessa tried to ask him a question about math.

"He used to have a crush on you!" Bree said at lunch, when Nessa told her about the change. "Remember when he would drop homemade brownies off at your locker last fall?"

"Yeah," Nessa said. "I hope he's worse at building bombs than he is at baking, because those brownies were really tasty."

Luc's reaction to the wolf-militia movement was less nuanced than Bree's. "This whole thing makes me ashamed to be part-human," he said, ripping a wolf poster off the wall by his locker at the end of a school day. They were heading out to his truck to go for a run in the woods. After Nessa and Jack's encounter, they were trying to double their time patrolling, though Luc was finding more time to be out in the woods than Nessa was.

His dad had flown to Arizona for a work conference and his mom was up in the UP, so he was spending nights in the cabin. Stopping by after a patrol, Nessa had seen a pile of blankets on the floor, under the shelf on the wall, the sleeping bag and cushions appearing untouched. She suspected he was using them to make a sleeping nest, wolf-style.

"That's how you think of yourself?" Nessa asked him now, when they were in the truck. "As never really having been a human?"

"Yeah," he said, shifting gears. "That bother you?"

Nessa had forgotten gloves, and she held her bare hands up against the truck's barely functioning heater. She remembered the first time she'd transformed, how her hands became blocky and she hadn't been able to open a door. She wiggled her fingers now, noticing how flexible they were. Human hands—they were a gift Nessa didn't think about much, but she was thinking about them now. Luc was willing to give that up, she knew. Could she ever?

"I don't think of myself as half and half," she said. "I become a wolf, but I never stop being a human."

"I've never felt fully human," he said. "And really, why would I want to be? Technology and science and government and prison."

Nessa sighed.

"What's happening to your mom—an innocent woman stuck in jail—that's humanity in a nutshell. You do realize that, don't you?"

"I've got to get back to the clinic," Nessa said, forcing her mind back to the task she had to succeed at. She had to help her mom. "Even if I'm not working there, I have to keep looking around. I've got to figure out what she was up to."

"Okay," said Luc. "But I don't think the answers you're looking for are going to be found in a cage. They never are." He gestured to the window through which they could see passing trees. "The answers are going to come from out there."

Nessa followed his gaze. The forest, a series of bare gray lines making a pattern as the truck whizzed by, seemed almost to tap out a rhythm, one Nessa had been listening to all her life.

Maybe, she thought now, *the rhythm is also a code?*

That night, after Bree drifted off, Nessa's brain kept working. What if they couldn't find anything at the clinic that would explain what her mom had *really* been up to? Or worse, what if they only found things like the bank statement—things that, rather than answering Nessa's questions, only created new ones?

After Nessa tossed and turned for almost an hour, her shoulder started to throb. She went into the bathroom, took two ibuprofen, and examined the wound. It wasn't deep and there was no tissue damage, thank goodness, but the longer she looked at it in a state of half-awake, dream-like contemplation, the more disturbing the idea of the wound became. Her skin was broken. Her human skin. But the wound wasn't deep, mostly because as a wolf, she'd been protected by thick fur. Wolf fur. She was 100 percent wolf when she had been bitten. She was 100 percent human now.

How could she possibly be both things?

Animal cells and plant cells were almost exactly the same, weren't they? A Paravida wolf was not like a natural wolf, but he was a wolf regardless. And besides—something Luc had told her—most of the wolves in the United States were actually wolf-coyote hybrids. Everything in nature had been altered by time, by chance, by need, by luck. Nothing was ever exactly what it seemed.

She shook her head, as if she could clear it with the gesture. Then she went back to Bree's room, and by the light cast from her phone, wrote Vivian a letter. It was short. It didn't mention anything going on at school.

Dear Mom:
One question: Who is DH?
Love,
Nessa

There were questions she had the power to find answers to. There were other questions she didn't know if she would ever understand.

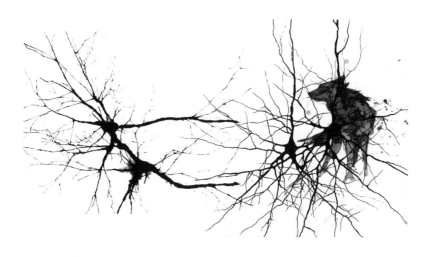

CHAPTER SEVENTEEN

Nessa mailed the note first thing Monday morning. On Wednesday, she had some version of an answer when a text came through while she was getting ready for school. It was from a number she didn't recognize and she expected it was someone in AP Bio with a Hail Mary question about the homework. Surprisingly enough, Nessa was the most likely person out of all of them to understand the assignments.

But it wasn't an AP Bio classmate.

This is Zach Chandler, your mother's lawyer. She told me I could reach you this way. Can you meet me?

She quickly consulted the bus schedule, then wrote back:

I'll be at your office at 10 a.m.

He wrote back instantly:

Not my office.

Then:

Meet me outside the courthouse. There's a bench across from the fountain. The corner of Ionia and Lyon.

Two minutes later:

Wait . . . don't you have school?

Nessa wrote back a lie she was confident a grown-up without school-age kids would believe.

Spring break.

After all, it was only a week away.

Bree dropped her in the center of town on their way in to school, and Nessa boarded the bus alongside Tether commuters heading to work in Grand Rapids. She slept for most of the ride, then, after climbing out of the bus in Grand Rapids' downtown, she walked to the courthouse.

The minute Nessa sat down on the bench Zach had directed her to and caught her breath, she realized that she was starving. She also knew Zach Chandler could appear in the next five minutes. If she got up to get food, she might miss him.

So Nessa waited, listening to the rumbling of her stomach, watching the groups of young, suit-wearing attorneys and junior attorneys checking their phones, laughing, and talking to one another. For once, it felt like spring was coming. No one was wearing winter clothing. A single tulip in the decorative beds surrounding the courthouse had bloomed. The contrast between the quasi-festive demeanor of the passing pedestrians and her own unsettled feelings of hunger, fatigue, and mounting nervousness made it hard to sit still.

She saw a homeless man shuffling along and what looked like a field trip's worth of elementary school children; then she caught herself watching a man in chinos and sneakers. He looked familiar, though she couldn't say from where, and then she realized. He was that man she had sat next to at her mother's bond hearing, the one scribbling on a steno notebook but who had not registered as a reporter. What was he doing here now? Never one to beat around the bush, she resolved to get up and ask him.

But just then, Zach Chandler appeared, and Nessa stood too quickly, bringing on a head rush. Why in the world hadn't she rummaged in the fridge for one of Stephanie's oatmeal-flax-chia bars? They weren't *that* bad.

"Hey, Nessa," Zach said. "You made it." He looked vaguely surprised.

"I took the bus," she said and immediately felt stupid, like she was a little kid announcing to the whole world she had just ridden her bike to the store all by herself.

"Okay," Zach said. He was out of breath, speaking fast. "I wanted to tell you. I met with your mom yesterday." He pulled out his Big Boy glasses, polished the lenses, and slid them on.

"How is she?" Nessa said. "Is she still sick?"

"I'm not going to lie to you," he said. "I think she was feverish when I saw her. I told her to go to the infirmary, to get some antibiotics or something, but she said she was handling it."

"Yeah," Nessa said. "My mom never takes medicine." She didn't even like to give antibiotics to Nessa, Nate, and Delphine—

they had to have strep or a really painful ear infection before Vivian let them have penicillin.

"But why I wanted to meet with you—" Zach continued. "We were discussing her plea. That's the next phase of the pre-trial proceedings. It's when the defendant has the opportunity to declare him- or herself guilty or not guilty. We're going to say 'not guilty,' but I want you to know, we might have to change that."

Nessa's heart sank. When she'd gotten Zach's text, she'd imagined he was going to have good news. Or at least *new* news. Now this was just one more brick in the impenetrable wall of bad news. "But she *isn't* guilty," Nessa said.

"Of course," Zach said. And then he lowered his voice. "But here's the thing, Nessa. At some point before the trial begins, the government is probably going to get in touch with me and tell me some of the evidence they have against your mom. If it looks bad for her, my boss is going to want me to settle."

"Settle my mom's case?" Nessa said.

"Yes. Maybe she could admit she did some but maybe not all of what she's being accused of, we all avoid the trial, and she accepts a shorter sentence."

"She would do that?" Nessa asked.

"No," Zach said. "That's the thing. Your mom's made it clear she's taking the 'Not Guilty' response all the way through. You're a minor and I can't discuss the details of the case with you, but I can tell you that given the resources my office can put to bear here, this is not going to work out well for her. If she's fighting these charges, your mom needs significant, serious help. I've never seen anything like them. My *boss* has never seen anything like them. Most federal prosecutions are drug-related but they're all unique and complicated in their own way and I have forty-five of them to manage right now on top of your mom's. Honestly, my advice to you is to find an attorney who can handle this. Someone who wants high-profile action. Someone who can take you pro bono, wants the publicity for some reason, because billing on this case, it could run up to $100,000. At the least."

This isn't fair, Nessa thought, digesting the weight of what had just been explained. Zach Chandler shouldn't be telling her these things. These things shouldn't be happening. In a fit of anger, she spat out, "Are those even prescription lenses or do you just wear them in a pathetic attempt to look old enough to help people?"

Nessa thought he'd be hurt, but Zach actually smiled. "I'm sorry. I shouldn't even be telling you this stuff. I just—look, you seem like you have a nice family and if it was my mom in there, I'd want to know what I'm telling you."

He took off the glasses, and looked down at them in his hands. "And I know I look ridiculously young. I am, I guess. I'm twenty-nine. But I was number three in my class at Columbia, and I've been working in this court for three years. I'm good. I'm getting better every year. But you need someone phenomenal. Someone experienced. A Johnnie Cochran type or something. This case is going to be huge."

"Okay," Nessa said. "So that's why you asked me to meet you here? To tell me I have to find my mom a new lawyer?"

"No." Zach passed her a folded piece of paper clearly taken from a yellow legal pad. "Here," he said. "I'm not supposed to pass messages, but your mom gave me this to give to you. She told me to tell you she thinks the letters going in and out of the jail are being read, so she wrote this when I was meeting with her yesterday."

Nessa held the paper. She felt like it was burning the skin on her fingers. Zach stood. He looked at his watch. "I have to run. You going to be okay? You have a ride back to Tether? Oh, wait, right, you took the bus." He smiled gently.

Nessa forced herself to smile back, though she wanted to tell Zach this wasn't funny. That he wasn't her camp counselor. He hoisted his briefcase and headed off down the sidewalk. Nessa shoved her mom's note deep into her jacket pocket. She would wait to read it until she knew for sure she was alone.

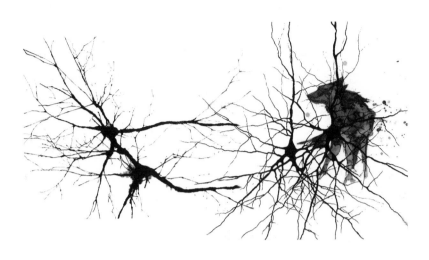

CHAPTER EIGHTEEN

Coke, please," Nessa said. "And a buttered roll."
She was finally eating breakfast, at a little café a block from
the courthouse. She realized Coke for breakfast was not the
healthiest, but she only had eight dollars with her, and the bus
fare would take up four of them so she needed to stretch what
was left into something that equaled energy.

The irony wasn't lost on her that she needed $100,000 to
hire a lawyer—from where she didn't know—and she didn't
even have enough money to buy an egg for her roll.

Except, of course, she did have hundreds of thousands
of dollars. Or she and Delphine did. Vivian did. In the bank
account filled with transfers from the mysterious Daniel Host.

Suddenly a five-dollar bill appeared on the counter, clutched in a large hand wearing a gold wristwatch. A man's voice—one she recognized—told the guy behind the counter to put some "bacon, egg, and cheese on this young lady's roll, if it's all right with her."

Confused, wondering whether this could possibly mean her, she looked up into the man's face and suddenly recognized him.

"Mr. Thomas?" she said.

It was Cassian's dad. Cassian, whom Nessa had spent the first two and a half years of high school crushing on. Mr. Thomas was one of Tether's few lawyers, and though Nessa didn't know him well, seeing him here, when she was among strangers, she might as well have bumped into her best friend.

She nodded at the guy behind the counter to let him know she accepted the extra calories on her breakfast sandwich. Why hadn't she thought of Mr. Thomas already? Why hadn't she gone to him right away? Cassian had told her his dad loved following her running career. He'd known her practically her whole life. Of course he could help!

"What are you doing here?" Nessa said. And then she felt immediately stupid. This was a courthouse neighborhood. The man was a lawyer. Duh.

"I have a case on in family court," he said. "It's two blocks from here."

"Oh," Nessa said. She ducked her head. "I'm here because of my mom."

"I figured," Mr. Thomas said, as Nessa's sandwich, Coke, and his coffee were delivered.

He led her over to a counter against the plate-glass window, the only seating the café had to offer. Nessa was assuming he'd ask how her mom was doing, ask how the case was going. Would he offer to help? Did he know anyone who might? She had high hopes for the conversation.

But when, instead of asking about her mom, Mr. Thomas said, "How's training? Are you looking to break any more records this spring?" Nessa nearly choked.

"Um, I've been training through the winter on my own?" she said. The question mark was there because she couldn't really believe he was interested in this information. Not when so much more was at stake. "Coach Hoffman can't hold practices, but we're having Captains' practice until the spring."

"Break is next week. You'll start in after?" Mr. Thomas took a swig of his coffee, then lifted his wrist to check his watch. She realized he was probably late for something. He was probably down here for a reason. If she was going to ask for his help with her mom, she had to do that now.

"Listen, just to get back to what I'm doing down here in Grand Rapids—"

"Now Nessa," Mr. Thomas said, cutting her off. "I—"

"My mom," Nessa insisted. "You know, she's in a lot of trouble. The FBI accused her of stealing from Paravida, and the public defender, he says she's facing charges he's not really used to handling and we need to hire our own lawyer, and I don't even know where to look for one, and then suddenly I've bumped into you, and—well, do you think you can help me?"

All the while Nessa had been speaking she'd been watching Mr. Thomas's face. It was clear to her he was trying to maintain a neutral expression, but he was having difficulty not wincing. It almost seemed like he was embarrassed by what she was asking.

"We don't have a lot of money," she went on, guessing this was the issue. "But we have our house. My mom could sell her car."

Mr. Thomas put up a hand. "Nessa," he said. "Stop. I wish I could help you. I do. It's just that—do you know what 'conflict of interest' means?"

"Yes," Nessa said. Her Social Studies teacher had explained the concept when Donald Trump was elected president. "It means when you can't be trusted to act in a nonbiased way in government because you have some kind of connection to one of the businesses the government oversees."

"Exactly," said Mr. Thomas. "In a court case, it means you can't work for one person in a case if you're also involved in another part of it. For instance, if the judge had Paravida stock he'd need to recuse himself and have another judge handle the trial."

"Okay," Nessa said.

"And," Mr. Thomas went on, brushing invisible dust off his immaculate suit jacket, "while I don't own any Paravida stock, I am representing them in a different matter. Unfortunately, I can't even talk to you about your mother's situation."

"You can't?" Nessa said. She felt like a balloon that had suddenly sprung a leak, all hope draining out of her body.

Mr. Thomas smiled, a handsome smile that reminded her of Cassian, but even as he was smiling, he was shaking his head no. "I'm sorry," he said. And then he was looking out the window like he'd just seen someone he knew across the street. "I've gotta go," he said. "But I wish you the best of luck."

He was out the door before Nessa could register how

unlucky it was that Mr. Thomas had been retained by Paravida when he was the only lawyer she knew. She really could have used his help.

Was it because he believed Vivian to be guilty?

Taking a half-hearted bite of her sandwich—up until the minute before it had been hitting the spot—she watched Mr. Thomas hurry toward one of the other court buildings, the wind picking up his tie and blowing it over his shoulder as he moved.

"You know," she heard a voice behind her say. "That's actually a tactic, hiring all the good lawyers in the local area so they can't help the person you're trying to put behind bars."

Nessa turned. Sitting right behind her—how did she keep missing his entrances and exits?—was the man from the courtroom, the one with the shaggy gray hair. Now that he was up close, she noticed his slate-blue, heavily lashed eyes.

He pulled out the stool next to hers and sat down. "I'm David Bergen," the man said. "I write for the *Saginaw Sentinel*. I covered Dutch Chem's pollutive meltdown in Tether extensively, and ever since Paravida bought the facility, I've been following them as well. In fact, because of Paravida, I'm investigating the shady intersection of medical research technology and government surveillance."

Slowly, Nessa lowered her sandwich onto its paper wrapper. He didn't look like her idea of a reporter. In the courtroom, she'd thought he might even be homeless!

"You're writing about what's happening to my mom?" Nessa inquired, her voice sounding hollow. She could see David Bergen looking at her closely.

"I'm mostly writing about Paravida, but I can't get any

answers when I try to get someone to explain your mom's role in all of this. Something feels off to me. There are a lot of holes in the story. I was hoping maybe you could fill me in." David Bergen glanced down at his reporter's notebook and looked up at Nessa as if to say, "Okay?" Nessa nodded.

"Can you tell me what exactly your mother's relationship is to Paravida? Did she ever work for them in her capacity as a scientific researcher? Why is no one asking about the links between the work she did as a scientist and Paravida's illegal experimentation with humans and wolves?"

Nessa stopped breathing. She stared. She felt the way she did in the woods when another wolf was growling, lowering its head and looking at her. This man wasn't going to help her. He was just another reporter. Except this time, he had access to information that Nessa didn't think anyone else had, information that would make things even worse for her mother.

Nessa couldn't believe that for two minutes she'd almost trusted this guy when all he really wanted was to pump her for information. Without another word, she picked up her sandwich, wrapped the paper back around it, and dumped it and her soda cup into the trash. She pushed the door to the café open without looking back, and once she hit the sidewalk, started to run. Her bus wouldn't arrive for over an hour and it was only a ten-minute walk to the stop, but she didn't care. She needed to get away, to feel the ground gripping her feet, to be rid of everything and not think anymore.

Nessa needed help, not to become a ten-second celebrity in a news story. She needed someone who was going to get her mom out of there and put her family back together, someone who could stand up to Paravida.

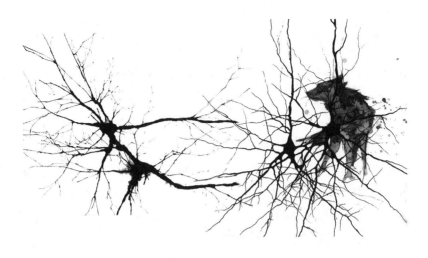

CHAPTER NINETEEN

aiting for the bus to come, shivering, Nessa sat on her hands, closed her eyes, and replayed the images of Cassian's father's big gold watch, the look of embarrassment on his face, the information that her mother's story was about to become headline news, the words "the intersection of medical research and government surveillance."

It was too much. It made her think that maybe she *did* want to transform into wolf state forever and spend the rest of her life in the woods. As a human, she felt lost and confused and angry and desperate all the time. She needed help and had nowhere to turn to get it. She kept trying not to give in to her feelings, but it was starting to feel that the waters of her emotions were rising higher and higher, and pretty soon, the dam she had built was going to give way.

She took out Vivian's letter, unfolded the page, and was greeted by her mother's tiny, cramped handwriting. Her eyes filled with tears at the familiarity of it. She'd always thought her mother's handwriting was bad because she had never taken school as seriously as she should have. But now, she realized her mother must have used this same writing to take notes and record experiments she'd set up in labs. She must have written first drafts of scientific papers with the same half-completed r's and a's that sometimes looked like u's and sometimes looked like o's.

Dear Nessa:

You ask about DH, so I assume you have found the bank statement. If I'd had time I would have hidden it better and not had to reveal it to you. I am sorry to burden you with the knowledge of what you cannot have.

Do not touch the money. No matter what. Do not attempt to contact DH. If he contacts you, don't respond. I can't explain it now, but you must take my word for it.

Take care of your brother and sister. I am so proud of you. Of how strong you are. Destroy this letter as soon as you have read it.

Love,
Mom

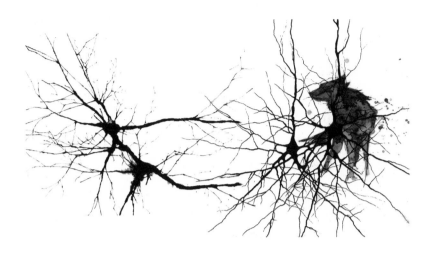

CHAPTER TWENTY

By the time the bus pulled up in front of Tether Town Hall, Nessa felt like she'd been traveling for days.

School was ending and she could have used a nap, but when Bree picked her up, they drove to Dr. Morgan's. Nessa felt certain now more than ever that she had missed something her mom meant her to see.

Bree passed her a half a tuna sandwich to eat on the way, and between bites, Nessa updated Bree on her conversations with Zach Chandler and Mr. Thomas and the content of her mother's note.

"I just don't get it," said Nessa. "How can Mr. Thomas walk away from helping my mom? They grew up together. Can't he just tell Paravida he's not going to work for them anymore? Do you think he really believes my mom is guilty of doing what she's been accused of?"

"Maybe?" Bree said. "It's like my dad. No matter how many times I explain to him ..."

"Your dad thinks my mom is guilty?" Nessa asked.

Bree looked pained. "Kind of?" she said. "Nessa, he's acting angry, but I know him. He's just scared. I've never seen him this scared. He keeps saying he's looking for some logical explanation to even cast doubt on these accusations against your mom but can't find any."

Nessa looked out the window. She couldn't argue with the logic. And what would Bree's dad say if he knew about Vivian's secret bank account? Nessa felt her jaw tense. "My mother didn't know about those engineered wolves when we discovered them last fall. She was surprised, remember?" Her voice had risen. She knew she sounded mad.

"Of course she didn't," Bree said. "My dad just doesn't have the information we do. And look. This is not the time to get angry."

Nessa knew Bree was right. The priority was to help her mom. "Okay, fine, it looks bad," she admitted. "Mom was definitely up to something. There were things about her past that she didn't tell me. But she's my mom. She didn't do the things people think she did. She couldn't have."

"Maybe we'll find something today that will help us understand," Bree said. "Let's review the plan."

"Good idea," Nessa said.

"So first ..." Bree prompted.

"Ignoring the fact that my last paycheck was delivered by

mail, I present myself at Dr. Morgan's to say I haven't received it," Nessa diligently recited. "While Ashley is checking for it, I wait until Dr. Morgan is called into an exam. I make an excuse about needing to use the bathroom. You engage Ashley in conversation. You offer to show her a new Pandora station she'd love, you get her to turn it on, and then be sure to leave it playing.

"This will give me one more chance to look around. And if there's anything good, I'll take pictures."

"Good," Bree said, smiling like Nessa was a third-grader who had nailed the seven times table. "Remember, just open cabinets and doors and take pictures. We can blow them up later and really take a look."

It was a long-shot plan, Nessa knew, but she appreciated Bree's coming up with it. It was better than nothing.

"Are you nervous?" Bree said.

"I can't afford to be nervous," said Nessa.

Bree gave her a skeptical look.

"Okay," she finally said. "I guess I'm nervous anyway."

When Nessa and Bree arrived at Dr. Morgan's, the parking lot was empty. Strange. They parked and walked around from the back. The outdoor kennels were empty. Also strange.

"Where is everyone?" Bree whispered, exchanging a glance with Nessa.

"I don't think you need to whisper," Nessa said, but she was whispering too.

When they got to the door, she saw through it that the waiting room was dark. It looked as if the clinic was closed. How could this be? Where was Ashley? Where was Dr. Morgan?

"Nessa, look," Bree said, pointing. Yellow crime-scene tape crisscrossed the door.

Bree ran around to the side of the building. Nessa followed, not sure where Bree was going. She stopped at a window on the opposite side and peered through it, covering her eyes with her hands to avoid the glare. "Nessa, look, quick!" Nessa joined her. "You can see into the break room from here," Bree said.

And sure enough, from where they were standing, they could see through the kennel room, into the open door to the break room. If you squinted, you could get a view of the back of that room, where a bookcase had stood.

Only the bookcase was gone. In its place they saw a gaping hole in the wall.

"There's something back there!" Bree said. "It's like a little closet or something."

Nessa peered through the window glass. "But it's too dark to see inside."

"Did you know that was there?" Bree asked. "Was it storage or something?"

"Not that I ever knew of," Nessa said. "There was a storage closet behind the kennels, in the back."

"Now what?" said Bree.

Nessa shrugged. She wanted to break through the glass with her hand, and find out what was in that room. If it was a secret room, what had it been used for? The work her mother referred to the night she'd been arrested?

All that was clear was that the FBI had been here. Who knew when they would come back? "Let's go," Nessa said. "I don't want to get caught here. The last thing we need is to have two members of the Kurland family put behind bars."

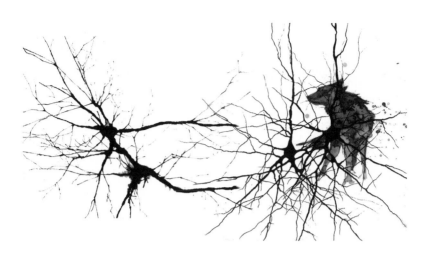

CHAPTER TWENTY-ONE

fter getting back to Bree's house, Nessa went out for a run. She knew she should work on getting her 5K time down by running as a human, but she transformed and ran as a wolf and headed straight for the natural wolves' territory. She needed to feel her pack beside her. She needed to remind herself that no matter what happened with her human family, her pack would still be there.

The puppies were out when she got there and she found herself immediately playing with them, rolling and chasing them in circles, letting them play-bite her ankles and knees, flipping them on their backs and shaking a stick until they grabbed on for tug-of-war.

Just as she was getting ready to go, Luc approached with a wolf whose smell Nessa did not recognize until they approached and she realized it was the pups' father, Jack. He trotted into the area where the pups were playing as though this was completely natural to him. He sniffed noses with Big One, bowed to Mama, then joined in the puppy play just as Nessa had done.

Luc stood back, watching, his gaze traveling from Nessa to Jack and back Nessa, as if to say, "Look. See?"

She did see, and when they left together and transformed back to human form in the woods behind Bree's house, she told him, "So Jack's living with the pack now?"

"Seems to be," Luc said. He looked pleased, Nessa could see.

"And you think they can all do what Jack has done, don't you?"

He came up behind her and put his arms around her waist. "Come with me for spring break and see for yourself," he said.

Nessa laughed, feeling happy and free. "It sounds pretty great," she had to admit, the idea of running as a wolf day after day, forgetting about Vivian being in jail, and Delphine and Nate being so far away. If she did, would Luc change his mind about letting her consider transforming for good? Would she want that? She closed her eyes for a second, relishing the idea that she could play with Sister and the Brothers, watch the pups grow and change, see the world not always split in half but as two separate things.

"So you'll join me?" Luc asked.

"Maybe," said Nessa. She knew she was supposed to spend the week in Milwaukee. "At least a few days?"

When Nessa got back to Bree's, the oven was turned up high, warming the kitchen. Stephanie was making pizza—a Wednesday night tradition at Bree's house. Wearing matching aprons, Bree and Stephanie were grating the cheese and rolling out the dough, drinking twin cups of tea and laughing at something when Nessa brought a breath of wind and darkness into the room.

"Want to join us?" Bree said, the laugh she'd just been sharing with her mom lingering in her voice. For a second, Nessa thought Bree and her mom could be sisters. They had the same dark curly hair, long eyelashes, tawny skin.

But no, Nessa did not want to join them. Seeing Bree and her mom together, something caught in her throat, and she wanted nothing more, all of a sudden, than not to be staying with Bree and her family. She wanted to be in her own kitchen, cooking with her own mom, the windows steaming the way they always did when Vivian attacked a sink full of dishes with water so hot it would scald anyone not wearing rubber gloves. And if not that, then the woods. With Luc. Unlike Tether, the woods were a place where she knew she was wanted.

"I think I'm going to get some . . . homework done," she said.

"You sure?" said Bree, but she was speaking to Nessa's back. Nessa shrugged.

"I might just need a nap," she added.

Stretching out on the air mattress, propping her head on her pillow, Nessa didn't think. She didn't want to think. She didn't want to think about how her mom was running out of options, how the wolves were closing in, how risky Luc's plan for spring break the next week might be, how even if she used the money in the bank account to hire a lawyer, she didn't even know where to begin looking for one.

She reached for her phone and dialed Daniel Host's office. Again. She wasn't thinking she would reach him. At this point, calling the number at all hours of the day had become a habit, a reflexive gesture to try to make herself feel as if she were at least trying.

One ring. Two.

The British lady's greeting usually came on sometime between rings four and five, but this time Nessa heard the sound of the line engaging after ring number three. She stopped breathing. She sat up in bed. And then there was a man's voice. "Hello."

Nessa didn't know what to say. Should she answer? Should she ask who it was? What if it was Daniel Host? Then what? Somehow, "How come you sent my mom more than $800,000 in an FBO account in my sister's name and my name?" didn't roll off the tongue as easily as Nessa had thought it might, and she said nothing at all.

"Hello?" the man said again. Just then the door to Bree's room flew open, bringing the heat and noise of the pizza night festivities with it. Nessa hadn't realized how loud the music Bree and her mom were blasting had gotten until the door was opened and she felt the full force of it. The light from the hallway cast a solid gold stripe into the room's shadowy blackness, causing Nessa to cover her eyes and squint.

"Nessa, there's someone on the—" Bree had started to say before she noticed that Nessa was holding the phone to her ear. Bree clapped a hand over her mouth. "Oh, you're on the phone?" she whispered. "Sorry."

Panicking, Nessa hung up. "It's okay," Nessa said. "It's no one."

"Okay," Bree said. "That's probably just as well because I think you need to come downstairs."

"Oh, sure," Nessa said, trying to sound polite. "Is dinner ready?"

"No," said Bree. She turned to face her. "Nessa, your Aunt Jane is on the phone. And I think it's urgent."

"I just heard from Zach Chandler," Jane said. "Your mom's cold has gotten a little worse."

"Is that . . . bad?" Nessa said.

"Maybe," Jane said. "It's hard to get information. Apparently, she's been running a temperature for days, and had some sort of collapse getting to the cafeteria for breakfast this morning."

"Okay," Nessa said. She knew she shouldn't panic, that that would just make everything worse.

"They admitted her to the infirmary inside the prison. She's been on fluids and antibiotics while the prison doctor tries to figure out what she has."

Jane explained further: Vivian's plea hearing was being postponed. Aunt Jane was driving in to see her in person. Jane would hire an aide for Nate and come right away.

"Do you want to come with me?" she said. "I think it would be really great for your mom to lay eyes on you."

"Of course," Nessa said. "I'll be there."

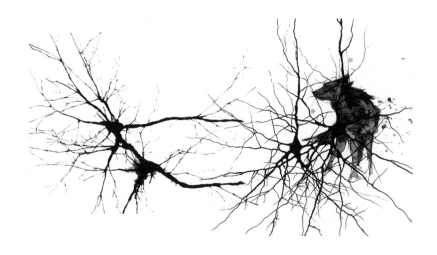

CHAPTER TWENTY-TWO

The jail where Vivian was being kept looked innocuous enough. It was on the outskirts of Grand Rapids, at the side of the road, surrounded by a tall fence topped with loops of barbed wire. There were multiple old brick buildings inside. The one with the security check-in looked a little bit like an elementary school from the outside.

As Nessa and Jane waited in the interminable line for the privilege of being sent through the metal detectors—and then waited even longer for the privilege of being patted down, and waited again to be interviewed about what they were carrying— Nessa kept thinking: *Wow, Coach Hoffman was right. This really* would *make a good college essay.*

In high school, [Nessa wrote in her mind] *I stood in a lot of lines. The cafeteria line every day at lunch. The line to sign up for clubs in the gym* [well, she was planning on joining some clubs as soon as things calmed down], *the line to sign up for cross-country my freshman year, a decision that would change my life, lines to pick up bib numbers, lines to sign up for visits with college recruiters. But during the middle of April of my junior year, I found myself in a line I hadn't ever imagined would be part of my high school experience. I was in the line to get into jail.*

It's not as bad as it sounds. I hadn't been arrested. I wasn't being booked for a crime. I was there to visit my mother, the woman who had been there for me since I could remember, who had taught me to ride a bike, who had cooked me more meals than I could recall, who had brought me cold washcloths when I had fevers, who had told me I was feeling sorry for myself and to get back out into the cold when I'd tried to drop cross-country my sophomore year.

How had my mom ended up in jail?

"You have to prepare yourself. Your mom is going to look pretty sick," Aunt Jane kept saying, in a way Nessa thought was as much for her own benefit as for Nessa's.

So Nessa prepared herself. But in the hospital bed, Vivian looked worse than Nessa had imagined. Her hair was limp. She'd lost weight. Her skin seemed ashen and her eyelids appeared to droop.

But still, she was Vivian. She was Mom. Nessa saw Vivian make the same half-smile she always made, as if to smile fully was to tempt fate. From her quick intake of air, Nessa could tell that Vivian was maybe on the brink of crying.

And she felt a little teary herself.

Jane kissed Vivian on the cheek, then announced that she was going to look for the doctor and left the room. Vivian reached out a hand. Nessa walked toward her, felt her mom grasp her and pull. For someone who looked as sick as she did, Vivian was surprisingly strong. Leaning down to hug her mother, she noticed Vivian smelled different. Woodsy.

Wolfy.

Nessa pulled away. Maybe she was smelling herself? Maybe the heightened emotionality of the moment was causing her to release something wolfy into the air?

And then she forgot all about it, because it was just so good to be with her mom again, to feel her looking at her, to remember that she was real.

"Come here," Vivian said, gesturing for Nessa to come closer. As Nessa leaned in, Vivian whispered, "Everything we say is being listened to. We can't talk openly."

"Mom," Nessa said, whispering back. There was a guard with them, but she was sitting at the other end of the room, staring at her phone. "Mom, you look so sick. Are you going to be okay?"

Vivian cleared her throat. "Don't worry about me," she said. "Worry about yourself. Worry about getting that scholarship. About taking care of Delphine and Nate."

"No, Mom, let me help you," Nessa said. As quietly as she could, she spoke into her mother's ear: "I know more about what's happening to you than you think."

Vivian closed her eyes. Shook her head. With her thinned hair and sunken cheeks, she looked beautiful in a tragic kind of way.

"Mom, I know how strong you've had to be, raising me

and Nate and Delphine on your own, but now you have to take care of yourself," Nessa said. "You need a lawyer. A lawyer who specializes in this kind of thing. The one you have, Zach Chandler, he even told me so. He told me when he gave me your note. And you're right. I found the bank statement. We have the money. We can do this."

Vivian's eyes were glittering. She had been leaning against a pillow but now she sat forward. "Look," she said. "You might think you know what's going on but you don't. There *are* things I have to tell you. We don't have much time."

"Yes," Nessa said. "Daniel Host. Tell me about him. Who is he?" She got close enough to her mother that she could whisper. "He gave us money. Why?"

"That money is tainted," Vivian spat out. Her mouth was pursed. Her eyes were narrowed. "We can never, ever touch it. I didn't use it when Nate could have had a private aide, when I could have sent you to running camp, when I knew what an upgrade on the computer would mean for Delphine. I'm certainly not going to use it for myself. Not now."

Nessa lowered her voice as far as it could go. "You can't *not* use it," she insisted. "Mom, we need you to get out of here. We need you to come home." She was speaking so quietly she assumed Vivian would need to be able to read lips to understand her.

"Oh, sweetheart," Vivian said, squeezing Nessa's hands. "You just don't understand, but please trust me. You can never contact Daniel Host. Never believe what he tells you. I can't explain more."

She fell back on her pillows, coughing a hacking cough. Eventually a nurse came in with a cup of water and two pills.

She looked at Nessa, annoyed, as she watched Vivian put the pills on her tongue, take a sip of water, and swallow. The nurse turned to go, but Vivian must have swallowed the water awkwardly. She started choking and then the choking quickly turned into a hacking cough. Vivian's hands were trembling so much, the water was spilling onto her gown.

Rather than helping Vivian, the nurse turned to Nessa. "Time's up," she said. "Visiting hours are over."

"She needs help!" Nessa called after the nurse, taking the cup of water herself. "Where did my aunt go?"

The nurse only pointed again to her watch. "Visitors need to be out," she said. "Now."

The nurse looked at the guard pointedly. The guard stood, finally putting her phone away.

Vivian gasped for air, then started coughing again. Finally, Jane rushed in. "What's going on in here?" she cried.

Jane started to move toward the bed, but the guard blocked her. "I'm afraid you're both going to have to leave now."

"Mom," Nessa said, leaning around the guard so she could see her mother one last time. "I'll come back. I'll keep fighting, okay?"

Vivian shook her head, her hand on her chest as if she could relieve the tightness she was feeling.

The last thing Nessa remembered seeing was the nurse's back as she leaned over Vivian to administer a shot.

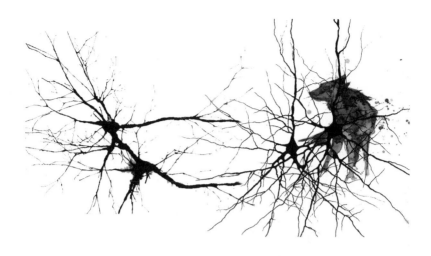

CHAPTER TWENTY-THREE

T he phone rang just as Nessa was getting out of the shower after a run. She wrapped herself in a towel and, fumbling to pull her phone from the pocket of her running jacket, answered before checking the number.

"Hello?" she said, feeling how strange it was to answer a call when you didn't know who it was going to be. In the fogged-up bathroom mirror, she saw a blurred version of herself with the phone at her ear.

"Is this Nessa?" It was a man's voice. "This is—" For a second Nessa wondered if it might be one of the reporters from Vivian's bond hearing. She suddenly felt bad for all the celebrity vacation or swimming-at-the-beach pictures she'd ever looked at in one of Bree's magazines—here she was dealing with a reporter when she was wrapped in a towel with soaking wet hair. It wasn't fun.

The call turned out to be about so much more than a reporter, though. "Nessa," the voice on the other end of the line announced. "This is Daniel Host."

Nessa stopped breathing.

"I understand you've been trying to reach me."

"How do you even know my name?" Her heart was racing, but her mind felt sharp. Yes, she knew she'd been calling him, but she'd never once left a message.

For some reason, this question made Daniel Host laugh, a short little bark. He sounded like they knew each other already, like she might be kidding or referring to an inside joke. "Of course I know your name."

"Who are you?" she breathed.

He cleared his throat. "You don't know?"

"No," she said.

"Your mother never told you?"

"No."

On the other end of the line there was a pause. Then that same cough of a laugh, expressing disbelief or exasperation, Nessa could not tell. "Nessa," Daniel Host said, "I'm your father."

Nessa sat down on the edge of the toilet lid, hard, bringing her other hand up to the phone to keep herself from dropping it.

"You're what?" she said.

"Your father," he said.

"I don't believe you," Nessa said, the words coming out before she had time to think. But she knew, in the moment, that she was right. Her father was a man she remembered—

she couldn't picture his face, but she could remember a smell, a feeling of being carried. She'd never thought about it, but if she'd heard his name, she assumed she would recognize it.

Except, now that she came to think of it, his name had always been in her memory: "Daddy."

Not Daniel Host.

Right?

"I realize this is probably big news. We haven't seen each other or spoken in a very long time."

"No," Nessa said, not meaning to sound as if she were agreeing but rather wanting to say no to this whole proposition. Her father had done something bad. She didn't know what but it had caused her mother never to speak of him, to act as if he had never existed. Her father was gone.

And Daniel Host was not him. Daniel Host was a name on a bank account. He was trouble her mother had gotten herself into.

"You haven't seen me since you were three years old, though I did try to visit. Do you still have that blanket? The blue one? You thought she was a person. You insisted everyone address her as 'she.' You called her Blue-y?"

Nessa's mind traveled to a shoebox she still kept beneath her bed, containing the remains of the blanket she'd slept with every night until she was ten and there wasn't much of it left. It had been called "Blue-y." She *had* thought of Blue-y as a person. Of course Blue-y had been a girl.

"How can you be my *father*?" Nessa managed to choke out, embarrassed that she seemed to be crying. "I don't even know if my father is alive. I thought—I don't know. He's gone."

"I'm not gone," the man on the other end of the line said.

"I'm actually relatively close. And I tried, Nessa, I did. But your mother wanted me to be completely gone from your life. I respected her wishes. At the time, it seemed like the right thing to do." His words were traveling deep into some place inside Nessa she wouldn't have been able to say was even there. It was almost like being tickled, the emotions rising to the surface like laughs. "But now, Nessa, you've called me. Well, I'm glad. I've been wanting to reach out to you for a very, very long time."

Nessa slid from the edge of the toilet seat to the floor.

"Nessa, I've been following what's happening to your mother. In the news. I'm so sorry. I want to help. Can you come see me?"

"Wait," she said. She had the urge to retrace her steps through the conversation, rewind it. Had she missed something? "I saw your name on the bank account," she said. "When Mom got arrested, Delphine and I found it."

"Delphine?" Daniel Host said. "Delphine! How is she?"

"She's great," Nessa said. "She's—" Nessa didn't know what to say. Was this man really Delphine's father too?

"Look," Daniel Host said. "This isn't going to be easy. I know it must feel like it's all come out of nowhere. But Nessa—I don't want you to think that for even a moment I haven't been thinking about you. That bank account. I know it's not the same as being in your life, but that was my way of supporting you. Of doing what I could."

"It did nothing!" Nessa said, her confusion tunneling into anger. "Mom never touched your money. She said I shouldn't even be talking to you."

"She hasn't used the money?" Daniel Host asked, and for the first time he didn't sound relaxed and happy and just glad to be talking to Nessa. He took in a deep breath and Nessa registered that this news had come as a surprise to him. "But it was for *you*. For you girls," he said. "I knew your mom wasn't earning much. She—she really *never* touched it?"

Nessa shook her head no, before remembering she was on a phone call. "No," she said. "At least, not that I know of."

"And this case—the charges against her," his voice was raising in urgency as he thought out loud. "I looked it up. She's in trouble. Is that why you've been calling?"

"Yes!" said Nessa, because as surreal as it felt to be talking to this total stranger who said he was her father, it felt good just to know that someone else understood her mother was in serious trouble. Finally, someone else could help.

"She isn't even using the money to pay for legal help," Nessa explained.

"But that's absurd," Daniel Host said. "The case against her—I've been reading the accounts in the press. She'll need experts. A team of lawyers. How will she pay?"

Trying not to sound like she was telling on someone, Nessa explained. "It's just this public defender. He's a nice guy, but he's busy."

"A public defender?" Daniel Host said. "Who . . . is *busy*?" He couldn't keep the scorn out of his voice. "Your mother! I'd almost forgotten how stubborn she can be."

Out of loyalty to her mother, Nessa kept quiet. But as Daniel Host continued asking her questions about her situation, she found herself telling him more and more, trusting the intelligent way he spoke, liking how quickly he seemed to understand how dire things were.

"Look," he said at last. "Nessa, I won't lie to you. I was a pretty poor husband and maybe a worse father. I was very hurt when your mother left. I didn't know the best thing to do. Frankly, I was angry. I'm used to being good at things. Being successful. And I failed. But I've come to see things differently now. I've had experiences that have—let's just say—opened my eyes. When I saw you'd been trying to reach me, I was thrilled. I want to make it up to you."

"Okay," Nessa said, feeling more overwhelmed than anything else.

"I want to help you. I want to help your mother. And Delphine. Look, come see me, can you?" he said. "Can you get out of school?"

Nessa was so surprised by the request, she found herself able only to think in practical terms. "I have break next week, actually."

"Next week? That's perfect. That will give me time to make some calls. See what I can set up to help your mom. Help you and Delphine."

"I have to ask Aunt Jane," Nessa said, though really what she wanted to say was that she needed to think about it, that she couldn't, in the course of ten minutes, go from learning that she had a father, to committing to spending a week with him. Then something occurred to her that made her laugh out loud. "And I don't even know where you live."

"Of course," he said. "Of course." For the first time she wondered if this wasn't a little bit overwhelming for him as well. "I live in Oregon. About five hours from Portland. It's a little remote, but I get in and out quite a bit." He paused like he was looking at a calendar. "Just let me know what date will work for you and I'll send a plane."

Somehow, Nessa agreed. She didn't have much choice, frankly. This was the only person who had offered to help her mom. She had to track him down.

But after hanging up, Nessa realized that the way Daniel Host had phrased the suggestion that he'd arrange for her to fly out to see him was weird. He'd said, "I'll send a plane." Not "I'll buy you a ticket." Not "I'll come get you in my car."

Did that mean he had access to a private plane? Daniel Host, Nessa's father, a man who had given away close to a million dollars, who was he?

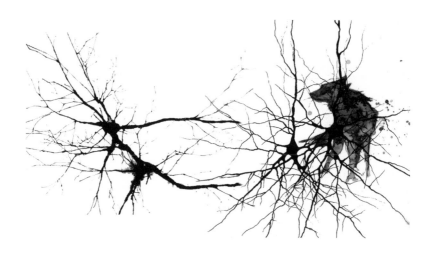

CHAPTER TWENTY-FOUR

To Nessa's surprise, Aunt Jane said it would be okay for Nessa to visit Daniel Host. First, Jane insisted that she and Daniel have what Jane referred to as "a very long talk." This happened over the phone while Nessa was in school Friday morning. Nessa couldn't wait until the end of the school day to hear how it went. She called Jane during a free period to find out what Jane had thought of Daniel Host. But all Jane would say was, "Well, he is your father, that's for sure, and he really does seem to want to help Vivian, so if you want to go see him, you're welcome to."

By lunch, Nessa was huddling with Bree at a table far from the group they usually sat with, going over and over the call and the pending visit.

"What do you think he did that made your mom so mad?" Bree said. "Can you ask him? Is your mom going to be mad that you're talking to him now?"

Nessa shook her head. She took a bite of the sandwich Stephanie had hastily thrown together that morning—cracked wheat and spelt bread with tahini and low-sugar jam.

"Water!" Nessa choked out, reaching for her water bottle, her voice raspy as if she'd been lost in the desert for days. "Can't talk."

"Hey, my mom made that sandwich," Bree said defensively. Then she took a bite of her own. "Ooh, yeah," she said. "It is kind of dry. But don't try to change the subject. Nessa, this is huge! What are you going to do about this guy?"

Nessa shrugged. "I don't know," she said. "I mean, he sounds kind of nice. He wants to help. And, honestly, Bree." For the first time, Nessa named what she was feeling for real. "It's kind of a relief, you know? That someone—an adult—is going to step in and take care of things."

"And an adult with access to money and lawyers no less," Bree added. "Not to mention a private plane."

"Whatever," Nessa said.

"Whatever?" Bree said. "A private plane is not whatever." That night, while they were supposed to be doing homework together up in Bree's room, she passed Nessa her phone. "Check this out," Bree said. "Apparently there are private planes, and then there are *private planes*. Next time you talk to him, try to find out if he owns it outright."

"I'm not going to do that!" Nessa said. "I don't really care."

"I know, but it could be important," said Bree. "I mean,

how rich is he? Because there are executive sharing options for planes, kind of like timeshares people have on condos, and even those are pretty expensive. But if he actually owns an airplane, Nessa, he's gotta be *so rich*."

Nessa looked at a few pictures of plane interiors that looked more like living rooms in RVs. Really fancy RVs. "You think I should go, right?" said Nessa. "I mean, my mom said I shouldn't even talk to him and now I'm planning to visit. Shouldn't I listen to her?"

Bree got serious. "That's up to you," she said. "But he is your dad. I think you owe it to yourself to at least meet him. And if he wants to help, I mean, you said it yourself. It would be a huge relief."

Of all the people in her life, Luc was the only one who told her to stay. "Nessa, you don't even know him," he said. They were eating ramen in his cabin after a session running with the pack. It had been nice to get out into the woods, even if there were so many Paravida tracks Nessa felt certain the wolf population had increased from the 70 Ted had said the National Guard counted with their heat-detecting satellite equipment.

But they'd been working with the pack that afternoon—at first tracking Paravida wolves with Brother and Mama, pushing them back. After they'd cleared the area, Sister, Jack, and two of the pups had joined them on a short excursion. They'd been so busy chasing squirrels, it had taken an hour to travel only a quarter-mile from the den, but still, it was a big day for the pack. The pups were getting stronger every day. And Jack looked almost comfortable with them. Only once did he do something strange—he started scratching his side with his back leg and just kept doing it over and over like he didn't know how to stop. The other wolves had just stared at him, until Luc plowed into him, distracting him through play. When they disengaged, Jack seemed to have lost the insatiable urge to scratch.

Luc slurped some soup and opened the door. Maybe it was the warming air, but Nessa was noticing that more and more, Luc was opening windows and doors, as if he could no longer tolerate the feeling of being enclosed. Or maybe it was just the conversation that was making him act like he needed air. He wasn't the kind of person to tell anyone else what to do, even when asked. Was this too much pressure for him?

"A week ago you thought your father might be dead," he said. "Your mom said not to even talk to Daniel Host and now you're flying all the way to Oregon? What if he's some kind of psychopath?"

Nessa shrugged. "You could be right," she said. "But still. Over the course of the last few weeks, so many things have turned out to be not what I thought. So many secrets." Nessa thought back to the last moment before she'd found out Daniel Host was her dad—the glimpse of herself she'd had in the fogged up mirror. "I feel like we need to break something open. Blow open the safe, you know?"

Luc blew air out of pursed lips. Nessa could tell something was continuing to bother him.

"What?" she said.

"It's nothing."

"What?!"

With an expression of defeat, Luc said, "Well, spring break, Ness? This was supposed to be our time. I was hoping to put in some longer wolf days."

"Right," she said. "Could you—I don't know—wait for me? I'm not going for the whole break."

Luc shrugged, noncommittally. Nessa knew: What he was doing wasn't just about them. He was on a mission. "But what if you get stuck? It's too early for you to think about that." Again, Luc's expression was noncommittal.

"Wait, seriously?" Nessa said. "You seem like you're upping the timetable."

Luc gave Nessa a long look. He wasn't going to talk about it—she could see that. She sighed, fixating for a moment on the idea that she was only giving him a hard time about it because she was jealous. What if she just joined him in wolfdom? It would be so simple. Just the two of them. Nate and Delphine could stay with Jane, and her mom . . . well, Nessa didn't know who her mom even *was* anymore.

"Are you really going to be okay out in Oregon?" Luc said. He stood in the open doorway, looking out into the cold. "Don't forget—it's going to be the full moon next week. You're going to have to transform while you're there. Don't put off finding a good place for it. If you don't have a plan, you're more likely to transform where you'll be seen."

Nessa, who had finished her bowl of ramen now, stood up and set it down on the table. She went to the door and stood behind Luc. There were buds on the trees. This was the last time she'd come to the cabin before break. When she got back, there would likely be leaves as well. Things were changing. She never would have imagined it, but now she wished she could move time back into the long, cold winter of running patrols.

She reached for Luc, her hand on his shoulder. She felt him

relax against her hand. She knew he was worried about her. And no, she didn't want this to change. "It's Oregon," she said, her voice steady. "Land of endless woods." She didn't know if this was true. She didn't want to admit—even to herself—that she was just as worried as he was.

Luc shook his head and sighed, then turned away from the view of the forest and wrapped his arms around her waist. "I'm going to miss you, you know that," he said. "I know I don't always talk about stuff like that, but I'm thinking about it. Loud and clear."

Nessa felt herself smiling. She knew she had to go to Oregon, but wow, was she going to miss him too. She was going to miss all of it—being here, with him, in the woods. It was the only place she felt truly herself. "If you really can't keep the Paravida wolves away from town without me, you call, agreed?"

He looked at her sideways. "What?" he said, wrapping his arms around her waist. "You'll zip right back? You'll have your dad send you over on his private plane?"

Nessa smiled as she kissed him. "Don't be too impressed," she joked. "It might just be an executive share."

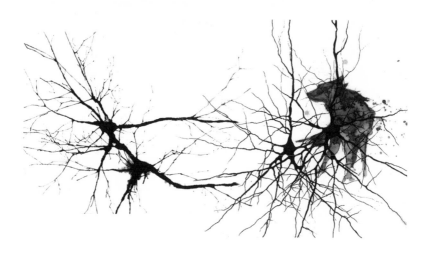

CHAPTER TWENTY-FIVE

*O*n Saturday morning, bright and early, Bree and Nessa loaded their bags into the Monster and started out on their first-ever interstate road trip, driving from Tether all the way around the southern end of Lake Michigan and on to Milwaukee. The second the Monster roared past the Tether town limits, Nessa could feel the stress of her mother's arrest and her serious illness, the Paravida wolves—everything—slipping away. She and Bree listened to the radio, ogled cute guys at the rest stops, ate M&M's and turkey sandwiches, and checked in with Ted every forty-five minutes (his idea), stopping at three different outlet malls along the way so Bree could shop for shoes.

In Milwaukee, everything seemed to be going well. Delphine and Nate had been living with Jane for two and a half weeks, but from how comfortable they looked, it might as well have been forever. Jane was behind at work from taking Thursday off to see Vivian at the prison hospital, and she was looking stressed, but was also filled with stories about funny things Nate had said. Delphine whispered complaints about Aunt Jane's cooking, but all of the rubbery chicken and raw rice was made up for by the school. She took Nessa and Bree to the Saturday night basketball game, and on the car ride over talked on and on about the computer programming department and the friends she'd made.

The one thing Delphine seemed not at all interested in talking about was Nessa's upcoming trip to Oregon and the reason behind it. On Sunday morning, after Nate made banana bread for breakfast—he had discovered baking—Nessa asked Delphine if she wanted to take a walk. "A walk?" Delphine said, suspiciously. "You *run* everywhere."

Nessa rolled her eyes. "Aunt Jane's out of milk," she said. "We can go to the corner store." Delphine agreed, and after they'd gone about two blocks, Nessa said, "So it's a little freaky, isn't it?"

"What," Delphine said, uncharacteristically sulky.

"That we have a dad now."

"*You* have a dad," Delphine said, wrapping her arms around herself tighter. It was a warm enough morning that she could have worn a light jacket and been fine, but she'd chosen to wear just a sweater and looked cold to Nessa. "Poof. Out of nowhere. And he seems to want to talk only to you."

"You're mad?" Nessa said.

Delphine stopped walking and turned to face her. "Of

course I'm mad!" she said. "Tons of divorced parents wish the other one would just die in a hole but the other one doesn't just say okay and disappear! How come he never came to see us? And if he's all, 'I was sending money so I'm helping,' shouldn't he have checked to make sure Mom was using it? Or at least just sent us a lousy gift card to Old Navy once in a while, say, on our birthdays?"

"So that's all it would take?" Nessa said. "An Old Navy gift card?"

Nessa was just kidding but Delphine was not in a mood to notice that. "How about a phone call to *me*?" she shouted. "Don't you think it's a little strange, how he's all 'Nessa, let me send the private plane . . . '?" She seemed to run out of steam there. "Though a gift card wouldn't hurt."

Nessa laughed and Delphine even cracked a smile. "What? Clothes are important! And you know what? Screw Old Navy. If he's as rich as Bree keeps saying he is, it would have to be Anthropologie." She cracked a smile. "I've never been able to afford anything there."

"That's it?" said Nessa.

"Yeah," said Delphine. "Except Nessie," she said, using the family nickname Nate still used but Delphine had dropped around the time she started middle school. "Why do only you get to go? Why *didn't* Dad ask for me?"

"I wish I had an answer, but I don't," Nessa said. She didn't tell Delphine what Aunt Jane said: that in the conversation Aunt Jane had had with Daniel Host she'd suggested both girls come together and he'd said, "Not just yet."

"Maybe because I was the one who called him?" Nessa tried. "Or because he can't handle two people at once? Maybe he's shy? Or maybe he doesn't have room in his house?" She was pretty sure someone with a private plane wasn't going to have that problem.

"I think he's scared," Delphine said. She sounded angry and bitter, but even so, Nessa realized that was the closest to an answer that sounded plausible of anything she'd heard so far.

What did their father have to be afraid of?

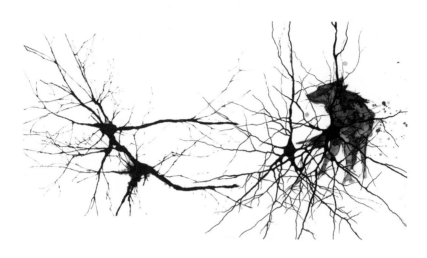

CHAPTER TWENTY-SIX

ater that morning, loaded up with a "travel tunes" playlist and three pieces of leftover banana bread, Bree headed back to Tether. Jane drove Nessa to a small secondary airport on the outskirts of Milwaukee where Daniel Host had told her to wait for the plane. He wouldn't be there himself. He was traveling on business through Sunday night, so she wouldn't see him until after she'd arrived at the house.

Jane left her at the door of a building marked 'Charter Flights'. After promising her aunt that she would call when she arrived, Nessa walked into a lounge where she was greeted by a uniformed flight attendant. "I'm Belinda," she said. "And you must be Nessa? I've heard a lot about you."

"You have?" Nessa said, somewhat incredulously. She was a) surprised that her father's flight attendant would have heard about her, and b) surprised that he even had a flight attendant. What exactly did a flight attendant do when there was just one passenger on board? How many sodas was this woman expected to pour?

"Of course," Belinda said, sunnily. Nessa thought Belinda wasn't that much older than she was—maybe early twenties? She had the kind of wholesome smile that would make her perfect for orange juice commercials. "Your dad flies a lot and since most of the time he flies alone, we get to talking." Belinda led the way up a few flights of steps. "That is, when he isn't working. Work, work, work! Never a quiet moment at Chimera." She threw up her hands, giving Nessa two insights: one into the personality of this man she didn't know; and two, how to say the name of Daniel's company. Kai-meer-ah. Nessa wondered if Belinda knew Nessa hadn't been *quite* certain how to pronounce it.

Belinda escorted Nessa past a TSA checkpoint staffed by a single agent who took a cursory glance at Nessa's school ID. She nodded them through, and as Nessa followed Belinda onto the airplane, Nessa actually gasped out loud. It was beautiful. The seats and armrests were upholstered in cream-colored leather, and the rest of the interior seemed to be created out of highly polished wood, like the inside of a yacht. There were lots of little touches of elegance: A row of crystal drinking glasses secured with a leather strap in a tiny alcove under a spotlight so the cut crystal refracted light in patterns. On the desk, a row of gold and black fountain pens stored in a shallow depression next to the leather-topped writing surface.

This was definitely not an "executive share," Nessa concluded instantly. Unless the other executives wanted to fly with a giant Chimera Corp. logo stenciled faintly on the left interior. Nessa studied a photo over the desk, which showed a rolling, hilly forest seen from low in the air. The forest vista was drop-dead beautiful, and Nessa sighed seeing the acres and acres of pine trees beneath an endless, glowing evening sky—hill after hill after hill, each casting a different shade of purple, blue, or green. Nessa could not turn her eyes away from it.

"You like that?" Belinda said. "Your dad does too. That's why he bought it." With a smile, she knocked briskly on the cockpit door.

"The photo?" Nessa asked.

"No, silly," Belinda said. "The trees—all that land in the picture belongs to him. Thirty thousand acres and he's in negotiations, he tells me, to buy five thousand more." She said this casually, as if she'd just told Nessa he was putting an addition on his back deck. Belinda then knocked briskly on the cockpit door. "George, we're on board. Any time you're ready."

The door opened from the inside, and a man in a pilot's uniform smiled crisply. "You're Nessa?" he said, his eyes crinkling. "Well," he winked at Belinda, "she doesn't look like him at all, does she?"

"No, not at all," said Belinda, laughing.

Nessa couldn't help but feel proud and then she quashed that feeling. She didn't want to feel proud of her dad.

As George taxied the airplane toward the runway, Nessa sat down in one of the passenger seats, an armchair that made her feel like she was floating. Belinda showed her how to control the sound system and offered her a soda or a meal. She laughed, as if they were playing a game. "It's not a very long flight, but what's your pleasure? Steak dinner? Movies and popcorn? An ice cream? Your dad's been crazy about this small-batch chocolate harvested in the Andes mountains ..."

"I'll have a Coke," Nessa said, and then because she missed Bree, "Do you have M&M's?"

"Of course," Belinda said. Stepping into the back, she emerged with a polished wooden case secured with a gold latch. Nessa suspected it to be filled with cigars, but when she opened it, she saw instead every kind of standard-issue commercial chocolate candy she had ever seen. She had her choice of dark, mini, peanut, or regular M&M's. She selected regular and then, thinking of Bree again, whipped out her phone.

"Mind if I take a few pictures?" she asked.

Belinda gestured to the cabin with her hand. "Of course," she said.

But when Nessa tried to text them to Bree, the text would not go through. "That's weird," she said, showing Belinda the error message after the third time.

"Oh, right, I should have told you. Daniel has his own VPN—a virtual private network—installed on the plane. He's got very tight controls over the media that can be transmitted over it. There's one at the house, too. It just makes everything a little more secure." Belinda flashed her adorable smile one more time, wrinkling her nose. "Cozy, no?" she said, like the block was just one more amazing feature of the plane for Nessa to admire.

Nessa nodded politely, even if actually, "cozy" was not exactly the word she would have used. More like "Big Brother creepy."

But she soon forgot all about it as she sank deep into the cushions of her seat, her hands soaking under the heated towel Belinda had brought. Looking out the window, she watched the houses and streets and factories grow smaller and smaller. Ninety minutes later Nessa looked for and spotted the Rocky Mountains as they passed over them, and then she drifted off to sleep.

"Recognize the view?" someone said. She stirred, forgetting for a minute where she was, just feeling deeply relaxed and rested. Realizing it was Belinda's voice, she opened her eyes and followed the direction Belinda was pointing. "The view," Belinda said, still pointing. "It's the same as in the photo."

Looking back and forth from the poster to the view out the window, Nessa realized Belinda was right. Though now, the light on the forest below was different. It was all yellow, tinted with flashes of dark green—late afternoon light. "We'll be landing in just a couple of minutes," Belinda said, sliding a small glass of orange juice into the drink holder next to Nessa's chair. Nessa took a sip, feeling the cabin pressure change. As the plane descended, she watched the forest getting closer. It seemed to go on forever, an uninterrupted ocean of trees, a moving, living blanket draped over the hills below. The image in the poster had barely captured its size and scope.

"Wow," Nessa said.

"Your dad will be glad to hear you like it," Belinda said. "This forest means the world to him."

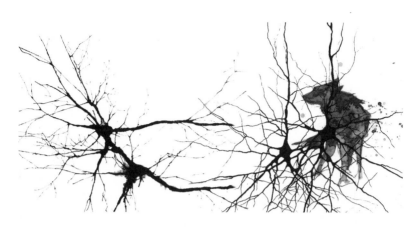

CHAPTER TWENTY-SEVEN

essa knew that Daniel Host wasn't going to be at the house when she arrived, and she was almost grateful to have the opportunity to take it all in while she was still relatively alone. Her father's assistant, Milton (hers had been the impersonal British voice Nessa had heard on his answering service), greeted her on the private landing strip and ferried her in a golf cart over to the house. Milton looked almost like a boy with her clipped hair, bit of bangs, neutral collared shirt, and dark pants. All business.

Without explaining whether Milton was a first name or last, she drove the golf cart along a series of paved roads that led through the woods. At intersections, Milton pointed the way to different lab facilities. Nessa gleaned that the lab employed about thirty people, most living on site. "Security is of course an essential concern," Milton explained as if answering a question she was sure Nessa was about to ask. "We keep the team deliberately small and most of our employees plan to be here the entirety of their careers. Working with your father is an opportunity of a lifetime."

The golf cart took a series of jackknife turns up a steep blacktop road. Nessa wondered what to expect from Daniel Host's house. Daniel Host—she still had a hard time thinking of him as "Dad"—was clearly wealthy and powerful. Would the house be enormous? She pictured two stone wings and a veranda. Were there going to be columns?

Bree is going to die, Nessa thought.

But the house was only a modest single story, so carefully blended into the woods you couldn't even see it fully through the trees. It wouldn't have been out of place in Tether. Even though she was trying not to care, Nessa couldn't help but feel a little disappointed.

She lost that sense of disappointment once she'd stepped inside. The first hint of luxury came from the thickness of the carpeting. It was so springy that Nessa wondered for a second if memory foam was involved. Then, as she passed through the otherwise modest entryway into the living room, she understood that what made the house remarkable went beyond cloud-like carpeting.

The room was not only understated and calm, but also just simply enormous. Nessa was pretty sure you could run the 50-meter dash from one end to the other. There were multiple living rooms' worth of furniture inside—three couches set up in a U near an enormous flagstone fireplace as well as other more intimate arrangements throughout the room. All the way at the end, there was a dining room table that looked like it could have easily seated thirty people.

But the view stole the show. The long wall of the rectangular room was constructed entirely of glass, with sliding panels leading to a deck high above the treetops. Nessa walked to the window almost involuntarily, turning to Milton, who was discreetly straightening a pile of books on a table. "How far can you see?" Nessa asked.

"Oh, at least twenty miles. And you know, this all belongs to the house and the lab. Let me show you your room."

Milton then led Nessa down a flight of stairs—the house was not a single story after all, but multiple floors built into the side of a forested cliff like a giant tree house. Leading Nessa down a hall with a polished wood floor and soft lighting, Milton opened a door to something that looked like it had popped right out of an HGTV special on eco-luxury hotels. The plain wood-paneled walls, the crisp edges of the low bed, the drawers flush with the walls seemed designed not to distract from the view, a repeat of the one upstairs, but to make you feel like you yourself were sleeping inside of the forest, tucked into a tree house miraculously balanced in the canopy.

Nessa had a private deck and once Milton had closed the door, Nessa dropped her ratty duffel at the end of the bed and stepped outside, leaning on the wide teak railing, caught up by the feeling of the forest, the sight of the trees swaying in the breeze, the sound of birds she could not see, the rustling of squirrels.

Snapping pictures, she texted Luc:

Still wondering if I'll be able to find a place to run and

transform?

She pressed Send.

She'd forgotten about the private network blocking image texts. A second later, when she saw the error message she remembered. *Oh, well*, she thought. *I'll show him all the pictures when I get back*. Instead, she sent him a text:

got here safely. miss you. lots of woods. barefoot no problem.

Milton had said she could take a rest and relax—dinner would not be for over an hour. So Nessa bathed in a tub that sat beneath a large plate-glass window. More views of trees. She got out of the tub when the secretary called her room phone to say Daniel Host would meet Nessa in the dining room at 7 p.m., as he was flying himself in on the little plane and would want to shower and change before meeting her.

OMG! Nessa texted Bree. He has TWO planes!

Again, the text went through.

Nessa called Aunt Jane, getting the latest update on Vivian's health—learning that Vivian had had a good day but still had a troubling fever and would stay in the infirmary—and then Delphine got on the line. Nessa told her about the flight and the house. "I wish you were here to see it for yourself," Nessa said. "There's probably all kinds of stuff I'm missing that you would notice."

"No kidding," said Delphine. "You're taking pictures?"

Nessa explained the security protocol that prevented her from sending them. As she finished the explanation she felt Delphine's discomfort. "That's weird, isn't it?" Nessa asked.

"Yup," said Delphine. "But they'll be tiny anyway and Nessa, just enjoy! What are you going to wear for dinner? Please tell me you brought something decent."

Nessa just laughed, but after getting off the phone, still luxuriating in the softness of the robe that had been neatly folded next to a stack of towels by the bath, she surveyed her clothing, a collection of beat-up sweaters and jeans. Their tears and threadbare sections made them fit her like a glove, but she realized they might not work so well in the context of the giant room upstairs.

Fortunately Bree had insisted Nessa bring along a pair of Bree's simple black pants that she had bought and not yet hemmed and a silky blouse that billowed comfortably and rolled up to three-quarter sleeves. It was wrinkled, but would do. Nessa dried her hair, dressed in her borrowed clothes, and checked herself in front of the floor-length mirror on the back of the bathroom door. She almost didn't recognize herself in a muted blouse that fit the style of the house, her hair falling straight down her back. At 6:58, she left the room and headed down the hall.

At the foot of the stairs, Nessa suddenly felt so nervous she didn't think she could climb them. She couldn't face the enormous beige and tan living room fronting the wall of glass. She couldn't face the enormity of what she was about to do. This man was her father and she didn't know him at all. What was she even going to say?

Take a deep breath, Kurland, she told herself. *This isn't about you.*

This was about helping her mom. She had to go, and putting one foot in front of the other, she went.

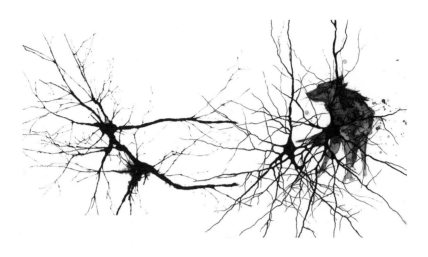

CHAPTER TWENTY-EIGHT

$\mathcal{G}$eorge the pilot was right, Nessa realized on first seeing her dad. He was standing at the end of the table as Nessa walked through the long room toward him, and except for the fact that he had brown hair while she had Vivian's blonde, she recognized his features as her own. He had her square forehead, straight, if maybe slightly too large nose, strong chin, wide cheeks. He was looking at her head-on, and Nessa recognized her own habitual determination there as well. Maybe he was masking nervousness also? She remembered what Delphine had said about Daniel Host probably being scared.

This thought made her predisposed to feel sympathy for him, and when he smiled a wide, open smile, Nessa couldn't help it. She smiled back.

Daniel didn't try to hug her—she was grateful for that—but settled for clasping her by both shoulders and holding her there for a minute so he could look at her. "Wow," he said. "You are all grown up."

"And you are—" Nessa started and then immediately regretted her choice of words. She didn't know what to say. She didn't remember his face but she didn't want to tell him that. "Here," she finally came up with.

"Yes," Daniel agreed, covering up how awkward that had felt.

Up close, Nessa noticed Daniel looked older than she'd been expecting. His dark hair revealed streaks of gray. His skin was weathered. He was dressed in a soft-looking brown sweater and tan pants that looked halfway between something you'd wear hiking and something you'd wear to an office. Daniel turned to face the windows, where the view was completely transformed from what it had been earlier. The trees were now a black mass, the sky a purple-blue glow, a blank canvas for the pinpricks of light made by a single star as well as several planes. Nessa knew without having to even think about it that the moon, when it rose, would be large—it was only two days away from full.

"Do you like it?" Daniel asked.

Because she knew he meant the forest, not the house, Nessa nodded and then added, "It's amazing," her voice betraying how *much* she liked it.

"Thank you," said Daniel. "And now, are you hungry?" He gestured for her to sit down. She did, and then carefully followed his lead as he pulled the napkin out from under his fork and took a sip of water from his glass. When Nessa lifted hers, she noticed how heavy yet perfectly balanced it felt in her hand. Was this what it was like to be rich? Every single object you took for granted in your regular life was somehow better made and more beautiful? Why had her mother been so clear that she didn't want this for them?

"You know," Daniel said, his eyes crinkling as he smiled. "I ran cross-country in high school, too."

"You did?" Nessa said.

"I wasn't state champion, but I had my fair share of personal bests and the occasional course or team record."

"Do you still run?" Nessa asked. It was strange to think she might have inherited running from Daniel. Vivian didn't even like to hike. She would laugh and say Nate was her form of exercise.

"A lot of my lab workers do," Daniel replied. "There's not much else to do out here in the way of recreation. But not me anymore, I'm afraid. My knees are shot. I grew up in New Hampshire where running involves climbing a lot of hills."

Nessa laughed. "Yeah," she said. "The nice thing about running in Tether is it's basically flat." And that was how their conversation began, talking about running and training and courses. Daniel encouraged her to tell the story of winning States and asked all about the training regimen that got her there. As a man in a white apron and chef's jacket emerged from the kitchen to put a plate of salad greens at each of their places, Nessa told Daniel about the recruiters who had started visiting the day after she'd won and the Paravida Prize and her worries that the slow times she'd been running after taking the winter off—combined with Vivian's arrest—would cause the company to rescind the prize.

"Don't worry about that," Daniel said, spearing a tomato that he'd just told her was grown in a greenhouse at his lab. "Nessa, I want you to understand something. Now that we've reconnected, you're not going to be looking for scholarships anymore. You want to go to cross-country camp? It's done. College tuition? I'm covering that. For you *and* Delphine. I want to get to know you both. I want to be your father again as much as you'll let me. Even if you don't want the relationship—I understand that—I want to cover your expenses. I want you both to have every opportunity to succeed."

Nessa leaned back in her chair. She felt her eyes filling with tears. Even her fantasies of leaving Tether, and what her life might one day be, had never been *this* rich.

She was grateful that just then the small, quiet man who was cooking for them emerged with two more plates—a simple steak with cut potatoes, both covered in some kind of creamy sauce flecked with scallions.

"That looks incredible," Nessa said, both because in the days approaching a full moon her relationship to red meat always got a little—well—intense, and also because she didn't quite know what to say to this man who had just offered to change her life in the most dramatic of ways.

"I know all of this will take a little getting used to," Daniel said quietly as soon as the chef was gone, taking their salad plates with him.

For the first time all night, Nessa laughed.

"Maybe that's the understatement of the century?" Daniel said, solicitously.

Nessa smiled, sawing off a bit of steak and taking a bite. And then, as soon as she started chewing, she forgot about the conversation entirely. "Oh, my God, what *is* this?" she said. "It's the most delicious meat I've ever tasted."

Daniel smiled. "It's wild game from the preserve here. We harvest it systematically to create a balance in the ecosystem."

"It's venison?" Nessa asked. Living in Tether, where lots of people hunted, she ate and knew venison steak. It was full of flavor but a bit tough to chew. This was tender and melted in her mouth.

"Not *exactly* venison," Daniel said, and then moved on before Nessa could ask what he meant by that. "It's something we created in the lab."

"You created something in the lab that's 'not exactly venison'?" Nessa asked, laying down her fork. She looked at her plate. But then suddenly she felt her fork lifting to her mouth. Okay, just one more bite.

Daniel took a sip of wine. "I wonder how much your mother might have told you about me? About herself? Her work?"

Nessa slipped another bite of whatever this meat was into her mouth; because it was so delicious she forced herself not to be creeped out by it. She noticed how much more relaxed she'd become over the course of the meal. Had this man really just said he was going to pay for her to go to college? To cross-country camp? "What did Mom tell me?" Nessa said. "Um . . . Let's start with nothing."

"I see," Daniel said.

"Mom's worked as a vet tech my whole life," Nessa continued. "She made it seem like she hadn't made it all the way through college. After she was arrested—well, then Aunt Jane told me Mom worked as a scientist. But I don't know anything more. I've only seen Mom once since she was arrested. And she was too sick to explain much."

"She's sick?" Daniel said. He asked this question casually while looking into his wine glass, the way you might ask about the health of any casual acquaintance.

"Yeah, she has a fever. They don't know why. It's really scary."

Daniel looked up at the ceiling. Only then did Nessa notice how the room's lighting emerged from a series of tiny fixtures recessed into the walls at ceiling height, as well as through the simple chandelier globes suspended every twenty feet throughout the room. The lights gave her a feeling of peace and calm and balance. It was just plain hard to be worried here. Even when she was explaining how Vivian being so sick was "scary," the word felt muffled by the extra-soft carpeting and the expanse of trees.

"Look," Nessa said, thinking that if she named that feeling, she'd be protected from complacency. "Now that I'm here, everything feels really—well, far away. It's really nice and all, but I'm having trouble believing any of it is real. A week ago I didn't know you existed. Three weeks ago, Mom was still at home. I just—I just don't understand. How she had this other life. Where you fit in. Where—I don't get any of it. Can you explain?"

Daniel put down his napkin, pushed his plate away, cleared his throat. "Your mother was simply the most creative scientist I've ever worked with and I've worked with some of the best," he said. "Our personal relationship aside, that's where all of this begins. I think it's a travesty she's been hiding that fact from you and Delphine and I want to fix it, starting now. You should know."

"Okay," Nessa said. She took a bite of potato. "Where did

you meet?"

"We met in graduate school," he said. "Your mom was younger than me—she was a prodigy who finished college in two years, and once we started working together I could see why. She wasn't *just* an excellent technician, though that was part of it. When we met, human DNA had yet to be sequenced and that was all anyone was thinking about. The professor we worked under was developing technologies to use for mapping, but your mom was already thinking beyond mapping. Mapping was happening. She was thinking about what could be done with the map. She was thinking about manipulating DNA."

Nessa smiled.

"What?" said Daniel.

"My friend Bree said that when she asked her mom why the sky was blue, she said God only had enough yellow paint for the sun and he had a lot of blue left over from the ocean. Mom never told us stuff like that."

Daniel furrowed his brow. "Why would anyone say that?" he said. "It's not true."

Nessa shook her head like she was trying to shake away a déjà vu or strange association. "The way you just said that," she told Daniel, "you sound just like Mom."

Daniel laughed. "Your mother and I are the same in many, many ways. Or at least we used to be. We weren't together long—just seven years—but our connection went deeper than most because we saw eye-to-eye when it came to our work. The work we eventually did together—the company we built together—was successful because of how closely we were able to track each other's thinking. When she left, well, it took me a while to build my own work back up."

"What was some of the work you did?" Nessa asked.

"Well, our first big breakthrough was that we circumvented the clumsiness of manually manipulating DNA. Your mother had the idea of using combinations of proteins to change the DNA pattern. We weren't the only ones working in that area but your mom had a gift for selecting the enzymes that would work best—they're not all created equal. We made an absolute killing on the patent."

"So why did you stop working together?" Nessa said. "What . . . happened?"

Daniel paused, as if trying to think of the best way to express what he had to say. "Nessa, I wasn't a good husband." He cleared his throat, looking uncomfortable. "I didn't always keep my promises." He made a point of looking Nessa directly in the eyes. "I wasn't a good father either. I just want you to know I acknowledge that."

Nessa remembered Delphine's questions. If this man wanted to be her dad, he was going to have to answer them. "Why didn't you fight harder for us?" she said.

"What can I say, Nessa?" Daniel said. "Everything sounds like a feeble excuse in retrospect, but at the time, I felt convinced the right thing to do was to respect your mother's request that I remain out of her life. And yours. The circumstances of our split were, well, let's just say I was at fault."

He didn't elaborate and Nessa's mind immediately jumped ahead. Had he had an affair?

She didn't want to ask.

"We were having disagreements about the direction of our work. When your mother left, we were on the threshold of several new discoveries and I believed at the time we had to follow up on them immediately. It was just me, working alone. As I said, it was hard to adjust but for a while I thought it was better that way. Better for you and Delphine to have things appear to be simple. As soon as Chimera started to make real money, I sent some to your mother. It truly does surprise me that she didn't use it."

"She told me it was tainted," Nessa said. "She said we could never touch it."

Daniel shook his head. "Still cutting off her nose to spite her face, I see." He sighed, heavily. "Vivian was a rigorous thinker— so careful, so intuitive, so disciplined. But the rigor would tie her up into knots when it came to ethics. She'd back herself into a corner where she would end up thinking being paid for your work at all invalidated your findings. Totally unrealistic. Labs are expensive and—" He laughed. "Scientists have to eat, right?"

Nessa laughed along with him, but she was also thinking, *Do you need to always eat like* this?

"Enough," Daniel said. "Enough talk. You must be exhausted. I have some reading to do to prepare for a meeting in the morning." He explained that he'd be working when she got up, but she should feel free to roam around and explore, go running if she liked, and he'd be done by mid- to late morning. He wanted to show her the lab.

"Sleep well," were his parting words. Nessa came close to answering, "Ha!" After all she'd learned, she assumed she would be up all night putting the pieces together.

But once she got downstairs and changed into pajamas and lay down she realized the mattress was—heavenly. The eiderdown quilt made her feel like she was wrapped inside a cloud. Her phone had blown up—Delphine wanted to know what Daniel Host was like, Bree wanted to know what she'd worn, and Luc checked in on whether she'd scoped out a good location to transform. She sent back brief texts to Bree and Luc, but called Delphine. Nessa was not a detailed storyteller but she tried to remember everything and pass it on to her sister. It wasn't fair that she got to be here and Delphine stayed home, but as the conversation wore on, Nessa almost thought she'd trade places with her. The sound of Nate chatting in the background made her homesick and the day had been long. As soon as she and Delphine got off the line, Nessa fell asleep quickly and slept hard.

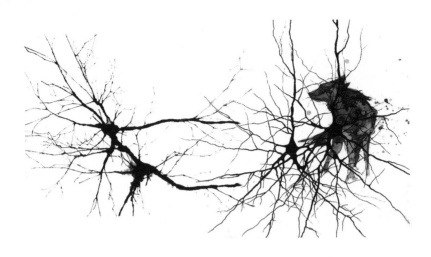

CHAPTER TWENTY-NINE

essa woke up feeling rested in a way she hadn't in a long time. She heard a soft knock on the door, and when she opened it, found a cream-colored shopping bag with brown raffia handles. Was this a present?

Bringing it into the room, she looked inside, and then, realizing what it was, carried it over to the floor by the window and began pulling out the bag's contents: two Adidas tanks, shorts in three styles, a pair of running tights, a hoodie, SmartWool socks, a Chimera Corp. wicking running hat, and a pair of her favorite sneakers. In her size. In fact, everything looked like a copy of what she'd brought in her bag, except all of Nessa's things had come from Walmart and Target, and the new items were top-of-the-line.

One of the packages was actually wrapped in gift paper. Nessa tore it away and found a Garmin GPS-enabled running watch.

"How did you know?" she asked out loud, holding it out in front of her the way Daniel had held her the night before. Nessa had *always, always* wanted a Garmin.

A note in Milton's tiny, all-caps handwriting explained:

NESSA: THE WATCH WAS PLANNED. THE REST DANIEL HAD ME ORDER FOR YOU LAST NIGHT—APOLOGIES FOR LOOKING THROUGH YOUR THINGS TO SEE WHAT YOU NEEDED, BUT HE INSISTED. THEY WERE FLOWN IN THIS MORNING. –MILTON

And then, a note from Daniel:

Nessa: I mean it. You're not a scholarship kid anymore. –D.

Nessa didn't know if the "D" stood for "Daniel" or "Dad." She didn't care. Ripping off tags, sliding on the new clothes, lacing up the shoes, Nessa was up the stairs and out the front door in minutes, remembering just how much she loved the woods, loved running, and exalting in how glad she was to be somewhere new where she wasn't carrying the weight of life in Tether.

Nessa turned left on the blacktop, running on the high ground the house was built on, knowing that if she headed the way the golf cart had come the night before, she'd be running straight down a punishing hill toward the airstrip. She turned right at the intersection and took off.

She always felt like she shaved 10 percent off her pace when she wore new shoes. Luc did too—back in February, kind of as a joke, they'd gone on a "shoe date," each taking out a pair of new shoes on an inaugural run. Dorky, but fun.

Or just dorky, according to Bree.

Nessa felt disloyal switching to new shoes without Luc. But mostly she felt like she was running faster, which always felt good. She was running—no, she was flying—finally hitting the splits her Paravida sponsors had been expecting.

Not that she needed them anymore.

It's really hard to believe, she thought as she let her stride lengthen and settled into the run. Hard to believe that this man was her dad. She tried to picture Daniel Host with her mother, and she could almost see it, as much as she could imagine anyone that old being young. What if, while sitting at the dinner table the night before, she'd turned around and seen her mother in the living room? What if instead of growing up in Tether, Nessa had grown up here, her mother reading a magazine on one of the giant couches or warming her hands at the slate-stone fireplace?

She tried to imagine Daniel Host in Tether, her parents together, standing next to each other at a track meet or a cross-country race. Nope. She couldn't quite see it.

She tried to imagine them standing side by side in front of a laboratory bench, wearing white coats and safety goggles. Instantly she wished she could have known Vivian as a scientist. Nessa thought of her mom's hands—how she had such a gift for calming an anxious animal. How her sutures were tight and even, neater than Dr. Morgan's. How she always seemed to know just what to do when an animal was presented in the garage-clinic. How she kept ahead of the research on Nate's diagnosis and often countered with her own treatment suggestions. How she was almost always right.

Nessa thought of Bree and Luc with a pang. If she'd grown up here she would never have met them. But still, the fantasy was powerful. What if her mom had been sitting at that dining room table the night before, flying around the country in a private plane, having important meetings and doing important work? What had Daniel said? That Vivian was "the most creative scientist I've ever worked with"?

How could an affair have made Vivian walk away from all that? Couldn't she have just set up her own lab, the way Daniel had?

Just then, Nessa heard a noise in front of her. She was passing a tall clearing where a single deciduous tree was growing up among the firs. Deciduous trees here were still bare for the winter, but it looked like this one was covered with small, dark leaves. Nessa heard the noise again. A cracking sound in the woods behind the tree—it was the sound of a stick breaking, Nessa thought, though it probably would have been inaudible to a person without wolf hearing.

As if in reaction, the leaves lifted off the branches of the deciduous tree, duplicating the tree's conical shape about ten feet in the air. The lifting motion made it look like the tree was breathing. And then, as if caught in an updraft, the cone of leaves flattened into a pancake shape, still suspended in the air. Then the leaves organized themselves into a line, flying up in a spiraling shape.

Those weren't leaves, Nessa thought. They were birds. A flock of birds. With iridescent green bellies and yellow beaks.

They were beautiful.

By now, Nessa had stopped running just to stare up at them, her hands on her hips, her heavy breathing causing her chest to rise and fall. She'd been running hard. She was standing in this position when another runner emerged from the woods up ahead, about twenty yards past Nessa, heading toward her. *Is there a trail back there?* Nessa wondered. And then she realized the runner heading toward her must have been the one who had disturbed the birds in the first place.

Shaking her head at her own confusion, she continued her run, wondering for a minute if the runner might be her father—then quickly realizing it wasn't and noticing that she was disappointed.

As she passed the runner, she saw he was much younger than her father. Closer to her age. He was running fast, a phone strapped to his arm, earbuds in. Nessa could hear his music almost as well as he could—Beyoncé. They nodded as they passed each other and she thought that would be that.

Soon after passing him, Nessa came to a fork in the blacktop road and turned left again, then right at another fork, then left. Estimating she'd run about three miles, she turned, hoping to be able to reverse the path she'd followed. But none of the forks looked familiar and she was starting to wonder if she was hitting the turns correctly. Where was the tree the birds had lifted out of? Shouldn't she have seen it by now?

She rounded another bend and saw the same runner she'd seen before. He was running toward her . . . again, which either confirmed that she was totally turned around or that he was. *I guess I could ask him for help if I'm really lost,* she thought. But that kind of thing—flagging down strangers—was not how

Nessa rolled. She ran past him again, ignoring the quizzical look he was giving her. Noting at the same time that he had chiseled features and was smiling at her like he knew something she didn't. Did he know she was lost? Was he laughing at her?

Who was he? He looked young to be one of the workers from Daniel's lab.

Feeling suddenly shy—and missing Luc—Nessa took a little hop to propel herself back to top speed, blowing past the runner while looking studiously out into the trees.

She ran left. She took a right. She was heading up an incline she didn't think she remembered running up before. She came to an overlook that she *definitely* did not remember. It was a breathtaking view, showing a steep-sided gorge lined with tall pines, a rocky river sided by meadows of dried grasses below. But where was she?

For a moment, she thought she might have to transform in order to find her way back. As a wolf she could navigate by smell. But that option wasn't ideal. She didn't know where she was, but she knew she was close to civilization. She'd just seen another runner, after all. As a wolf she might scare people. She could get shot. She was going to *have* to transform in a day or two—the full moon was coming. But by then, she'd have a chance to get the lay of the land.

Turning, Nessa ran back in the direction she'd come. Turning left, then right, then left again, she found herself standing by the clearing with the single tree, the one she'd seen the birds take flight from. At least she was close now. And then there was the runner—again!—coming toward her.

She knew she should stop him. Bree would stop him. But something kept Nessa from doing it. He was looking at her with that same knowing smile. Then she heard him call out to her when she was just a few steps beyond him. "Hey!" he called out.

Nessa turned. Had she done something wrong? Was she trespassing? There hadn't been any signs . . .

The jogger was breathing hard, his hands on his knees. He had to catch his breath while she waited for him to form the next words. "What's a guy gotta do to catch you? Your dad said you'd gone for a run—he was worried you'd get lost."

"My dad sent you?"

The jogger held out a hand to shake. "Sure. I'm Gabriel." He flashed a straight-toothed smile. Nessa noticed the glow of his copper-colored skin, his bright black eyes, and tight, curly hair. "You looked like you were having such a good time out there, I didn't want to break your focus. I just kept looping around the paths so I wouldn't lose track of you."

He was breathing heavily, his hands on his knees. "Do you *always* run in repeating circles when you have access to a 30,000-acre preserve at your disposal?"

Gabriel's warm smile made Nessa see that his teasing was good-natured. Maybe she had been a little ridiculous—or maybe he was just being a little flirty? "I guess I kind of have independence issues," she said. "I don't like to ask for help."

"No worries," Gabriel said. "I think I was about to start having issues keeping up with you. If this is your nice casual jogging pace, I'd hate to see you race."

Nessa laughed. She wondered for a second what he would think if he saw her run as a wolf.

"Hey, listen, I'm going to have my butt handed to me if I don't bring you back. Will you do me a favor and join me?"

Nessa laughed again. Since Milwaukee, she'd been alone or

with adults. This guy—Gabriel—seemed closer to her in age. She felt as close to normal with him as she'd felt in a while.

She liked the way he was looking at her. It made her feel like she was pretty.

They started jogging and Nessa was careful not to go too fast. As they ran, Gabriel told her he was a Biology graduate student at Stanford, and working for her dad as a lab assistant. "Isn't Stanford kind of far away from here?" Nessa asked.

Gabriel laughed. "You think?" he said. "Seriously, it would be if I was still taking classes, but I finished my coursework last year, and I'm in the research phase of my degree. When I need to get to campus I can usually hitch a ride down with Daniel. He goes down once a week to teach a seminar." He explained that he met Daniel when he was taking his class and was lucky enough to land one of the rare Chimera internships.

"They have interns here?" Nessa said. "I thought no one who worked here ever left because of all the security issues." She was kidding, thinking Gabriel would roll his eyes at how uptight Milton was. But Gabriel didn't. "That's why the internships are rare," he said. "Unless something goes wrong, there's an assumption they'll turn into your life's work."

"Okay," Nessa said, glad Gabriel hadn't seemed to pick up on the sarcasm. "You look a little young to be signed on to a job for the rest of your life."

"I am," Gabriel said, smiling again. "I'm only twenty-three. But I don't feel tied down. I feel lucky. Chimera Corp. It's kind of a dream research job. You get to do stuff that's simply groundbreaking. Daniel makes it possible for brilliant scientists to have the space they need and none of the red tape of grant-funded work." They were approaching a turn-off—the one Nessa had been looking for.

"That's the way to the house, isn't it?" she said, pointing to the left.

"You're getting it," Gabriel said. "But, hey, you don't want to see the lab, do you?" He looked at his watch. "I'm supposed to go check on my mice about now. You could meet them."

Nessa had to admit, she was curious. And it was obvious Gabriel wanted to spend more time with her. That felt nice. "Sure," she agreed. "But just promise me when it's time to get back, you'll draw me a map."

Gabriel laughed as they turned to the right. "You bet," he said.

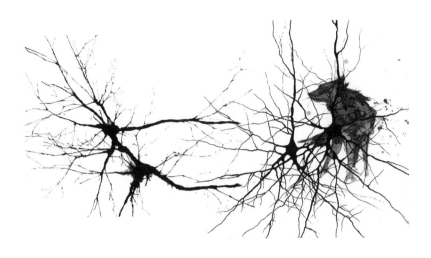

CHAPTER THIRTY

rom the outside, the lab looked like the house, appearing to be only a modest one story, with a flat roof, wood trim, and glass window walls extending from floor to ceiling. Seeing it from the outside, Nessa thought it didn't look much bigger than Dr. Morgan's.

But after stepping inside, Nessa realized the visible part of the building was only the entrance hall. Passing through it, Nessa found herself standing in a glass atrium, a greenhouse-like facility with a glass roof and glass walls separating various plant-filled chambers. In the center of the room, a circular railing marked off something that, when Nessa approached, she realized was the top of a silo reaching many floors down.

Looking down, she saw a series of hallways and closed doors on every level. They were all white and clinical, but up here she felt like she was in botanical gardens like the ones she had visited in Detroit on a school trip. With all Daniel's talk the night before of DNA mapping and viruses, Nessa had expected computers and test tubes, but she could hear the trickle of running water. The air was humid and warm and she could smell flowers blooming.

"You're working on plants?" Nessa said. "I thought my dad was doing genetics."

"Well, yeah," said Gabriel. "And so was Gregor Mendel, who invented genetics. Remember that guy?"

"Oh yeah," Nessa said. "Beans."

Gabriel smiled. "Come here," he said. "I want to show you something." He led her down a hallway, passing a series of rooms separated by glass walls. He stopped to fill two water glasses at a mini-kitchen built into the hallway. "One of the few rules here is that you can't use plastic water bottles," Gabriel explained. "We're highly eco-sensitive."

"Okay, fine," Nessa said and she followed Gabriel into one of the glass-walled chambers, where what looked like different varieties of grasses were growing in trays.

"Do you know what this is?" Gabriel asked her.

"Uh . . . wheat?" Nessa said.

"No, but close. It's rice. I don't know how much you know about growing rice, but there's something dramatically different about these."

"Mostly what I know about rice is that you eat it for dinner sometimes," Nessa said.

"Yeah, okay, that's definitely a starting place," Gabriel said. "But I bet that the rice you eat was grown using a lot of water. Traditionally rice is grown in paddies, which get flooded. Look here." He stuck his finger in a tray of soil. "No water," he said.

"So this rice isn't as thirsty?" Nessa said. Speaking of thirsty, she took a sip of her own water.

"Actually, that has nothing to do with it," Gabriel said. "The water in rice paddies isn't for the rice plant. The water is like a natural pesticide. What's going on with paddies is that the rice plant can survive underwater and most of the organisms that eat the rice plant cannot."

"So it's like diving underwater to get away from mosquitoes and horseflies?"

"Spoken like someone who has gone swimming in the north woods," Gabriel said. Nessa laughed.

"So . . . *rice*," she said. "This is what you're dedicating your career to?" She couldn't help but wonder how someone who was only twenty-three was willing to decide to spend the rest of his life working for Chimera Corp.

"Are you kidding me? I could dedicate, like, two careers to it," Gabriel said. "Rice accounts for about 20 percent of all humanity's caloric intake. When you're looking to address world hunger, rice is a great place to start."

"Okay, when you put it that way, it does sound kind of important," Nessa said.

"The world is changing. Global warming, globalism, overpopulation—humanity is going to need food. Some of the developments that have been made include making rice that can survive flooding by seawater, rice that produces more grain and less plant. These varieties here are pest resistant—that's why you don't need the water. In another place, we've got varieties that don't resist the pests, but resist the pest-killers. Pesticides."

"But aren't pesticides bad?"

"Maybe," Gabriel said. "Or maybe not. Certainly if you're using them on food crops and humans who ingest those crops are then ingesting the pesticides absorbed into their food. But what if you can develop food crops genetically engineered not to absorb the pesticide?"

"I don't know," Nessa said. "Spraying poison just doesn't seem like a good idea to me, period."

"Yes, exactly," she heard behind her. She and Gabriel turned at the same moment to see that Daniel had entered the room. "But let's say a pest evolves that can attack even the genetically modified rice seeds. And water is not available. What if the choice is between a pesticide that's harmless to humans and starvation?"

He rested a hand against a tray of rice. "The point is, Nessa," Daniel said, "we aren't building tools to shape the world here. We're building tools to save it. And we don't always know what the world will need saving from. Our job is to tinker, invent, and let the politicians and big pharmaceutical companies and the industrial agricultural complex decide what they want and need from the toolbox we've filled for them. Some of what we build here has never been used. Never *should* be used. Other innovations have been enormously effective. There are entire countries reshaping their agricultural policies using products created at Chimera."

"But I thought there were only thirty people working here."

"Yes," Daniel said. "We're just creating prototypes. We hold the patents. Manufacturing, implementation—we leave that to others. When one of our patents gets used, we make money and use it to fund more research." Daniel turned to Gabriel. "I had assumed you'd be showing Nessa the *other* rice you'd been working on."

Gabriel smiled. Why had Daniel said "other rice" like it was some kind of an inside joke?

Gabriel and Daniel led Nessa to an elevator bank off to the side of the railing overlooking the silo of labs. While they waited for it to come, Daniel said, "Look at this." He showed her a display, like in a museum: an aerial photograph of the park set under a glass dome. Daniel touched Nessa on the elbow. "That's the Chimera campus," he said, pointing down. "All of this here." She saw the house, the airstrip, what looked like a hangar.

"This is employee housing," said Gabriel, pointing to the other side. "Look, you can even see the roof of my little studio. You can *really* see the bigger roofs of the more senior employees. They have houses." Nessa saw a jungle gym, a pond, a canopied park pavilion. But what most impressed her was the undisturbed forest.

"There's nothing out here?" she said, pointing away from the campus, to the vast expanse of trees. She looked at her dad. "How come?"

At her question, she thought her father and Gabriel exchanged a look, but whatever it was passed so quickly she convinced herself a moment later that she'd only imagined it.

"We think of the rest of the park as a living laboratory," her father explained. "It's actually the greatest strength of our facility, worth more than all the rest of our equipment put together. So much of genetic science is out of our control. On the one hand, we've made strides in the past few years that are mind-blowing. They would have been inconceivable just decades ago. On the other hand, the mechanics are still blunt. There's massive tracts of the science no one has begun to understand. We're trying to tinker with evolution, understand the growth of embryos with incredibly complex systems we only get to see very small parts of. Sometimes the best we can do is make a change and release it into the wild, see how nature absorbs it, corrects it, makes use of it."

As he spoke, their elevator arrived and they had stepped in. As they emerged at the lower level, the bright sunshine of the atrium and greenhouse floor gave way to LED lighting that was nearly blinding against the white walls and floors. Nessa could hear the hum of machinery as Gabriel led them into the lab with a press of three fingerprints to a touchpad.

The rows of cages inside reminded Nessa of Dr. Morgan's. Striding forward to see the animals inside, she saw scurrying. White fur. Red eyes. Lots of gray. Mazes in some cages. Bright lights in others. One had music playing—it was Motown—coming in on tiny Bose speakers set up in the upper corners of the cage.

"Mice," Nessa said, looking from her father to Gabriel, glad that at least one of the puzzles that had been presented to her she could solve.

"Look again," Gabriel said.

Nessa did. Getting closer to the cage with the music, she saw that the creatures were larger than any mice she'd seen before. The ears—they were larger too. The teeth. A longer tail. And strange, rounded eyes.

"What are they?" she asked, the tone in her voice conveying

204

the "skip the games and just tell me" urgency she was feeling.

"They're our other form of rice," Gabriel said, looking at her with trepidation, smiling with wary hope. "Get it?"

"That's not funny," she said. "That's ... "

"We call them chimeras," her father said. "All joking aside, they're amazing creatures." Opening the cage door, he removed one and held it in the palm of his hand. "We injected mouse DNA into a rat embryo and had our first success about a decade ago. Since then, we've been using them as the basis for genetic experimentation."

Nessa could not contain her feeling of instant revulsion. There was something about this that just felt wrong. Unnatural. Ugly.

Maybe Daniel was able to read the feelings on her face. "Don't be scared," he said. He stroked the top of the creature's head and Nessa saw it begin to relax beneath his touch. This did nothing to make her feel less nauseated.

"This mouse-rat chimera was one of our first successes."

"That's what it's called, a chimera?" Nessa asked. "That's what you named your company after?"

"Yes," Daniel said. He laughed. "A chimera is a mythical beast that combines several different species. It's also a scientific term for any organism that contains genetic material from two individual zygotes—or two species. It occurs naturally— occasionally mothers will contain strands of their children's DNA for years after giving birth. Hematopoietic chimeras show up in cattle populations—the result of the exchange of hematopoietic stem cells between twins."

"Hemato-what?" Nessa said, laughing.

"Sorry," Daniel said. "That just refers to blood. Our chimeras connect across more than just blood though. They exchange organs, anatomical features, habits, and capabilities that tell us their brains are affected for sure."

"That's ... amazing," Nessa said. Though she herself was not feeling so amazing. As if the air blown into the room was not as rich in oxygen as it should have been, she felt herself growing light-headed and dizzy. Gabriel laughed at her jokes, looked at her in a way that made her feel attractive. She couldn't help but respond to the attention, but what was she doing? She felt herself flushing, thinking of Luc, which only made her feel more queasy inside.

"We like to think so," Daniel went on. Nessa struggled to focus on what he was saying. She reached for the cage behind her, thinking to steady herself by holding on to it, but suddenly she could not shake the idea of the mice-rat chimeras inside scrabbling up the outside, their claws digging into the skin of her hand, taking nibbles of her flesh. Ingesting her DNA, absorbing it into their own bodies.

"Of course, the implications for medicine are far-reaching," Daniel was saying. "We've already started to see applications. You can grow mouse or rat organs and safely transplant them into host animals from either species. We've seen success with this, Nessa. We haven't been able to test this in human subjects—" He broke off here and laughed, casting a glance in Gabriel's direction.

"Except for me," Gabriel said, and blushed in a way that Nessa had to admit was adorable.

"It's the researcher's dilemma, especially the *young* researcher," Daniel said, turning to Nessa with the air of someone explaining an inside joke. "Sometimes we want an answer so badly that we are tempted to make our own bodies our unofficial test subjects."

"It's just so much faster than waiting for approval," Gabriel added, also directing himself to Nessa, though he kept glancing at Daniel as if seeking approval. He slapped the interior of his wrist, like he was about to draw blood. "I've probably lost a quart of my own blood doing research in this lab. My sister just had her first kid and it was all I could do not to ask her to give me the umbilical cord blood. It's loaded with stem cells. I could have thought of a dozen different projects I could have used them for."

Daniel laughed and slapped Gabriel on the back. "Now, now," he said. Gabriel blushed some more. "We aren't *actually* testing on human subjects. But we have reached an 80 percent cure rate bringing lab-grown pancreas transplants into diabetic mice."

"You're growing extra organs for them in the lab?" Nessa said, suddenly realizing two things:

One, her father was engaged in the same kind of work that was going on at Paravida.

Two, she was about to throw up.

How far beneath the ground were they? The elevator ride had been short, but she knew they'd passed several levels before exiting. The mice, or "rice," or whatever—continued to scurry. The tinny speakers continued to play Marvin Gaye. The LED lights were unrelenting. The ventilation system continued to hum.

Could she get out of the room and make a run for the bathroom without pressing her fingerprints into the touch-screen?

She could feel the periphery of her vision starting to blur. Her hearing was dimming as well. Her father's voice: "Nessa? You okay?"

Gabriel said from far away, "She doesn't look so good."

She felt for a minute just the way she did when she was about to transform: Everything inside her body was moving, like in one of those ocean wave-producing machines where a Plexiglas box filled with ocean water rocks back and forth on a pedestal until waves start to slosh across the water's surface.

Oh God, Oh God, thought Nessa. Suddenly the idea of throwing up all over this incredibly cute guy and her nice-to-meet-you dad wasn't the worst scenario imaginable. *Don't turn into a wolf*, she begged her body. *Don't let me turn into a wolf.*

And then suddenly Nessa didn't care about any of those concerns any longer. Nessa felt herself falling, her feet growing light, her head lifting off her shoulders like it was a helium balloon.

She floated backward into memory. An old memory. She smelled her father's soap and the beeswax smell that sometimes came off his skin. She was sleeping. She had fallen asleep somewhere that wasn't her bed and her father was carrying her to the car.

And then another memory. She was sitting somewhere. She was crying, the way little kids do, without trying to stop. She was in a car—the back seat, but it was parked. She could see her father but something was wrong. She smelled something acrid and burning and then behind his head, above a low roofline—a garage?—she saw flames.

She slowly came to, realizing there was no car. There was no bed. No fire. She was in the lab. The basement lab. The mice.

The "rice." But still, her father was holding her as he had when she was a little girl. Was it a memory she'd woken to? Or just a feeling? If she'd felt she could sit up and push away from him she would have, but she was too woozy to move.

Still, something had changed. Daniel wasn't a stranger anymore. She remembered him as her dad. "I think maybe we should get you back to the house," he was saying. "I'll have Milton come by in the golf cart."

"Here," Gabriel said. He was holding out a glass bottle of apple juice, the glass in the shape of an apple.

"Right," Nessa said, taking it from him, taking a sip. "No plastic."

Gabriel laughed.

At first, Nessa was more embarrassed by the fact that she'd passed out than anything else, but as she recovered in her room—the chef from the night before brought down a tray of pastries and a bowl of fresh cut-up fruit while Nessa snuggled under the super soft comforter and watched TV—she began to wonder if maybe her fainting had something to do with the moon. It was set to rise the next evening. At some point during the next twenty-four hours she was going to have to slip away and transform.

Her chance wouldn't come very soon. That night at dinner, Daniel invited her to join him at Stanford the next morning. He had a seminar to teach, and then held his office hours afterward. He had made a request for a meeting with the cross-country coach. Admissions would give her a private tour.

"Stanford?" Nessa said. "Really?" She'd been on their

website more times than she cared to admit. She would need a mind-blowing scholarship to get to go there, but still, she was holding out for it. Her first choice.

Nessa supposed she'd just have to wait and transform when they got back.

She texted Luc as soon as dinner was over to tell him the good news. She'd been so busy it hadn't occurred to her that he hadn't yet replied to her text from the night before. She was planning on calling him, but after getting out of the shower, she saw that he had finally replied.

Sorry. Busy. PV getting worse. Working with Jack. Other PV may join us. I'm mostly barefoot these days.

The minute she saw the message, Nessa tried calling, hoping to catch him, but Luc did not pick up. After a long talk with Jane, who filled Nessa in on her frustrated attempts to have Vivian seen by a doctor outside the prison system, Nessa tried Luc again. Still he wasn't picking up. Had he transformed again? The thought made her literally ache to transform herself. She missed him. She missed his cabin. She missed running together as a human and as a wolf. She missed the way he would look at her and without saying anything, she'd know what he was thinking. She missed the way nothing got to him—she'd always thought of herself as mellow and not judgy, but Luc set a new standard.

At the thought of running with Luc, of running as a wolf— the two had become inextricably linked in her mind—she felt her skin prickle, almost like she was going to transform in spite of herself. Was she going to make it until tomorrow night?

She was going to have to.

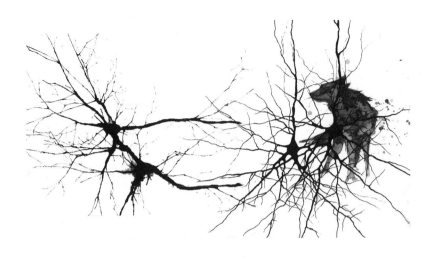

CHAPTER THIRTY-ONE

The next morning Nessa felt a little bit better. More relaxed. She wasn't nervous climbing through the narrow doorway of the tiny four-seater plane with her dad. It was exhilarating actually, sitting in the co-pilot spot, equipped with a full set of controls. The itchy, need-to-transform feeling was still with her, but it receded to the background and she hoped it would stay there.

The night before, Daniel had asked her about her plans for college, her career goals. She hadn't been able to believe she'd even been having the conversation. Nessa wore the same outfit from the night before because she didn't have anything else remotely appropriate but she felt grownup nonetheless, twirling creamy pasta onto her fork as Daniel identified the four different mushroom species they were sampling, trying to look not grossed out when the chef brought a whole broiled fish to the table, eyeballs and all, and lifted up the skin so he could slide sections of the flesh onto Daniel's and Nessa's plates, as they talked about which schools offered the best programs, not *just* which school would grant the best scholarship to a Michigan state champ. Daniel had asked all the right questions. He'd treated her like an adult, listened to her plans, offered a few suggestions. Had she considered living abroad during her junior year? Had she considered spending the coming summer at a pre-college institute some colleges offered, to get the flavor of the college experience?

She asked him about his parents—her grandparents—and he told her that they died together in a car accident when he was still in high school. "You were actually named for my mother," he said. "Did you know that?"

Nessa felt a chill come up her spine. She shook her head.

"Vanessa Host. She was a bookkeeper in a factory—she had an almost photographic memory for numbers. My father was a foreman—the kind of person who kept every hinge in our house oiled, who would jack up a house and readjust the foundation if it started to sag. My older sister—she was a teenager already when I was born—she had a rare genetic disease, and there was no cure. She died a few years before they did. I suppose that broke them. And it's probably also what got me interested in genetics in the first place."

"You wish you could go back and save your sister?"

"Save my mother," Daniel said. "My sister—I know this will sound callous, but because of her illness, we never had much of a connection. She was much older, and by the time I could remember her, she had already lost the ability to speak or move around on her own. To me, she was just the monster in the downstairs bedroom. My mother left her job to nurse her and I always resented the time and attention my sister received. No matter how many academic awards or trophies I brought home, my sister's illness ruled the roost." He toyed with the base of his knife for a moment where it lay next to his plate. "You know how kids' minds work."

Nessa nodded. Daniel looked up at her, straight into her eyes. "'Nessa' was your mother's invention. My mother's name was *Va*nessa. Funny how you've turned out looking a bit like her."

"I never knew I was named after anyone at all," Nessa said. "Is Delphine?"

Daniel smiled. "Delphine was your mother's idea. She was thinking 'truth teller.' You've heard of the Oracle of Delphi, from Greek legends?"

"Of course," Nessa said. Nate had gone through a major Percy Jackson phase and cataloged everything Greek myth related over and over.

"The oracle would speak truth, but in ways no one could understand. Unraveling the riddles of her predictions would drive men crazy. Given the work we were doing—our research to try to read the genome—that idea had special resonance." Daniel laughed. "Also, it's pretty. We both liked it." For a minute, Nessa thought she saw a look of wistfulness in her father's eyes. But then the look passed. He cleared his throat. "Though to be honest, it wasn't my first choice for your sister. I wanted Abigail."

"Abigail?" said Nessa. She'd never particularly liked that name and couldn't imagine her sister walking around with it. It sounded so plain and ordinary compared to Delphine. She was about to say so when she caught the expression on Daniel's face. He looked like he was about to say something really important—his eyes had taken on a serious expression and his jaw was set.

But then all he said was, "Abigail means 'father's love,' so that's probably not the most appropriate, is it?" He laughed, sounding as sad and lost as Nessa had ever heard him. He'd said he regretted not being part of his daughters' lives. But she hadn't felt how much until now.

After the meal, Daniel had coffee while Nessa was served a dish of ice cream and a cup of peppermint tea and they talked about Vivian's case. "I have five lawyers in mind. I'm interviewing the last two this evening and then I'll sign with one of them. We should be able to have an injunction soon. To at least get your mom back home."

"That's so great of you," Nessa said. "Thank you."

Daniel waved away her thanks. "I appreciate your gratitude, but this is really the least I can do. Nessa, I know that it's difficult to know who or what to believe right now. Please know I'm here for you. I want to make up for not being in your life."

Now, as Daniel went through the pre-flight checks, she found herself watching him, questioning him a bit. It was difficult to know what or who to believe. The memory of him that had come back to her when she woke up from fainting— she was starting to see that that memory made her feel connected to him now. It was an unsettling feeling, like straddling an international border, one foot in the United States and one in Canada, but it made her feel lighter, like she didn't have to worry. She knew where she came from. She knew he was her dad. Funny that her understanding of her father was developing *now*, at the exact moment that her understanding of her mother was slipping away.

Once they had reached cruising altitude, Daniel turned to Nessa. "Want to fly her?"

"Me?" Nessa said.

"I don't see anyone else in the plane."

"Uh . . . sure," Nessa said, and Daniel explained how the controls leveled the plane, how to move gently into the turns, what the pedals did, how to gauge the airspeed and heading, how to read the altimeter. "Make only the smallest adjustments," he told her. "Planes are extremely sensitive and you'll feel it."

He was right, Nessa realized as she grasped the yoke with both hands and lifted her left ever so slightly and felt the plane bank right. "I did that?" she said.

"You did," Daniel replied, a wide smile opening up his face.

Nessa experimented with keeping the plane level, asking questions. Daniel seemed delighted to explain aerodynamics, GPS technology, small plane engine design. While she was flying, she felt the least wolfy she had all day. Maybe it was the focus she had to bring to the task at hand?

Whatever the reason, once Daniel took back control of the plane, Nessa had a sudden surge of wolf drive, telling her to grab the control back from her dad. She wanted to keep flying!

Uh-oh, Nessa thought. She'd long come to realize that right before she transformed, her mood got a little weird—she'd cry at the drop of a hat, or fly off the handle about something that wasn't a big deal.

She pressed her hand against the window glass, feeling the cold, willing herself to think about anything besides running in the woods. It was hard not to think about Luc when she felt so much like she wanted to turn into a wolf. Once, when Luc had mistimed a transformation—thinking he could make it to the end of the day and then realizing halfway through that was going to be impossible—he'd punched his locker, making an ear-splitting noise that reverberated throughout the hall and left his hand bleeding and his locker door so badly bent the handyman had to come with a crowbar to get it back open again.

Daniel broke the moment of silence. "You know, it was your mother who first got me interested in chimeras. As an undergrad, she'd had a professor who was obsessed with the implication chimera creation might have on endangered species. Maybe you have a species on the verge of extinction and you can save it, at least in part, by combining its DNA with another species quite similar to it and creating something new, but very similar to what came before."

Would Nessa have made the connection to Luc if she hadn't already been thinking about him? "A friend of mine back home who is really into wolves, he told me that most of the wolves living in the U.S. are actually not pure wolves, but carry coyote DNA."

"That's true," Daniel agreed. "The main difference between interspecies cross-breeding and what we're doing is that we're seeing features presenting in our chimeric constructions that are directly tied to the separate species."

Nessa considered this for a moment. It seemed important, but she wasn't sure exactly what it meant.

"How did you actually get the DNA from one of the species into the other?" she asked.

"Well, you have to insert the DNA as the organism is forming—at the embryonic phase when you just have a bunch of stem cells that don't yet themselves know what they're going to become. That's what we did with the mouse-rat you saw. We injected the mouse embryo with rat stem cell material. Or really, not injected. We infected, using that same virus-DNA manipulation technology your mother invented."

Nessa tried to keep the disgust out of her voice and her expression—it was bad enough she'd passed out in the lab the day before. "In a test tube or something?" she asked, hoping the question came off as disinterested and polite.

Daniel laughed, but looked a little sheepish. "Sorry to horrify you, Nessa. I'm in Lab Mode. I know it sounds a little creepy. But the natural order of *my* universe includes controlling nature. We all have to challenge the unfamiliar. Don't let taboos stand in the way of progress." Nessa smiled politely. Daniel looked back down at the control panel and adjusted a dial. "To answer your question, we tried test tubes and they never worked. Right now, we can only get an organism with two sets of stem cells to grow in utero. There's something about the natural sequence of chemical signaling that occurs in utero that allows stem cells to grow into variegated cells, such as heart, kidney, brain—you name it."

"Have you tried this with humans?" Nessa said.

Daniel laughed. "That, my friend, is the question of the hour," he said. "It's where all this will lead one day, but currently the concept raises a lot of legal and ethical questions. What happens if you have a pig with a human hand? How about a human brain? Once you get into reproductive tissue, the issue gets even more complicated—could a pig give birth to a human baby? It's fascinating. And repulsive. But you have to acknowledge this much. Imagine how many human lives would be impacted if we could grow replacement kidneys inside a lab animal."

Nessa shivered. She flashed on the scene of the human ear coming out of the Paravida wolf. She wanted to tell her father about it. But a gut instinct made her stop.

"What?" Daniel asked.

"Nothing," Nessa smiled bravely.

"The implications for organ transplantation science are astounding," Daniel continued. "Right now there are more than one hundred and twenty-five thousand people in the United States waiting for life-saving organ transplants. Most of them aren't going to get them."

Daniel met Nessa's gaze. "Our work with chimeras is going to change the world someday."

Still thinking of Paravida, Nessa asked, "Are there lots of companies doing this work?" She tried to keep this question casual and looked away in case her face betrayed her extreme interest in Daniel's response to her question.

"Successfully? No. We're one of the few. And what we're making money on right now is our patents. We've developed tools and techniques that make chimeric creation accessible to other labs. The pace of development right now is such that everyone's willing to pay top dollar for it."

"I see," Nessa said, though her mind reeled with all the things she *couldn't* see.

It was as if her father—and her mother—had access to special glasses that allowed them to see deeply into living beings and see their patterns of DNA. To read the combinations there like they were letters, an ancient language in which were encoded the secrets of history, of evolution, and of time.

Nessa could barely take in the information she was learning about her own family.

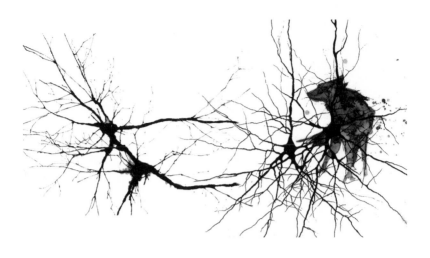

CHAPTER THIRTY-TWO

fter the plane landed, they were met by a driver from the university. As they settled into the backseat of an SUV emblazoned with the Stanford seal, Daniel's phone rang.

"Sorry," he said to Nessa. "It's Milton." But after he answered with a cursory, "Yep," his tone changed. "Oh, that's bad," he said. "How did it happen?" He paused to listen. "He was . . . what? Oh. God. That's awful."

When he hung up, Nessa looked at him inquiringly. "A colleague of mine, another geneticist, was just attacked," he said. "He's in the ICU. No one knows if he's going to make it."

"I'm sorry," Nessa replied. She wondered if she was supposed to do something to comfort Daniel. He seemed upset. "Was he—um—robbed or something?" she asked.

"No, that's what strange," Daniel said. To Nessa's relief, he was already texting out a message on his phone.

He was attacked in the woods. They think by some kind of an animal.

Nessa froze. That sounded like what had happened to her.

"He's going to die," Daniel said, still typing, shaking his head. "Brilliant guy too."

They rode in silence a few minutes, while Daniel continued to type on his phone. He seemed to be texting several people at once. As they passed through a gate, under a Stanford University sign, Nessa said, "What was he attacked by?"

Daniel looked at her blankly; he seemed to have already forgotten.

"Your friend?" she said. "What kind of animal?"

"Oh, Thomas," Daniel said. "He was more like a competitor, really. 'Colleague' is the diplomatic term. He was attacked by a coyote. A pack of them. Which is weird, right?"

"Really weird," Nessa said.

"I guess coyote attacks on humans are getting increasingly common, especially in California."

"That's where he lived?" Nessa said. "Did he teach at Stanford also?"

Daniel laughed. "No," he said. "There's no department in the world that would have room for the two of us."

By that point, they'd reached the lab building, where they were greeted by the director of admissions, a tall woman in a business suit, and a tour guide, a perky admissions intern named Bailey. The director shook Nessa's hand professionally. "Nice to meet you, Nessa," she said. "While your father's teaching, you can get to know the campus better."

"Great," said Daniel. He looked at Nessa. "When you're done, we'll eat lunch at the faculty club."

Daniel rushed off to his class and the director of admissions, after asking Nessa if she had any questions, returned to her office. Bailey and Nessa started walking toward the center of campus. "I'm a sophomore," Bailey said. "But I've been coming here since I was a baby. My dad went here and his dad and his dad. So I'm the perfect person to give you the scoop. It sounds like you're coming in on the inside track also."

Gross, Nessa thought. It was nice to have her dad telling her she could afford to go here, but the idea that she was on an inside track? Nessa resisted the impulse to tell Bailey that her mom was a vet tech who was in jail. *How's that for inside?* she thought to herself.

"What's funny?" Bailey asked.

"Nothing," said Nessa, smiling. She looked out beyond the building they were passing into a grove of trees and suddenly wanted to lunge at the squirrel running up one of the trunks. *Uh oh.* That was the kind of thought that generally came to her when she was about to transform. Was she? Maybe she could ditch Bailey at some point and find some woods to run in before she had to get back on the plane to go home? She was lucky she'd made it all the way down without transforming.

Bailey led her through the library and showed her around the freshman dorms, but saved the most passionate and detailed comments of her talk for describing the personality types associated with each sorority on campus. Nessa half-listened, soaking in everything that Bailey wasn't pointing out—the students who looked like they were smart and had someplace they needed to be, the way the teachers inside the classrooms were laughing with their students and speaking to them like they were equals, not criminals in training one step away from their next suspension. The beauty of the buildings, the plantings, the idea that this might someday be a place she could live—it all combined to make Nessa feel dislocated but in a pleasant, pinch-me-I'm-dreaming kind of way.

She had been on the website, but somehow she hadn't realized just how large the campus was, how impressive it would be in every way. The swimming pool, the athletic facilities, the cross-country course, the laboratories, the dorms—everything was bigger and brighter and newer than Nessa had thought it would be.

When they dropped into a lab, a junior described her research assistant job. The girl seemed smart but also cool and down to earth as she explained that she was working on a research project creating a nanoparticle with a magnetic core that had applications in cancer therapy. Nessa couldn't believe she was only a junior. Her work sounded like something that she might have been learning about at Chimera. At the same time, she couldn't deny the second thought rising into her mind.

I could do that, she thought. *That could be me.*

"Okay," Bailey said as they were leaving the Bio building, tossing her long blonde hair over one shoulder. "Next I can show you the boat house, and I highly recommend that, because the guys on the crew team are totally hot. But my boss said you could also go see any professors who have office hours right now, like if you want to talk about your major or something."

Bailey extended an iPad with a listing of professors. She was pinching the pad between two fingers as if it might be leaking a toxic substance onto the ground and she wanted to be sure to keep any from spilling onto her shorts. With her free hand, she pointed with her thumb toward some trees. "The boat house is that way."

Nessa took the iPad, partially because it looked like Bailey was about to drop it. Who treated iPads like they were disposable? The Kurlands didn't even own one, even though Delphine had been dying for one since they first came out.

"You know, you've been really awesome," Nessa said. "But I kind of just want to wander around a bit on my own. Do you think I could borrow this?" Nessa asked the question just to make the girl snatch the iPad back. But Bailey shrugged.

"Take it," she said. "Even if you don't bring it back, I'm sure no one's going to say a word. You've got one of those gold stars next to your name in the book. Did your dad donate a building or something?"

Nessa laughed. "Hardly," she said, but then she had to wonder. Had he?

Bailey pointed to the iPad. "That listing's searchable," she said. "So just type in the topic you're interested in and if one of the professors here is an expert in it, you'll find out."

As soon as Bailey was out of sight, Nessa consulted the campus map. She scanned for any kind of area large enough for her to transform. But it was worse than she'd thought. The campus was a series of quads and lawns. There were trees, but there was nothing like the kind of space Nessa would need to run as a wolf. And beyond the campus, Palo Alto was crowded with houses.

She took a deep breath. Exhaled. Shuddered. Out of desperation, she opened up the search box and typed in "werewolf transformation."

It was a strange thing to do. She got that.

What was even stranger? That a name actually appeared.

A professor: Maxine Halliday, PhD, Assistant Professor of Anthropology and Folklore. Among her many areas of research listed, Nessa saw "Eastern European and Slavic werewolf traditions and mythology." Professor Halliday's schedule didn't show her as offering office hours that afternoon, but apparently she was giving an upper-level lecture, *Agrarian Legend and Ecological Truth in Post-Medieval Eastern Europe*, this very minute.

Possibly the most exciting combination of fancy multisyllable words Nessa had ever heard. And the building was in the next quad. Checking her phone to confirm she had time to get to the lecture before meeting her dad at the faculty club, Nessa took off at a jog.

As modern and up to date as the rest of the campus had been, the lecture hall for Professor Halliday's class felt like something out of the 1950s. The room was dimly lit, with leaded glass windows and wooden seats in rows descending steeply down from the door in the back of the room where Nessa entered. You could see dust motes in the beams of light. Professor Halliday stood at the front. Her blonde-gray hair was drawn back in a tight bun and she was wearing a tailored gray wool suit, black knee-high boots, and thick black-framed glasses. She spoke with an accent and looked up inquiringly when the hinges on the seat Nessa pulled down to sit on protested loudly. Even as Professor Halliday stared at her, Nessa could not read her expression. The lenses of her glasses were thick.

Professor Halliday returned to her lecture. "The variation in the 'cz' pronunciation village to village was reflective of geographic barriers as we have discussed . . . "

Somewhat disappointingly, the lecture had nothing to do with werewolves. Instead, Professor Halliday was describing Eastern European linguistic patterns—how words and grammatical structures evident in local languages testified to cultural traditions but were also possible to link with geographic land formation.

The lecture was dry and technical and would have been hard to follow even on a good day. Given Nessa's state of mind (or state of body? state of wolf?) it was impossible. She felt claustrophobic in the dry and dusty room.

When the class ended, a boy sitting three seats away from her closed his notebook and leaned over. "Are you new in this class? I haven't seen you before."

Nessa held up the iPad. "I'm just touring the school."

"Well, don't judge it based on this one class. I'm dropping."

"This late in the term?"

"Yeah." The guy had long reddish hair and his shorts showed off muscular legs, short socks, Pumas. A skateboarder? "It's worth it. She gave me a D on the midterm. She grades like the ghost of Nicolae Ceaușescu or something." Nessa didn't know who that was but he sounded mean, and she could tell she was supposed to laugh, so she did. "I only know who that is because she mentions him every other lecture even though he has nothing to do with the subject."

"You're generally *not* interested in," Nessa consulted the iPad and read, "'Agrarian Legend and Ecological Truth'?"

"Look," the skateboarder said, throwing up his hands in mock exasperation. "I only took this class because I needed humanities credits. But you get the feeling—" He rose to stand, leaning toward Nessa, his voice low. "You get the feeling that she actually believes there once were rat-headed kings and vampires and werewolves roaming the fields."

"Wow," Nessa said, as the skateboarder packed up. This was the first thing she'd learned in the entire lecture that actually sounded interesting. She looked down the rows of chairs to where Professor Halliday was sliding her folders and books into her black leather shoulder bag.

"Uh, thanks for the heads-up," Nessa said and trotted down the stairs to the base of the amphitheater, following Professor Halliday as she headed for the door behind the lectern.

By the time Nessa got to the bottom of the room, the professor had disappeared. Nessa charged through the door and caught up to her as she was exiting the building, heading back out into the bright blue afternoon. "Professor Halliday!" Nessa called, jogging a bit to catch up to her. The woman started to turn toward Nessa, the sun glinting off her glasses, which were the kind that turned dark when exposed to sunlight.

"I told everyone inside," Professor Halliday said, in an aggrieved tone. "There are going to be absolutely no extensions—" but something about Nessa made her stop short. She narrowed her eyes and let her words die on her lips.

"You're not one of my students," Professor Halliday said, making a statement more than asking a question.

Nessa held up the iPad as if it might explain her presence

on campus. "This says you teach about werewolves," she blurted out, and then, realizing how strange that might have come across, added, "a guy—I don't know him, but he was sitting next to me in your class. He said you believed they were real."

Professor Halliday shifted her briefcase from her left hand to under her right armpit. Nessa noticed the professor's gray hair was actually silver, and that she had kind, crinkly smile lines at the corners of her eyes. Nessa could just make them out behind the owlish shades of the professor's glasses—she was beautiful in the way of older European women in skin-care commercials. "Well," she said, exhaling. "It's hard not to when I'm standing face-to-face with one so obviously about to transform."

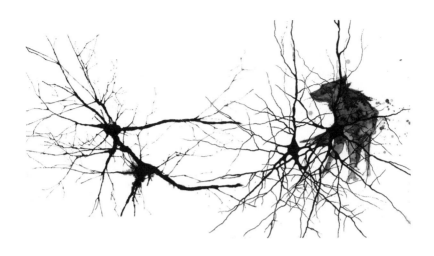

CHAPTER THIRTY-THREE

on't worry, your secret is safe with me," Professor Halliday said, smiling gently. "No one else would be able to tell," she explained. "You are emitting a pheromone I've developed the ability to detect. If you're looking for somewhere you can run, Palo Alto doesn't have a lot to offer, but there is Foothills Park. Just be careful."

"No," Nessa said. "I'm okay, I'm supposed to meet my dad in a few minutes anyway. I don't have time." She rocked forward slightly on her feet. Another prickly wave of nausea swept over her and she felt a soreness in her throat. Maybe she wasn't okay? She laughed. "I *think* I'm going to make it."

Professor Halliday looked up at the sky. The moon wasn't

visible but somehow Nessa knew that the gesture referred to it. "I guess you know yourself best," she said skeptically. "But I hope you'll get wherever you're going soon." She paused as if considering whether to ask a question that had just occurred to her. She must have decided to go ahead. "You're not a scientific wolf, are you?"

"A what?" Nessa asked.

Nessa saw the professor narrow her eyes. "You don't know what I mean?"

Nessa shook her head.

"Come, walk with me," the professor said. "Where are you headed? You said you have lunch plans?"

"I'm meeting my dad," Nessa said, feeling a little false calling him that, but not wanting to sidetrack the professor with a long explanation. "At the faculty club."

"Oh, okay," Professor Halliday said. "I'll walk you over there." Without missing a beat she said, "A scientific werewolf is someone who becomes a wolf not through a bite—as I'm assuming you did—but through injection. In some cultures, people who are to become wolves are raised with the knowledge that they will transform. But looking at you, I'd guess you probably were chosen by a wolf community. Is that right? Those two ways are how it has always worked in nature."

"So what's a scientific wolf?" Nessa asked. "They're not part of nature?"

"That depends on your definition of 'nature,'" Professor Halliday said. "But that's a debate for another day. I should explain. Starting in the nineteenth century, scientists began injecting themselves in ways meant to replicate the wolf bite initiation."

"They turned themselves into wolves?" Nessa said. "That actually worked?"

"No," said Professor Halliday. "Mostly it was a dismal failure. Best case, the scientists died immediately. Worst case, they died, taking others down with them."

"Brutal," Nessa said. "Why would they do that to themselves?"

"When someone's that curious about the world, about the human body, how could they possibly leave their best test subject out of the equation? That's the untold story of scientific experimentation, you know—scientists testing their experiments on themselves when they can't ethically experiment on other human beings." Gabriel's words from yesterday about testing on yourself reverberated in Nessa's ears. Professor Halliday cleared her throat and went on. "With tragic results. And this was no exception—the first injections were wolf blood, but after the discovery of stem cells, I've heard some scientists have created an infusion that is less . . . fatal. The wolf stem cell material works its way into your DNA without endangering your own human functioning. It spreads to each cell, taking over, like . . ."

"A virus?" Nessa asked.

"What?" the professor said. Her eyes narrowed. "You've heard of this?"

Nessa was thinking: Mom. Her father had said her mom invented a technique for changing DNA through viral technology—proteins designed to make targeted changes in subjects' DNA. Her father had said it was being used by scientists all over the world. Maybe her mom had helped to invent the mechanism used here?

Nessa ignored the professor's question. "Did you think I was a scientific wolf?" Nessa said. "Why did you ask me if I was one?"

"Only because I thought you might be looking for the antidote. That's mostly who's tracking me down these days."

"What does the antidote do?" Nessa said. "Turn you back into a full human?"

"No." Professor Halliday laughed again, as if at Nessa's naïveté. "It only suppresses the actual transformation. As long as you inject it monthly you will be able to keep from transforming into wolf form."

"Wow," Nessa said.

"Yes," agreed the professor. "It's like having HIV. All you need is a steady supply of AZT and you won't get sick. Of course, if you don't have the steady supply . . . "

"You start transforming again?"

"No. Then you just get sick. Your body can never transform again. At least not in any case I've ever encountered. You're lucky this isn't your situation. It's never good. And the only person I know manufacturing the serum died last year—I have my eye on someone else who might be able to replace him, but it's delicate. We haven't discussed it yet. I don't know if he stockpiles the serum or has even made it before, but if anyone here would, it would be him."

"I—uh—think I'm okay," Nessa said.

"Okay," Professor Halliday said. "So what can I do for you?"

Nessa hesitated. All this talk of transformation and decisions you could not take back—it was making her think of Luc. Maybe Professor Halliday could settle their transform-for-life debate once and for all.

"What would happen to someone who wasn't born a wolf but wanted to become one forever anyway?"

"You're asking about getting stuck?" It felt funny to Nessa to be thinking about this next to the manicured lawns, the sprinklers gently watering the uniform plantings in the flowerbeds. What she was talking about belonged in the woods at Tether—where tree roots were old and gnarled and snow clung to dead leaves matted into a frozen carpet on the forest floor.

"No, not stuck," Nessa said. "This would be someone choosing to stay as a wolf?"

"What about it?" Professor Halliday shrugged. "You stay in wolf form long enough, then you're a wolf. Some think that in seven years you get a choice to come back again, but I have never met anyone who has returned after that much time."

"I see," said Nessa. She swallowed. "But why do people born as werewolves expect it, but it's not okay for people like me?"

At a penetrating look from the professor, Nessa rushed to clarify. "I'm not thinking about this seriously. Just curious." The professor was still looking at her. "Very curious." Which of course made her sound like she was lying. "It's really a friend of mine who is thinking about this. I was kind of hoping that maybe he could do it for a month or so and then come back if he wanted."

"No," the professor said simply. "It doesn't work that way. You're in or you're out. If your *friend*—" (clearly she didn't believe Nessa) "—isn't sure, he shouldn't even think about crossing over. And now we've reached the club." Nessa looked up and sure enough, the building they were standing in front of was the faculty club, complete with umbrella-topped tables on a second-story terrace that was dripping with plantings. "Take this," said Professor Halliday. She fumbled in a pocket on the outside of her briefcase and fished out a business card. "I'm more than a little curious to hear your story. I collect stories like yours. And if you have any more questions, or just need help, I'm happy to be of service. To you or your . . . friend." She smiled knowingly and Nessa, not wanting to fight a losing battle, smiled back.

She was reaching for her phone to call Luc again—why hadn't he texted her?—when she noticed the time. She was late. She put the phone away.

Over lunch—Nessa didn't get past "bacon double cheese-burger" when scanning the menu—Daniel asked her how her morning had been. "Do you think it would be a good fit for you here? Or do you want to look at Yale? Princeton maybe?"

Nessa cocked her head to one side. She smiled, thinking about the idea of Yale or Princeton. *Yale or Princeton?!* She could get used to life with Daniel Host as a dad. "Not a good fit," she said. "A *great* fit. Better than I ever would have thought."

"Excellent," said Daniel. "I'm pleased."

Just then, the club's maître d' arrived. Daniel, who had collected the admissions office iPad from Nessa, passed it to him, asking if he'd return it, and then they began talking about the fish specials. Nessa felt her phone buzz in her pocket. Taking a peek, she saw the call was from Aunt Jane.

Please call.

Nessa excused herself and called Jane from the ladies' room, but to her surprise, it went straight to voicemail. Nessa checked the time stamp on the text. It had been less than five minutes since Jane had sent it. Nessa would try her again a few minutes into lunch, she decided.

But all during lunch, people kept coming over to her father's table to say hello, clapping her dad on the back, shaking Nessa's hand warmly. A lot of these people seemed to have important jobs in the university. She kept hearing the words "dean" and "provost," and when Daniel introduced her as his daughter, they would tell her how glad they were to meet her, how important her dad's research was. Each time, Daniel gave her a secret, friendly, but also modest smile. She didn't know if he was deflecting their praise or making a comment about how weird it was that he was calling her his daughter, this man who two weeks before she hadn't known existed. Either way, the smile felt honest and real. She was really starting to like Daniel.

And it was just plain fun to be the daughter of an important person. After Daniel told one of the deans that Nessa would be applying to schools the next year, the dean offered to set up a special meeting with the track coach for later that afternoon.

"Do you want to?" Daniel said to her.

Nessa did want to. She wanted to very much. She had met the Stanford cross-country coach once before at a recruiters' meeting and had trusted and liked him. But she also knew that if she didn't get back to Oregon pronto, she was going to explode. Already the slight nausea she'd been feeling that morning had intensified. Maybe it was the bacon double cheeseburger? The first few bites had been so delicious . . .

She had to call Jane. She'd gotten up twice to try to call her and both times had only gotten voicemail.

Daniel must have picked up on some reluctance in her expression, because he turned to the dean and said, "I think maybe another time," and within the hour they were back on the Cessna. Nessa didn't even try to hide how gross she felt as they lifted off into the air. "You going to be okay?" Daniel asked, glancing over in her direction frequently. "Want some Dramamine?"

Nessa shook her head. This wasn't motion sickness. She felt

nauseated, yes, but she also felt her throat closing up, the way Delphine's did when she was exposed to freshly mown grass. Only Nessa didn't have any allergies. And last time she checked, having your palms itch was not an allergic reaction.

"I think I just need to get some fresh air when we get back," Nessa mumbled. "Maybe I'll go for a run."

Daniel fumbled in a compartment and passed her a barf bag. "For what it's worth, you don't exactly look like someone who is up for running."

Nessa nodded, closing her eyes. She couldn't even hear the word "running" without thinking about transforming. She focused on the sound of the engine, repeating over and over in her mind, *I am in an airplane. I am a human. I am traveling with my father. I will not transform.*

She didn't know how she managed to make it through the flight, only that she did. When the Chimera Corp. forest preserve came into view, she thought she'd feel better knowing she was close, but the desire to transform only intensified. She could take only shallow breaths. The skin on her fingertips appeared to wrinkle, the way it might when you've spent too long in the bath.

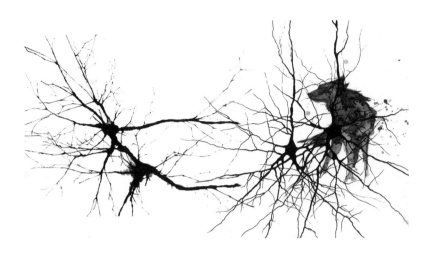

CHAPTER THIRTY-FOUR

hen the plane landed, Milton was waiting in the golf cart. Nessa thought all she would have to do was survive the five-minute drive to the house, but Milton was holding out a phone. "Nessa, your aunt has been trying to reach you," she said. "I promised you would call her the minute you landed."

"What is it?" Daniel asked Milton. He looked at Nessa and if she'd ever wondered if he cared about her, if he wanted to be in her life, she felt the last of that doubt removed now.

"I'm sorry," Milton said. "Your mother's gotten sicker."

Nessa took the phone from her hand. It was already ringing Aunt Jane's line, and when Nessa heard Aunt Jane's familiar voice, so much like her mother's and yet *not* her mother's—

the tightness in her chest kept her from speaking. She gripped the edge of the seat, her knuckles showing white from the squeezing.

"Nessa, I'm so sorry, but you have to come back," Aunt Jane said. She sounded flustered and scared. She wasn't even trying to maintain her usual "we grown-ups have this all under control" veneer. "She's being transferred to a higher level of care. Nessa, no one knows why she isn't responding to antibiotics. In the last twenty-four hours it's gotten so much worse. I'm starting to wonder whether she's being poisoned by whoever trumped up those charges."

"Oh my God," Nessa said, hating how Jane's listing Vivian's symptoms was only making her think about her own body, how she felt like she was going to either explode into wolf form soon, or die.

"Your mom says she is having a hard time breathing," Jane said, and Nessa felt an intensification of the tightness in her own chest. Was she only imagining it? She couldn't think. "I'm going to visit her but I can't get away until the weekend."

"I'll leave now."

"Okay," Jane said, taking a deep breath. "I wish I didn't have to go to work, but if I get fired, everything's going to get even worse."

"I understand," Nessa said. They made a plan for Nessa to fly home. Nessa would go immediately, and Jane, Delphine, and Nate would leave Saturday morning.

When Nessa hung up the phone, she turned to her father. "I have to go home," she told him. "Mom's getting really sick." She explained what Aunt Jane had told her.

"Of course," said Daniel. "I'll alert my legal team. We'll get

Vivian out of there. And I'll arrange for a flight back for you first thing in the morning tomorrow."

At the house, Nessa fast-walked inside, took the steps down to her room at a trot, threw on her running clothes, and shouted, "See ya" to her father, who was still standing in the foyer, looking through the mail.

"Uh . . . Nessa?" she heard him say, but she let the door click behind her as if she'd missed it. There wasn't time to explain. She just had to get far enough away from the house and the lab buildings so she could transform without the risk of being spotted.

But of course, Nessa knew she couldn't transform just anywhere. She had to get far away from the house and lab first. From the time she'd spent studying the map of the Chimera Corp. campus, she was pretty sure she knew what direction to head in—all of the buildings were clustered at the south-eastern edge of the park. The portions to the west and north had no buildings. The loop road went through, but for the most part the only markings on that end of the map indicated the existence of trails.

Just as she was about to leave the road and head into the woods, she heard the sound of a golf cart approaching along the road she was about to cross. The golf cart came into sight and stopped directly in front of her, idling in the center of the intersection and she realized that it was Gabriel behind the wheel.

He was dressed for running, too. Her brain, clogged with the effort of remaining in human form, could not quite connect the dots. If he *was* running, why the cart?

"Out for a run?" he said. Nessa's impatience was spiking but she held back from saying, *Stating the obvious, Gabriel?* At least out loud.

Nessa must have been making a face at him because Gabriel raised both hands in the air in a gesture of self-protection. "Sorry," he said. "I guess that's obvious. I guess what I meant was, want company? Your dad told me you'd gone out and I thought I'd try to catch up with you."

Nessa put her hands on her hips, grateful that the difficulty she was having drawing even breaths could be explained by the fact that she'd just stopped running. What had she ever found attractive about Gabriel before? Now he just seemed older and very . . . unwolf-like. She missed Luc. He was so much more . . . Luc-like.

"Oh," said Nessa. "That's cool." But actually, this wasn't cool. She had to go. She had to go now. And she had to go alone. "I'm running pretty long," she said. "You think you're really up for it?"

Gabriel drew back his chin. "How far?" he said.

Nessa tried to calculate how far she thought he could go. Then she doubled it. "Ten?" she said.

"I don't usually go past seven, but I guess I could try . . . " he started.

She shook her head. This was not going to work. "Look," she said. "It's—there's been a lot going on. I need some time alone. To clear my head." She smiled, trying to think about how Bree would say something like this without hurting Gabriel's feelings. But it was hard to think about this because she couldn't imagine Bree going on a ten-mile run and *not* wanting a cute guy to come along. (To be honest, she couldn't imagine Bree running ten miles period.)

"Okay," Gabriel said. "Fair enough. It's just—" Nessa couldn't think what he was going to say now. She was getting a chill standing here talking and she rubbed the sides of her arms. *Oh my God*, she thought. She felt something unfamiliar under her finger pads. Was that . . . fur? On her skin?

She had to get going. Now. "I'm sorry," she said. "I'm going to start cramping up if I don't get going." She started to move.

"Yeah, okay," Gabriel said. "Want to go hear music later?"

"Music?" Nessa called out over her shoulder.

"In town," he shouted. "There's this place."

She gave him a wave. She was booking now.

Had he just asked her out?

As she put another mile between her body and the spot where his golf cart had been, she wished she didn't feel so freaked out. She wished he hadn't followed her. She felt disloyal to Luc and gross because before she'd liked the feeling of his being interested in her and . . .

How had he even known to come looking for her? How had he found out so quickly that she'd gone running? She'd just left, shouting her plan to Daniel even as it had been forming in her mind. He'd been standing in the hall, casually sorting through his mail . . . had he radioed Gabriel immediately and sent him after her? Maybe Gabriel had already been dressed? Had been about to go? Had stopped by the house on his way out and just happened to drop in there the second Nessa had gone? Maybe Daniel had said, "You can catch her if you take the golf cart"?

Nessa didn't know and almost as soon as she'd formed the thought Nessa no longer cared. She cut into the woods, crashing through the brush and feeling the sweet relief of shifting into wolf form.

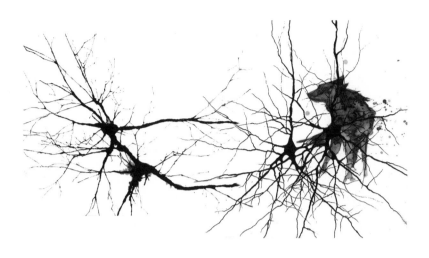

CHAPTER THIRTY-FIVE

As Nessa unfurled her clenched fists into paws, letting them sink into the loamy forest floor with each lunge forward, she felt herself breathing into the spaces between the pads. She felt like she was breathing into her own being. This was what was right. This was who she was supposed to be.

She didn't have a plan. She didn't have anywhere she had to be. She ran in circles. She chased her own tail. She breathed deeply for what felt like the first time in forever. She picked up a stick in her mouth and broke it in half, enjoying the way the bark felt against her tongue.

She had never transformed anywhere but the woods around Tether, and the change in the feeling of the ground beneath her feet, the smells of what was growing and what was rotting, the amount of humidity in the air—it was almost overwhelming. Nothing was familiar. Nothing felt exactly safe.

But at the same time, she could feel something sweet and promising in the air. Her wolf mind felt optimistic the way she did as a human when she smelled flowers. Lilacs. Lilies. Peonies. Roses. Bright and sharp and hopeful and smelling of who and what she wanted to be. She didn't think anymore, just tore through the open spaces between majestic firs, kicking up the inch-thick carpet of downed needles as she dug into her sprint. The sky was not yet dark, but the moon was visible. She could feel the power and the pull of it.

She felt it watching over her. It was the same moon that drew the wolf from inside of her when she was in Tether. Its cold, clear light shone honestly, the same on snow as on water, granting no warmth, only sight, a constant in an otherwise changing world.

Nessa felt her heart expanding, oxygen plumping hungry alveoli. Her heart was beating in time, playing the music she could dance to, her soul blooming, rising, singing, alive.

She came to the top of a rise. There was no view here, but the way the wind traveled, it gave her a chance to get some perspective on what filled this forest.

She smelled so much: squirrels, their trails, their discarded shells; birds, hawks, rabbits; colonies of ants chewing through plant matter; spiders spinning webs, flies caught inside them; water dripping off branches, seeping into rock; moss clinging to the effluence. Scat, skins, bark, resin, animals whose smell patterns she recognized only through ancestral memory, as they were long gone from the Tether woods—bobcat, lynx, panther.

There were animals whose smell made no connection to anything Nessa knew as a wolf, though they reminded her of animals she knew. One in particular reminded her vividly . . . of the meat she'd eaten on her first night with her father. What had he said it was? Venison. No . . . she suddenly realized. He had never said exactly what it was called.

But then she forgot about the meat, because she heard another wolf. Singing. A territorial marking song that sounded like a variant on the songs she and Luc had been belting out all winter long.

There was answering music—still miles away, not near. Then another wolf song. A chorus of barks. Triangulating the distance, using wolf brain functioning that no computer could quite match, Nessa determined the lay of the land: twenty wolves. To the northeast. She was not in their territory now, but she didn't want to take a chance of entering it. Not alone.

Nessa loped off toward the northwest. No wolves seemed present in this direction. Strange. That was not the way wolves worked. If there was land, they would hunt it.

Nessa came to a grove of trees that were larger than anything she'd seen in other parts of the forest. The trunks thick as four people standing together, taller than cathedrals, shooting straight up to the sky. But the massive, impressive trees were not where the power of this place lay. Within ten steps she could count hundreds of different shapes of young leaves, a dizzying number of species.

She took a swipe at the ground and saw a web of roots, and in between them the soil that was so much more than soil. She could smell but not see fibers and filaments and fossils and crevices left behind by the organisms that consumed them. Gases released by those absences and decay, a fruitful cocktail of time-rot-regeneration-residual humus, as unrepeatable and precious as the smell that lingered on her mother's clothes or the one memory of her father carrying her, waking her from sleep.

Nessa the wolf shook herself from head to toe to shed the pleasure of remembering and the pain of knowing how much had been forgotten. She was too old to climb back into everything she could half-remember. She was too young not to wish she could try. But she would come back here.

She sprang forward. She needed to see what else this forest had in store.

When she did encounter a human smell, it was faint and old. In Tether she might not have registered it at all. She followed it and found a track in the woods. She had no idea which one. She didn't know how far into the park she had come.

But where the trail crossed the stream, she looked up and saw an unnatural tree, which on closer inspection revealed itself not to be a tree at all, but a pole cemented into the ground, at the top of which was a camera. Nessa ducked away from its electronic eye. She knew she would not present anything unusual—there were already wolves in these woods. But what was the camera set up to follow, trained as it was on a series of holes in the ground from which she could sense the unmistakable odor of chipmunk emanating?

Wait, *were* those chipmunks? She took another sniff. Or black squirrel? She sniffed again. Or . . . something else? How could an animal smell like itself and like something else all at the same time?

The word rose into her mind. *Chimera.*

Spooked, Nessa's wolf body sprinted away from the chipmunk holes.

She crossed over a steep rise and down the other side of what seemed to be a cliff face, a rocky outcropping where she nearly lost her balance scampering down. At the bottom she encountered a streambed, water foaming and rushing over gray stones, dead leaves on the water's surface riding the current, eddying and rippling, then dragging the leaf under.

Nessa relaxed, again lulled into complacency by the magic of the place, the richness, the on-and-on quality, nature left alone to make its own rules, shape its own future. She ran and ran, traveling farther and farther north in the park, wondering how far she could keep running, stopping frequently to listen for the other wolves, the other animals. She wished Luc were with her. She wished they were running together as wolves, communicating questions without using words. She could just imagine the way Luc would lift an ear, looking long at whatever was making him suspicious. Wolves were not meant to travel alone, trying to decipher the tapestry of smells coming with every new gust of wind without help. Without each other.

Nervous now, Nessa redoubled her speed. By her calculations she could run for miles more before reaching the end of the property and she fully intended to. But she stopped short at the intrusion of a chain-link fence, twelve feet high, reminding her of nothing so much as the fencing surrounding the jail where her mother was being housed, reminding her of the fence surrounding the Paravida facility. Razor wire on the top and a sign posted to warn of electric current.

This fence, she thought, *this should not be here.* It wasn't just encountering something fabricated in such a deeply natural place. She remembered the map she'd seen in the lab—this fence had not been on it.

Following the fence's perimeter, she came to a gate and a road leading through it. Also missing from the map. At that very moment a vehicle approached. Nessa sank into the shadows, watching as the headlights materialized: a van emblazoned with the logo of Chimera Corp. It passed through the open gate. Nessa followed, keeping off to one side of the road, running under the cover of trees.

About a quarter-mile from the gate, the road terminated at a building—one that looked like a smaller version of the lab Nessa had toured with Gabriel and her dad. A pair of techs emerged from the van, walked around to open the back doors, pulled out some boxes, then entered the building. Nessa noticed that they were wearing what looked almost like armor—Kevlar vests, ballistic helmets with masks, thick gloves, heavy pants, and boots.

The second the door to the building opened, Nessa smelled something distinctly animal, though which animal she could not say. What would a pig be doing out here? An octopus? A snake?

After a few minutes the door opened again. The techs emerged. The boxes were gone. One of the techs was examining his sleeve. "Another tear!" he said. "That's the second time this month."

"I hate coming out here," said the other, sympathetically. "But you can't let it get to you. Do you wear the ear plugs?"

The one with the ripped sleeve shook his head. "I should. I know. You've told me."

They climbed back into the van and as they headed back down toward the gate, Nessa realized she had to leave with them or risk getting stuck when it closed. She ran, reaching the gate ahead of the van, watching the tech punch in a simple code into the pad—9653. She waited for the van to pass through, for the gate to close, and then she transformed back to human form. Nessa punched in the code on her own and left the enclosure herself.

Running back to the house, the sound of her footfalls seemed to beat the bushes, flushing her mother's voice out of the hiding place Nessa had assigned it to.

Please trust me. You can never contact Daniel Host. Never believe what he tells you.

Nessa hadn't listened to her mother. And now here she was miles from home, alone in the woods, alone with the knowledge that Daniel Host had a secret.

Nessa wondered: *Am I going to regret not listening to Mom?*

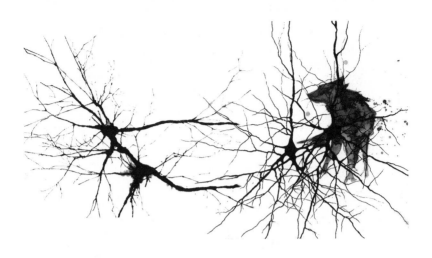

CHAPTER THIRTY-SIX

y the time Nessa returned to the house, it was nearly seven, the dinner hour. Her father wasn't in the living room, so she headed for the office he had mentioned but not shown her, in the back hall. She would have called his name to announce her presence but she wasn't sure what she would call him. She wasn't ready for "Dad" but "Daniel" felt wrong as well.

Nessa knocked lightly on his half-opened office door. When there was no answer, she pushed it open. The room overlooked the same view the living room did—the tippy tops of trees. She scanned the horizon line, looking out over the expanse of the park. Nothing. Nessa could look at it now without feeling her body contract in a spasm. But she also couldn't help but wonder: What was in that distant laboratory that had to be *more* secret than any of Daniel Host's other top-secret projects?

The same satellite-view map of the Chimera Preserve that Nessa had seen inside the lab was mounted on a wall across from her father's desk. Stepping toward it, she scanned the northern portion of the park, looking for some sign of the building she'd found in the woods, or the road leading to it. She almost wondered if she'd imagined it. The idea of a little building in the middle of the woods with a mysterious smell was something out of a fairy tale. Little Red Riding Hood, Hansel and Gretel, Snow White?

But no. She knew what she had seen. She hadn't imagined it—not the Chimera Corp. van, the techs in body armor. Nothing out of fairy tale legend there. She scanned the map, looking for the building. It just didn't make any sense. In the main lab area, every building was marked and labeled, no matter how small. But up in the northern portions of the map, it appeared as if no Chimera facility existed at all. Pulling out her phone, Nessa snapped a picture. She didn't know who exactly she wanted to show it to, but she felt like it was important.

In order to get the whole of the map into the frame, she had to walk behind her father's desk, and after she took the picture, she accidentally jogged his computer keyboard. The monitor on his desk lit up, and Nessa saw a newspaper article and headline.

Scientist, Nobel Laureate Thomas Raab Killed in California Woods

Nessa felt the air pushed out of her lungs.

Her father's "colleague" attacked by coyotes. The rival geneticist, such a big mind he couldn't share a university with Daniel

Host. He was Dr. Raab, the doctor running the experiments on Tether's children at Paravida?

And now he was dead?

"Nessa!" she heard, and there was her dad, standing in the doorway. "You're back." Was it just her imagination, or was there a tone of sharpness in his voice?

If there is, it shouldn't be surprising, Nessa thought. Here she was, sneaking around in his office. Feeling herself flush, she rushed out from behind his desk.

"I was just . . . uh . . . looking for you," she said. "And then I saw the map of the preserve." She pointed to the wall. "I was trying to figure out where I'd run."

"Oh, yes, of course," Daniel said. "And where *did* you go? You were gone for a while. You must have run far."

"I—" For about half a second, Nessa thought she would tell him where she'd gone. She should be able to trust him, shouldn't she? After all, he was her father. He wanted to help her. Take care of Vivian, take care of all of them. Send her to college. Why wouldn't she just come out and ask him about the other lab?

Don't trust him, her mother's voice said in her head. *Don't contact him. Don't touch that money.*

"It was just so beautiful," Nessa said. At least that much was true. "I went everywhere. Just all over. I found some trails in the woods. So many unusual plants. Animals we don't have in Tether."

"There're plants and animals out there you don't have anywhere in the world," Daniel corrected. He headed toward the window as if to scan the woods for them. "I think I was starting to tell you about this earlier. We use the forest to test how our chimeras do in the wild. Once nature takes over, the true miracles begin."

Nessa laughed without meaning to.

"That's funny?" Daniel said.

"No, it's just . . . well, it's kind of frightening actually," Nessa said. "It makes it sound like nature's going to take over. You know, wrap us all up in kudzu. Bring down another Ice Age."

"Oh, no, nature's definitely not winning these days," Daniel said. "There's a tipping point, where human-directed change overwhelms nature's capacity to absorb it. We're definitely reaching that point on this planet." Striding away from the window, toward the poster, he gestured to the wide-open space Nessa had just been studying on the map. "This part of the park is nature's last stand. That's why we need all thirty thousand acres."

"And all completely undeveloped, right?" Nessa added. "Other than the buildings around here, there's nothing?" She made sure to look straight into her father's face while she asked this question. What would his reaction be?

"Completely undeveloped," he said, his gaze steady, his tone sincere. She would never have known he was lying if she hadn't seen the building that afternoon with her own eyes.

But she had seen. He *was* lying. It took every ounce of Nessa's self-control not to shout out an accusation.

"I'm proud to have tracts of old-growth forest embedded in the preserve," Daniel went on. "Eventually I want all of it to return to that state."

Nessa heard her mother's words again. *Never believe what he tells you.*

"Won't that take centuries?" she asked.

"It will," Daniel said. "But you have to start somewhere,

right?" He walked around the back of the desk and laid a hand on top of the monitor Nessa had been reading. "You saw the story?" he said. "I saw you reading it when I came in."

"I knew him," Nessa blurted out. "I didn't realize when you were talking about it this morning that your friend was Dr. Raab."

"You . . . what?" Daniel said, losing his composure for the first time that Nessa had seen. "*You* knew him?" Daniel asked. "How? Did your mom—? No, that's impossible, he entered the field after she left."

"He ran a health study in Tether," Nessa explained. "On kids who were at risk for health problems from the Dutch Chemical contamination."

"Oh, I had no idea he was doing that type of work. How . . . noble."

"That's one way of looking at it," Nessa said. She didn't want to get into what Dr. Raab had actually been doing. To this day, when Nessa thought about little Billy Lark, the young boy in Tether who had died while Paravida "researched" the effects of the Dutch Chemical spill, she could just cry.

"Anyway," Daniel said. "I believe dinner is about to be served. I'm going to have to leave first thing in the morning— before you're up—so I want to go over some details about your mother's case tonight."

"Yes," said Nessa, leading him out of the study, taking one last look at the map. She looked again at the blank space where she'd spotted the second lab, where she'd smelled the mixed-up animal odors, where she'd seen what he was hiding.

What else was Daniel lying about?

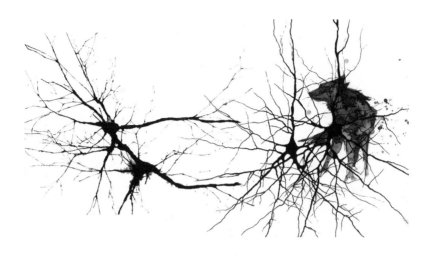

CHAPTER THIRTY-SEVEN

The next morning, Nessa's flight was set to leave at ten but she woke up like a shot at 6:15. She couldn't stop thinking of her mother, and what state she'd be in when Nessa and Jane reached her. But a thought kept pinging her about the secret building in the woods. Finding it had changed everything, and left her with more questions than had been answered.

Nessa slipped into her new running clothes and headed out into the preserve. This time, there was no Gabriel in a golf cart following her, and she wondered again if maybe her father had sent him after her the day before.

As soon as she broke free from the area surrounding the lab facility, Nessa allowed herself to transform. Even though she didn't technically have to, it still felt good—coming as a relief after the day before. She ran right for the northwest corner of the preserve. A small part of her brain hoped she wouldn't be able to find the secret building again, that she had imagined it after all, that if she did make it to the gate, the code would no longer work. Maybe then she could just jog back to Daniel's beautiful house, board his beautiful plane, and forget that any of this had ever happened?

But she did find the gate, quickly. Nessa transformed to punch in the code. It did work and there the building was, set off in the cleared meadow as she'd seen it the day before. Low, flat-roofed, white, glowing as if lit from within amid the waving grasses that were yellow in the morning sun.

The coast was clear—there was no van in the driveway, no techs carrying in boxes. There were two entrances to the building that she could see: the side door the techs had passed through and a set of stairs leading up the back of the building, where there was a setback second story and a deck.

Nessa approached the door she'd seen them pass through the day before.

She didn't know exactly what her plan was going to be and ended up taking the most direct and simple route: knocking. When no one answered, she tried the same code in the keypad there and found that it worked for the second time. She opened the door and found herself standing inside what looked like a suburban kitchen. An out-of-date kitchen that reminded her of the community kitchen in the basement of the church Vivian dragged them to on Christmas Eve.

A kitchen no one used. The counters were strangely empty— no toaster, no microwave, no jar holding spatulas and mixing spoons, no dish towel on the oven door, no magnets on the fridge. It didn't smell, even residually, of toast or spilled milk or old garbage or baking banana bread or chopped carrots.

Nessa heard the low sound of a television coming from another room and headed in that direction, stepping lightly to test for noise before putting her weight on the floorboards. It felt dangerous, entering what she had to believe wasn't a lab at all, but someone's home.

This was what her father felt the need to hide away in the park? Why? It wasn't like the other labs weren't highly secured. Why would he want to hide this totally innocuous church-basement-feeling boringness?

Suddenly Nessa heard a scream. Her heart began to race and she was running across the room before she heard the follow-up: applause.

A laugh track.

Music.

She froze in place. This was TV.

Breathing hard, she thought: *Maybe this is a secret R&R facility where all those Stanford-educated, type A lab workers come to pretend they have normal lives with kitchens and families and TV?*

Then she remembered the Kevlar body armor the techs had been wearing. The gash in one of their suits. This wasn't R&R.

Heading toward the sound of the television, Nessa left the kitchen and walked across a hallway that was set up to look like the center hall of a colonial house. There was a door, which Nessa tried only to find that it wasn't real—just a doorknob attached to the wall and some carpentry trim work to make it appear a door was there. On closer inspection, the light coming through the windows was fake as well. Projections of hedges, other houses across the way.

It's like a doll's house in here, Nessa thought.

Opposite the door was the staircase. Or what Nessa assumed was a staircase. She wondered if it led to the second story of the building. It didn't matter. The stairs had been completely blocked off.

Like a baby gate, Nessa thought, examining a barricade. A thick layer of plywood ran alongside the stairs floor-to-ceiling, covered in sheet metal, reinforced with chain link, closed with a chain and locked with a padlock that was about ten times larger than the one on Nessa's school locker back in Tether. Only the edge of the stairway banister was visible. *That's some baby.*

Nessa continued on, peering into what appeared to be a living room but, like the kitchen, was strangely unliving-room-like. The couch was made of what looked like rubber or plastic—something indestructible. The lamps were attached to the walls with metal bolts. And again, important smells were missing—no fires had burned inside the fireplace. No cheese and crackers had been laid out on the coffee table. Ever. The pillows had not been fluffed by human hands. The couch had not been curled up on.

Had she stepped inside a human-scale version of a dollhouse? Rooms designed to be inhabited only by plastic dolls, tables only ever laid with plastic food?

The sound of the television had grown louder, and by now Nessa could tell what the show was—*Keeping Up with the Kardashians,* something even Delphine disparaged. For a moment she considered transforming into a wolf for her own protection but then she thought better of it. She didn't want to scare the living daylights out of whoever (or whatever) was watching TV.

As she finally turned the corner into the room glowing blue from the TV's light, she was prepared for that room to be empty like all the others, the television just another stage prop for this unlived-in house.

But someone *was* watching it.

There was no door to the room—only bars like a jail cell, which Nessa thought was odd considering the room otherwise looked like it was styled for a little girl. It had white furniture, pink lampshades, ruffled curtains, a pink shaggy rug. There was a large picture window that looked out over the woods, buzzing with filtered green light. The wood paneling—bleached, reclaimed—gave the room a luminous glow that further obscured the recessed lighting and sisal carpeting.

The TV was built into the wall, behind Plexiglas fastened by large bolts in easy view of a white couch that was a perfect half circle with a high back and thick cushions. Sitting on the couch, her back to Nessa, was a girl.

A girl Nessa would have recognized anywhere.

It was Delphine.

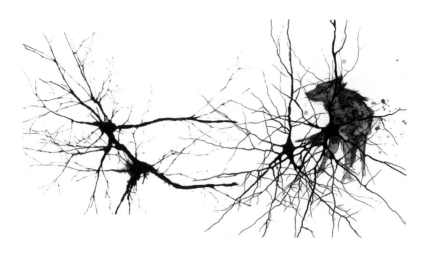

CHAPTER THIRTY-EIGHT

*I*t wasn't just the hair, braided the way Delphine had just started wearing it. Nessa would have recognized anywhere the way Delphine held her head when she watched TV—slightly cocked as if she were thinking. Or listening.

Nessa's brain was flooded with questions. Wasn't Delphine with Aunt Jane? Nessa had talked to her on the phone just the night before.

Did Delphine know Nessa was here? Why wasn't she turning around?

And more to the point, what was she doing here?

Just then, Delphine turned her head to face Nessa, and as she did, Nessa realized that something terrible had been done to her sister.

Delphine wasn't . . . herself.

Delphine wasn't . . . human.

From the back, all Nessa had seen was Delphine's long hair, braided in pigtails lying across her shoulders. With Delphine now facing her, Nessa could see that her sister had thick, spotted fur like a baby deer's on her lower face extending down her neck and chest, and as she made eye contact with Nessa, Delphine's ears unfolded and pricked at attention like a . . . bat's. They were located too far down the skull to *be* a bat's, but they certainly were bat-ear-shaped.

"Delphine, what happened to you?" Nessa said, hearing how faint her voice sounded, noticing that her knuckles were white where she was grasping the bars of the cage.

Who was this? When the creature stood, she was naked save for the fur that ran from just below her shoulders to just above her knees. On her left side, Nessa saw a human knee, a calf, an ankle, a foot, but the creature's other leg was the leg of an animal. Nessa couldn't identify which animal exactly but the knee bent the wrong way, and the calf—under fur—appeared to be composed mostly of sinew and bone, the way a deer's would be. Nessa couldn't imagine how this creature could walk, and as it took a step toward her, she saw that it couldn't. Not really. It balanced its swollen version of a human hand on the back of the sofa for support, dragging the human leg forward then swinging the stiff animal leg around. Nessa saw that the left arm was covered from bicep to a few inches below the elbow with reptilian scales.

What *was* this?

The creature leveled Nessa with a cold stare, peering

through blue, human eyes—eyes that belonged to Delphine—and with chilling certainty, Nessa realized: This was one of Daniel Host's chimeras.

What had he said? The "researcher's dilemma" was to hold back from using their own bodies as test subjects? Had that somehow extended to the bodies of his children—or the biological matter belonging to his children—to Delphine? There was never a better time, Nessa knew, to harvest stem cells than at birth. The umbilical cord was loaded with them.

As these thoughts made Nessa feel her brain was going to shut down, the Delphine chimera continued to move toward Nessa, its eyes fixed on her. It was only when it got close that Nessa realized how very large it was. About a foot taller than Delphine. A good head taller than Nessa. Its shoulders were broad, its chest broad. It bared its teeth, then shook.

Nessa's wolf senses were on high alert, telling her that it was better to be safe than sorry, that she should go. She could be a wolf in seconds, be running. But from what? She felt she needed to know.

"What are you?" Nessa said.

"My name is Delphine," the Delphine chimera said.

The voice alone was like a metal fork scraping a dinner plate. It was all Nessa could do not to cover her ears. Nessa tried not to show on her face how much she hated this thing, but she took a step backward as the chimera took another forward, and opened its mouth painfully to form another word: "Ness-aaahhh."

"What happened to you?" Nessa whispered back.

"Don't you remember?" the chimera said. "The fire?"

Nessa froze.

"Oh, God," she said, covering her mouth. How had this Delphine chimera pulled out a memory that Nessa didn't even have full access to?

It cocked its head as if listening to a voice Nessa could not hear, and Nessa shivered. Because she *had* remembered a fire. When she'd fainted in the lab, she'd had a glimmer of a memory. But now, that glimmer was taking full form.

Nessa's brain flashed to Vivian and her father arguing, Nessa and Delphine in car seats in their old station wagon, seeing his face looking down at her, billowing smoke behind him, flames in the distance.

The chimera version of Delphine had trouble closing its mouth. Each time it spoke, saliva drained out of the corner, perhaps because its teeth were an uneven mix of shapes and sizes. When the Delphine chimera waved both its hands in Nessa's direction, almost as if it were trying to spook her, Nessa saw that one of its hands was significantly larger than the other, and some fingers on each were furred and terminated in long claws.

"What fire?" Nessa said.

The Delphine chimera approached the bars separating Nessa from the rest of the room. "You know which one," the Delphine chimera said. "You were there."

Nessa shook her head. "I don't remember," she said, though that wasn't quite true. The Delphine chimera began to shake the gates, never taking its eyes off Nessa. It was coming to get her. Nessa had to run. There was nothing she could say or do to change the situation. The chimera had the mind of an animal, Nessa reminded herself. The way in wolf form she could only think in present tense. There was no conditional.

263

"You do remember," the chimera shouted, continuing to rattle the bars of its cage. "I know you do." Nessa heard a tearing sound, as if a wooden stud inside the wall had splintered. What looked like half-inch bolts that secured the bars to the ceiling were coming loose.

As the bars pulled out of the walls and the Delphine chimera lunged at her, all Nessa saw was the creature's mouth—the uneven teeth, the fur pulled back behind taut lips. Above the mouth, the familiar blue eyes of her own real sister were narrowed in disgust. Nessa's wolf instincts took over.

Nessa twisted as the Delphine chimera lunged at her side. She spun in the air and landed in a crouch, ready for the next blow. Somewhere while she was twisting, she'd become a wolf.

Nessa kept her eyes on its hips, as Luc had taught her, missing the feeling of the pack behind her, wanting nothing more than just to be home in the woods of Tether, knowing that she had her family to guide and protect her and all of the lonely craziness of this house in the woods was just a dream.

But it wasn't a dream. It took all of Nessa's cunning and sense of timing to deflect the blows and leap out of the way. She knew that if the Delphine chimera ever truly got hold of her, she'd be a goner.

The chimera's teeth dug into Nessa's flank, and Nessa bit the creature back on its deformed hoof. *Don't hurt her*, Nessa thought. But she didn't know where the thought came from, or why. Maybe because even though the Delphine chimera was attacking her, she looked enough like Nessa's sister that she couldn't bear to hurt her.

As she made her way through the house to the door, Nessa could hear her blood pumping in her ears. The Delphine chimera moved with fury and abandon while Nessa retreated, knowing that her only chance for survival was keeping her head.

Nessa saw with relief that she'd left the door of the building slightly ajar. Staying in wolf form, she was able to push her way through it, then sprint across the meadow that stood in for the lawn.

The Delphine chimera followed her outside but stopped herself a few feet from the building. Only then did Nessa notice the small flags planted in the lawn. Was this strange building surrounded by an invisible fence, barricading the Delphine chimera in like a dog?

Nessa was both grateful the Delphine chimera wasn't chasing her and guilty to imagine what a powerful jolt of electricity it must take to enclose a creature with the strength to pull steel jail bars out from the walls.

Nessa sprinted nearly all the way back in wolf form, transforming a few miles from the house and then running in human form the rest of the way.

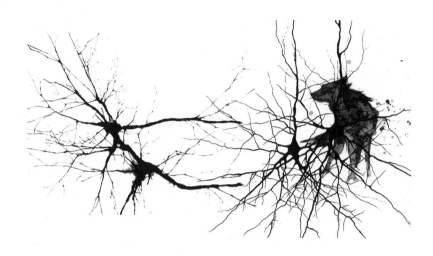

CHAPTER THIRTY-NINE

The closest airport to Tether was in Grand Rapids. After the plane touched down, Nessa disembarked, walking across the tarmac with Belinda. They said goodbye after Belinda was buzzed into what looked like a back door between two docking bays for airplanes. She pointed to a set of stairs inside. "Follow those," she said, wrinkling her nose as she smiled one more time. "They take you into the terminal and you'll be able to find your way from there."

Nessa's sneakers squeaked on the rubber matting on the stairs and the sound echoed against the cinderblock walls. Ambient noise returned once Nessa pushed through a second door into a crowded loading area—a flight was departing for

Miami and passengers were starting to board. Nessa took in the soft music, soft pretzels, soft neck cushions strapped to overloaded carry-on luggage. She felt like she had stepped back into reality after a dream.

Had she been to Narnia?

No. What she'd seen that morning was stranger even than talking fauns and evil queens.

Suddenly all she wanted was to get home. And not home meaning an air mattress on the floor of Bree's room. *Home* home. With Nate watching TV, Delphine tinkering on the computer, Vivian cooking dinner while talking to Aunt Jane on the phone. Nessa started to walk, scanning the overhead signs marked 'Exit', navigating her way through a crowd spilling out from a Fort Lauderdale flight that had just arrived.

Nessa felt her panic rising. She'd told Belinda that Bree was coming to get her, but in fact Nessa had only assumed this. The plan was unconfirmed. What if Bree hadn't seen her text? For the past few days Nessa had been able to relax in the protective custody of Daniel Host, where every need she might have was taken care of. Now she was returning to a world where every-thing was up to her.

She passed by the magazine shops, the ticketing counters, the baggage carousels, and then the automatic sliding doors automatically slid open and she was standing outside again, on the curb by the pick-up and drop-off zones. Nessa shivered. Away from Daniel Host's forest, the air felt dry and unnatural. She noted the casual litter blown up against the side of a bench and became aware of how much was paved here. She had the sudden urge to have all the buildings razed, the pavement jackhammered to sand, the entire state of Michigan returned to its primeval, forested state.

Get ahold of yourself, Kurland, she thought, pausing to put on her sweatshirt, shaking her hair from under its collar. *Deep breath.*

And then she saw it, about thirty feet up the curb: the Monster, beloved in its shabby enormousness, waiting faithfully, Bree at the wheel. *See?* Its presence seemed to be saying to Nessa. *You can do this.* Nessa headed toward it.

Bree looked great—she was wearing giant sunglasses with pink frames and had pulled her hair back into a ponytail, which bobbed with authority as she checked behind her before pulling into traffic. As Nessa sank down into the broken springs and worn velour of the passenger seat, pulling at the Monster's familiar if somewhat overprotective seat belt, it occurred to her she'd never even seen Daniel Host's car. But she imagined his seat belts were perfectly calibrated to make you feel like you weren't even wearing one. "Was it nice there?" Bree asked.

"Yes," she said. "It was nice. But I am very, very glad to be home."

Bree smiled, putting the car in gear. "Tell me everything," she said as they exited the airport, heading for the highway. "And I'm warning you. I don't want the stripped-down Nessa version. I want it all—detail, color commentary, the whole thing." Nessa laughed. "But first—are you hungry?" Bree went on. "My mom gave me money and there's a Starbucks at the rest stop. I have enough for us to split a Frappuccino."

"Yeah, about that," Nessa said. She pulled out her wallet, opened it to show Bree the ten crisp twenty-dollar bills Daniel had left with her (just for the trip). The cash had come in an envelope with the $500 Anthropologie gift card for Delphine (on the last night, at the end of dinner, he'd asked what she might like), and matching smartphones for both of them. "The Frappuccinos—plural—are on me."

They pulled off at the next rest stop and forty minutes later were still sitting across from each other at a small table under a skylight at the rest stop's café. On the table between them stood two spent Frappuccinos, the wrappers from two pesto-tomato-mozzarella paninis, and the last crumbs of a package of chocolate-covered graham crackers. Nessa had just finished describing her interaction with the Delphine chimera.

"Get OUT," Bree said. She slapped the table and pushed back her chair. "Your sister Delphine has a freaky, half-monstrous mutant identical twin clone?"

"She does," Nessa said, checking to make sure no one was listening before pulling on the last of her Frappuccino dregs.

"And your dad is rich and you get to go to any college you want?"

"Yup."

"Is your mind basically blown, like—" (Bree held her hands out to the sides of her head as far as they could go) "—this wide?"

"You got it," said Nessa, and she could feel herself smiling. The situation was crazy, yes, but she couldn't deny the fact that hearing Bree encapsulate it in her very Bree way made it seem slightly more manageable. Or maybe it was just great to feel that she wasn't dealing with all of this alone anymore.

"So," Nessa said, as they headed into the parking lot. "Did anything happen in Tether while I was away?"

She asked the question casually, expecting the answer to be no. After all, not much happened in Tether in general and she'd been gone for only five days. But then she caught the look on Bree's face. "What?" Nessa asked.

"I better tell you in the car," Bree said. "We have to be getting back or we'll miss curfew."

"But it's not even two in the afternoon. Have your parents gone crazy?"

Bree shook her head. "It's not my parents' curfew," she said. "There's a curfew on the whole town. Tether is on military lockdown."

Now it was Nessa's turn to feel like she was propelled backward in her chair. "How were we sitting there for two hours with me talking, and you never thought to mention this? Is this in the news?"

"It's all happened really fast," Bree said, shaking her head in disbelief as she unlocked the driver's side door. "News crews started arriving yesterday." Leaning across the bench seat, she flipped open Nessa's lock—the power locks in the car hadn't worked since the Bush administration. "It's so awful, Ness, I guess I wanted to wait to tell you. But okay, here's the deal. It's the wolves." She looked sideways at Nessa to see how she would react. "The curfew started yesterday. There are vans and vans of soldiers in town. Suddenly no one's allowed to leave home after dark or soldiers will pull you over and escort you home."

"Are the wolves okay?" was Nessa's first question, but she didn't give Bree a chance to answer. "And what soldiers are you talking about?"

"The National Guard," Bree said, then took a second to focus on backing out of her spot. "The governor called them, but they were only supposed to be here to give the police advice on what to do. Then yesterday, boom, they're everywhere! There's a meeting today at the school gym to update everyone. I don't know if you want to go? My dad thinks maybe the wolves did something really bad that caused the Guard to go into active mode, and they're going to tell us what it was."

"What does your dad think the wolves did?" Nessa asked.

"Go get me some gum first?" Bree said. Bree had pulled up at the rest stop's gas pumps and was pointing to the convenience store with her chin without answering Nessa's question. "I've gotta pump."

"Okay," Nessa said. After paying for the gum and the gas, she got back to the car. "Bree, you can tell me," Nessa said, leaning against the Monster's side, squinting in the harsh, clear light.

Bree lowered her glasses so she was looking over the top of them. Nessa could see her large eyes. Nessa had always wondered how it was possible anyone could have eyes that round, with lashes that long. "My dad said there's no way the Guard would have gotten involved at this level unless someone's been attacked. And killed."

"By a wolf?" Nessa said. She felt something shift inside her.

"Yeah. Dad said the Guard's probably not saying anything about it because they don't want to set off a town-wide panic."

"But Luc was saying he has things under control."

"Has?" Bree said. The pump clicked. The Monster's seemingly bottomless tank—Bree generally could afford to put only five or ten dollars' worth of gas in at a time—was finally full. Nessa had insisted on prepaying for a full tank with some of Daniel Host's trip money. Bree pulled the nozzle out, tapping it on the threaded rim of the tank to take care of any gasoline drips. "Or had? When was the last time you heard from him?"

Nessa didn't answer. She turned away from the car, taking the steps to the passenger door and feeling woozy. She hadn't heard from Luc in over twenty-four hours. She'd texted him from the plane and again as soon as they had landed, but he still hadn't replied. Was he okay? What if something was wrong?

Back in the car, navigating toward the highway on a series of rest stop merges, Bree spoke again. "You know, I saw him in town on Monday. He was in the library, taking out this huge stack of books, and he didn't look well. He hadn't shaved. He didn't look like he'd been showering much either."

"Okay," Nessa said, her gaze directed out the window. The trees in the woods were dotted with thin green leaves. One spindly sapling a good distance in had bloomed white. "I'll track him down. He's probably out at the cabin."

"Nessa, you can't go out there!" They'd reached a stop sign before merging back onto the highway and Bree slammed on the brakes as much for emphasis as for traffic rules. The Monster's overprotective seat belt nearly broke Nessa's ribs.

"Jeez!" Nessa complained, pulling at the strap.

"Sorry," Bree said. "But seriously, Nessa. Things are different now. You have to promise me. No running. Not in the woods. Not as a wolf. You're going to get shot, okay? It's not like it was before. You have to listen this time."

Nessa said nothing.

Cars were stopped behind them now, waiting to enter the highway, but Bree wasn't taking her foot off the brake. "Promise," she said. One of the drivers lay on the horn.

"Okay, okay," Nessa said. "I promise."

Bree gave the Monster gas. "I know you're going to end up

just doing whatever you want," she said. "And look, I trust you. But honestly, Nessa, this might be a good time to lay low and stay safe, let the Guard do what they need to do."

"Okay," Nessa said. "I'll keep that in mind."

As the Monster sped toward Tether, Nessa checked the texts on her new phone yet again. She'd gotten everything all set up on the plane, but the screen was so clear and the resolution so sharp . . . the pleasure of using it almost eclipsed the fact that there was still nothing from Luc. She scanned Bree's Instagram, asking questions to find out what Bree had been doing. Get-togethers. Breakups. Seniors were making their college decisions. Things felt normal again.

Sort of. Was Luc not texting her because he was busy? Or was he in danger? Did he know he might get shot?

The National Guard . . . this was serious. Were there going to be soldiers walking up and down Tether's Main Street? Nessa couldn't imagine it would be that bad.

In fact, it was worse. As Nessa and Bree crossed into the Tether town limits, they encountered the first of several checkpoints that had been set up by the Guard. Bree slowed the car and came to a stop in front of a roadblock reinforced by piles of sandbags. A woman in an olive jacket and pants ballooning out over black boots, with an assault rifle held in two hands, approached the car. "Are you girls Tether residents?" she asked. "If not, we're asking all traffic to detour around."

Bree pulled her driver's license out of her purse and showed it to the soldier, who took a long time scrutinizing it before handing it back, leaning in close to look them both in the eyes. She had slicked-back, short black hair, acne scarring on her coffee-colored skin, and an intense gaze. The soldier looked at

Nessa long and hard, and Nessa wondered if she knew she was looking into the eyes of a wolf.

"Is there a problem here?" Nessa said, meaning her voice to project confidence, but ending up with a burble of Frappuccino-fueled nerves instead.

"Just trying to get to know the residents," the soldier said, her eyes cold and aggressive in a way Nessa recognized from the woods. Without breaking her gaze, the soldier stepped away from the car and patted the roof of the Monster to let Bree know she could pull away.

"Jeez, be careful," Bree said. "You don't want to call attention to yourself."

Nessa knew Bree was right, but she stayed quiet until they were almost at Tether's downtown. "That meeting?" Nessa said. "It's happening now?"

"Yeah, 'cause they want everyone to be able to get home before dark."

Nessa shifted under the seat belt one more time. "Okay," she said. "I think we should go."

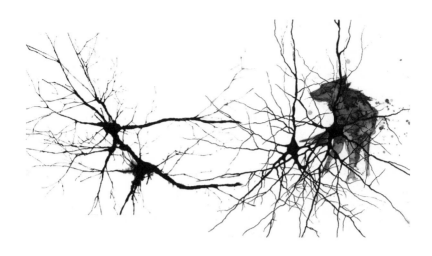

CHAPTER FORTY

The parking lot at the high school was packed. There were cars and pickups all the way to the edge of the soccer field, blocking access to the dumpsters, and on the grass near the turnaround where the school buses generally picked up and dropped off.

Nessa and Bree had to park the Monster on Ferris Street, more than four blocks away. As they approached the main entrance to the school, they saw that the attendees weren't just Tether locals—several news vans were parked outside the school doors, their satellite dishes and antennae ready to project the video feeds of the proceedings to televisions across Michigan.

"You think this will make the Detroit news?" Nessa asked Bree.

"Nessa!" Bree said. "Small-town America has been overrun by aggressive, oversize wolves? This is going to be on the news all over the world."

Nessa remembered the reporters outside her mother's bond hearing. She was glad she'd thought to put on a baseball cap in Bree's car. She pulled the bill down low over her face. She tucked her hands into the ends of her sleeves, too—as if that would do anything to keep her identity secret. She hunched her shoulders and tried to look small.

As they passed through the vestibule and into the gym, Bree, always energized by a crowd, threw back her shoulders and lifted her chin, scanning the room, pushing her pink sunglasses up onto the top of her head, tightening the knot in the plaid shirt she'd tied around the waist of her jeans. She waved at Andy Carlisle who was sitting with a group of other kids from their grade on the top row of the bleachers. After spotting them, Nessa was quick to look away. She didn't want to be seen.

But no matter where her eyes traveled, she saw people she knew: kids from school, neighbors, distant cousins, a group of Delphine's friends, owners of animals Vivian had treated in her garage clinic. Then Nessa's eyes landed on Luc.

So he *was* alive!

It was all she could do not to run across the room waving her arms and shouting his name. But she held back, contenting herself with staring at him, willing him to glance in her direction.

He was leaning against the wall by a side exit, one foot up behind him so a knee stuck forward. He had his hands in his pockets, staring forward, eyes unfocused, his straight black hair falling forward over his ears. She could only imagine how much he was hating this whole show. He didn't like a) large groups of people and b) controversy. When teachers tried to get debates going in class, he'd slide down in his seat and shoot his feet forward under his desk, crossing his arms across his chest to let the teacher know: "Even if you call on me, I'm not really taking part."

What is he even doing here? Nessa wondered. If he was alive and well, why hadn't he texted? She remembered Bree's description of him coming out of the library, unshaven, carrying a stack of books.

Come to think of it, wasn't that the same shirt he'd been wearing on Friday, when they'd said goodbye?

Up on the dais, she saw Tim Miller's dad, the mayor. She saw Cassian's dad. She wondered if he was up there because he was representing Paravida. There was Principal Sarakoski. There were two older men with short hair and no-nonsense glasses. They were dressed in uniforms—Nessa assumed they were officers from the National Guard. They were conferring, and Nessa could just make out some of the words: "get started" and "at capacity." Then, clearing his throat, one of the guardsmen called the meeting to order.

"Okay, thanks all for coming. I won't waste your time with introductions, just ask that the lights be dimmed if that's possible. I think there's something you all need to see." A screen descended behind him.

A projected image showed a satellite view of the area around Tether. Nessa could see the spiky tops of bare trees, the fuller masses of evergreens, neat squares of farm fields and pasture, black twisting roads and silver rooftops glinting in the day's bright sun. *This day's* bright sun. Unlike Google Street View, this wasn't showing a picture taken months before. This was live—the trees in the map were the same degree of not-yet-leafy early spring.

The map was dotted with red circles, many of them moving, collecting, dispersing. Nessa thought of movies she'd seen where sharpshooter assassins would use beams like these to line up a shot.

"I think that's the map my dad told us about," Bree whispered. "The one that tracks wolves by their body heat."

"Oh, right," Nessa said, remembering Ted describing the meeting he'd gone to back when Nessa had first started staying with Bree. It seemed so long ago.

"There's so many of them," Bree said, under her breath.

She's right, Nessa thought. The red dots could have been stars in the night sky. How many had the Guard estimated before? Seventy? Now it looked like at least a hundred. Nessa noticed something else about the red dots, too. "Bree, look," Nessa whispered. "Do you see anything going on there?"

"Uh . . . a lot of red dots?" Bree whispered.

"Look at the groupings." Nessa pointed out what she was seeing—a few clear clusters had begun to emerge. There were a few to the east of town, bordering the state land and grouped on either side of the river, others toward the south, past the farm fields where there was more undeveloped land. There were even a few north of Tether, near the Paravida facility. "They're forming packs."

"You're right," said Bree. She pointed to the river. "But look at what happens when they go in the water."

Bree drew a line with her finger and Nessa saw that when the eastern wolves reached the river, they vanished from the map. An entire line of wolves began crossing just then and Nessa watched the red dots approach the water, disappear as soon as they entered it, and then show up again on the other side.

"The water must be freezing," Bree said. "At this time of year, it's all snowmelt. Maybe their body temperatures drop?"

"Could be," Nessa said.

Just then, a man in the audience stood. Nessa knew him—it was Mr. Wood, who ran the hunting and fishing club as well as the local chapter of the National Rifle Association. He had white hair and a white beard. He was wearing a camo flak jacket and work boots. "I just have one question," he said. "If you're saying all those red dots are wolves, how is it anyone still thinks they're endangered? Rather than sitting around here doing nothing, why don't we get out there and do something about the problem? I don't want to lose my hunting license, but I'd consider it a privilege to hang a wolf hide on my trophy wall."

There was immediate cheering in the room. Nessa glanced at Luc. She could see by the way his shoulders were bunched up around his ears that the cheering was like fingernails on a chalkboard to his ears. And suddenly Nessa thought she understood why Luc had come to the meeting in the first place. He was here for the wolves. He wanted to learn everything he could so he could better protect them. But how? Was he going to say something? He would be just one voice, and a kid's voice at that. Few people knew him. His family had lived in Tether barely a year.

She felt pain in her chest, thinking about how helpless Luc

was. How helpless she was, too. Especially in contrast with her dad. Visiting him, she'd seen what wealth and power looked like. It looked like a few phone calls that could change the course of a legal battle or her future.

Luc still didn't seem to have seen Nessa. His attention was focused entirely on the dais, where the guardsman presenting the map rocked back on his heels, his hands clasped in front of him, his arms held low. Nessa's attention was pulled away from Luc by the shrill voice of a woman in the audience, calling out, "What about Vivian Kurland?"

Nessa felt her back stiffen. She'd been keeping herself hidden underneath the brim of her cap, but now she nearly pulled it off as she found the source of the comment. She felt Bree's hand on her arm, holding her back from rushing into the crowd. Bree was right. She didn't want to rush the crowd. Nessa contented herself with a growling, "Not this again."

Bree shook her head. "But look who it is," she said. "Who cares?"

Bree was right. The woman who had spoken was someone Nessa knew from Dr. Morgan's clinic. Her name was Susan Moddaugh. She wore her thinning hair in a topknot and had on a sweater that looked older than Nessa—its embroidered flowers were unraveling. Bree sighed and leaned to whisper to Nessa, "Isn't she the one with the cat colony in her backyard?"

"Dr. Morgan said she's crazy," Nessa whispered back, remembering how Vivian had told Nessa that Susan Moddaugh fed the cats even though she could barely afford to feed herself. But she saw the cats as her mission, and Vivian's mobile spay/ neuter clinic had basically been her mortal enemy.

"Vivian Kurland's clearly the problem," Susan Moddaugh

was continuing. "She did something to these wolves. She always told me my cats were getting an unnatural advantage but she was the one making the wolves unnaturally strong." She fished out a newspaper clipping from her purse. "See, it says that right here in the newspaper!"

"That is so unfair!" Nessa hissed to Bree. "It was Paravida!"

Bree's hand on Nessa's arm increased in pressure. "Don't react," she said. "Most people don't think your mom had anything to do with this. They're not stupid."

As if to prove Bree right, the man whom Nessa recognized as the manager of the grocery store stood. Nessa remembered that he'd brought his dog to Vivian's informal garage clinic the night his dog had been hit by a car. "None of that's been proven," he said. "I've known Vivian Kurland for years. I don't see how she could have done what they're saying she did."

Another voice shouted from the crowd, "Vivian Kurland is one of us."

Up on the dais, Cassian's father stood, flashing his handsome smile. "Now, Susan," he said. "Let's leave poor Vivian Kurland out of this. What we have to do now is eliminate the threat. As you know—" he said, as he looked out to the room at large, "I'm representing Paravida here tonight and they've very generously offered to install electronic surveillance equipment outside every home in Tether. They're also going to be delivering food and drinking water to any of us that requires it. Pet food will be part of their emergency supplies. I think that ought to make you happy. I think we can all agree these measures are the kind of forward-thinking action that will help us get started in returning things here in Tether back to the way they used to be."

There was cheering again in the room. Mr. Thomas held up his hands in a gesture that showed that he appreciated the response, though he couldn't take credit for Paravida's actions personally.

But then another man in the crowd spoke out. Nessa could see just the back of his head, but saw that he was looking at notes on a notebook held in one hand as he did, and Nessa *did* recognize that notebook. And then she recognized the man's gray, bushy hair. When he turned she remembered that he had a bushy moustache as well. It was the reporter she'd seen at her mother's hearing, the one who scribbled on a paper rather than accosting her for comments from a news van. The one who had talked to her that day in the coffee shop and explained why Nessa wasn't going to be able to hire a lawyer to help her.

She'd run away from him when he started to pump her for information about the connections between her mother's work and Paravida. But now, after her visit to her dad's, she wondered: *Maybe these are the questions that most need to be asked?*

"That's him!" Nessa whispered to Bree. "He writes for the *Saginaw Sentinel*."

"He does?" said Bree. "They're famous. They win Pulitzers even though they're only this tiny paper."

"Mr. Thomas," the reporter said, "since you are Paravida's representative here at this meeting, I wonder if you can provide a comment from the company on the record. I have received information suggesting that the wolves menacing Tether were in fact bred and genetically altered not by Vivian Kurland but by Paravida, as part of ongoing organ transplantation research. I have also heard that they were released accidentally by the company last fall. Is this something you can confirm?"

Mr. Thomas lifted his hands as if in self-defense and started speaking, but his words were drowned by a roar of boos and yells from the crowd. When the noise finally died down, Mr. Thomas looked at the National Guard officers as if to ask for assistance. One officer gave a subtle nod—his face had remained impassive all this time. Flashing his handsome smile again and taking his seat, Mr. Thomas said, "I've never heard of anything more absurd."

The officer stood and the room instantly quieted in the presence of his cool authority. He waited until things were quiet and then he started to speak.

"The 'Tether Wolves,' as they're being called," he began, "are an active threat. They are not related to medical research. We're tracking them coming in from the north. We don't yet know if they are a new, emerging species of wolf, or if they are the offspring of particularly large and powerful animals, which is also a possibility."

The room was silent as everyone in the audience strained to listen to the officer.

"Someone asked about hunting. At this time, there has been no alteration to the hunting ban against wolves, and we strongly advise all hunters to stay at home. These animals are smart. You might think you are hunting them, but from what we have seen out there, the likelihood is that they are hunting you."

This statement produced a different kind of noise from the audience. Less boos and cheering and more the sound of people speaking to those near them in the room.

One of the reporters who had moved to the front of the room approached to ask a question, her cameraman right behind her, shining a light in the officer's face. Nessa was so busy listening to all the confused conversations taking place among people in the crowd that she hadn't trained her hearing on the reporter's question. After Nessa saw the impact it had on the officer, however, she wished she had. He frowned, shook his head, and blanched slightly.

Enough people around the reporter had noticed what Nessa had, and turned to shush their neighbors, that when the reporter repeated her question the room had quieted enough so that everyone could hear. "Do you believe the wolves are responsible for the deaths of six Paravida workers late Monday night?" the reporter asked.

For a minute, the room was entirely silent.

The National Guard officer was entirely silent.

Then, as if on cue, the room immediately exploded in reaction, everyone speaking at once. Bree had both hands grasping Nessa's upper arm. "Oh my gosh!" she said. "My dad was right!"

But Nessa was barely aware of the reactions around her. She was looking at Luc. He still did not appear to have seen her. He was staring directly at the floor, his eyes on the polished boards of the gym as if he was reading something written there.

Because of her wolf hearing, Nessa was able to pick up a private conversation taking place on the dais—Luc could too, she was sure. Covering the microphone with his hand, Mr. Thomas was saying to the officer, "I thought we weren't going to release that information."

"That was before we got asked a direct question about it," the officer replied. "We need these people to keep faith in us. To listen to us. We need them to stay home."

As the officer and Mr. Thomas continued to confer on the

dais, the chatter—and the outrage—in the room was getting louder. Nessa heard people saying things like "We can't let the kids out, even in the yard" and "I'd thought I'd be safe as long as I was in my car, but now I don't know . . . "

A couple of Tether residents stood, shouting, "Was anyone planning on telling us this?" and "We need a plan!" Their voices became lost among the general noise, all of it rising toward the gym ceiling, the room reverberating with sound the way it did during packed basketball games in the winter.

Turning to face the townspeople, the officer put a hand out to block the camera's light and the second Guard officer approached the front of the platform to stand beside him.

Nessa instinctively recognized the power of this other man.

Though both men were tall with close-cropped hair, the officer who came forward now had a slightly smaller build. Nessa noticed that his chest was covered with a solid two inches of ribbons.

"We're asking that everyone remain in their seats," he said. His voice had a special authority and the room quieted slightly. "Please have a seat," he said again, and a few did. "Settle *down*," he repeated, and the room settled. Nessa thought: *Alpha*.

"I believe the families of the men killed in the attack on the Paravida van are still being notified," the new officer began. "Some were harder to track down than others and Paravida asked that we not announce their names until then. But yes, the report is true. A van transporting a team of six scientists into the Paravida facility was attacked late Monday by a pack of wolves."

The sound of one person's cough echoed in the otherwise

silent space. Nessa felt the hair rise on the back of her neck.

"My dad is going to freak out," Bree whispered.

"The attack took place at night," the guardsman began, "on a Paravida access road. We are actively investigating several key features of the attack. Any information you all can provide might be of great value, especially if you were an eye witness."

The reporter who had asked the original question stepped forward again. "I have a source who suggests that some elements of the attack imply human involvement. Can you speak to that?"

The officer shot a look of annoyance in Mr. Thomas's direction, then resumed speaking in his calm, measured way. "I cannot speak to that as the attack is currently under investigation. What I can tell you is that the attack involved knowledge of human technology, understanding of its vulnerabilities and how to exploit those vulnerabilities, as well as a desire to kill for sport rather than sustenance."

"What are you saying?" shouted a man from the audience.

"When were you all planning on telling us?" a woman's voice joined in. "My kids can't walk to school—now I can't even drive them?"

The officer remained calm and steady. Nessa wondered if he spoke so slowly and carefully to hypnotize the crowd to a calm.

"A tire on the van showed signs of tampering. We believe that when the driver of the van stopped to inspect the flat, a pack of what we estimate to be twenty wolves overwhelmed the passengers who remained inside at the same time they ambushed the driver."

Mr. Wood was standing again. "Were they armed?" he

asked. "I never hunt without a pistol for self-defense when your rifle fails you. They might have wished they'd done the same."

The officer swallowed, waited for Mr. Wood to finish speaking. "The scientists were armed and I believe trained in the use of the weapons they were using. A few wolves were killed on the scene and some died as they ran away, but for the most part, the forensic evidence suggests that those in the van did not have much time to defend themselves."

Nessa felt her own insides churning.

"Nessa, is that possible?" Bree said. "Could the wolves know how to give a van a flat tire? Could they track it down?"

"I don't know," Nessa whispered.

"Do you think Luc—" Bree stopped. "I mean, Nessa, you said he's been working with the wolves?"

"Helped them *murder* six people?"

"Of course not," Bree said. "I forgot about the murder part."

Bree put a hand on Nessa's shoulder to indicate there was something happening on the stage. Nessa saw the reporter with the notebook—he'd told her his name before but she'd forgotten it—was waving the pad to get the guardsman's attention. He looked like someone's dad—or grandpa—shouting at the ref from the sidelines of a kids' soccer game. "I heard the same reports about the van," he said. "But I have sources who indicate that the van was carrying not Paravida scientists, but security personnel, sent in to eliminate the wolves. Can you confirm that this is true?"

The officer made a show of laughing a bit here. "Soldiers for hire?" he said. "Why on earth would Paravida be sending in soldiers for hire when the National Guard is already on the scene? No offense to whatever outfit you might be referring to, but no private fighting force is going to be able to match the National Guard in terms of technology, personnel, firepower, and training."

The officer looked at Mr. Thomas, who nodded with authority.

The journalist waved his notepad in the air for emphasis. "Can you comment on an internal memo, leaked to me by an undisclosed source, that stated the Paravida mercenaries were in fact regular Paravida employees who had served as guards while these same wolves were being bred in captivity and were believed to know the animals and how to capture and kill them?"

By now the officer was red in the face and sputtering. "Are you calling me a liar?" he said.

"Not at all," said the reporter, his voice calm and even. "I'm just wondering if the deaths of these Paravida security guards might be linked to allegations of wolf abuse on the Paravida campus made last April by People for the Ethical Treatment of Animals? According to a Freedom of Information Act request I filed last month, accusations filed with the Animal Welfare Society of Michigan were never investigated by Michigan courts or by state law enforcement. I think it's highly coincidental that Paravida's name is involved at both ends of the story of these wolves in Tether. I wonder if anything is being done by the National Guard on the investigation end?"

The reporter had barely gotten the words out before he was roundly booed by the people sitting around him. A woman cried out, "Did you not hear? Those wolves are murdering people in cold blood!"

Someone else shouted, "If Paravida's bringing in soldiers to fight them off, good!"

Mr. Wood stood up on his chair. "The only good wolf is a dead wolf!" he shouted.

"Dead! Wolves! Dead! Wolves!" someone called out and he was almost instantly joined by others. The room seemed to rock and pulse with the cheer. People were stomping their feet. "Dead! Wolves! Dead! Wolves!"

Nessa felt her ears burning and her fingers start to twitch. She willed herself to stay calm, but her wolf hearing picked up the tiny hissing noises people were making when they got to the "-s" of "wolves," the spray of spittle collecting in the corners of their lips, their moist tongues sucking against the back of their teeth. She could hear the squeak of rubber sneaker bottoms on the highly polished wooden gym floor, the ping of loose change and key rings jingling as the stomping moved the contents of people's pockets.

A man near Nessa turned to his companion and said, "I knew a guy once, kept one of those wolf-dog hybrids. You know how a dog will come barking at you when you get up a driveway?" The other man must have nodded because there was a pause before the first man went on. "This wolf-dog creature didn't do that. He managed to get himself up on that guy's roof and once he was up there he didn't make a peep. When you came up the driveway he wasn't warning anyone. He was just waiting for you to get close so he could kill you."

Nessa wanted to turn to the man and shout, "Do you know what humans have done to wolves?"

By now, both National Guard officers were standing at the front of the stage with their hands up, trying to quiet the crowd, but the people of Tether weren't having it. Nessa knew this wasn't rational, but she worried the noise they were making would somehow flush the wolves out of the woods. She looked up at the screen, watching the red dots move. What did the collection of swirls and eddies mean? How had the wolves managed to put a hole in the van's tire? *Had* Luc helped them?

Nessa glanced in his direction only to see that he was gone, the space where he'd been standing empty as if his presence had left a cloud no one was willing to penetrate.

How long had he been gone? How much had he heard? Nessa pushed through the crowd that had come in behind her, keeping her head low so as not to be recognized.

A few seconds later, she was standing on the front steps of the school, scanning the parked cars sparkling in the late afternoon sun. There was no sign of either Luc's truck or his tall form slinking off toward the woods or lounging on the steps, as she'd half-hoped she'd find him, waiting for her.

Had he seen her? Had he left anyway? She'd been texting him for two days. Why hadn't he replied?

All the feelings Nessa had been doing such a good job of keeping at bay descended on her. Her town was imploding, her mother was in the hospital, wolves were murdering humans, and if she wasn't careful, she herself was in danger of being shot. Without Luc—loyal, unflappable Luc, her partner in the woods, the one person who knew her as a human and as a wolf—how was she supposed to take any of this on?

She didn't realize Bree had come to stand at her side until she spoke. "We should go home," she said, her voice low but serious. "Nessa, I know a lot of things are safe for you that aren't safe for me, but right now, you have to come back with me. I'm sure Delphine and Aunt Jane are worried."

Nessa knew Bree was right so when her friend said, "Come on," she felt herself following her down the steps, covering the blocks near school until they reached the Monster, climbing in. She heard herself talking to Aunt Jane over the phone, saying she had arrived safely and discussing the time and place they would meet on Saturday.

Nessa talked to a legal assistant from the firm Daniel had hired to represent Vivian—Vivian had been transferred to a civilian hospital that afternoon. Her lawyer was sending a car to pick up Nessa in the morning.

Daniel had texted and left Nessa a voicemail on her new phone, but every time she saw his name she couldn't help but think about the Delphine chimera hidden in the woods. She did not reply.

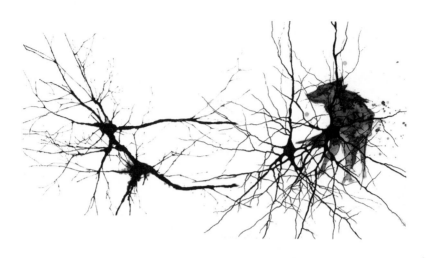

CHAPTER FORTY-ONE

s Bree and Nessa settled in to go to sleep that night, Bree started catching Nessa up on what break had been like in Tether. "I can give you one word," Bree said. "The most boring break on record."

"That's like . . . a lot of words," Nessa pointed out.

"Okay, I lied," said Bree. "Honestly, there are a lot of words I could use to describe the desolation to my social life that is the town-wide curfew but that might be the only thing *more boring* than living in a town with a town-wide curfew. With the exception of that meeting—which was no fun, by the way—we've all just been trapped inside doing nothing." She punched her pillow and rolled over to face Nessa. "You know how Simone Clarke was bragging all month that her parents said she could have a party in her basement and they promised not to even come into the kitchen—she could have complete privacy as long as no one drove home drunk?"

"Yeah," Nessa said.

"Well her party was yesterday and you know what she had to do? It was worse than having a party with your parents around. She had to have a . . . brunch."

"Like, they made breakfast food and stuff?"

"Her parents were like, 'You can still have the basement'!" Nessa snorted.

"None of the boys even went and it ended up being just a bunch of girls sitting around eating bacon and giving each other pedicures."

"Was that fun?"

"Actually, yeah. Simone's dad makes really good muffins . . . but still, Nessa. Muffins. Do you know how hard it is to carry on a flirtation with Andy Carlisle when all I'm doing is hanging out with a bunch of girls, eating muffins?"

Nessa laughed. It was so nice to feel like just a normal person for a minute, to forget that earlier that morning she'd been running through a forest as a wolf, confronting the dark parts of the forest, thinking that maybe that was where she belonged. She started to say something about that to Bree, but then Bree started telling her about Andy Carlisle. "It should be like the Blitz in London," Bree said. "People feel like they could get killed by a wolf at any moment. So they're hooking up like crazy."

"They're more likely to get shot by the National Guard," Nessa said.

"Whatever," Bree yawned. "The point is we're all facing death. Carpe diem, Andy. You'd think he'd make a move." She yawned again. They lay in silence for a few minutes and then Nessa heard Bree's even breathing and realized her friend was asleep.

She might have drifted off herself, but was finding the faint barking sound coming from the woods annoying. It didn't even sound like barking. It sounded like a person barking. A person barking while whispering. Now why would someone do that?

Nessa sat up in the bed, careful not to let the rustling of her sleeping bag wake Bree.

Someone would whisper-bark because they knew that only one person in the house was capable of picking up on a whisper from 100 feet away. And the only people who knew that were Bree—who was sound asleep—and Luc.

Slipping a sweatshirt on over her pajamas, Nessa moved as noiselessly as possible through the carpeted upstairs hall and down the stairs, tiptoeing through the wiped-down kitchen to the back glass slider that led to the deck. Sliding open the door, she took a step into the cool night air, feeling the damp of the slightly slimy decking under her feet, scanning the dark edge of the woods for any sign of Luc.

There he was, a few feet behind the tree line, the lights that had come on in the back hitting his khaki pants and his face. Nessa figured he had seen her. Suddenly he broke out into a smile that seemed—at least in her mind—brighter than the moon itself. She could feel herself smiling in return.

Luc took a few steps toward the end of the woods, and Nessa jumped off the deck. Even though the ground was freezing on her bare feet, she ran to where he was waiting. Wrapping his hands around her waist he pulled her in a spin move behind a tree. "Feet! Cold!" Nessa whispered, and stepped on the toes of his Timberlands, holding on to his waist to stay balanced.

"Hey," he said, after he'd kissed her, hard and long. He leaned back against the tree and she had no choice but to lean on top of him, still a little off balance from standing on his toes.

For a moment they just held each other. Nessa didn't want to make too big a deal of it, but as she breathed in the smell of his fleece jacket mixed with the piney scent on his skin, she felt tears come to her eyes.

"I have so much to tell you," she said, pulling away at last, trying to keep from getting too emotional.

Luc cleared his throat. "Me too." From the look in his eyes, she saw that the hug had meant as much to him as it had to her.

He put a hand on her shoulder, let it trail down her arm, and took both her hands in his. "It's pretty intense out here right now. The wolves—"

"Yes, tell me about the wolves. I kept texting you."

Luc ran his hand through his hair. "Yeah, sorry, it's been a really crazy thirty-six hours," he said. He repositioned his hand on the back of her waist. "I *have* been making progress. The wolves—Nessa, they're learning so fast. They're changing. Most of them are just so scared. I'm trying to teach them to let go, to give into their wolf selves. To just be. To just be wolves."

This was a long speech for Luc. She could tell more from the way he was holding his body how hopeful—and also exhausted—he was. Even though she'd last been close to him less than a week ago, he had lost weight. His arms beneath his sweatshirt were ropy and lean. Wolf-like.

"I could see them," Nessa said. "On the heat map. The

Paravida wolves are massing, aren't they? Forming packs?"

"They've finally got leaders. And the others are getting smart enough to see that not everyone gets to be in charge. They're lining up."

Nessa took a deep breath. "I heard this thing," she said, figuring it was better to get it out into the open now. "Remember Dr. Raab?"

Luc nodded.

"My dad knew him—so I found out yesterday. Dr. Raab died." She could feel Luc's chest—he was holding his breath, waiting for her to finish. For a second she wondered whether he already knew what she was going to say. "He was killed. Attacked. They think it was coyotes."

"*Coyotes?*"

"I guess California has a coyote resurgence?" She leveled him with a "get real" look. "It was wolves, wasn't it?" she said.

"From here?" Luc said.

"You tell me. If they could figure out how to ambush a van of armed security guards, why couldn't they hunt down Dr. Raab in California?"

Luc ran a hand through his hair again. "I . . . I don't know what to say. I mean, I should tell you. There're three main packs of Paravida wolves, okay?" Pulling a hand off Nessa's waist, he drew a map in the air. "One to the east, right? One to the south and one in the north. I've been working with the southern and eastern ones. The northern wolves I can't even get close to. Those wolves will kill you if you so much as look at them. They're bigger too."

"So you think it was them? Who took down that van of scientists?"

"You mean guards?"

"Whatever."

"Yeah," Luc said. Did she sense a new coldness coming from him? She remembered how he looked in the meeting. So tired. Nearly defeated. "Nessa," he said. "The northern pack is tough, but they're *wolves*, Nessa. They couldn't get to California. They couldn't—I don't know—figure out that Dr. Raab even lived in California."

"Okay," Nessa said, though she didn't feel convinced.

Luc shook his head. Even this gesture was muted—she so loved this about him, how his thoughts and feelings were hard to read for everyone but her. "The thing is, after that meeting today, I think we need to get the wolves out of here. Move them to somewhere less populated by humans."

"You think it will work?" Nessa asked.

He nodded. "As soon as the puppies are stronger—in a month or so—I can get the wolves up into the Upper Peninsula. Maybe even into Canada. There's space there."

"And . . . you'll go with them?" Nessa asked, realizing this was his plan only as she said it out loud.

Luc nodded, confirming it was a foregone conclusion. Then she saw him register her disappointment. Nessa forced herself not to look away from him.

Nessa felt the amorphous sadness she always felt when contemplating his taking on wolf form in a more permanent way. So this was happening.

"Whenever you talked about becoming a wolf . . . for real," Nessa said. "I always thought it would be later."

"Yeah, me too," Luc said. He sighed and looked at her in a way that made her insides go all melty. "I guess I always thought

I'd wait 'til I was done with high school. Like I was signing up for the army or something."

"Yeah," Nessa said.

"But I don't actually think a diploma's going to do much for me out in the woods."

"No," Nessa said, laughing at the irony.

He leaned his forehead against hers. "Actually," he said. "The only thing keeping me from wanting to go is you."

Nessa took a deep breath. Luc's eyes were looking straight into hers, so close they weren't quite focused. Mostly what she had from him was the feel of his body under hers, his musky, soapy, pinewoods smell. She felt so close to him in this moment.

"I can go with you," she said. "Just not now. With my mom in the hospital—"

"Ness," he said. "No."

"Luc," she felt her voice rising. Was this a fight?

"You're cold," he said. "Go inside. I'll text you tomorrow."

"Oh, you mean you will this time?" she said, wishing she'd done a better job of keeping the anger from her tone.

He rubbed her upper arms, both warming her and pushing her off his boots. "You're going to freeze your toes out here," he said, his voice determined.

She kept wishing that Luc's face would shift, would break into a smile, that he'd play-slap her on the arm and say, "Just kidding," that he'd let her back in. His expression did not change.

"Okay," she said finally, pride taking the place of desire. She wanted to lean in and kiss his cheek, but instead turned and checked the windows of Bree's house, hoping not to see a curtain moving in Ted and Stephanie's room. Luc was right. Her feet were frozen. Picking her way across the lawn, she returned to the house, checking once before she slid the door closed to see that Luc was still watching her, waiting for her to be safe before he took off into the night.

Back in Bree's room, she burrowed into her sleeping bag and checked her phone one last time. There was another text from Daniel.

> Are you back in Tether? Was the flight okay? Please let me know if there is anything you need. Please call.

She did not reply.

A Lincoln Town Car with a driver idled at Bree's curb the next morning at 6:45. Nessa grabbed a handful of dry cereal and jogged out to meet it. The car passed through Tether's downtown, something you'd miss if you blinked, though Nessa knew every square inch of it intimately. She found it shocking to notice the temporary trailers set up in the parking lot in the center of town as a headquarters for the National Guard. Soldiers with assault rifles seemed to be everywhere. By 8:00 she was standing at the nurses' station on the fourth floor of the hospital where her mom was being cared for.

Nessa found her way upstairs to the unit where her mom was housed, noting the difference between the jail's infirmary and this hospital. Outside Vivian's room, a single armed guard sat in a chair playing solitaire on her phone. Otherwise there was not a sign of security to be seen. There were framed posters on the walls, chair rail molding, unlocked doors.

When a nurse came up behind Nessa and said, "Your mom's been waiting for you," Nessa realized how nervous she suddenly felt. Throughout her life, she'd rarely gone more than a day without seeing Vivian, even when Vivian was working a lot.

Taking a deep breath, Nessa opened the hospital room door and pulled back the curtain.

And there Vivian was. Nessa immediately felt her breathing constrict, her eyes fill with tears. Yes, her mother looked like a stranger, but it was because of how ill she appeared, not because of the time that had gone by. Vivian's skin was gray and the texture of paper, her hair streaked with white, she'd lost twenty pounds at least. Her hands were gripping the bedrail in an effort just to hold her body in place. The only part of her mother Nessa recognized was Vivian's eyes. Blue, wise, humorous, knowing—everything that was her mother was still there.

"Mom!" Nessa said. "What's happened to you?" Nessa took her mom's hand in hers.

Vivian shrugged, her eyes showing the same strength Nessa had been guided by the entirety of her life. "I guess I'm pretty sick," she said, coughing with the effort of speaking.

"You guess?" Nessa said. "But what do you have?"

Vivian coughed some more, then seemed to get ahold of herself, taking a few low, wheezy breaths. The guard, who had been sitting outside the room, stood up to check on Vivian. Vivian held up a hand to signal she was okay, but the second the guard left the room again, Vivian started coughing some more.

Remembering how she'd felt when she'd been having trouble breathing on the plane ride home from Stanford, Nessa had an instant appreciation for how terrible her mom must feel.

"Are you having tests?" Nessa asked. "Are the doctors trying to figure it out?"

Vivian smiled ruefully, raised her eyebrows. She shrugged again. "Of course. They're testing."

Ignoring the fatalism in her mother's tone, Nessa took her words at face value. "What have they tested?"

Whispering, Vivian answered, "Come here." Nessa got close. Vivian pointed to a chair. Nessa pulled it toward the bed. "Sit," she said. Nessa sat.

Nessa saw that her mother's hand was moving, trembling almost involuntarily.

Vivian looked her straight in the eye. "Nessa, what I have, there's no test for."

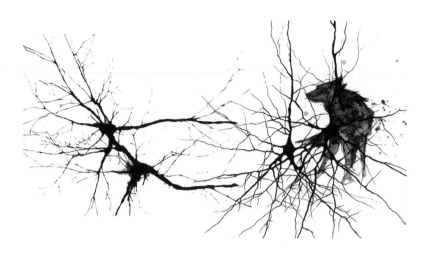

CHAPTER FORTY-TWO

"Mom, what do you mean?" Nessa said. She laughed nervously.

"The doctors." Vivian paused to get her breath back—she couldn't even get through a full sentence. "They won't even know. What I have."

Groping for the control pad wrapped around the bed's railing, Vivian raised the mattress so she was closer to a sitting position. She took a slow, deep breath, as if testing her ability to do so.

"There's so much," Vivian said. "I need to tell you. About your father. His work. *Our* work. You've seen what he does now?"

Nessa shrugged. "Why didn't you tell me?"

Vivian narrowed her eyes. "You're angry."

"I'm not angry," Nessa said, although she could hear the anger in her voice. "Well, okay, maybe I am. Don't you think I had a right to know who my dad was? That I even *had* a dad?"

"Yes, I do think that," Vivian said. "I just wanted to wait."

"Wait for what?" Nessa said.

Vivian blinked slowly. Nessa wondered if she had to think about the answer to her question or if this was something she'd been preparing to tell her for a while. "College."

"Okay," Nessa said.

Something about the way Nessa had said that—the fact that her "okay" meant exactly the opposite of how it sounded—made Vivian smile. "In college, I had such fresh eyes. Like you. I wanted so much from the world."

Vivian gestured for the cup of water beside her bed. Nessa held it to her lips and watched her drink.

"That's how your dad was also. We had that in common. We were both so sure we could find answers no one else could. We were so sure of ourselves."

"Mom, what does this have to do with your illness?"

Vivian held out a hand, indicating that Nessa should be patient. "When I was starting out," she went on. "I could stay up all night reading or working in the lab."

"Dad said you were the most creative genetic researcher he'd ever worked with."

"Dad?" She smiled ruefully. "You call him that?"

Funny, Nessa thought. She'd never used the word when speaking to him directly.

Vivian held up a hand as if to say, "Never mind that for

now."

"He told me you developed a technology that used proteins or viruses or something to alter an organism's DNA."

Vivian grimaced. She shook her head. "I don't know how to tell you this in a way that you will hear. But I just have to say it." She paused to suppress a cough. "You should not trust him. I know he's helping us and has power and got me out of that jail." She paused again, swallowing. Took a sip of water. "I imagine … he loves you and wants to be part of your life. I'm sure he's proud of you. But you just don't know what he is capable of."

Nessa thought with a shudder about the Delphine chimera. Did her mom know about her? She said nothing, waiting to hear what Vivian would say next.

"What exactly did he do that is so bad?" Nessa asked.

"It's not what he's *done*. It's what he *could* do. What he might do. What he would do." Vivian grimaced, frustrated by the difficulty she was having describing what she had against Daniel. Nessa could see how exhausted Vivian had become after just a little bit of talking.

"It just doesn't sound that bad," Nessa pushed. "It sounds like you're saying he didn't even do anything wrong."

"It's that he doesn't know where to stop," Vivian spat out, speaking quickly and with energy, which resulted in her coughing again. She coughed in a way that seemed to have no end, one racking series of coughs followed by gasping for breath and then embarking on still more coughing.

Worry for her mother quickly supplanted Nessa's anger and curiosity. "Stop, Mom, please stop," she said. "It's okay. Don't explain."

Vivian was gripping Nessa's arm, squeezing so hard it hurt.

"No," she gagged. Nessa offered the water glass. Vivian took a sip. She closed her eyes until the coughing spasm passed. "I have to explain," she said. "You need to know. We were both like that. I didn't know where to stop."

Nessa could tell that this was important to her mom. "You have to understand. The reason I'm sick. It's because . . . it's because I was like your father. I did things . . . I tried things on myself."

Nessa looked at her mom—this thinner, grayer version of her mom had already become someone Nessa was used to.

"Mom," Nessa said. "That was almost twenty years ago. How could something you did then make you sick now?"

Vivian shook her head. "Did your father," she said. "Show you his chimera?"

"Which ones?" Nessa said.

"Right," Vivian said. "He's made hundreds by now. He's infected the planet with them, like viruses introduced into unsuspecting populations for experimentation. But I have only myself to blame. I made the first one." A wave of horror washed over Nessa. *Her mother* was responsible for that mutilated version of her sister, tucked away in the woods? Vivian closed her eyes, opened them again. Fixed Nessa with a look. "I *was* the first one."

"You?" said Nessa.

Vivian winced. Nessa wondered if she was in pain in her body or if she was reacting to what she was saying. "I got interested." She took a breath, pushed on her chest with the flat of her hand to suppress a cough. "In wolves."

"Mom," Nessa said. What did wolves have to do with any of this? The way Vivian was looking at her—the significance in her tone—Nessa thought for a minute her mom was talking about the wolf in Nessa.

"You know. Graduate school," Vivian went on, as if that could explain. "I never should have."

Nessa felt her hands had gone numb. She felt her brain had been turned to icy slush and the blood running through her veins had gone cold. It was the opposite of the feeling she had when she was about to transform—instead of hot, sparkling heat and electricity, she was chilled to the core. Was her tongue swollen or had it been transformed into lead?

"I changed myself," Vivian continued. "I thought I could manage it. And I did for a long time." Vivian lifted a hand to her forehead, hiding her eyes, then peeked out from behind her hand, her unflinching, penetrating blue eyes fixed on Nessa's. "They found my supplies at Dr. Morgan's, I heard."

Nessa felt her throat closing up. "That's what you wanted me to find? The night you were arrested. You asked me to look for it, didn't you?"

Vivian nodded. "I was fine for years," she said. She was speaking in short sentences to keep the coughing at bay. "The mutation I caused inside my body. It could be controlled with medications. Only I knew how to manufacture them. But once I went to prison . . . I lost access. Now my work has been destroyed."

Vivian started coughing again and twisted her knees to the side, tucking her chin.

"Mom," Nessa said. "I want to try to help you. Please tell me how. Tell me how to make what it is you need."

Vivian opened her eyes. "No," she said. "Out of the question." She fumbled for the mechanism that controlled the bed, raised it up a bit, then lowered it. "Your father—"

Vivian closed her eyes again. For a moment, Nessa worried this meant that her mother was done talking to her, that she was going to remain as opaque on the subject as Daniel had. Then Vivian began to speak.

"Now," she said. "Your father—"

"Mom, you're exhausted," Nessa said. "I'll come back. Why don't you rest for a while?"

"No!" Vivian said with a force Nessa found surprising. Her cheeks were red, her eyes appeared sunken. "I have to tell you now."

"Okay, okay," Nessa said, worried that fighting her mom would only make this worse.

But then what Vivian said next did not make any sense. "Those wolves. The work Paravida was doing. That's the logical extension of what your father and I started. That's the kind of evil we unleashed on the world. You must understand that."

"Mom, you had nothing to do with what happened at Paravida!"

Vivian sniffed, letting her head roll to one side on the pillow. Reaching for the bed's controller again, she lowered the mattress down. Nessa could see that just sitting up was too much for Vivian now. "Mom, you have to focus on getting better. Don't worry about Dad or Paravida. Worry about yourself."

Vivian coughed out a laugh, her voice so weak Nessa could barely hear her over the sound of the bed's motor. "The damage is already done." She pursed her lips. "Though if things get very bad, the mutation may kick in . . . to save itself."

Nessa felt tears coming into her eyes and had to look away. It was time to go, she could see that. Her mother needed to rest.

But what did her mom mean, "very bad"? And what kind of a mutation, exactly, did her mother have?

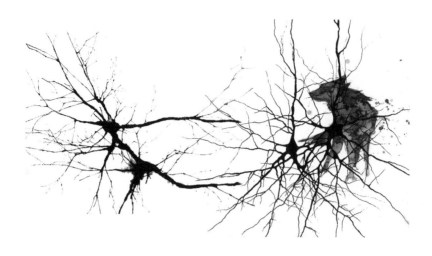

CHAPTER FORTY-THREE

The car that had taken Nessa to the hospital from Tether was waiting for her at the curb, the driver inside on his smartphone, a cup of coffee in his other hand.

Before getting in, Nessa searched her pockets. Where had she put Professor Halliday's card? Had she transferred it from the back pocket of her jeans to her duffel bag? She hadn't. It was still there. With shaking hands she dialed the professor's number.

Getting a voicemail greeting, Nessa took a deep breath, willing the trembling in her voice to stop. "Hi, this is Nessa . . . Kurland," she started. She wished she'd done a better job thinking about what she should say before dialing. "I met you earlier this week. I'm a high school student but I went to your class?" It went against her better judgment to actually mention wolves over the phone. "A friend of mine. A . . . different friend. She has that condition you were describing. The scientific one."

She didn't like how desperate she sounded, but couldn't do anything about it. She *was* desperate. Was she also right in her guess about what had happened to her mom? She could only hope so. She left her number quickly, and then hung up.

Once in the car, she told the driver to take her back to Bree's. The car glided through a few intersections, making its way north, easing onto the highway. During the course of the ride, Nessa closed her eyes, feeling very alone with a thought she'd been trying very hard to avoid since the minute she'd seen how sick her mom really was.

What if Vivian didn't get better?

Nessa knew she shouldn't go there. She took a deep breath. She needed to focus. She called Aunt Jane.

But the second she heard her aunt's voice, her own became feathery and light, her fear for her mother taking over any conscious effort she had made at control.

"Nessa?" Aunt Jane said. "What's wrong?"

Nessa gave Aunt Jane the details without mentioning what she and Vivian had covered in their conversation. Jane didn't even let her finish.

"Okay, I'm coming out there," Jane said. "I don't care if I do get fired. I'm bringing Nate and Delphine. We'll leave first thing in the morning tomorrow and be there before noon."

What was Aunt Jane going to do? She was powerless against the National Guard, the Paravida wolves, against whatever was making Vivian so sick. Still, Nessa couldn't help but believe that once her family came back together, everything would be okay.

On the way back to Tether, Nessa's driver was stopped at the same checkpoint Nessa and Bree had driven through the day before. Nessa looked for the soldier with the slicked-back hair and acne but the soldier talking to the driver was a man with red hair (as much as you could tell from his crew cut). The soldier who had examined Bree's and Nessa's IDs wasn't part of the group of about six milling around by the sandbags on either side of the roadblock either. How many soldiers were there?

When the car dropped Nessa back at Bree's, Bree greeted Nessa in the doorway. She was still in her pajamas, holding a bowl of chocolate chip cookie dough in one hand, a wooden spoon in the other, and had put her hair in two adorable pigtails.

Walking into Bree's house, which smelled like freshly baked cookies and grilled cheese sandwiches, Nessa let herself fall backward into one of the chairs at Bree's kitchen table. "I just saw my mom," she began. She put her head in her hands. She wasn't sure she even had the energy to cry. "I need to get her some medicine and I need to tell Luc something but I can't get him on his phone."

"You need to take a nap," Bree said. "You're about to fall over, you look so tired." Bree gave her a second, diagnostic look. "You want a grilled cheese?"

Suddenly Nessa realized she was starving. A grilled cheese sandwich was about the closest to Nirvana Nessa might ever achieve.

As Bree cooked and then Nessa ate, Bree listened to Nessa's

account of her visit to the hospital with her mother. When Nessa finished she asked, "So you actually think your mom turned herself into . . . a werewolf? Like you?"

"Not like me," Nessa corrected. She explained everything she knew about the concept of a scientific werewolf. It didn't take long.

Bree shook her head as she pulled a batch of cookies out of the oven. Nessa checked her phone for what felt like the millionth time. Still nothing.

"Call her again," Bree said.

"After this cookie," Nessa said, reaching.

"Hey!" Bree said. "You can have a few, but don't eat too many. I'm bringing them to Andy."

"Andy?" Nessa said, her mouth full. "Why does he need cookies?"

"Because I told him I would make them for him. He's having a bonfire. His parents are away. Back in the woods behind his house."

"What about the curfew?"

"I'm sick of the curfew. Everyone is. We're all sneaking out and meeting at Andy's."

"Is that safe?" Nessa said.

Bree gave her a look. "You want to give me lectures on safety?"

Nessa reached for cookie #2.

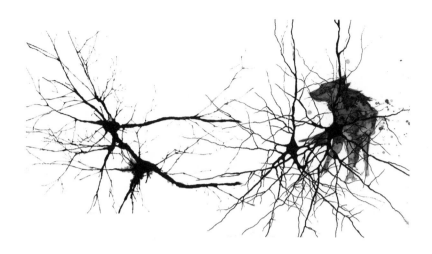

CHAPTER FORTY-FOUR

aybe the National Guard had the streets of Tether under control, but they clearly had no sense of what was going on in the woods. That night, after Ted and Stephanie were asleep, Bree and Nessa snuck out the back of the house, following trails, keeping their flashlights low. They saw no sign of soldiers as they met up with at least half of the juniors at Tether High, most of the seniors, and a good handful of sophomores as well. Andy kept the bonfire contained in a clearing far back on his family's property. Nessa was grateful for the darkness—only a few people recognized her.

It also made it easy to slip away into the shadows, back behind the couples sneaking away from the fire to make out.

Nessa noticed Cassian Thomas was one of them, leading a sophomore girl away from the fire, wrapped in his arm. *I guess he's moved on from Hannah,* Nessa thought, remembering the freshman on cross-country Cassian had been dating after Nessa broke things off with him. She shuddered. To think she'd wasted more than half of high school waiting for him to notice her. She shuddered again, appreciating the independence and her freedom of mind . . . and when the shudder was over she realized she had become a wolf.

And she was on the move. She relaxed into the feeling of looseness and speed as she kicked up her pace into a light jog. This was her first transformation since returning from Oregon and she felt the difference in the quality of the woods. Daniel Host's preserve had been magical—at times terrifying—but Tether was home.

Then, within seconds, Nessa knew: Something was wrong.

The change in the Tether woods was unmistakable. First, the smell of the Paravida wolves had grown nearly overwhelming. It was everywhere. And that wasn't the biggest change. Now—traveling on the air, left behind on the forest floor, absorbed into the pores of emerging buds and leaves, embedded into the bark of trees—there was a smell unmistakable to a wolf. The smell of fear.

It was sour and penetrating, like milk gone bad, or like the odors coming off fermented fruit. For five or six steps, she'd think she had run through it or past it, but then a fresh wave of it would break over her and she'd realize the fear was so thick that it was almost like the entire forest was afraid.

Running a wide arc around any part of the woods that bordered houses or buildings or even farm fields, it took

Nessa about twenty minutes to get close to Luc's cabin. As she approached, she hoped for the odor of woodsmoke that would indicate he was inside. There was nothing. When she came within sight of the clearing, she saw the cabin's doors and windows were shut tight. Transforming back into human shape, she stood at the doorway for a moment trying to catch her breath. "Luc?" she called out in case he was nearby and might hear her. "Anyone here?"

There was nothing but the sounds of the night in response—squirrels moving through the upper branches of trees, the calling of frogs in a marsh nearby. Ducking her head, Nessa pushed open the cabin door. "Hello?"

Even to her human nose, the room had a wolfy smell that worried Nessa. The sleeping bag was stowed in its stuff sack, the cushions he'd been sleeping on top of were pulled neatly together to form a bed. Which on closer inspection was covered in fur.

Had Luc been sleeping as a wolf?

Luc, she thought, *where are you?* Then, as if her wish had summoned him, there he was, standing in the doorway of the cabin. As human as human could be.

"What are you doing here?" he said, though the way he twisted his mouth as he said it, she could tell he was happy she was there. She let him hold her, breathing deeply. She didn't want to think.

Eventually he asked how she'd gotten out of the town curfew and she explained Andy Carlisle's bonfire. She explained her mother. The story she'd heard. While she was talking they went inside and he boiled water. They drank tea and sat on the cushions. Nessa didn't ask Luc if he'd been sleeping on them.

She didn't ask him if he'd been sleeping as a wolf.

"I've heard of those synthetic wolves," Luc said. "I don't think it's easy for them."

"I don't get that," said Nessa. "Why would it be harder?"

"I don't know," he said. "It just is. It's like . . . you know, I was learning in Bio, there's this thing with trees in old forests. Like, rainforests and stuff. You take one tree out of that forest and try to grow it somewhere else and it dies. It needs the other trees around it to live. And scientists think it's because there are these microbes that live in the soil. They carry information or nutrients. I don't remember. I guess scientific wolves—they're missing out on the process. They're like that one tree, trying to grow away from all the relationships that make it easy for a tree to be a tree in the forest."

"Is that like you?" Nessa said. "Being a wolf, and knowing you were a wolf from when you were a kid?"

Luc stretched his long legs out in front of him. He looked at Nessa straight-faced and calm, his straight eyebrows neither raised nor lowered, his long chin relaxed, his high cheekbones and calm eyes giving his face an ageless look. "Yes," he said. "I think it is."

He didn't make any further comment about it.

Luc sighed, pushed his hair back off his forehead. "We need to get the wolves out sooner than I thought."

"Why's that?" Nessa asked, feeling herself getting sleepy next to Luc. It was hard to believe she was going to have to leave the cabin in just a few minutes.

"The National Guard—I don't know what they're planning but I think it's something major. I've seen their cameras. They're everywhere. And I can smell something just . . . off."

"Yeah, I smelled it too," Nessa said. "It smells like fear."

"The pack is almost ready," Luc said. "Except the pups." He sighed. "I honestly don't know how we're going to get them out." He shook, wolf-like, as if to rid himself of that thought. "But I'm thinking maybe next week," Luc said.

"Next week?" Nessa said. She sat up. She wasn't sleepy now. "But I thought you were talking a month? The pups can barely walk a mile."

"In the center of town, the Guard's set up a headquarters. It's those temporary trailers, you know?"

"I saw them," said Nessa.

"I've been listening outside them," he said. "I heard them talk about some kind of action. You know, like an extermination. If you hear anything, will you let me know?"

"Of course," Nessa said. She checked the time on her watch. "But now I've got to get back. Andy Carlisle's party is probably wrapping up."

"One more thing," said Luc. "Take these." He was holding out a set of keys on a chain she knew well. "You should hold on to them."

"Luc, that's your truck key!" she said.

"I know what it is. I haven't been driving much lately. I thought you could use it, getting back and forth to see your mom. I parked it near Bree's. Shouldn't be hard to find."

"Luc!" Nessa said. She buried her head in his neck. Felt his hand smoothing the hair on the back of her head. "You're making it sound like you're leaving me."

It had been a day of shocks.

When she got back to the bonfire, it was burned to the ground and Bree and a bunch of other girls—the only ones left at the party—were pouring water over the embers. "Where have you been?" Bree asked. "I've been looking for you. All the guys took off. They're such jerks."

"Even Andy?" Nessa said in a low voice.

"Yeah," Bree said. "There was definitely something up. They wouldn't tell us but kept giving us meaningful looks all night. And then, a half hour ago, without cleaning up a single thing, without putting out the fire, they just disappeared."

Nessa had a bad feeling about what they could be up to. "Do you have any idea?" she asked.

Bree grumbled that they'd probably hear about it the next day—after the boys got caught. "Yeah," Nessa laughed, helping pick up the last of the cups before heading off with Bree down the path, flashlights held low. She just wanted this long day to end. To get into bed and forget everything her mom had told her, forget how sick she had looked, and forget what Luc was not saying: that he would stay.

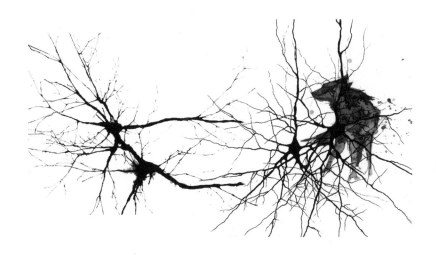

CHAPTER FORTY-FIVE

The path to Bree's meandered into the woods around Tether before looping back toward town. As Bree and Nessa pushed into the deepest pocket of forest, Nessa caught the unmistakable smell of a Paravida wolf on the wind. She put a hand on Bree's elbow and a finger to her lips.

Bree's eyes were immediately opened wide. Nessa could feel her fear as if it were a temperature shift on the wind. "It's okay," Nessa said, even though she had no idea if that was true.

Nessa took another whiff. It wasn't just one wolf—this was a small patrol—maybe five or six wolves altogether.

Not good.

The only bright spot in this terrifyingly dark picture

was that she and Bree were downwind of them—essentially invisible. All they could do was keep moving and hope they stayed that way.

Then she smelled something else.

Humans.

Uh oh, she thought. Wolves + humans. This could not be good.

"Go home," she whispered to Bree. "Run."

"Without you?" Bree said, her voice a strangled croak. "What is it, soldiers?"

"I don't know," Nessa said. "But get yourself somewhere safe. I can be careful." Nessa passed Bree her light.

"Don't you need it?" Bree asked. Bree held the light so it cast demon-style shadows on to her face, highlighting how scared she looked.

"I'd rather go by smell," Nessa said.

"Oh, right." Bree swallowed hard. Nessa could smell Bree's fear mixing in with the rest of the fear in the forest. "Go," Nessa said. "Run." Bree took off at a sprint.

As soon as she was gone, Nessa left the path, picking her way as best she could over tree roots and brambles until she transformed and could manage much better on four legs. She covered a quarter-mile or so and then stopped to assess the swirl of smells in the dark again. She'd been hoping that the human smells and the smell of the wolves were coincidental and that when she got closer she'd confirm they were nowhere near one another.

But now that she was close she was able to tell this was not the case.

And also? These human odors, she recognized them. In the

back of her mind, she'd been hoping they were soldiers, who could at least try to protect themselves. But it wasn't soldiers. It was Tim Miller and some of the other guys who had been organizing the anti-wolf activism in school.

Andy Carlisle.

So this was what the boys were doing instead of cleaning up the cups and other garbage back at the bonfire.

Stupid.

Nessa ran faster. She hadn't been able to tell if the wolves were actually with the boys, though she knew they were close to them. Maybe they'd pass each other by? Maybe the Paravida wolves would be smart enough by now to leave the humans alone?

Unless they were stalking them?

Oh, God . . . What if this patrol had come from the northern pack, the ones Luc said were out of control? The ones who hunted humans?

Nessa heard the crack of a gunshot. As she did, she heard shouting—human shouting. The sounds of boots pounding out an uneven rhythm on the forest floor. She heard the snarls of wolves, barking, growls, the crunching of sticks and rustling of leaves. Everyone was running, crashing through brush and turning on a dime to avoid trees. *Who was chasing whom?*

At a full sprint, Nessa quickly reached the spot where the gun had been fired. What she saw there didn't so much surprise her as confirm her worst suspicions. Tim Miller was standing in a clearing in the woods, his flashlight shining on the ground beneath him—the emerging blades of grass and young ferns disappearing into the dark outside the flashlight's beam. Nessa could only make him out in silhouette form—his camouflage baseball cap rocked back on his head as if it might fall at any moment, his Carhartts slipping down around his hips, his arms out at his sides as he spun in a slow circle, lifting his light to take in the sight of one snarling wolf after another.

Nessa didn't know where his friends had gone. She assumed they'd all run after the shot was fired. The sound of the gun. Had this been a hunting party? The dots were connecting: Nessa remembered there was a deer stand nearby, a rough platform and ladder built onto a tree that hunters used when staking out deer. Was that where they'd started their "hunt"?

While Nessa had been taking in the visuals, her brain had been absorbing the smells as well—more distinct and more disturbing. Fresh blood. As her brain connected the odor to what she was seeing, she let her eyes follow her nose just as Tim's flashlight passed over the Paravida wolf at the edge of the clearing.

In human form, Nessa might have gasped, but as a wolf she only blinked, feeling every cell in her body go still.

Nessa knew she would have to act quickly to save Tim's life, but she didn't know how. There were six wolves facing him, and wolves were all about numbers. They did not walk away from a fight where they so clearly had an advantage.

How could she possibly convince them to back off? If only Luc were with her . . . He had ways of communicating with the Paravida wolves that she had not mastered.

She also wished Luc was with her so she would feel less alone.

"Help!" Tim called out. "Someone help me!"

Hearing the desperation in his voice, Nessa felt her heart pounding in her chest. She had to do something. But to charge the wolves would be suicide.

She had to be smarter than that.

One of the Paravida wolves took a step closer to Tim. A female. She seemed extra aggressive, and Nessa noticed her belly was rounded. Was she pregnant? That meant she was an alpha in her pack. And she had a lot to lose.

If the female's mate was nearby this whole situation could get a lot worse . . .

Without meaning to, Nessa let out a whine of anxiety. The wolf next to the alpha female turned to look at her. Nessa froze. But then the wolf next to that one turned as well, and suddenly Nessa had an idea.

She charged the pregnant female alpha wolf and nipped her in the ankles. Before the wolf could spin around, Nessa was gone, leaping away in a game of what—if her life had not been at stake—might have resembled "Guess who?"

The pregnant alpha would have no doubt found her within seconds if Nessa hadn't next nipped the male wolf standing next to the pregnant one. The protector wolf had been so focused on growling at Tim, he hadn't heard Nessa behind him until she crashed into his flank. Turning to see who was there, he confronted not Nessa—she had already moved on—but the pregnant female. The two pack mates did not immediately start fighting, which Nessa took as a sign that they truly were learning what it meant to travel in a pack. But still, they were discombobulated enough that they lost their focus, sniffing each other nose to tail as if needing to reorient themselves entirely.

Nessa played the same trick on the other wolves in the circle and soon the pack was in chaos. Knowing the window of opportunity was very narrow, Nessa did not hesitate, but rushed Tim, who remained frozen in fear.

She couldn't use words to tell him to run. From the look in his eyes, she knew he thought she was about to kill him herself. Instead, she could only push at him with the side of her head. He got the idea and began running from her. She kept pushing, showing him the direction he needed to go in.

Sending up a baying cry, the Paravida wolves realized he was escaping and were soon after them, but Nessa pushed on. Soon Tim seemed to understand where she was heading and corrected course, navigating on his own toward the hunters' tree stand, then scampering up the rough ladder.

Nessa knew she could not afford to wait to make sure he was all right. She galloped on, zigzagging through the trees at a sprint, hoping that the wolves would be distracted enough by Tim to leave her alone. And hoping that he would be okay up there, that the wolves would eventually leave so he could climb down and limp home.

She did not stop sprinting until she'd made it to the woods behind Bree's house. Emerging from them in human form, Nessa took a minute to catch her breath, making sure to stay in the shadows where she wouldn't be seen. She couldn't help but remember standing here with Luc just last night. So much was changing, so fast.

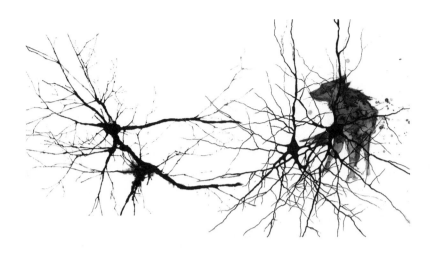

CHAPTER FORTY-SIX

*B*efore going to sleep, Nessa checked her phone. Professor Halliday had still not returned her call.

The next morning, the first thing Nessa did on waking was check the phone again. Still nothing.

Because of the wolf threat, Ted insisted on driving Stephanie to work, so the girls were alone for breakfast. Over cereal at the kitchen table, Nessa caught Bree up on what had happened in the woods. Bree was horrified, and then, checking her texts, saw that everyone was talking about Tim Miller.

"He sprained his ankle," she said, scrolling through her phone on the table while lifting a bite of cereal to her mouth with her other hand. "Everyone's going over there later for hot dogs. We should go!"

"No thanks," Nessa said. "I'm going to the hospital."

"Oh, right," said Bree. "Do you need a ride? I could skip Tim's and drive you."

"Actually," Nessa said, thinking of Luc's keys still in the back pocket of the jeans she'd been wearing the night before. "I've got the truck." She didn't have the heart to tell Bree why.

After breakfast, while Nessa showered, Bree loaded some game apps onto Nessa's phone. "Have you talked to your dad yet?" she asked idly, making little adjustments to the phone's settings as Nessa was getting dressed.

Nessa didn't answer her question. She hadn't. She wasn't sure she wanted to. How could she, after everything she'd seen and heard had so drastically changed her impression of who he was?

Daniel had been calling her, however. Every time she checked to see if Professor Halliday had responded, she saw the notification of the missed calls. While she was driving, Nessa felt her phone vibrate with an incoming call. She pulled over onto the shoulder, fished the phone from her pocket, and saw that this time it wasn't him. She answered.

"This is Professor Halliday returning your call," she heard. With the flat of her palm, Nessa covered the ear on the opposite side of her head, she was so intent on being able to hear every word Professor Halliday had to say. "As soon as we hang up I'm going to text you a phone number. You call that number and tell the man who answers that you got his number from me. Explain what you're looking for. I don't know if he has ever made it before, but he's the best bet."

"Thank you," Nessa said. "I can't tell you how much this means to me."

"You can thank me by deleting my text as soon as the call has gone through. Delete my name from your contacts as well. Keep the card, call me when you need to, but I prefer not to leave an electronic trail if you would be so kind."

When the call was over—it had lasted less than a minute in total—Nessa stared at her phone, willing it to show a new message coming in. When it finally did, she felt like she had summoned it from sheer force of will.

Nine digits lit up in blue. Strange to think that was all that might separate her mother from being the person Nessa had always known rather than the skinny, exhausted, coughing person she had become.

Without studying it further, Nessa hit the number with her index finger, quickly moving the phone to her ear.

When she heard "Hello?" Nessa was surprised. She sat up straighter and commanded her brain to focus. She had to be wrong. From just one word, could you ever really be sure who was on the other end of a phone line?

Nessa could. Nessa was sure.

"Dad?" she exclaimed. "This is you?"

"Nessa?" he questioned.

The gears in Nessa's brain were spinning. Daniel and Professor Halliday worked together at Stanford. It made sense that Professor Halliday would think of him—Daniel's company was called Chimera Corp. What was more of a chimera than a wolf-human hybrid?

"Nessa, I'm so glad you called. I was just starting to really worry. I—"

Before he could finish his sentence, she disconnected the call and turned off her phone.

Her father—he could help with a lawyer. But not this.

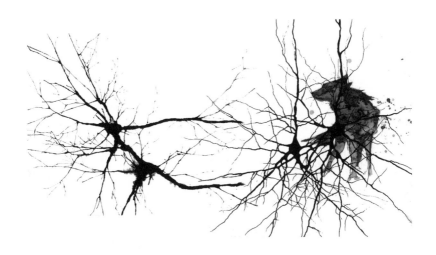

CHAPTER FORTY-SEVEN

efore she had even reached her mother's room in the hospital in Saginaw, Nessa saw Delphine coming toward her in the hallway. Delphine was carrying Vivian's mauve plastic water pitcher and Nessa assumed she was taking it to be filled at the nurse's station. Delphine was looking down, her eyebrows pulled together in an expression of obvious worry, her dark hair pulled back in a bushy ponytail.

"Delphine?" Nessa called and she got to see her sister's pretty features shift from surprise to joy. Nessa felt a smile spreading on her own face as well as she and Delphine hugged hello—something they rarely did. They weren't used to being separated long enough to need to.

"When did you get here?" Nessa asked. "I wasn't thinking you'd be here until lunchtime."

Delphine explained that they'd left Milwaukee after Nate got back from school, eaten dinner on the road and checked into a hotel near the hospital just in time to get to bed. "Aunt Jane wanted to be in the room first thing this morning." Delphine's expression darkened. "Nessa, Mom's so sick and I heard Aunt Jane talking to the doctors. They don't have any idea what's wrong with her and they've run through all the tests."

Nessa debated telling Delphine her mother's secret. Secrets, Nessa was coming to believe, were basically bad for families, and Delphine had the right to know. But she felt instinctively that this was not the right time.

"She's going to be okay," Nessa said. Delphine looked at her skeptically. "I'll tell you all about it later, okay?"

Delphine could tell something was up. "You know, I'm not a baby," she said.

"I know," said Nessa. "I promise I'll tell you everything soon. Just not now, okay?"

Maybe Delphine saw something in Nessa's eyes. Whatever it was, she backed off her insistence, passing the water pitcher to Nessa like she was giving up on something. "I'm going to take a walk around outside," she said. "I'll see you in there in a few?"

When Nessa pushed aside the curtain just inside the door to Vivian's room, she saw that Aunt Jane was sitting in the chair Nessa had been using the day before. Nate was closer to the door, standing, leaning with his back to the wall, his face buried in Aunt Jane's iPad, his leg jiggling. Nessa put a hand on his shoulder—she'd always been good at judging just how much physical contact he could tolerate—and he looked up. He didn't smile, but she didn't expect him to. His dark blond hair looked unwashed and his face was drawn.

"Hey, buddy," she said. "I missed you."

"That's okay," Nate lifted the iPad. "You're seeing me now, and Aunt Jane just let me download *When Trains Attack*, premium. I'm already on level three."

Nessa showed him a thumbs-up and Nate's attention went right back down to the game. Nessa hugged Aunt Jane and let her kiss her cheek. "Oh, sweetie," Aunt Jane said, squeezing her arm.

"Hi, Mom," Nessa said, turning toward the bed and taking her mother's hand in hers. Vivian's eyes looked dull and tired as they met Nessa's. Even with a nasal cannula blowing oxygen-rich air right into her nose, her breathing was shallow.

Was it really possible that Vivian's illness was a symptom of synthetic werewolfism? Yesterday, hearing her mother's story, Nessa had thought of nothing but action—of getting the serum, of fixing her mother—but now, seeing Nate and Delphine in the hospital room, knowing that her dad was the only one who had the power to save her mother, the entire situation was beginning to feel surreal.

Jane stood. She put a hand on Nessa's shoulder, leaned down to kiss Vivian's cheek. "Nate and I are going down to get a snack," she said. "We'll be back in twenty minutes." Still holding Nessa's hand, Vivian nodded.

Nessa took a deep breath, as if to compensate for Vivian's shallow ones. She tried to look not too worried.

"Mom, I have some great news," she whispered, taking advantage of the fact that they were alone in the room. "I think

I've found someone who might be able to make that serum."

Vivian's eyes shot open wide, as if she'd just gotten the shot of oxygen she needed. "You have?" she said. She narrowed her eyes, suddenly suspicious. "How?"

Nessa swallowed. She had never been able to lie well to Vivian and that wasn't out of principle—it was because Vivian had a way of looking at people that made them nervous. Made them feel she could see inside their heads.

"When dad took me to Stanford I sat in on a class and the teacher—she knew a lot about wolves. So I called her, thinking she might know where to help. I didn't tell her about you. I kept it very vague, but she knew what I was talking about. She gave me a phone number for a guy who might be able to make the serum."

Her mother's entire face had gone still. She was looking at Nessa with a fixity that made Nessa want to squirm and look away. But she kept her eyes on her mother's. Finally, Vivian asked a question. "Who is it?"

"Well," said Nessa, swallowing hard. "You have to understand, this professor—the one I called—she works at Stanford. So it only makes sense that the person she sent me to works there also." Nessa stopped there. She tried to open her mouth to finish answering her mother's question but found that her lips could not move. Air could not be pushed up from her lungs into her throat to speak.

"Who is it?" Vivian repeated, her question more of a command than a request.

"Okay," Nessa said. "Here's the thing. It was my father. It was Daniel. Dad."

She didn't know what she'd expected—that Vivian would

start coughing again? That she would sit up in bed and shout "Noooo!"?

Vivian just closed her eyes. She half nodded. She opened her eyes again. And she said, "Of course."

Vivian's grip on Nessa's hand had strengthened. Nessa looked down at her mother's fingers—thin and claw-like. Had she lost weight even since yesterday?

Suddenly, with her other hand, Vivian was reaching for something. No, she was pointing. To a table on wheels pushed up to the bed.

"Water?" Nessa asked, remembering how much her mother had drunk the day before.

Nessa quickly poured some water from the plastic pitcher Delphine had passed off. But Vivian wasn't satisfied. Nessa noticed a small cup holding three pills next to the water pitcher. "These?"

Vivian nodded and Nessa passed the pills to her mother to swallow. Nessa remembered her mother popping the occasional Ibuprofen when her back hurt. She would put three in her mouth at a time, and get them all down with a rushed swallow of coffee. Now, Vivian's hand trembled so much it was hard for her to place the pills on her tongue. She got them down eventually, one at a time.

"What are they?" Nessa asked.

"B_{12}," Vivian said. "If I take enough . . . I can breathe." She took a breath as if to demonstrate and ended up coughing. "For a bit," she clarified when she could speak again.

After the next breath she took, she was able to keep from coughing. She breathed again, clearly savoring the feeling of air in her lungs. Nessa saw her mother's nostrils flare with the effort. Vivian's nose had always been large for her face, a sign of strength and personality. Nessa suddenly felt how much she had missed her. How much had she been holding back from letting herself feel the loss of her mom?

"I appreciate you trying to help," Vivian said. "But your father—Nessa." Vivian breathed again. "He's not to be trusted."

"You've said that," said Nessa. "But what if he's the only one who can help you? Wouldn't you want to take a chance?"

Vivian shook her head. Nessa had the feeling the head shaking wasn't her saying no in answer to Nessa's question, but just her mother's expression of general sadness about the impossibility of the situation.

Vivian took Nessa's hand and pulled her closer until Nessa was leaning down, their faces so close that Nessa could see individual pieces of dry skin flaking off Vivian's chapped lips. At least her mother seemed to be breathing more regularly and deeply now. But she needed medicine, she needed the serum.

"I need to tell you why I left."

"Mom, you shouldn't be talking too much," Nessa said.

"No!" Vivian held up a hand. "You need to know this."

"Okay," Nessa agreed. She passed her mother the water. It was amazing. Even sick in a hospital bed, barely able to breathe, Vivian could make Nessa feel like she was a little girl all over again.

"When I was starting out," Vivian began. She was talking very quickly, whispering. Nessa understood almost every-thing she said, but occasionally Vivian would drop a word. "I felt invincible. Any time I heard someone mention a concept I hadn't heard of before, I'd hit the library and research not only that concept but others that one would lead me to."

"What's wrong with that?" Nessa said. "What's wrong with being excited about science?"

"I didn't know where to stop. I always wanted more. I wanted to know—" Vivian paused here, and she looked pained. "We were talking only in theory back then, but the idea that we could rewrite the genetic code of a mouse, of a bird, was so thrilling. I was thinking the same thing everyone else was: Could we use this on ourselves?"

She gestured for more water. Nessa gave her another sip, then Vivian continued. "Chimera," Vivian said, and there was such disgust in her tone that Nessa wondered if Vivian might actually spit after saying the word.

"When I turned myself into a wolf, I kept practicing science, but I knew," Vivian continued, "I'd gone too far. Yet I kept going. There was no way to stop. Living on the edge of invention— that's a heady place to be. You feel powerful."

"Okay."

"Your father was the same. Is the same, I assume. It's part of what brought us together. I pushed aside the voice in my head telling me there had to be a limit. But your father—I'm not sure there was even a voice to push aside for him."

Her mother paused to catch her breath again. "And then you were born. And Delphine. Nessa, having you—in spite of all I knew about the creation of life, I felt like I was witness to a miracle. I began to change the way I was thinking about the work Daniel and I were doing. I pushed him, too. I kept saying: Take a more natural approach. We can't be gods. We have to be students. Be humble."

"Did he listen?" Nessa asked, though she was pretty sure she already knew the answer. She'd seen Chimera Corp.

Vivian shook her head. "He didn't. Things were starting to come together for the company. We built a house and a lab. Outside of Portland. In Oregon. It wasn't like what he has now, but it felt big then.

"After Delphine was born, we talked less. He loved you— but he lived for his lab. He disappeared into it. I started to read—history of science, environmental writers. I stopped asking questions about the work in the lab. And then one day, he was out, and I stepped into the lab to look for something and I saw . . ."

Vivian stopped speaking for a minute and Nessa realized she herself had stopped breathing. "What, Mom?" she said, whispering. She didn't want to break her mother's concentration. "What did you find?"

"Keep in mind, our labs were the size of small airplane hangars. Daniel had a few primates. There were kennels and rooms and cages. He was interested in interspecific pregnancy. We needed it for our work."

"What is that?" Nessa asked.

"It's impregnating one species with the offspring of another. It's the only way to generate a chimera—there's no such thing as an artificial womb. There are tricks you can play to ensure the host accepts the transplant—I invented a few of them." Vivian smiled and Nessa could see that in spite of her mother's disavowal of her work, she had been proud of her accomplishments. "Sometimes you can wrap an embryo in the tissues of the host species. That sort of thing. I'd had some success with rodents and smaller mammals and I knew he was continuing the work. He'd told me a chimp called Lulu was pregnant. I assumed she was carrying one of the chimp-based chimeras

Daniel had been working on. I decided to visit her.

"But when I found Lulu, she was alone, and—" Vivian paused, her face recalling the pain.

"What was wrong with her?" Nessa said. "Could you tell?"

"She told me," Vivian said. "She was adept at sign language and kept signing over and over for her baby. I remember thinking that something must have gone wrong with the fetus and Daniel hadn't told me. But then, as I crossed the lab to leave, I saw a door I had never noticed before. These labs were large so I wasn't surprised—depending on the scope of our work we were often building out new rooms where certain conditions could be maintained. But since Daniel hadn't mentioned any new line of inquiry and I'd been surprised he hadn't told me about Lulu, I decided to open the door.

"And what I found—Nessa—I've never told anyone what it was."

Nessa held her breath.

"The room was...odd," Vivian said. "It didn't look like a lab. It looked . . . well right away I noticed the crib. The changing table. Fake windows—curtains and frames backed by wall. A shelf stocked with board books.

"And sleeping in the crib was Lulu's baby. Or at least, I assumed that this was the baby Lulu had been carrying. But this baby hadn't come from Lulu's genetic material. I'd known that much—Daniel had told me. He'd said he implanted a chimera chimp-deer-bat hybrid. But this was no chimp-deer-bat hybrid. This baby was human. Or at least partially human."

Vivian stopped speaking again. She pressed her lips together. She closed her eyes, as if she was trying to keep herself from seeing. "And Nessa, the human parts of this baby, they were Delphine."

Nessa shuddered. She felt sick. "The baby was barely alive," Vivian went on. She was concentrating so hard on what she was saying, she was speaking almost normally now. "It was tiny like a preemie and hooked up to a respirator and feeding tubes, living inside a tented bubble—I realized Daniel must have collected Delphine's stem cells from her umbilical cord blood."

"Isn't that . . . illegal?"

"Of course it is. Scientists often will run experiments on themselves—that's certainly what I had done. But you don't experiment on embryos. There are ethical issues. You don't mess with human embryos. You don't make human-non-human chimera embryos. And you certainly don't bring those embryos to term!"

"How did you know it was Delphine?" Nessa asked.

"It was the eyes. And a birthmark on the shoulder. Her beautiful baby fingers." Nessa rarely saw her mother cry, but now Vivian's eyes had filled with tears.

"Daniel had taken one of our precious, natural creations and distorted it. The baby—she was dying—anyone could see that. I was watching my own daughter die—slowly, as a laboratory subject."

"What did you do?" Nessa said.

"I had a moment of clarity," Vivian said. "*Extreme* clarity. I realized that the work your father was doing . . . it was wrong. The work I was doing was wrong. We are not meant to play God. We should not be altering what nature has created. We should not be altering our planet. I had turned myself into a wolf! Your father had created a monster. Who knew what that . . . child's life would be, short as it was? I realized that our work—it

338 ●

had to be destroyed."

Vivian pressed the fingers of her left hand to her temple. "I rescued her," she said.

Nessa raised her eyebrows. That Delphine chimera Nessa had encountered at her father's lab hadn't seemed particularly *rescued* to her.

But Vivian wasn't looking at Nessa. Her eyes had lost focus as she returned to the memory. "I unhooked her from the equipment and I wrapped her in a blanket," she went on. "I held her. I sang to her. I don't even know if she was still alive anymore by the time I carried her out of that room and handed her over to Lulu."

"The chimp?" Nessa inquired.

"The chimp. Her mother. Lulu deserved the chance to say goodbye. I gave Lulu a backpack of food and I let her out into the small preserve we had attached to the lab. She carried the baby in her arms. I called a contact at the zoo and told them to send someone to pick Lulu up.

"I released all the animals from Daniel's lab and from my own. I went back to the house—Nessa, I'm telling you about this as though I was calm and rational, but at the time I was sobbing. On the one hand, I was thinking with extreme clarity and on the other, I remember that once I got back to the house, I was trying to make you a sandwich and I was just staring at a jar of peanut butter and I couldn't remember what the order of operations was—did you dip the bread? Spread the jam first? While you were eating lunch, I packed up a bag for you, one for myself, one for Delphine. I loaded them into the car, strapped you and your sister into your car seats. I remember telling you I had to do one more thing before we left to go see Grandma and Grandpa.

"Nessa, that's when I left you in the car and went back to the lab. I knew what I had to do, but I kept thinking that there had to be a better way."

"What did you do?"

"I burned down the labs. Daniel's and mine. They were filled with equipment and information we'd spent our entire professional lives developing. Most of it irreplaceable. I found lighter fluid and gasoline in a maintenance shed. I doused the outside of the building and threw on a match."

"You didn't try to even talk to Dad?" Nessa said.

Vivian shook her head. "His car pulled in just as I came back to the driveway. He got out. He must have smelled the smoke before he saw the flames rising from behind the garage. He asked what I was doing. I told him. I said I was taking you and Delphine. And then I watched his face."

Vivian took a deep, ragged breath. Nessa could tell it was getting harder for her to breathe, that the tightness in her throat was returning. "The look in his eyes, Nessa. That told me more about him in one minute than I'd learned being with him since I was twenty years old. At that moment, he made a choice. He chose the lab."

"Did he think the animals were inside?"

"No. I told him they were all in the woods." Vivian shrugged. "I don't know how much of it was left by the time he got to the labs. The fire was burning pretty hot. As I drove away, I could see it in the rearview mirror and I passed the fire trucks he must have called. I take comfort that all the genetic material he'd likely amassed from you and Delphine—it was all gone. The zoo would find Lulu. The other animals could be collected as well."

"But the baby," Nessa said.

"Nessa, I can tell you without hesitation that unhooking that baby—letting her die naturally as opposed to slowly over the course of weeks, during which she would have been subjected to all kinds of medical tests—that was the hardest and worst thing I've ever done, but I've never regretted it."

Vivian's eyes had filled with tears. Nessa could hear that her breathing had become labored again.

Nessa put a hand on her mom's shoulder and leaned in. "Mom," she whispered. "That creature you saw—the one that looked like Delphine? The baby. I saw her. At Chimera Corp. She survived."

Vivian began to cough. She gasped for breath. "She's still alive?"

And then Vivian was consumed. She coughed like Nessa had not seen her cough before. She was writhing on the bed, gasping for air, her fingers clawing for purchase.

One of the machines she was hooked up to started ringing an alarm.

"Excuse me, please step aside," Nessa heard. A nurse had rushed in and inserted a nebulizer into Vivian's mouth, holding the back of her head for support. "Close your lips down, that's a good girl." The nurse put Vivian's hand on the button. "Press the button when you're ready to take your best, deepest breath. Go."

Nessa watched as her mother broke out into a sweat from the coughing, her dark blonde hair sticking to her forehead in streaks. Vivian held the air from the pump in her lungs for a long moment, then released it. The nurse pushed the hair up off her mother's forehead.

"I think that's just about enough talking for her for today," the nurse said to Nessa.

Nessa nodded. "Of course."

The nurse added a new pillow under Vivian's head, and as she let herself be moved, Vivian's eyes searched for Nessa's, giving her a look, begging Nessa to do something. Nessa couldn't think what she could do just then.

What did her mother want from her? Nessa thought but before she could answer that question, she heard the curtain that separated the room from the hallway move and Delphine stepped in, flushed from her walk. "It's cloudy outside," she said. She put a paper cup down on Vivian's tray. "And I got you some more ice chips on the way in. Do you want any?"

Vivian nodded and Delphine fished out a spoonful of crushed ice with a plastic spoon and gently placed it in Vivian's mouth.

By the time Jane returned with Nate, Vivian had had her fill of ice chips and was lying back on the pillows, the skin on her face nearly as pale as the pillowcase.

Nessa could see that Vivian was tired; even the little conversation they'd had, had been exhausting for her. When Aunt Jane returned with her coffee, she must have seen it too. "We should go," Jane said gently. She bent down and kissed Vivian gently on the cheek, but Vivian had already fallen asleep.

They rode the elevator in silence. Nessa glanced over at Nate and Delphine. They should be here, but seeing Vivian like this was wearing them down. She wondered if she looked as crushed as Nate and Delphine, or if she was better able to mask her feelings.

Heading toward the hospital exit, Jane said in a voice full of cheer, "Who's up for a movie? Or lunch? Nessa?"

Nessa tossed her newly acquired truck keys in the air. "There's a hot dog grilling thing going on," she said, trying to look like the kind of teenager whose social plans were her number one priority at the moment. "Bree and some kids I know will be there."

"That sounds nice," Aunt Jane said. Nessa felt guilty about lying, but what was she going to do? Explain that she'd promised Luc she would try to listen in at the National Guard headquarters? While Aunt Jane was right there? Things were moving so quickly.

By the time Nessa reached Tether, the midday sun had broken through the morning's clouds and it looked like it would be one of those perfect early-spring afternoons when you can finally enjoy being outside. The parking lot where the National Guard had set up temporary headquarters was not far from the town green, and since it was so nice out, Nessa sat on the steps of the gazebo, feeling the sun's warmth penetrate her jeans and fleece sweater. She played around on her phone a bit, listening to the sounds coming from the buildings: a soldier saying, "And then I was like, lady, look . . . "; a throaty laugh; a phone ringing; radio static; the beeping of what she assumed was a microwave—someone heating up a cup of coffee that had gone cold?

She let the noise coming from the buildings fade into the background of her thinking. The sun warmed her face as she squinted in its glare, taking in a regular weekday afternoon in Tether. Men in quilted plaid shirts and work boots parked their pickup trucks in front of the hardware store—contractors and tradespeople. Retirees stopped by the post office. Moms and their toddlers emerged from Story Time at the library.

Tether, Michigan. Nessa had always thought that growing up here had been a foregone conclusion, but there had been a moment in time where Nessa and her family might have lived out an entirely different life. As Nessa let herself relax in the familiar landscape, she couldn't get the images of her mom's story out of her head. She saw her mom standing in the driveway of a house Nessa couldn't remember, two little kids in infant and toddler seats in the back, the trunk full of bags, her young mom facing off with her father and then driving past approaching fire trucks, flames behind her.

How strange to think that Vivian, Nessa, and Delphine had driven straight from there to the house Nessa remembered her grandma living in. Aunt Jane had told her Vivian had come back when her grandpa was sick with cancer. Nessa didn't remember him. She didn't remember any of this but now she wished she did. Maybe then it would make more sense.

Would she ever have the courage to change her life that dramatically, to give up so much? To be so sure of what she wanted?

She checked her watch—it was just after 1 p.m.

What if she did go with Luc, living in wolf form for good? She knew she would miss her family, but the simplicity of the life appealed to her. Wolves did not keep secrets from one another. They didn't worry about having enough money or finishing school or winning races. They didn't interfere with nature and have to figure out what was too much and what was enough. They *were* nature.

What would it be like, she wondered, never to have to sneak out to transform? And there was this: If Nessa was right about Vivian, being a wolf hadn't made her mother sick. It was *not* being a wolf. It was suppressing the ability to transform by injecting herself with the serum.

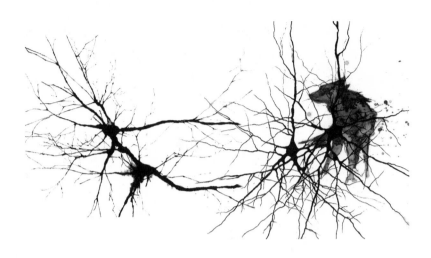

CHAPTER FORTY-EIGHT

essa stood, stretching, feeling very wolf-like in the moment. She'd stopped for a hamburger—well, a few hamburgers—on the drive back to Tether, but even so, she felt vaguely hungry. She was thinking of giving up on the National Guard and texting Bree to see if she could meet up with her at the hot dog party, and then she heard a voice say, "I saw you at the meeting yesterday, trying to hide underneath that baseball cap."

She looked up—it was David Bergen, the reporter from the *Saginaw Sentinel*. Nessa had pretty much run away from him when he'd tried to talk to her at the coffee shop in Grand Rapids, but after the tough questions she'd heard him ask at the town meeting, she'd begun to wonder if he wasn't different from the other reporters, who seemed only interested in the most salacious of the stories they covered.

He had come up the back steps on the other side of the gazebo and now he sat on one of the benches inside. Nessa was in the sun on the front steps. He was in shadow. For a second she wondered whether that was to keep it from seeming obvious he was talking to her. Who did he think he was hiding from?

"In spite of everything going on, Tether's still a pretty nice town, huh?" he said. She said nothing. He seemed to be making casual conversation, but Nessa detected something more in his question. Or maybe she was just a tad freaked out by the fact that his question put into words exactly what she had been thinking.

"Your mom's a pretty amazing person, you know that, right?" he said. Nessa remained silent. She thought about walking away from him, but the sun was warm on her face.

"I know you don't trust me," the reporter said. "And I don't blame you. But I'd like to help you. I'd like to help your mom. There's a lot more going on in Tether than this idyllic scene suggests, and I'm starting to get the feeling that the truth is on your mother's side."

"Uh-huh," Nessa said. She wasn't looking at the reporter but she could hear the scratchy sound of something sliding toward her—she turned quickly and saw that he'd slid a business card across the bench.

David sighed. "Okay, I'll tell you what I know," he said. "I know Paravida's behind Tether's wolf problem. I know your mom is not who everyone thought she was all these years. I know there's some pretty sophisticated science at play. But I don't understand nearly all I need to understand if I'm going to expose Paravida and get to the bottom of what's really happening."

Expose Paravida, Nessa thought. *That sounds pretty good.* But still, she didn't turn around. She didn't talk.

The reporter let the silence extend between them, but eventually he broke it. "If anything comes up," he said, "or you'd just like to talk about some of the answers I've been uncovering, my number's there. I can tell you something. I've seen people in trouble. I know what trouble looks like. And you look like this might be your time for it. I know I look old, but I know how to text and I'm happy to talk in whatever way is easiest for you. Don't be afraid to ask for help."

She met his eyes briefly. He was right. They were not young eyes. They were not penetrating like her mom's, or quick and intelligent like her father's. They were tired, like they'd seen too much. They were eyes Nessa felt she might sometime in the future want to trust.

But not now. "Thanks," she said, turning, hearing how cold and sullen she must sound.

She heard the creaking of the old boards beneath him as he stood. A few beats passed before she heard departing footsteps.

He's right, Nessa thought. She did need help. But not from him.

Picking up her phone, she scrolled through recent calls, found her father's number, and paused for a brief moment with her index finger poised above the screen. Then she tapped, watching as the call went through.

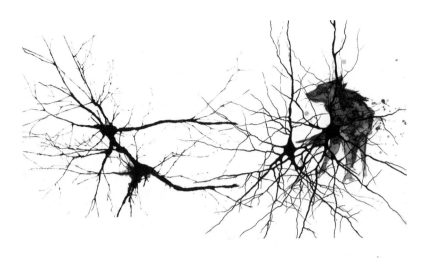

CHAPTER FORTY-NINE

*D*aniel answered Nessa's call on the first ring.

"Hello, Nessa," he said, guardedly. He paused as if to give her the opportunity to speak first. When she didn't, he said, "I'm glad to hear from you. Is everything all right?"

"Well, no," Nessa heard herself saying. There was a bit of an echo on the line, so she could hear her own voice, sounding younger than it did to her own ears. "I thought . . . well, do you know Professor Halliday from Stanford?"

There was a pause. A careful one. "I was just speaking to her this morning," Daniel finally said, his tone letting her know that there was more he knew than he was saying.

"Yeah, well, small world, me too," she said.

Daniel laughed at her attempt at a joke and Nessa joined him more out of nervousness than any appreciation of her own humor. "About that," she said. "Professor Halliday gave me your number." Nessa paused. Briefly, she considered hanging up the phone. How furious would her mother be if she knew Nessa was passing on the secret she'd confided in Nessa . . . and to the person she trusted least of anyone in the world?

Nessa went forward anyway. She had to save her family. She had to save Vivian, and Daniel was their best source of help.

He could make things happen—the special tour of Stanford, the private plane, getting her mom out of the prison hospital and into the private one. Nessa needed something to *happen* now.

The words came pouring out of her mouth. "Professor Halliday said maybe you might be able to make this special serum that someone who has a 'bit of a wolf issue' might want to ingest."

"Oh, dear God, Nessa, I've heard of the phenomenon but I didn't realize you—"

"It's not me," Nessa said.

There was silence on the other end of the line. Was this the sound of Daniel not believing her? "It's, well, it's Mom."

"Your *mother*?"

"You didn't know?" Nessa said.

"No, of course not," he sputtered. This was the first time she'd heard Daniel sound flustered.

"It's just a guess," Nessa said.

"So how did you know to call Professor Halliday?"

"I—uh—" Now it was Nessa's turn to sound stumped. What could she say? That she googled "Werewolf Expert" and her name came up? She ended up using the same line that had worked on her mom. "She mentioned werewolves in a lecture I sat in on and made a comment that made me think she might know something about what was happening to Mom. I was desperate—she was the only person I could think of."

"I see," Daniel said.

"Can you make the serum?"

"I'd better try, hadn't I?" he said, laughing dryly. "I'm going to need a few days . . . at least."

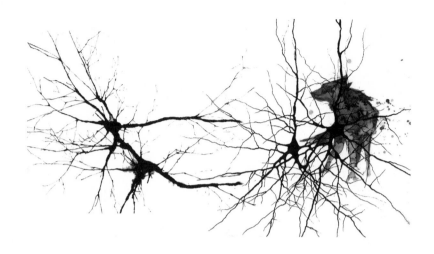

CHAPTER FIFTY

The next few days were some of the longest in Nessa's life. Time ground to a halt as she waited to hear from Daniel to say if he could make the serum, as she drove back and forth to the hospital, as she sat with her mom, watching her sleep and cough. Jane wouldn't set foot in Tether, given the wolf threat and military curfew. Everyone in the family but Nessa was living in a nearby hotel.

When Vivian was napping, Delphine and Nessa played *Words with Friends* on their new matching smartphones—Delphine beat Nessa in every game—or they took turns looking up model train websites with Nate, while from the corner of the room Jane answered emails and prepared reports on her laptop, pretending not to notice that Vivian was getting sicker and sicker.

The B$_{12}$ was no longer working.

Finally, a call came in with an Oregon area code. Nessa was opening a pack of Skittles she'd just bought at the newspaper stand in the hospital lobby and she accidentally managed to both tear open and drop the bag as she fumbled to answer her phone. There were Skittles everywhere but she just turned her back on them.

It was all she could do not to ask, "Is it ready yet?" instead of saying, "Hello." When it wasn't Daniel's voice that answered, she felt all the momentary hope she'd inhaled seeping out of her body.

"Hey, Nessa," she heard. "This is Gabriel." For a second, her mind was a blank. "From your dad's lab."

"Oh, right, hey!" she said, her enthusiastic greeting an overcompensation for not immediately recognizing who he was.

"Hey," he said, and she was grateful to him for sounding casual, for not mentioning the fact that the last time they'd spoken he'd been chasing her down in a golf cart, suggesting they go hear some music together, and she'd been sprinting away from him as fast as she could run.

Nessa was still not clear if his invitation had come from his wanting to date her or if he had been spying on her at her father's request. Come to think of it, she didn't care. Back in Oregon she'd thought Gabriel was cute. Now that she was back with Luc, he seemed impossibly slick and disingenuous.

"Listen," he said. "Daniel's working on something. He's been locked in the lab for two days. I think he might even be sleeping in there. None of us knows what the project is or anything about it, but he asked me to call you."

"Okay," Nessa said.

"He said he needed something of your mom's?" Gabriel choked out an embarrassed laugh. "This may sound crazy, but he wanted something personal—maybe a piece of her hair." Gabriel laughed again. "I don't want to freak you out or anything, but also, he said, um, a cheek swab would do the trick. He said you'd understand, but if this makes you uncomfortable, I can just tell him."

"He needs DNA, is that it?" Nessa said. She might not be a Stanford graduate/intern but she knew enough to know what a cheek swab and a piece of hair had in common.

"Well, yeah," said Gabriel. "But you know, I have divorced parents myself and one thing I've learned is that as much as I love them both on their own, I don't get mixed up in anything going on between them."

"Good to know," said Nessa. "But this isn't a divorce thing. It's, well, just tell Daniel I'll send what he's looking for."

"Okay, then!" Gabriel said and his tone was so nice and normal, Nessa was able to remember—just a little bit—what she'd liked about him. "Sounds like you and Daniel are on the same page about this. How much time do you think you'll need to gather a sample? He said he'd really like to have it by tomorrow morning."

"Um . . . I need five minutes," Nessa said.

After hanging up, she went back up to the room, pretending to have lost her car keys, "found" them in her bag after all, and, in giving her mother one last kiss on the cheek goodbye, lifted a hair from the pillow. A white hair. Vivian's streak of silvery-white was spreading.

In the elevator on her way back down, Nessa realized she hadn't talked to Gabriel about how to get the hair to Daniel. Was she supposed to mail it? But once back in the lobby, she was greeted by a man from a courier service hired by Chimera Corp. He was dressed all in black, like a celebrity bodyguard, and was wearing dark glasses. Nessa handed him the hair wrapped in a tissue and he slipped it into a plastic sandwich bag like he was collecting evidence.

It was the kind of detail Nessa couldn't wait to share with Bree, except every time she tried to connect with her best friend these days, Bree seemed to be with Andy Carlisle. And Tim Miller. After his "one-on-one moment" with a wolf in the woods who saved his life, Tim Miller had done a 180 and switched from wolf hunter to wolf activist.

Instead of organizing anti-wolf protests, he was organizing a movement for increased human-wolf understanding. Andy was second-in-command and Bree had made herself an indispensable member of the team. There were a lot of late-night sessions planning strategy and drafting petitions. At some point, Bree and Andy had made it clear that they were as interested in each other as they were in wolves, and now Nessa never knew where to find Bree when she came back from the hospital.

"You're not exactly that easy to reach either," Bree had explained to Nessa when they'd talked about it. This was true. When Nessa wasn't in the hospital, she was making up one excuse after another to lurk around the town square, listening to the chatter coming out of the National Guard headquarters.

Which for the most part was a whole lot of nothing. The officers in command, the ones who had spoken at the town meeting, had flown away in a helicopter early in the morning the day after the town meeting and, as far as Nessa could tell, had not returned. The only conversations she overheard from the offices were about what to have for lunch or the minutiae of the National Guard's pension benefits and terms of enlistment.

At night, the headquarters were empty. Nessa would pretend to go to sleep, but then sneak out after Ted and Stephanie were asleep. These were her favorite moments—running in the woods with Luc.

Only then did Nessa wish time could move more slowly, rather than faster. She and Luc ran shoulder to shoulder, visiting the packs and checking on the pups' progress with long journeys, communicating with the leaders of the emerging Paravida packs. Nessa got to know the pack leaders and underlings, played with their offspring, watched the way they communicated with one another, and memorized their individual odors (Luc could discern each separate wolf's scent, and Nessa was starting to learn them herself). Jack—the Paravida wolf who was the father of the pups—often came with them. But he was also spending more and more time with his own pups and Sister, learning about what it meant to be a wolf dad.

And not a minute too soon. The puppies were getting bolder and stronger day by day. That night, playing tug-of-war with Brothers Junior Number One—he'd gotten hold of a stick that somehow smelled *exactly* like a dead frog—Nessa loosened her grip and was surprised by the power with which One wrested it away from her. And Biter's bites were actually starting to hurt.

As she played tug-of-war with One, Biter sank his teeth into Nessa's back ankle, and she turned on him and growled before she could remind herself he was only playing.

"He's one of those pups who needs a lot of instruction on social biting cues," Luc said when they were back in the cabin, laughing at the fact that that was an enormous understatement. Nessa laughed too, because . . . well, Biter. And, well . . . Luc.

She just loved the way he put things.

Also, she was the kind of tired where laughing came too easily. They had gone out later than usual after her long afternoon waiting for news from the National Guard headquarters. Luc had joined her and they'd heard one of the junior officers mention that the lead officers were flying back that afternoon and had waited in case there was further information—there hadn't been any.

Now, Luc and Nessa were back in human form, sitting on the bench Luc had built outside the cabin's front door. It wasn't exactly warm enough to be outside at night, but Luc was increasingly uncomfortable indoors, even in human form, and he didn't seem to notice the cold. Nessa found herself surprisingly okay with the weather as well, at least once Luc had wrapped an arm around her shoulders and covered her legs with a sleeping bag, carefully tucking it around the sides of her body and shoulders.

This was the first time in days that Nessa felt her human self relax. Luc took a deep breath. Reflexively, Nessa took a breath as well, feeling it warm her entire body. She rested her head on his shoulder, and he leaned his face in to give her a gentle kiss. She couldn't believe that Luc might be leaving, that little moments like this would be gone from her life when he took off into the woods.

He must have been thinking the same thing because he tightened his grip around her arm and lowered his face down to hers. "This," he said, like he was pointing something out he expected her to be able to understand.

"This what?" Nessa said.

"This right now. This is what I wish I could have forever. This moment here with you."

Nessa felt her breathing tighten. Luc had said exactly what she was thinking, and yet hearing it come from him she suddenly felt she was about to cry. How could something feel so sweet and at the same time so sad?

In an attempt to hide her ragged breath, she buried her face in Luc's neck, but his familiar, pine-needle smell just made her more aware of how much she wanted to hold on to him, to keep him right where he was now. She wanted to always have the exact roughness of his cheek against hers, the feeling of his silky hair under her hand.

"It won't be for a month, right?" she said. "The pups aren't ready."

"I think sooner," Luc nearly whispered. "Those soldiers, Ness, they're not waiting a month before they move in."

"No," Nessa said. "They're not. But I could go with you if you just had more time . . ."

"Don't," Luc said, and she could hear the pain in his voice. "Let it go. Please. You're killing me."

"I'm trying to be strong, you know?" Nessa said. "But sometimes—I know I can't do this alone." She didn't know where those words had come from, but once she started in, the words found their flow. "In the hospital every day . . . walking through this town where half the people would shoot me on sight if they knew what I really was . . . where the other half maybe think my mom is the one responsible for the Paravida wolves being here in the first place . . . it gets old."

"Yeah," Luc agreed. She loved that he laughed. That he got exactly how much her life sucked. "It's not easy to go through life feeling hunted."

Luc was looking up now, to where the stars were visible through the break in the trees. Nessa followed his gaze, trying to guess what he was thinking, wishing she could tell the future in the stars—divine from the patterns they made what she should do and where she should be.

"How are you supposed to protect those wolves?" Nessa said. "You need to remember to protect yourself."

"And you," Luc said. "You're supposed to protect an entire town." He reached across her body, under the sleeping bag, and grabbed her hand. He pulled it to him, their fingers interlaced. "You, Nessa Kurland. Don't forget why you were chosen. There's something here, some way to rescue everyone, that only you have the power to see."

Nessa didn't look away from him. She let his eyes bore into her. Was it possible that he was right? She didn't feel she had any power at all.

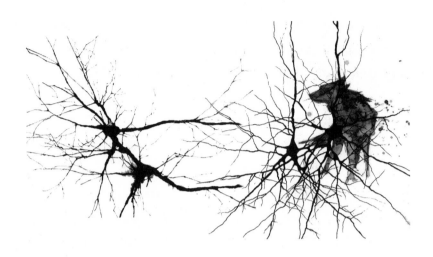

CHAPTER FIFTY-ONE

When Nessa woke the next morning, Bree was sleeping in after a late night—Andy, Tim, and a few other boys were sleeping in the basement where they'd crashed so they wouldn't violate the curfew. Nessa was careful not to wake her friend. Slipping on her sneakers, grabbing a glass of juice from the fridge, Nessa headed out for a run, making her way into town and finding herself at the gazebo as usual.

Everything looked the same as it always did. She saw David Bergen going into the coffee shop to get his coffee. His movements in and out of the town hall, the library, and the coffee shop were as regular as the bells in the high school still ringing out class changing times, even if no one was in school.

Bracing her arms by placing her hands on her knees—she'd been running pretty fast—Nessa took a few minutes to catch her breath, straining to listen for activity in the National Guard headquarters. She wasn't expecting anything to happen this early in the morning.

Until suddenly it was.

She heard the rustling of paper, the scraping of chairs, liquid being poured into a cup . . . and then someone clearing his throat. That someone then said, "Thanks, all, for your patience over the last few days while we met with the governor." Nessa recognized his voice. It was the officer who had spoken first at the town hall. "I want to assure you that the plan we are about to review has been fully vetted and approved," he went on. "At all levels." There was a pause during which Nessa heard the rustling of paper. "Jean, can you make copies of this, please?"

And then, just as the officer launched into what Nessa expected to be the meat of the conversation—the words she had been waiting for days to overhear—the sound of the copy machine kicked in.

Nessa was used to the high-pitched squeal combined with the complaining rattle of whatever combination of rubber and ventilation and electricity-fired engine apparatus formed the guts of this tired-sounding copier. She knew it well enough to realize she wouldn't be able to hear even blood-curdling yells while it was operating. All she could do was hope it didn't stay on during the whole of the conversation. Perhaps there weren't very many copies to make?

There were. As the machine groaned and squealed, rattled and roared, Nessa could hear only whatever word was spoken at the moment the machine got to the end of spitting out one sheet and paused before scanning the next. She heard: "capability." She heard "nexus." She heard "sightlines." She heard "between."

Nothing helpful. Nothing to hint at a meaning she could stitch together until the machine finally, blessedly, ceased its labors and she heard " . . . briefing on the operational objectives for tonight, if we're going in we'll need . . . " And then the machine started back up again.

Nessa stood, frozen in place, not bothering to even appear to be stretching anymore.

The voice she heard. It was now the *other* officer speaking. The one who had appeared to be more senior. The one more definitively in charge.

Had he said "tonight"?

She offered up a silent prayer that the machine would stop.

She moved closer and, pretending to be doing high-knee exercises and then lunges, she headed toward the parking lot.

The machine was finally done. "Yes, again, the governor is aware. And no, waiting is not my recommendation. What happened the other night with those boys. We're just asking for more of the same if we don't take the wolves out now."

The less senior of the two officers chimed in. "If you'll look at your instructions—thank you, Jean—there're just two parts I'd like to call your attention to. We'll close in with flank units from the east and west, and then come up from the south—our aim is to eliminate as many as possible."

Someone asked a question that Nessa could not hear. "Yes," the officer answered. "We will be receiving air support if necessary but we'd like to avoid it if possible. The last thing we need is the people of Tether waking up to a war zone."

Another mumbled question. "That's right. We begin at 1900."

Forgetting for a moment about her mother, about Professor Halliday and Daniel Host, Nessa took off at a sprint. The time 1900 hours translated to 7 p.m. Air support. Elimination. She hated to think what that would mean for the wolves. She needed to find Luc.

But as Nessa, still in human form, raced toward the woods, her phone buzzed.

She checked the number: Daniel Host.

She answered the call with shaking hands.

"Nessa," he said, not even waiting for her to say hello. "I'm calling from the air. I'm an hour from Saginaw. Can you meet me at your mother's hospital room?" Nessa remembered that this crisis in the woods was not the only one. Daniel was a card she was playing in another game.

"Uh . . . yeah," she said. "I can be there."

She texted Luc. She repeated to herself: 1900 hours was 7 p.m. It wasn't enough time but her mom's situation was even more dire. Maybe she could be back in time?

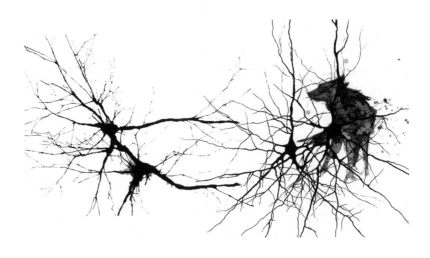

CHAPTER FIFTY-TWO

hile Nessa drove Luc's truck to the hospital, her mind kept traveling in circles. The text she'd written to Luc had read:

You need to get the wolves out tonight. Guard is coming in at 7 p.m.

She'd paused before she'd sent it. Once it was received, she knew that Luc would begin to get ready to leave. He would take the wolves out of Tether and he would go with them. Maybe there could be another way? Maybe her mom could do something once she'd been injected with the serum? Get out of bed, talk to the people in Tether, get them to go to the National Guard? Maybe her father would help? Maybe she herself could do something?

Who am I kidding? Nessa thought, as she drove past the National Guard checkpoint. *There isn't enough time.*

Halfway to Saginaw, she pulled over and wrote another text, this time to Bree.

Please call David Bergen. Tell him the National Guard will be rounding up all the Tether wolves at 7 p.m. tonight. This is a story he can't miss.

Maybe, somehow, he could stop the exodus. If he did, then Luc could stay.

Daniel was waiting for Nessa outside the revolving doors of the hospital's main entrance, holding a small and discreet cooler. He was wearing a beige blazer, his chocolate-colored hair brushed neatly across his forehead.

He looked, as always, composed but also curious—he had a habit, Nessa had noticed, of leaning forward on his toes. It made him seem over-eager. She realized that this was the first time she'd seen him since that last dinner at his house. Since then she'd learned so much more about him—about what he had done, how he had done it, who he had lied to in order to make it happen. About where curiosity could take you.

When he recognized her behind the wheel of Luc's old red pickup, his eyes opened a little wider. "This is what you drive?" he asked.

"Yeah," said Nessa, stepping down—the hospital had valet parking and if ever there was a time to use it, the time was now. "It's actually my boyfriend's but he loaned it to me."

All her dad did was blink. Slowly. At the word "boyfriend." But it was that blink, and maybe the studied absence of any other major reaction that let her know something was shifting in the way he saw her.

She was glad. *It's high time he sees the real Nessa,* she thought. Not the one sitting at attention at the fancy dinner table in borrowed clothes but the one who mostly wears the same pair of jeans and can handle the stick shift in a seventeen-years-young Chevy.

A smile crept across his face. "I guess you can take the girl out of Michigan . . ." he said.

"Or not," said Nessa.

He smiled even wider, clearly appreciating the intelligence of her rebuttal. He didn't try to hug her. He gestured to the door. "Shall we go in?"

They walked through the lobby and into the elevator without speaking but when the elevator was climbing, Daniel said, "Does she know I'm coming?"

Nessa nodded. "She does," she said. "But I didn't tell Aunt Jane."

Daniel nodded. He took a deep breath. "Delphine will be there?" Nessa looked at him sideways and nodded in return. Was he . . . nervous?

Before Nessa drew back the curtain surrounding Vivian's bed, she poked her head around it and said to Jane, Delphine, and Nate: "Uh, guys, someone's here to see Mom." Too late, Nessa realized that what was about to happen was something she might have wanted to prepare them for.

Prepare Vivian for.

Would she summon all her strength and look Daniel

straight in the eye as she said, *Get out*? Or would Aunt Jane do that for her?

Drawing back the curtain, Nessa thought, *There's only one way to find out.*

"So, yeah," Nessa said. "This is Daniel Host."

Jane, already half-standing in her chair, froze.

Nate was looking up as if startled by a loud noise.

Delphine was just staring at Daniel with what Nessa could instantly see was an expression of both recognition and pain.

As Daniel's sharp black eyes darted from Vivian in the bed to Jane in the chair, Nessa could see him taking it all in. And all of them looking right back at him.

His eyes finally landing on Vivian, Daniel went pale. "That bad?" Vivian said.

Daniel composed his face. "No, you look fine. It's just—well, it's been fourteen years."

"That's a long time," she said. Even those few words made her cough. But she caught her breath enough to add, "And now you've come."

"I have," Daniel said, his voice cowed, strangely empty.

"I asked him to," Nessa added, and then to the others as much as to her mom: "He has the medicine for you, Mom. I asked him to make it."

"That's right," Daniel said.

"You did?" Vivian said.

Nessa looked her mom in the eyes and did not let go of her gaze. "Will you take it?"

For a minute, Vivian just stared at Nessa, then at Daniel, then again at Nessa. Instead of answering Nessa's question, she addressed Daniel. "You used the Eisenhower formulation?" she asked.

Daniel nodded, and Nessa had the realization that her parents shared a language that only they understood.

Vivian dipped her chin. "Okay," she said. "We can try."

Nodding briskly like he was Milton, or any other one of his own attentive staff, Daniel took a few swift steps toward Vivian, releasing the seal on the cooler even as he was moving. With the efficiency of a skilled clinician, he slipped on a pair of surgical gloves, prepped a syringe, found the free port dangling near the permanent IV, and temporarily closed off the drip from Vivian's fluids to make way for whatever he was bringing in his bag.

Vivian had her eyes closed and was leaning against her pillow with an expression of resignation, but Jane jumped to her feet when she saw the syringe. "Wait a minute," she said. "What in the hell do you think you're doing? What's going on? Who do you think you are?"

"It's okay," Nessa said to Aunt Jane. "He knows what he's doing." She paused. "You know this is my father?"

"I do know that," Aunt Jane said sarcastically. "I was worried that he was clearly not a doctor but now that I know he's a man your mother despises, it's perfectly fine he's injecting her with—what *is* that?"

"It's—" Nessa said. "I can explain later."

"Let him, Jane," they heard, and all three turned to see that Vivian had spoken. She held up a hand. "Spare me," she said. "Let me see your calculations."

Daniel shook his head. "I knew you'd ask for that," he said. He pulled a paper out of the case and passed it to her. Vivian took the page, which shook in her trembling hands. She had to squint to scan it, but clearly she was able to make out what it meant. At one point she muttered, "Messy," but made no other comment until she had either exhausted herself or finished reading. She lowered the paper, letting it rest on the mattress, though she was still gripping it, wrinkling it, nearly folding it in half with the force of her twisted fingers.

"I had to make some significant guesses," Daniel said. "Do you think it will work?"

"Probably not," Vivian said, and she looked at Daniel in a way Nessa didn't recognize at all. There was a shared joke between them. Was there also longing in her mother's eyes— for the man she'd been in love with, the father of her children? For the life she'd given up? For life, period?

At the thought that her mother was afraid for her life, Nessa felt her own gut contract in reflexive pain and fear. That her mother might be dying—that was not possible. That could not be. But there it was.

Daniel finished filling the syringe. He uncapped the needle, inserted it into the extra port he'd found attached to Vivian's IV, and depressed the plunger with his thumb.

The serum was bright yellow, the exact shade of a lemon Starburst. Nessa saw Nate watching the yellow liquid travel through the port. Delphine had her face hidden in Aunt Jane's shoulder.

Vivian had closed her eyes. She was perfectly still. For one horrible second it occurred to Nessa that the serum might have killed her.

And then Vivian opened her eyes, but doing so seemed to be difficult for her. Clearly, she had not regained any strength.

"How long do you think it will take?" Nessa asked.

Daniel shrugged.

"It depends on the phase of the moon," Vivian whispered. "It could take . . . days."

"So you're saying," Daniel said, settling back into a chair as if to get comfortable, "that all we can do is wait?"

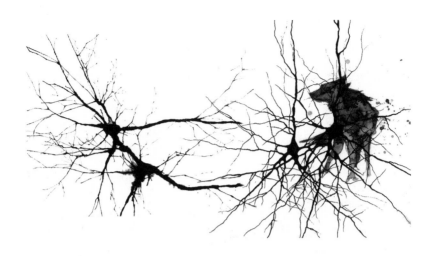

CHAPTER FIFTY-THREE

"I'm going to get a hotel room in Saginaw," Daniel announced, closing up his cooler, "in case I'm needed. I'll need to check her tomorrow, and I'd like to observe right now. I prepared a second dose from an alternate batch just in case."

Jane sniffed. Delphine looked up at the ceiling. Nate had his head buried in a video game. "That's fine," Nessa said, speaking for all of them. Just then, her phone buzzed. Pulling it from her pocket, she saw it was from Luc.

"Look," she said to all of them, "I—uh—I gotta go."

"You . . . what?" said Delphine, finally willing to look at her. She glared at Daniel then looked back at Nessa. "You're leaving us?"

"It's important," Nessa said. "I'll explain later."

Rushing down the hospital's stairwell—that elevator was way too slow—Nessa read his message:

I could use your help. You nearby?

Nessa texted back:

Heading your way. Give me an hour (sorry). Where are you?

Luc sent nothing in reply.

If Luc's truck had been capable of speeds greater than 53 mph, Nessa would have pushed it, but she knew the truck could barely maintain 53. It was torture, driving this slowly. But she was learning to overcome torture.

Finally reaching Tether, Nessa parked Luc's truck by the old trailhead at mile marker 12, sprinted into the woods, and transformed as soon as she was hidden by the cover of trees. For lack of a better idea, she headed toward Luc's cabin.

It stood empty, old leaves in the clearing blowing in the breeze.

Luc wasn't with the natural wolves either—in fact, their den was deserted, even the pups were gone.

On a hunch, Nessa headed west from the den, remembering that one of the new wolf packs had been gathering there the last time she had made the rounds with Luc. Sure enough, Luc was there with them.

She found him standing on a rocky outcropping with several of the larger Paravida wolves in the area. They appeared to be engaged in some kind of a council. Seeing her, Luc broke away from the group and ran a bit into the forest. Nessa followed, taking on human form when he did. They did this at times when they needed to talk.

"Luc," she said. "Luc, what are we going to do? The pups aren't ready to go."

"I know," he said. "But it's not just the pups. Communication has still been a little rough with the rest of the wolves, especially with the pack to the north. The south and the east packs are closer to being ready, but it doesn't take much for them to start fighting among themselves. But yes, the pups are going to be a challenge."

"Where *are* the pups?" Nessa asked. "When I checked the den they weren't there."

Luc rubbed one of his temples with his first two fingers. He didn't generally exhibit any signs of stress. This tiny crack in his composure spoke volumes about what was really going on inside. "Big One moved them this morning. They're up by the river now."

"Bree's calling that reporter from the *Saginaw Sentinel*," Nessa said. "He might be able to bring some attention to what's happening. Maybe it will slow things down."

"Okay," Luc said. He took a deep breath. He looked the way he did before a race, when he finally stopped pounding power bars or writing his name over and over in Sharpie on the race swag and went into this very deep, internal place. He looked at his watch. "We have a little over three hours. Why don't you go to Big One? Let him know he has to move—the pups have to go as fast as they can."

"Where should I tell them to go?"

"Big One will know. Tell him I'll meet them there. Tell him to expect company."

"But Luc," Nessa said. "The heat map. They're going to know

where you are. They have helicopters."

"I don't know what else to try," Luc said. "The alternative is to stand and fight and I don't know about you, but I didn't wake up today with suicide on my mind."

Nessa would remember those words later and wish they hadn't rolled off Luc's tongue quite so easily.

Brother was waiting for Nessa when she arrived at the spot Luc told her about—the wolves were camped out on a bluff where the river turned. The spot was wooded, but from the rock where Brother was standing, there was a view along the river course in two directions.

Nessa touched noses with Brother and then headed down the opposite side of the rock where she was immediately ambushed by the Brothers, Part Dos. The pups jumped her and then rolled on their backs when she dropped into a crouch of surprise as if to say, "Get me! Go after me!"

Nessa lay down so they could climb on her belly, feeling again how much bigger they had become. Princess and Biter came running to join in and she groaned as they landed heavily on her belly.

Rolling them off into one chaotic fur ball of fun, she stood. "I wish I could stay with you guys and just play," she wanted to say. How was she going to tell the pack what she needed to tell them? That they had to move?

She saw that the wolves were waiting for her. Mama was watching, Sister was nearby, and Big One stood in front of both of them. Nessa sniffed him, rubbed noses, and did a quick running circle, miming a gesture that, had they been playing, would have gotten him into running mode as well. They weren't playing, though. He was watching. She ran in the quick circle again, ending with her nose pointed north, her tail erect.

Big One lay down deliberately, lowering one paw after another carefully to the ground. Nessa knew the gesture meant that he had reasons for wanting to stay.

She insisted. She ran in a circle again, ending with the same north-facing nose. Just as she was giving up on the communication, thinking, *Didn't Luc go over this already? I thought they were just waiting for the signal!*, Big One got up off the ground and repeated Nessa's gesture. At first he did it at a walk, then a trot, then he made his way around the circle of adult wolves who had gathered, performing the gesture and then watching as each member of the pack repeated it.

Nessa had never seen anything like it. She wondered if even animal behaviorists knew that something like this could happen.

When Big One came to Sister, though, Sister did not repeat the running gesture. Instead, she lay down ceremoniously, the way Big One had. Was she speaking for the puppies? Saying they weren't yet ready for travel? Nessa could only assume so.

Big One repeated the running gesture in front of Sister. Nessa wondered if she was making the same calculation Nessa just had. This time, Sister repeated the running gesture.

Fascinating, Nessa thought. *Also time consuming*. She sat back on her haunches and let out an impatient howl. They needed to get going. They needed to get going *now*.

Suddenly, bounding out of the woods, Jack appeared. Trailing him was an adolescent Paravida male. *Is this okay?* Nessa thought, but then she realized they were both pack members now. They approached Big One and Mama and performed the appropriate sniff tests. Then after Sister conferred with Jack, Jack and the new male rounded up the pups into a little pile between them. All of them sat and stared at attention except Brother Two, who was digging. Digging and digging and digging, in his own world and seemingly oblivious to the ceremonious and serious exchange of information going on above his head. Soon the other pups could not resist Two's example—they began digging as well, pushing each other aside to get at whatever delicious smell Two had uncovered. Except Princess. She sat primly by, giving them a look that Nessa interpreted as, "I didn't go to Harvard so I could become a ditch digger."

Finally, Mama started to walk in the direction Nessa had pointed them to, following the course of the river north. Brother followed Mama. Next came the pups, prodded forward by Jack, the new male, and Sister. Last in line was Big One. Nessa walked side by side with him, relieved to be on the way finally and also starting to wonder where Luc was now.

Had he managed to get the wolves he was escorting to come along as well? Had they responded to the signal—the sense of danger? Could they understand the urgency or would they resist the direction of another wolf?

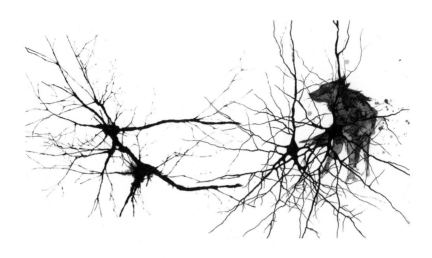

CHAPTER FIFTY-FOUR

The traveling started out auspiciously enough. Mama set a brisk pace and though the puppies darted away at every opportunity—apparently there was something interesting to smell behind nearly every rock and shrub—Jack, Sister, or the adolescent helper wolf would nose them back into line.

The snow had been melting over the course of the past few months and the river was running high, foamy white water breaking over gray and black rocks coated with moss. The crashing of the water created such a symphony of sound that Nessa couldn't hear her own breathing or footsteps or the occasional whine of a pup being told to leave a stick or leaf and move on.

The white water also interrupted Nessa's sense of smell—her nostrils were flooded with the cold, damp odors stirred up by the swirling water—the smell of crayfish and molds and rotting silt carried in the spray.

Distracted by the river, Nessa did not notice the wolves on the opposite riverbank until she happened to look up and see them—a whole line of them, with Luc at the front.

Luc had never seemed more perfect. Even in this moment of triumph—his plan was working—he was keeping it mellow. Brother's tail would have been held up like a flagpole, but Luc's was in a more neutral position, and he was trotting along like he was following a scent on a Saturday night in the woods, not leading a revolution.

They'd done it! She didn't know the time exactly but it wasn't close to dark yet—she guessed it was somewhere between 5 and 6 p.m. They had at least a full hour until the National Guard planned to attack. They had every chance of making it far away from anywhere the Guard would be hunting for wolves.

Nessa snorted. To think that these wolves Luc was leading were the Paravida wolves! Luc had been right. They could be turned around. Everything could be turned around.

She felt a rush of optimism and hope bubbling and crashing into her brain with the same force as the white water rushing below. Her tail high, Nessa felt that every single challenge would be resolved: Her mother would get better, her father would be the one to save her.

Wolves were beautiful—the slope of their dignified necks when they raised their noses to the moon, the hope and joy embodied in the slant of their tails, the grace of their long legs, the warmth and softness of their coats. Even these wolves, bred to be dangerous, were still wolves. Nessa could see this now. If she'd thought she could be heard, Nessa would have howled in joy. Here when so many things had gone wrong, when she'd lost so much, this was going as well as could possibly be hoped.

And then Biter lay down.

Princess kept going but her tongue was hanging out of the side of her mouth. The Brothers were dragging. Jack nudged Biter, trying to get him to stand up, and Biter tried, only to lie down again a few yards farther away.

Okay, Nessa thought, trying to collect her thoughts, trying to stay calm. The pups needed to rest. Fine. They could rest. For ten minutes. They had an hour. The only issue was that Nessa needed to tell Luc, but when she looked across the river, she saw he was too far away to notice what was happening. She couldn't get his attention unless she barked, and if she barked, she might throw all the wolves into a panic.

What were they going to do? How could they communicate to the other wolves that they needed to wait?

That question, it turned out, was moot, because just then, Nessa heard a sound layering in on top of the roaring of the water below. The sound was repetitive and rhythmic.

The rhythm wasn't coming from the water but from something in the air.

Thwok-thwok-thwok.

A helicopter. Nessa felt the word in her mind only seconds before she saw the bird in the air. It was the size of a boat, shaped like a gigantic insect, a small pilot's cabin for a head, and then a larger back body with open sides, soldiers' legs dangling over them.

There were enough ROTC-obsessed kids at Tether High

that Nessa had absorbed the name of the weapons this machine was carrying: She recognized machine guns, grenade launchers, autocannons, and rockets, but the soldiers' eyes were the scariest, the way they stared down at Nessa, Luc, and the other unarmed wolves impassively.

They don't see me as a human, Nessa realized. *These are U.S. soldiers but they will not protect me,* she thought, as the helicopter swooped down low, following the path of the river, taking advantage of the lack of trees to get a view of the wolves running on either side. *I am the enemy.*

What was the helicopter doing here? Nessa was sure she had heard 1900 hours as the start time for the mission. It couldn't possibly be that late. Were they here early?

Nessa looked across the river. Luc was still leading the pack but his tail was between his legs, his head down like he was a dog waiting to be reprimanded. He had glanced her way. The Paravida wolves behind him were stopping. Some were crouching. Some had run off. The natural pack was in disarray as well. At the sight of the helicopter, the exhausted pups had frozen in fear.

Sister pushed Princess with her nose. Mama tried to nudge Biter, but nothing took. Sister started to take rapid steps toward one of the Brothers, but Nessa could see Sister was disoriented and overwhelmed. Jack was reverting to his former self, snarling at everyone and everything, and then attacking Biter. Or at least that's what it looked like. Jack rushed Biter, knocking him down again—even though Nessa had always believed Biter to be Jack's favorite.

Big One and Mama stood protectively in front of Biter, not allowing Jack to get near but it did nothing to stop Jack's crazy actions. He dove this way and that, nipping at Big One or Mama in ways that generally would not have been tolerated. But with the sound of the helicopter returning and the rushing water, Big One and Mama did not attack Jack.

And then Jack managed to get past them. He took Biter by the scruff of the neck, and before there was time to gasp or rush him or think, "No!" he had tossed him over the side of the riverbank and into the rushing stream.

In shock, Nessa watched Biter travel downstream, his shiny wet head just visible above the white foam.

Wolves are comfortable swimming and don't mind even the most frigid water, but the river was flowing fast and it wasn't clear to Nessa if Biter could handle the current. She wasn't sure an adult wolf could. What had Jack been thinking?

She turned on him, growling. Every bad thought she'd ever had about Paravida wolves flashed forward to the front of her brain: They were monsters, they could never change. What did she expect, placing trust in someone like him?

Big One and Mama must have been having the same thoughts, because they were advancing on Jack now, teeth bared, heads lowered, shoulders up. Jack didn't seem to notice. He was barking at something. At Sister?

She was frozen, staring at him, whining as he continued to bark, but then suddenly she let out an answering bark and leapt into the water. Nessa had more confidence in Sister's ability to ford the white water and she suddenly also understood what Jack had wanted from her. She was going after Biter.

That is, Jack had *sent* her after Biter.

So he wasn't trying to murder him?

Nessa tried to spot Biter and barely had a glimpse of his tiny head disappearing where the river turned a bend. He'd gone so far. So fast. Walking would have taken at least fifteen minutes where the river had dragged him in only a few. Suddenly Nessa understood that too. Jack was saving Biter. Risky as it was, the white water would carry the pups farther and faster than they could ever move on foot.

As a Paravida wolf, Jack knew what humans were capable of. Jack knew that the helicopter would return. He'd understood that the risk of being shot was greater than the risk of drowning.

But now, as the helicopter approached for a second pass, Big One and Mama were still growling at Jack, getting closer to him. The adolescent wolf he'd brought along was backing him and Brother clearly didn't know what to do. He was jumping and pacing behind Mama.

Nessa made a quick calculation. Brother was a team player through and through. If Mama and Big One attacked Jack, Brother would stand with them. It would be two Paravida wolves against three smaller and less aggressive natural wolves. With the fate of the pups at stake, they could easily end up fighting to the death.

Nessa couldn't let this fight happen.

Picking up Princess by the scruff of her neck, Nessa tossed her into the river. Big One rushed Nessa with a ferocious snarl. Nessa ducked her head to show she did not want to fight him. Meanwhile, Jack picked up one of the Brothers Junior and tossed him after Princess. Down in the river, Nessa saw Princess and Little Brother's heads, swiftly disappearing.

The helicopter hovered close overhead and Nessa heard the crack of machine gun fire. Brother barked wildly. Big One ignored the noise and instead presented himself in all his intimidating bulk to Nessa, growling at her. She saw that no signs of deference she could offer were going to fix things. Big One was about to attack her.

But Mama attacked Big One first. She knocked into him. Then she nudged Brother Two toward the bank. Nessa could almost hear her thinking, *You go on now. It's going to be okay. You have to go now.*

The machine gun sounded again and this time it was closer. Nessa glanced at the opposite bank and saw one of the Paravida wolves Luc had been leading jump up and then fall.

Jack was tossing another pup into the water now, and the Paravida adolescent jumped in after her. Big One glared at Nessa. She barked at him. *Wake up! This is your chance to save your pack and yourself!*

Something shifted in Big One's eyes. Nessa barked again. Suddenly, as if it had been his idea all along, Big One circled the pack, pushing the remaining pups toward the bank, where Mama and Jack shepherded the last ones into the water. As soon as they broke the surface, Jack jumped in after them. Mama followed. Big One gave Nessa one last, long look and jumped in as well.

They were not a second too soon. The helicopter, which had been sweeping the opposite bank, appeared just above Nessa now, over the spot where they had all been standing. As machine gun fire rained down all around her, Nessa could see the dirt jumping up, the way the surface of a lake is pocked by falling rain. She leapt for the cover of trees, feeling the impact the bullets were making on the ground just behind her.

As Nessa continued to run away from the river, she saw a

half dozen Paravida wolves coming toward her. She froze in place but they rushed right past her toward the water.

Then she saw why. As she continued away from the river, toward Tether, she saw light breaking through the trees. At first she thought the light emanated from a single source, but then she realized she was seeing hundreds of individual lights, spread out in a line to the right and left that she could not see the end of.

She stopped, even before she realized that each individual light was affixed to a helmet, and each helmet was worn by a soldier. She was facing a line of them, heading in her direction, tromping through the woods in a human chain meant to compress the wolves closer and closer together.

"You're early," she wanted to shout. Had the plans Nessa overheard changed? Had she heard wrong? *This shouldn't be happening.*

Turning quickly before she could be seen, Nessa took off at a sprint, running behind the Paravida wolves, trying to make it back to the river, hoping that the helicopter might be gone, that Luc would still be there. They needed to regroup. They needed to make a new plan. Together.

But by the time she reached the river again, Luc was gone. Dozens of Paravida wolves lay dead on the opposite side of the river and among the wolves who were left standing, Nessa could not see a single one who matched Luc's coloring. Some of the wolves on the opposite shore were hiding under the trees. She could hear them and smell them. She sang out a question—

Luc, are you there?—and waited for him to respond but there was nothing. He might not have been able to hear her above the rushing water.

Nessa continued to hear the helicopter beating at a distance. Would it return? She called for Luc again, and again there was nothing.

Nessa's side of the river was crowded with Paravida wolves. They must have been flushed out of the woods by the approaching soldiers and reached the water's edge only to encounter the specter of the dead wolves.

Whatever social ties had brought these wolves together had obviously frayed to the point of breaking. They were attacking one another. They were sniffing like crazy where the natural wolves had been.

Nessa saw that the wolves on the opposite bank were watching them, looking like they were trying to track who was going to win the senseless fighting going on across the water. "You need to stay together," she wanted to shout. "You need to stay calm."

But Nessa didn't think the Paravida wolves were going to listen to her. They might know Luc but she'd been traipsing around her father's forest the entire time he'd been making his breakthroughs—they didn't know who she was.

To make matters worse, Nessa could hear the helicopter returning. It was visible now, and Nessa realized she had to try to do something. Taking a running start she made a wide circle around them, cutting them off at the riverbank and then running straight into the woods. A few followed her, out of instinct. Once she'd made it into the woods she stopped and turned on them, making her most ferocious growl. They froze.

Then she took off, making another looping maneuver, bringing a few more into the woods this time.

In that way, she managed to save perhaps seven or eight of the wolves. When the helicopter began strafing again, four were shot down.

It wasn't just bullets coming from the chopper this time, though. It released small capsules that hit the ground. They were smoking as they fell through the sky and when they landed, instead of the boom Nessa expected, there was barely a reverberation of any kind. Nessa thought the first few had been duds, and then she started to smell something rancid. She saw the smoke rising from the ground. Gas. For a minute, Nessa couldn't see the opposite bank of the river, and then she couldn't see anything at all. She'd gone blind.

With her eyes closed, she concentrated on what she could hear. There was the sound of the wolves nearby, the whines they were emitting, the rustling of their footsteps in the humus beneath the trees. There was the rushing of the water, the repetitive thrumming of the helicopter blades. Then the softer sound of soldiers approaching, calling to one another, the heavy tread of their boots breaking through sticks and squelching in the mud.

Nessa assessed the situation. The National Guard had the heat map. They had the helicopter. They had the soldiers. The wolves could run but they could not hide and a threat lay in every direction where they might turn. The wolves on the riverbank were sitting ducks.

Unless . . .

Nessa suddenly remembered something.

The natural wolves had swum for safety because that was

the only way the pups could travel. But there was another advantage to jumping in the river. The river would mask their presence. Once in the river, the wolves could not be seen.

Nessa felt her tail shoot up into the air behind her. Her nose lifted into the air involuntarily. She needed to be in charge. She needed to be big and bold. The helicopter was returning. She had to get those Paravida wolves to jump in the water. Maybe the wolves whose lives she'd saved by running them into the woods would follow her to the water? She could only try . . .

Nessa came at them from behind, biting an ankle the way she had when she was distracting the wolves who had surrounded Tim Miller that night in the woods. When the bitten wolves turned, she dodged them and ran for the river's edge, banking on the fact that they would follow. She couldn't see it, but she could hear the water. She could hear the wolves behind her as well. She stopped on the edge of the bank, but they had too much momentum and hurtled down past her, tumbling into the water, which immediately pulled them downstream. Maybe once they were embarked on the journey, they would understand.

Nessa ran back to collect the remainder of the wolves, shepherding them into the water as well, and when the last of them were heading downstream she herself crossed the river, climbed the opposite bank, and began the same maneuvers with the wolves on that side.

By this point, though, the soldiers on the bank she had just vacated had arrived and they were shooting. "Stop! Please stop it!!" she wanted to shout, her heart full of the sense of loss of life.

The soldiers did not understand wolf behavior. They did not understand that they were creatures who would track a meal for forty miles, only to share the kill with their sisters and brothers. They were creatures who fought a constant battle with starvation, who lay down to rest to conserve the calories needed for the pack to survive, their energy and life source not stingily withheld for their own use, but donated to others, the ultimate in team loyalty. How could the soldiers not value this? Not know? In the haze of her single-minded focus on her mission, in the haze of tear-gas smoke, Nessa did not understand how the soldiers could not see what she did.

Dodging bullets, she focused on getting one wolf after another into the water. She wasn't counting but she knew there were many floating downstream already. Finally, when the soldiers broke through to Nessa's side of the river, she made a quick decision to transform back to human form, and leapt into the water too, using her strong arms to keep her head above the surface, tears streaming out of her burning eyes, knowing she could not let the exhaustion overtake her yet.

The cold felt welcome, the water a rescuing force pulling her down, and already she was gone from the scene of the fighting. The Paravida wolves would stay in the river for miles, but as soon as the coast was clear, Nessa pulled her own exhausted form out of it. She lay panting on the riverbank, thinking only one thought. *Where was Luc?*

Nessa knew he hadn't been on the opposite bank of the river when she crossed. She would have seen him. She also knew he would not have left the scene without the other wolves. That left only one possibility: that his body lay with those of the wolves who had been shot. She felt herself crying, her tears working their way into the water already drying on her skin.

Eventually Nessa stood and started to make her way to a nearby farmhouse. She did not know when she had ever felt more alone.

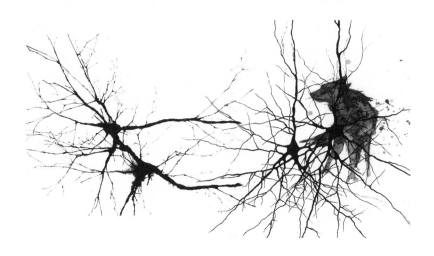

CHAPTER FIFTY-FIVE

*B*y the time Nessa reached Bree's—walking alongside the highway, she'd been picked up by a state police patrol—she was no longer dripping, but she was still wet. Her jeans were clinging to her legs. Riding in the back seat of the patrol car, she kept lifting the fabric, noticing that it was so stiff it formed a little tent. This reminded Nessa of the way Vivian had taught her to tell if an animal was dehydrated—you pulled at its skin and if it "tented," the animal needed fluids. Confusing her jeans with her skin, she thought, *Am I dehydrated? Is that why I feel so awful?*

At Bree's, Ted was the one who opened the door and let her in, nodding authoritatively at the Statie to let him know, in a man-to-man way, *We've got this from here.* He didn't say a word to Nessa to point out that she had been out after curfew. All he said was, "You all right?" when he saw her sorry state. He stepped back to let her in the house and then Stephanie was right behind him to put an arm around Nessa's shoulder, leading her straight to the bathroom. "Take a shower," she said. "I'm going to heat up some soup. Bree will bring you fresh clothes."

A half hour later, Nessa was sitting at the kitchen table, and Ted and Stephanie were very pointedly *not* asking her any questions about what had happened. Stephanie's delicious squash soup tasted like butter and thyme. She poured ginger ale over ice cubes in a tall glass and just inhaling the smell of it, Nessa felt the sugar quickening the flow of blood down to her toes.

Stephanie laid both hands on the table and leaned forward with a flat back, like she was stretching. "So ... your, um, father?" Stephanie said. "He called for you." Nessa nodded, to show that yes, she did have a father now. "He wants you to come to Saginaw. He's sending a car at nine. He said he didn't want you driving the truck."

Nessa nodded. Tomorrow morning at nine felt like a century away.

After Nessa had eaten, Stephanie said, "You're half asleep. Bree, take Nessa upstairs?"

"Nessa, I've been so worried about you," Bree said in a low voice when they were upstairs in Bree's room, under the covers with only one lamp on, even though it wasn't yet 10 p.m. "I called the reporter like you asked me to but it totally backfired. Somehow the National Guard found out reporters were coming and went in even earlier."

"They were killing wolves," Nessa said. "The soldiers were shooting at us. They had a helicopter like it was a war or something. There was tear gas." She closed her eyes but all she saw was the riverbank, littered with the bodies of dead wolves. "They—Bree, Luc is gone."

"He got shot?"

"I didn't see for sure but when the shooting started, I ran. When I came back, he wasn't there."

"Oh, Nessa," Bree said.

Bree seemed to want to say something. She opened her mouth. She closed it. She finally said, "If you didn't actually see him go down, there's a chance he's still out there. You have to have hope."

"Hope," Nessa repeated. She couldn't forget the blank look in the soldiers' eyes, the ones with their legs hanging over the sides of the helicopter, the ones who had been shooting at her, the ones who . . . oh, Luc!

"Luc was shot on the riverbank," Nessa said. She couldn't feel the pain she knew was lurking deep inside. "He was going to become a wolf forever. He was leaving me. And I was sad about it. The idea that I wouldn't be with him again. But this . . . now. He didn't even have a chance to be the thing he'd always wanted."

Bree put a hand on Nessa's shoulder, and Nessa finally broke down and wept.

When Nessa woke the next morning, her phone was ringing. Bree's bed was empty. Nessa let the call go to voicemail.

She didn't think she could move, she was so sore. She just lay in bed, staring at the ceiling.

What had been the last thing Luc had said to her? How would it be for his parents when he simply never came home?

Bree had said to have hope.

Nessa rolled over, burrowing her face deep in her pillow. Her phone rang again. When she answered, she heard a man's voice, but no one she recognized.

"Miss," the voice said. "I'm down in front. Your driver? Just wanted to let you know."

Just then she heard a knock at the door, and Bree stuck her head in. "The car your dad sent is here."

Nessa sat up, speaking to Bree and into the phone at the same time. "Got it," she said. Her mother. Her family. She had to go to them. "I'll be right down."

In the car, Nessa tried to keep from thinking about everything that had happened the day before. And when images did surface, she practiced looking at them without allowing any feeling to arise. She closed her eyes to block the sudden sensation that she was back on the riverbank, but the memory came anyway.

Nessa couldn't un-hear the roar of the water and the helicopter. She couldn't un-see the pups' small black heads struggling to stay above the surface of the churning white water. She couldn't not scan for Luc, again and again, looking, looking, waiting without satisfaction for the answering figure to emerge from the smoke across the way.

When the elevator doors opened on Vivian's hospital floor, Nessa saw a sight she could not have anticipated: Delphine with her head bowed in conversation with Daniel.

Delphine was carrying a pillow and wearing sweatpants—had she been sleeping in the hospital room with Vivian? Daniel still had on his jacket and was carrying the cooler he had brought the serum in the day before.

"And then?" Delphine said. It sounded like Nessa had walked into the middle of a story . . . Delphine was comfortable enough with Daniel now to be telling him a story? "The nurse on duty when we got here said something about how Mom exhausted herself until late last night speaking with some kind of reporter brought in by her new lawyer?"

"But no change?" Daniel asked. "She's the same as last night?" He glanced over, acknowledging Nessa as she approached, and included her in the conversation with his gaze.

Delphine looked up at Nessa too. "Hi," she said.

"Which reporter?" Nessa asked.

"It seems like Mom's exhausted now," Delphine went on, ignoring Nessa's question.

"What was he asking her?" Daniel said. He sounded anxious. Nessa suddenly realized that there might be things Daniel would not want Vivian to speak to a reporter about.

"I don't know," Delphine said. "Everyone from school messaged me what's been going on in Tether the past few days. Nessa . . . the Guard! They're hunting wolves! They're saying there was a huge showdown last night?"

"There was?" Nessa and Daniel spoke simultaneously.

Delphine turned to Nessa, giving her a skeptical look. "What, did you sleep through it?" she said to Nessa. Nessa didn't answer the question. She didn't want to think about last night. And she wished Delphine would stop wearing her hair in braids. Did Daniel think of the monster he had made when he looked at Delphine?

She studied Daniel's face for a moment. His gaze was calm and even. Did he know what Nessa knew?

"I'll tell you later," Nessa said. "But first, Mom's not—" She looked away from Daniel, then back at Delphine. "There's no change?"

Delphine shook her head. Daniel lowered his gaze.

"Did you try the second dose?" Nessa asked him.

He met her eyes again, shaking his head. "It didn't work. I'm sorry," he said. He put a hand on Nessa's elbow. "I'm going to stay here, though."

Nessa heard herself say, "That's okay, you don't have to." Even though she realized in that moment she did want him to stay.

"Nonsense," he said. "I'm your father. I want to. I want to help."

The second she saw her mother's gray face and heavy-lidded eyes, Nessa knew. What was happening to her could no longer be explained by the phases of the moon. The moon could not save Vivian. The serum had come too late. She tried to choke back a sob but one came anyway.

Vivian shook her head, lifted a hand a few inches off the mattress in what Nessa interpreted as a sign that she wanted Nessa to come closer.

"I talked to the reporter," Vivian said in a voice so soft Nessa had to lean down to hear. "He told me what happened. In the woods. How the army went after the wolves."

"Yes," Nessa said.

"He told me Bree had called him. You asked her to. She said you were helping the wolves as best you could."

"Yes," Nessa said. "I'm sorry. You probably didn't want me to?"

Vivian held her eyes closed for a minute. "You are doing things differently than I did," she said. She swallowed in a way that looked painful. Nessa realized Vivian was waiting to get enough air in her lungs so she could speak. "I think so." She drew a breath again. Waited. "I hope so. Your father will stay?" she asked.

"Yes."

Vivian opened her eyes and fixed Nessa with a look that still carried a great deal of power. "Good," she said. "You need him."

Slowly, as if it took all her energy to make the gesture, Vivian reached for Nessa's hand.

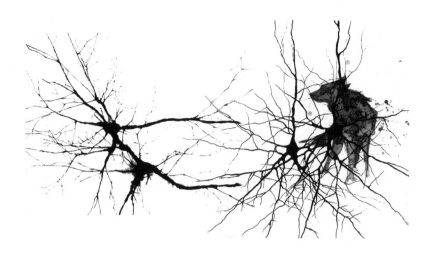

CHAPTER FIFTY-SIX

or three days they maintained a vigil in Vivian's hospital room, still holding out hope that the serum would take effect, watching the near-continuous coverage of the wolf crisis in Tether on TV. They saw the same footage over and over: wolf bodies piled on the riverbank. Shots of wolf dens, wolf footprints, interviews with wolf experts. Paravida's stock plunged, then recovered.

Then Nessa turned the TV off. Vivian got sicker and sicker. Her hair went from one streak of white to white all over. Her cheekbones pushed up and out and she became almost a different person—wide eyed, small, and strangely pretty, like Delphine. Jane bought a baby blue cashmere blanket at the most expensive gift shop in Saginaw and laid it over Vivian's shoulders. It gave Vivian a soft, unfocused look.

Jane was with her almost around the clock, taking breaks for three or four hours at a time to return to the hotel and sleep. Nate went back to his regular school but came to see Vivian every day at dinnertime as they ate takeout from every restaurant in Saginaw that would deliver—Chinese, burgers, fried chicken.

Delphine and Nessa kept hours similar to Aunt Jane's, buying hot chocolates and lattes from the hospital coffee cart. Vivian was mostly too weak to talk but she smiled faintly as Delphine told her stories about how things had been going in Milwaukee, featuring many allusions to Jane's terrible cooking.

To Nate, Vivian said, "Tell me about the trains I should remember," and he talked on and on, letting her hold his hand as long as he was reciting facts about engine capacity and timetables and track length. She would sometimes appear to be sleeping, but as soon as Nate's voice gave out, she'd stir and produce a question to get him going again. "What does an engineer do? I can't remember," she would say only for the pleasure of hearing his throaty, changing voice renew its obliviously confident monologue.

Sometimes while this was happening, Jane would leave the room. Once Nessa found her in the hallway, weeping by the elevator door.

That was when Nessa realized that the hope they'd been clinging to was slipping away. The serum had come too late. Her mother was going to die.

True to his word, Daniel stayed with them in Saginaw. The night when Nessa had battled for the wolves, he'd taken Delphine to dinner, made friends with her the way he had with Nessa. He and Jane had achieved an icy truce. He had the Lionel Trains catalog overnighted to Nate and the two of them pored over it together. He paid for all of the meals, for the hotel, for the parking, everything except the blanket Jane insisted should come only from her.

The lawyer visited briefly on the second day to announce that all the charges against Vivian had been dropped. Thanks to the interview Vivian had given him, the *Saginaw Sentinel* reporter had been able to connect the dots on the story of Paravida's involvement with the genetic alterations made to the wolves.

There was still no proof—Paravida would not be taken to trial—but the news coverage of the attack on the Tether wolves had ignited outrage among animal rights activists, and even the hunting community. Tim Miller had organized a rally in town that was covered in the *Detroit Free Press*, and Andy Carlisle and Bree were captured standing with clasped hands just behind the podium—the one bright spot in the continuous coverage. As photographs and video of mutilated wolf carcasses stacked by the dozens began to surface online, Paravida went radio silent and the National Guard withdrew from Tether.

The Guard claimed they left because the wolf problem had been mostly cleared up, and this was true. With the exception of one set of tracks spotted by a farmer out repairing pasture fencing, there had been no sign of wolves in Tether at all.

The lawyer reported all of this as if Vivian were personally responsible for it and should be celebrating. But as the conversation wore on, and he began to take in how very sick she appeared to be, the confident swagger with which he had opened descended into a more hushed and respectful tone. He spoke increasingly slowly and summarized more.

Nessa kept in touch with Bree and continued to call Luc's cell phone every few hours, but other than that, her entire world existed only within the four walls of Vivian's room.

Word about the dismissal of charges—and Vivian's rapid decline—spread quickly among the residents of Tether. Nessa and Delphine, and even Aunt Jane, began to be deluged by calls and emails requesting to see Vivian. In the end, she agreed to see four people: Bree, Dr. Morgan, Coach Hoffman, and Ann Lark, Billy Lark's mother. From the looks on their faces as they left her room, all of them knew it was goodbye. For once, Bree was absolutely speechless.

By the third day, Vivian was mostly sleeping, but in the morning, when Nessa happened to be the only one with her, she woke up.

"Mom," Nessa said, filled with a sudden bubble of optimism. Maybe her waking would be the beginning of Vivian's recovery?

But no. "Nessa, I have instructions," Vivian said, and Nessa's bubble burst. "Your father offered to take all three of you to live with him in Oregon, and I want you to go with him."

"You do?"

"I want you to bring my body," she said. "I don't want a service. I don't believe in any of that. I want you to freeze it, to make what I did to myself useful, perhaps to use what you can learn from it."

"Mom!" Nessa said. She didn't want her mom to be thinking about dying. She wanted her to be thinking about getting better.

Vivian then came as close to sitting up as Nessa had seen her attempt in days. "Whatever you do, don't put me in the ground. I have already spoken to Daniel about this and he has agreed. I am counting on you to make him keep his promise," Vivian said. "And I'm counting on you to take care of the others." She said all of this slowly and deliberately, taking shallow breaths every few words. "Can you promise me that?"

Nessa nodded.

"Say it," Vivian said. "Out loud."

Nessa swallowed. What her mom was asking of her was a lot. But she would do it whether she promised Vivian or not. "I promise," she said.

"One more thing," Vivian said then. "Your sister."

"I'll take care of her," Nessa said. "I already said I'll take care of both of them: Delphine and Nate."

"No," Vivian said, shaking her head a little bit. "Not that sister."

"Oh," Nessa answered. It took her a second to realize that her mother had meant the Delphine chimera.

"You need to take care of her too," Vivian went on.

"I—" Nessa said. "How?"

"She's more powerful than anyone can imagine," Vivian said. "But she needs help. You can save her. I know it."

Save her? Nessa had no idea what her mother meant but she didn't tell her that. She wondered later if that was a mistake. At the time, all she wanted was for Vivian to rest. For Vivian to recover.

"You'll see someday how it is," Vivian continued. "You think you can change the world, and then you think no one should even try. You think the world is an oyster and then you learn those whorls are the whirlpool and you are swirling toward the dregs. But I know one thing, Nessa. I believe in you. Don't walk away from what you know in your heart to be the way. No matter how wrong it all may seem."

Nessa tried not to let her mother see that she was crying.

"Find a way," Vivian said. "For me."

"Mom," Nessa said, but that was as far as she could get. She wanted to be strong for her mother and not cry. She wanted to be strong enough that her mother would get well.

Vivian did not get well. Late that night, when Nate had gone to the hotel to sleep, Jane, Nessa, Delphine, and Daniel held on to Vivian's hands and watched her take her last breath. She had been unconscious for hours, slipping into what appeared to be a deep sleep only a few minutes after Nate had gone for the night. And then she was still.

In the moments they continued to watch her body, Nessa realized she had never thought this would actually happen. She had remembered . . . there was something her mother had said when Nessa returned from Oregon. Vivian had hinted that her mutation might save her. That the mutation might take over her body when the disease was at its strongest—might save her in a moment of extremity.

But Vivian had simply . . . died.

Vivian, who had always been so strong. Who had never asked for help. Who had always known the right thing to do.

How could she be gone?

Delphine and Jane were crying and Nessa was holding on to her mother's hand. Holding it, and waiting, hoping, even as the minutes during which Vivian was not breathing stretched and solidified and it appeared to be incontrovertibly true that her mother was gone.

Daniel pulled his cell phone out of his pocket and left the room. Within the hour, a special team of undertakers had arrived. "Who knew? An out-of-state undertaker, all the way from the West Coast!" Nessa overheard a nurse saying to an orderly in the hallway outside the room. She said it in that way Michigan people do when they think someone is trying too hard to be fancy. Nessa scoffed and shook her head. The nurse could not have gotten her mother more wrong.

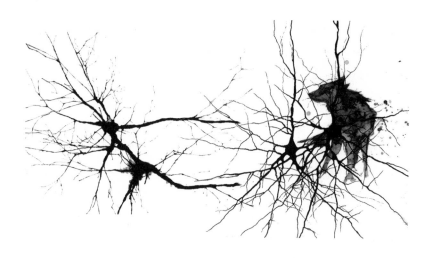

CHAPTER FIFTY-SEVEN

The next morning, over coffee in the hotel breakfast room, Daniel and Nessa explained Vivian's instructions to a shell-shocked Jane.

While Daniel spoke, Jane appeared to be absorbed by the task of pushing back the cuticles on her fingernails, her red hair blocking any view they might have had of her face. After Daniel finished, she raised her head and Nessa saw that her eyes were glittering with anger.

"I know I have no authority here," Jane said, glaring at Daniel across the table. "But I have something to say and that is this: No way. These kids already moved once this year—they've just *lost their mother*—they've been through hell. I am not letting them go."

Daniel held up a hand as if begging for a minute of Jane's time to let him begin to explain.

"No," Jane said. "Just . . . no. And I'll tell you something else. There's no way we're not having a service of some kind for Vivian here in Tether. There are people there who loved her, who grew up with her, who need the chance to say goodbye. Her kids need to see that happen. She was the queen of the disappearing act, but not this time." Daniel opened his mouth to speak but she cut him off again. "I know she wanted to donate her body to research. That's fine. We don't need a coffin, okay? A memorial service will be just fine."

Daniel sighed. "That's a good idea," he said. "A memorial service. And if you like, we'll leave everyone where they are for the rest of the school year. Nessa can stay in Tether, compete in track. Nate and Delphine can continue to live with you. It will give me time to get ready for them to move in with me in the summer. I've been thinking about installing a trolley system to connect the buildings at the lab. Perhaps this would be something Nate could help me design."

Jane looked surprised at how easily her point had been conceded. And there was no denying the fact that building his own train system would be just about the best thing that could ever happen to Nate. "They can see you on some weekends," Jane sputtered. "If you want to fly them out on your private plane."

"Good thought," Daniel said, ignoring Jane's sneering tone when she said the words "private plane."

"Is this what you want, Nessa?" he asked, turning to her. "Will this work for Nate and Delphine?"

"I'll speak to them," Nessa said. "It's all happening really fast and they might need time to think it over."

"Of course," Jane and Daniel said in unison, each quickly looking away as if embarrassed and hoping to ignore what had just happened.

Just then Daniel's phone rang. His finger hovering over the button that silenced the ringer, he glanced at the number. Whatever it was must have been important, because rather than ignoring the call, he stood, swiping to connect even as he was standing up.

"Tell me you have good news," Nessa heard him say, his tone abrupt and business-like. As he listened, a scowl emerged on his face. He stepped briskly out of the breakfast room, but didn't go far—Nessa could still hear every word of the call. "Empty?" he said. "The doors had been locked, right?" Whoever Daniel was speaking to must have explained something, but it did nothing to affect Daniel's highly irritated tone when he responded. Nessa had never heard anything like this coming from him before. "You think it was stolen?" Again, he listened to the caller only briefly. "I don't care. Figure it out. It must be found. Do I make myself clear?"

Nessa felt the flush of partial understanding rising, coloring her face. She looked at Jane as if she could hear, and in hearing, understand. Of course, neither was possible. Jane was staring forward, her gaze hitting the cereal dispenser towers unfocused, looking as if she had nothing left to hope for in the world.

Five minutes earlier, Nessa had probably been looking at the coffee urns in the same way. But not now. Now, she felt the tiniest, smallest, glimmer of hope.

And the way hope works, it turns out, is that a glimmer is really all you need.

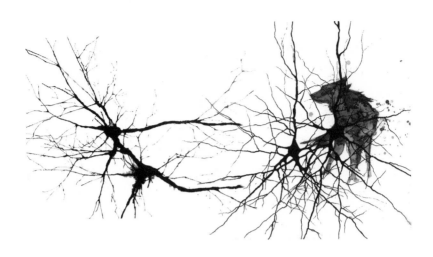

CHAPTER FIFTY-EIGHT

early every single citizen of Tether is here, Nessa thought, surveying the crowd at Grace Lutheran. Some, she assumed, were there out of guilt, for thinking the worst of Vivian when she'd been accused of genetically altering wolves.

Many people came to the service because, plain and simple, she was a cousin, or a friend, or a neighbor, and in Tether, people just naturally came out for weddings, funerals, and baptisms.

Others, Nessa learned, as the cards and notes flooded in, came because Vivian had touched them in some way. Set a broken leg for their dog and not charged them when money was tight. Held their hand after their cat had died and they could not face returning to an empty house. Brought a casserole to a potluck when someone was sick, or broke, or needed help. Many remembered her tireless activism during the town's fight against Dutch Chem. Many remembered Vivian in high school, winning state science awards, taking Advanced Calculus when she was still in the eighth grade.

"I remember when your mother came back to Tether with you girls," a neighbor wrote. "She was always so smart, I assumed she'd be too stuck up to talk to me. But then when my sister died, there she was with a loaf of bread and a can of tuna fish on her day off and saying sorry it wasn't something homemade but could she bring my kids over to her house for the afternoon as she was sure I could use a rest."

The notes and letters attesting to her mom's steady good sense helped bring back the version of her mother that she had always known.

After the memorial service, Jane stayed to help pack up the house as best she could. They would put it on the market, but for now Daniel was happy to pay the mortgage and it just needed to be closed up. Ted and Stephanie had said Nessa could stay with them through the rest of the school year. Daniel offered them money for her upkeep. They refused.

"Oh my gosh, Nessa," Bree was saying. "Do you think your dad is going to buy you a car?"

He offered, and Nessa said no. Not yet. Luc's truck was all that she had left of him. She wanted the truck. She wanted her mother back. She wanted Luc. The hope she'd been living on— the tiny spark of it—lived inside these desires.

Nessa returned to school, and life—such as it was—returned to normal. Nessa surprised herself: she wanted to be in school. She wanted to get up in the mornings. Was she in denial about what had happened to her? No. Nessa knew herself better than that.

She was looking for something. She didn't know what. Some sign that her hope was founded on fact. That there was a reason to fan the flames. She stayed away from the woods, though. The woods gave her nothing but the echoes of the wolves who had been there and were now gone.

Nessa sat down with Coach Hoffman the day she got back and he clicked open the Paravida training record she'd started and stopped maintaining before spring break began.

"Yeah," Nessa said, looking at the series of empty fields in the database where she was supposed to record her times and weigh-ins and cross-training routines. "I don't think I'm doing that anymore."

"Fine," Coach Hoffman said. "But you're going to need to be doing something. You're a good runner, Nessa. Last fall, you were a great runner. And no one's going to understand more than me if you can't make it happen this spring. But this could be something good to focus on while you're, you know . . ."

Nessa was grateful to him for not finishing the sentence, for not naming the loss.

And he's right, she thought. That afternoon, after a practice where she was huffing and puffing through what was really not a very intense sprint workout—plus throwing the javelin, which she did only because she had to—Nessa went for a longer, five-mile run. She didn't even consider transforming, and every hedge or bush she passed seem to remind her of Luc and their runs together.

She'd gone to his parents to ask about him, and they'd shown her a note Luc had left them, explaining that he was going on a "personal journey" and wouldn't be in touch for some time.

She didn't tell them her suspicions about his personal journey having ended on the banks of the river, that he had given his life to save others. She preferred they think of him as a wolf. As wild. As free.

Nessa was carrying certain memories with her all the time, but she didn't dare return to them too often. She didn't want them to lose their charge, to become stale. She went to them when she most needed to.

Then, she allowed herself to remember the sight of Luc waiting for her in the line of trees behind Bree's house when she first came back from Oregon. She remembered those days when she'd seen him running before they were a couple, his silhouette visible on the opposite side of a lake. That time when he held her under the sleeping bag in front of the cabin and she'd felt his pain at leaving her mixed with her own pain at his leaving.

The morning after her run, Nessa woke up early and went out again, craving the exhaustion that would follow. Practice that afternoon was even worse than before—the two back-to-back five-mile runs had left her exhausted—but after several days of running in the morning and again after school she began to feel her speed returning. Her sprint work began to show improvement as well.

Crouching at the starting line in spikes, feeling the back of her toe dig into the soft surface of the high school track, she was grateful that she had the focus to empty her mind. Bree started tracking Nessa's times again. She was getting faster by the day.

When the full moon arrived, she transformed, and the woods still felt empty and sad. She laid down some tracks and marked the boundary lines of the natural wolves' old territory, keeping it for them in case they ever cared to return.

At the thought of them—of Big One and Mama, of the pups—Nessa felt her heartbeat hollowing out a hole in her chest. She ended her run taking deep shaking breaths. She promised herself she wouldn't go back to the woods for a while.

But then a few days later, Nessa was running outside of town and she saw a perfectly still pond in the woods, off the side of a road. She could smell the loamy earth, the new ferns as tender as lettuces, the pine needles damp and redolent of spring.

Nessa couldn't resist. She sprang into the woods and within a few paces had transformed into wolf form. She ran a loop around the pond, and then up a rise, finding herself near the rock outcropping where she'd gone with the wolves when she'd first begun to transform.

As she made her way to the top, the path turned left and then right and then jutted out a bit so that she had a view of the outcropping she was heading for. And what she saw there quickened her breathing, and then her pace.

It was a wolf, silhouetted against the early evening spring sky. A white wolf like Nessa but larger. A wolf with a powerful smell. A wolf who wasn't trying to hide its scent.

Nessa had been running so quickly she had already passed

the spot where she could see the wolf by the time she registered the vision. She took a few steps back to see whether she could get another look, but the wolf was gone.

She ran up the rest of the hill anyway, sniffing like crazy when she got there. Sure enough, there was a wolf odor there.

A wolf! She thought. Another wolf.

Nessa ran in the woods every morning and every afternoon for the rest of the week, tracking the wolf she'd seen. She didn't want to let the thought in, but it came in anyway: the wolf was Luc. He was changed but he was still alive. Was it possible?

And after a month of track meets and conference calls with Daniel about his plans for Nate and Delphine's move to Oregon, a month of Bree and Andy Carlisle drama, a month of Tim Miller and David Bergen being interviewed by all the news media who had swarmed into Tether with the National Guard—Nessa continued to smell the mystery white wolf lurking in the woods around Tether.

She never saw the white wolf again, but she knew the wolf was there, bold and powerful and proud. It did not show itself to Nessa again, but it did nothing to mask its smell.

This wolf was not careful.

Maybe because it didn't need to be?

But given everything Nessa had seen—everything she had lost—Nessa was careful. She remained upwind of this wolf. She did not give herself away. Once, when she became convinced this wolf was tracking her, she left the woods entirely, sprinting to the trailhead where she had left Luc's truck and . . . gunning the engine, Nessa headed for the relative safety of Bree's house, hoping that whatever was out there had not decided to follow her home.

One day in early June, Bree burst into the cafeteria at the beginning of lunch and pulled Nessa by the arm away from the lunch line. "But it's taco day!" Nessa protested.

"This is better than taco day!" Bree said. "This is . . . just look!"

Bree shoved a printout from the library's computer into Nessa's hands. She saw that it was an email—a newsletter from an environmental blog. The subject line was: "50 Wolves Relocate to Grand Isle????!!!"

Once those words penetrated her brain, Nessa found her hands were shaking too much to read what followed. "What is this?" she cried.

"Grand Isle. Tim loves that place. It's this island in northern Lake Michigan where wolf researchers have been studying one colony of wolves for 50 years. Recently all the wolves died out and it was the saddest thing ever. The researchers still go back to check what's happening and just last week they saw this line of wolves swimming out from the mainland toward the island . . . and Nessa, they sound just like the Paravida wolves!"

Nessa grabbed the paper and . . . Bree was right. This *was* better than taco day. Way better! She left the cafeteria, still carrying the page, still reading. She went immediately to the library computer, clicked on the blog, and scanned the pictures, wishing they hadn't been taken in the air from helicopter height. Wishing they weren't so grainy. Wishing she could identify individual wolves. Were there puppies? Were Sister and Jack still together? Was Mama with Big One? The Brothers? The Brothers Junior? Biter and Princess?

Were these even the wolves she knew?

Nessa squinted, systematically examining each wolf she'd seen.

Were any of them large and gray? Were any of them Luc?

The white wolf, the gray wolf. She closed the browser window and squeezed her eyes closed. A little hope can be a dangerous thing.

Hope is the opposite of peace.

Nessa's running times improved. She performed well at meets. She made it to States. She took second place in the 400-meter. Daniel was there watching with Delphine and Nate and Jane. He'd flown them all in for the occasion, and afterward he drove them all to a restaurant in Detroit where Nessa was pretty sure their dinner cost more than most people in Tether earned in a month.

During the meal, Daniel kept directing the conversation to summer plans—activities he was planning for them, trips they might take, changes he was making to his house to make them all feel at home. Nessa felt the way she always did around him—caught between wanting to trust him and keeping two steps away, being always ready to sprint for cover if she needed to.

Back in Tether, Nessa was at a loss. Maybe it was time to face facts? Her mother was gone. Luc as well. Her family's house was up for sale, her friends were talking about summer jobs and parties that Nessa would not be there for.

On Nessa's last weekend in Tether, Bree planned a going-away party. She was running around getting ready for it and shoved Nessa out of the house. "Andy's picking up sodas and snacks. I'm taking care of the setup. You go!"

Nessa climbed into Luc's truck and decided to drive herself on a tour of the town. She started at her grandparents' old house where she must have visited in the years when her parents were still together. She didn't have any memory of it before her life in Tether.

She drove past Dr. Morgan's. Her elementary school. The high school and track, the fields where Delphine used to play softball, the health clinic. She drove out to the Paravida plant, past Billy Lark's house. She passed the trailhead near Joe Bent's farm, where she'd fatefully stopped to help a trapped wolf nearly a year ago. She drove past Mike's garage where Chayton, the first person to explain her transformations, used to stay.

She ended up at her old house—small, green, unremarkable, the lawn grown high with no one home to mow. She remembered the night of Vivian's arrest—the event that had initiated a chain of events that felt preordained now.

Opening the door to the truck, hearing the creak and groan as she pushed it closed, she walked around to the back of the house. Entering the woods in the back, she quickly located the path that she and Luc had worn away between the trees, passing from the cabin to her house and back.

How many times had she run this as a wolf? She thought about transforming now. The trees were in full leaf now. She could smell honeysuckle and skunk cabbage and the baked-wheat smell of freshly cut grass. But she didn't want to see it as a wolf. Not this time. She wanted to remember the Tether woods as a human.

It was a disorienting, but not unpleasant, feeling to hike in the woods as a human. She couldn't smell properly as a human and it made her feel both blind and deaf as she navigated the path. It was like watching a movie with the sound off, or navigating her way to Bree's bathroom in the pitch-black hallway at night.

Eventually, she came to the cabin. She hadn't been there since the afternoon the wolves had escaped. She could not see it without remembering her last night with Luc, huddled together on the bench in front. She imagined the cabin being as lonely as she felt, but as she got closer she saw that someone else had been there. The door was open and the glass in one of the windows was broken.

Nessa froze. What if the person using the cabin was in there now? She had visions of vagrants or drug addicts.

She was not expecting to see a wolf. But when the door opened farther, and first a snout and then a head emerged, Nessa realized that's exactly who was inside.

She considered transforming. This wolf could be hostile. It could be anti-human, but she did not want to call attention to herself. She was too curious to see more. Was this the wolf she'd spotted just after her mother died, the one she'd been tracking all spring?

As the wolf emerged fully from the cabin, Nessa thought it probably was. This wolf was huge. Its coat was a pure white. Its head was held high and its ears were graceful. As Nessa approached—against her better judgment, but she felt drawn to this wolf—she saw that the wolf's eyes were penetrating and blue and deeply, utterly familiar.

Vivian?

Nessa felt her breath quickening, her mind stitching

together everything Vivian had said about the mutation. She had said that in the end, the mutation that was sucking life from her body might be the only thing to save it. Daniel—Nessa remembered the phone call he'd taken during breakfast at the hotel. Something had been lost from the train. Now she knew what it was: a body. Nessa imagined the wolf nosing open the lid of a coffin, the wolf leaping from the moving train, landing on the ground and making her way back here.

Nessa took one last step closer and the wolf startled, stared hard at Nessa, and then ran out of the clearing, streaking for the cover of trees.

Nessa considered following the white wolf into the forest, but just then another shape appeared in the cabin doorway. And this time, Nessa didn't have to think for even a second to know who it was.

This second wolf was tall, gray, light on his feet, with quiet eyes and a relaxed demeanor. Seeing him, she gasped. She reached out her hands but didn't step forward. If this was a hallucination, she didn't want it to end.

The wolf was real, though. He trotted to her and she crouched down to open her arms. He held up his head and she petted him, then held her face next to his.

It wasn't the same as before when they were both wolves or both human, but his body felt comfortable under her hands and she knew that although she was leaving Tether, leaving everything she'd ever known, Luc would be here in the woods, running in whatever form he had now assumed, running as he had always dreamed of running, the white wolf at his side.

Heading out of the woods, Nessa felt herself newly aware of the life in the woods around her, the sounds and smells, the dappled light shifting as the trees moved back and forth in the wind. Birds landed on branches, insects churned the rotting branches back into the earth. To either side of the path, chipmunks scurried from one top-secret hiding place to another, rustling the leaves so that Nessa looked up several times, hoping for another glimpse of her mother or Luc in wolf form. She saw neither again though, and soon left the woods and was driving back to Bree's.

Behind her, however, crisscrossing the path she'd just left behind, a family of chipmunks slid out from behind the walls and doors. They were curious chipmunks—each had the brown body of a chipmunk, the telltale black-and-white stripe on full display. But the head of each chipmunk belonged to a mouse. And their tails were stumpy and short.

Nessa hadn't seen them as she'd made her way out of the woods. And as industrious as they were, unaware of the mutation in their genetic code, they'd paid no attention to Nessa either.

The End

ACKNOWLEDGEMENTS

First, I have to thank the wonderfully creative staff at Chooseco for giving me the opportunity to dig deep into Nessa's unfolding story with them. It was a pleasure to mesh minds with Shannon Gilligan, Melissa Bounty, Elizabeth Adelman, Liz Windover, Mieka Carey, Elisabeth Lauffer, and Dot Greene.

Chimera was inspired by great science journalism. Thank you to the scientists, writers, and radio/podcast personalities who keep those of us in the lay population informed of the heady discoveries taking place in genetics specifically and the universe in general.

This book would not exist without the hard work and encouragement of sales reps, bookstore staff, librarians, reviewers online and off, and readers. Thanks for "getting" what we thought was cool about Weregirl. Thanks also for letting us know.

In the reader category I have to send a special shout-out to my children and nieces. They are currently fighting over a single advance copy of Chimera and shushing spoiler conversations at the dinner table. Knowing how much this series speaks to them is inspiring. In the family category I also have to thank my entire extended clan for their love and support, especially Claudia Gwardyak, Rick Kahn, Max Kahn, and Eliza Kahn for their patience with me in the fast-paced drafting stages of Chimera.

C. D. Bell
August 2017

Jean Bourbon

About the Author

When she's not hanging out with her two children and husband in Brooklyn, NY, you can find Cathleen Davitt Bell writing in a decrepit RV clinging to the side of a hill in upstate New York, trying to teach herself to watercolor, or inventing her own recipes. She received her undergraduate degree from Barnard College and her MFA in Creative Writing from Columbia University, and is the author of the novels *Weregirl, Slipping, Little Blog on the Prairie, I Remember You,* and a co-author of *The Amanda Project.*